D0059217

ALSO BY

PHILIPPE GEORGET

Summertime, All the Cats Are Bored

Autumn, All the Cats Return

CRIMES
OF WINTER

Philippe Georget

CRIMES OF WINTER

VARIATIONS ON ADULTERY
AND VENIAL SINS

Translated from the French
by Steven Rendall

Europa
editions

Europa Editions
214 West 29th Street
New York, N.Y. 10001
www.europaeditions.com
info@europaeditions.com

First Publication 2017 by Europa Editions

Translation by Steven Rendall
Original title: *Méfaits d'hiver*

Library of Congress Cataloging in Publication Data is available
ISBN 978-1-60945-389-3

Georget, Philippe
Crimes of Winter

Book design by Emanuele Ragnisco
www.mekkanografici.com

Cover photo © gremlin/iStock

Prepress by Grafica Punto Print – Rome

Printed in the USA

Le vent se lève! . . . Il faut tenter de vivre!
—Paul Valéry

CRIMES
OF WINTER

CHAPTER 1

It sounded like a bubble bursting in Claire's purse.
A text message.
At 7 A.M. on a school vacation day.

Lying on a sideboard in the dining room, the purse was taunting him. It was a famous Spanish brand, a multicolored and multi-pocketed designer bag that the kids had given their mother for her birthday. Inside was her telephone, with the truth. The whole truth. The truth he'd been refusing to see for more than six months.

The past summer, Gilles Sebag had caught his wife in a flat-out lie. One day at noon, he'd come to her gym class to invite her to lunch afterward, but she wasn't there. At the time, he wasn't surprised. But the gym teacher's condescending smile had haunted him all afternoon. That very evening—without having premeditated it, he'd slipped a harmless-seeming question into the conversation.

"So, how was your gym class?"

"Exhausting," she had replied, calmly.

Over the following days, other disturbing signs had increased his concern. Claire went out a lot with her girlfriends, more than usual, and he had sometimes caught her being distracted while he was talking to her. Her thoughts seemed to be elsewhere. With another man, perhaps . . . And then she had left on a cruise with her girlfriends. As a teacher at the middle school in Rivesaltes, she had more vacation time than he did. And that year, for the first time, she had decided to take advantage of it without him.

She'd come back more in love with him than ever, and all the signs that had earlier worried him had suddenly disappeared. And he tried to forget his doubts. If Claire had taken a lover, the affair was over and it had been just a fling. It was him she loved, not someone else. They'd been living together for eighteen years; they'd raised two children together, Leo, who was sixteen, and Séverine, who would soon be fourteen, both of them great kids.

He had tried to understand that these days, love was no longer necessarily accompanied by eternal fidelity. That the desire to see herself as beautiful in another man's eyes could be stronger, and also the desire for another body, another skin, the desire for the first stirrings of interest, a first smile, a first rendezvous, a first kiss.

He'd tried to understand and he was still trying.

But his imagination made it harder. It didn't stop with a first kiss, it invented what came afterward, with increasingly painful details: raunchy images of shared erotic pleasure, sighs and tender words exchanged in bed or by telephone, maybe sometimes behind his back, by text message, for example.

Another bubble burst in the purse.

His experience as a cop had taught him that today there is no better confidant than a mobile phone. And no worse traitor.

For the past six months, he'd been struggling not to spy on his wife. That was a step he had always refused to take. Especially since he might be mistaken. His boss and his colleagues constantly praised his legendary flair. But for once, he might have gone astray, these feelings, this excessive love, and this jealousy that had flourished in him like a cancer might have addled his brains. Too much emotion, too close: his intuition might have gone off the rails. It was easier to let it guide him coolly in a police investigation.

Coolly?

The adverb wasn't right. He never conducted an investigation coolly. On the contrary, he always got emotionally involved. And it was this empathy, for the victims and also for the perpetrators, that made him a good cop. No, he wasn't mistaken: Claire had had a lover. Maybe she still had one, or at least was still in distant contact with him.

He was so sick of all these questions!

He went over to the open purse. The telephone wasn't in a pocket but simply lying on top of an incredible jumble of women's things. A little light was flashing on its right side, sending him vulgar winks, like a Bulgarian prostitute on a sidewalk in La Jonquera.

He reached out to take it, then changed his mind.

What was the point?

Claire was on winter vacation; she was still sleeping in their bedroom. The children hadn't gotten up yet, either. In a few days, it would be Christmas, why spoil everything right now? He decided that if he still hadn't succeeded in getting a grip on himself after the New Year, then it would be time to lance the boil. Finally to speak with Claire and remove the last doubts. For better or for worse.

But the light was still flashing.

Oh, for shit's sake!

He grabbed the phone and used his right thumb to bring up the screen. There were in fact two text messages. Two. He pressed the icon. A first name came up. It meant nothing to him. He pressed again and read the two messages. There was no longer any possible doubt.

He felt something like a rip in his belly, a fissure in his life. The world had just collapsed.

CHAPTER 2

Christine opened the window of the hotel room and lit a cigarette. Éric had left it for her before departing. He'd also given her his lighter. He was an attentive man. Was he in love with her? No. And it was better like that.

She took a long drag on the cigarette, looking down on the Rue de la Poissonerie. It was a narrow, deserted street, like most of the streets in the old quarter of Perpignan. The cigarette warmed her body, her mind, it prolonged the pleasure she'd felt a few minutes earlier. An intense pleasure spiced with the aroma of the forbidden.

She adjusted her glasses on her nose. She never took them off, even to make love. At first, Éric had tried to make her take them off, but he'd had to give up. She felt too naked without her glasses. It was only with Stéphane that she agreed to take them off. Sometimes, only sometimes. When she thought about her husband, she felt her mouth contract and twist to the left. A new grimace that she couldn't control. Éric had pointed it out to her recently.

She raised her head. Only two meters separated her from the windows of the building across the street. She had put her blouse back on, but still wore only her panties. Fortunately, the guardrail on the windowsill hid her from indiscreet eyes. If there were any: there had still been no sign of life behind the dirty windows of the buildings across the way.

She took another drag on her cigarette and bits of a song

rose up from the depths of her memory. A song by Charles Dumont, she seemed to recall. She hummed:

Ta cigarette après l'amour
Je la regarde à contre-jour
Dèjà tu reprends ton visage
Tes habitudes et ton âge.

She rubbed the place between her eyebrows with her thumb. Two vertical wrinkles were forming there. They'd appeared very early on, and were now threatening to separate her forehead into two equal parts.

Ta cigarette après l'amour
S'est consumée à contre-amour.

Heaven knows they were exquisite moments. An unexpected fountain of youth. Never had she imagined that she would experience that feeling again. Her index finger slipped over her crow's-feet and then over the little folds around her mouth. Her skin was inexorably drying out, despite all the care, creams, and sessions at the beauty salon.

But for the past few weeks she had grown younger in her soul. She was twenty again.

Christine had met Éric in her yoga class. She had not felt any particular attraction to him, but she had immediately perceived the spark in his eyes. Flattered to feel herself desired that way, she had enjoyed meeting him at every class. He had started smiling at her, politely greeting her, and even tried to exchange a few words with her. At first, she had remained reserved. This kind of thing was not appropriate for her—not anymore—so why yield to it now? Why say yes to him after having so often said no over the past eighteen years? But she had ended up saying yes. Probably because she felt that she was getting old . . .

And maybe also because Éric had known how to be patient, and to find the right words . . . The right guy at the right time. He had succeeded in overcoming her defenses, one by one.

Until they ended up in this room . . .

The cigarette was almost finished. She'd have to leave soon. It was already past 2 P.M. She stubbed out the butt on the windowsill and threw it out into the street. Then she closed the window and closed the gray curtains. The bittersweet effluvia of their lovemaking were still floating in the room. She picked up her black stockings and sat down on the bed to put them on. Her thighs still remembered Éric's caresses, on and under the nylon.

She looked for her skirt. Where could it be? She grabbed the bedspread and shook it. Her skirt, wrinkled because it had been too quickly taken off, fell on the carpet. She put it on over her stockings and smoothed out the fabric with her hand to make it look more suitable. Then she couldn't help folding the bedspread and putting it over the tangled sheets.

She liked this little room's bare, pale-blue walls.

The first time they had come there was in mid-October. She had been trembling all over and hadn't been able to relax. But she had liked feeling Éric explore her body. He had done it at first with his breath. In this domain as well, he had proven patient. And the intensity of their meetings had increased each time.

No, she hadn't grown younger, she wasn't twenty, she was really forty-seven, and it was not the body of young woman that climaxed but that of a mature woman blooming with new feelings in the arms of an attentive and experienced lover. She had never known that before, not even during what she had always considered as a youthful mistake. It was just after Maxime's birth. No, she had never known that before, and would probably never know it again. That was the whole pleasure of this adventure which would someday come to an end.

Necessarily.

He had his life, and she had hers. There was no question—not for him and not for her—of endangering what each of them had built in their own worlds.

She shivered and her mouth twisted again.

Before leaving the room, she was always gripped by uneasiness. Life was going to resume its usual course until the next time. Though she was fearful during the first part of her affair, Christine had found it increasingly easy to go back to playing her role as a mother and housewife. To return to her habits.

As if nothing had happened.

She had thought that she would be uncomfortable lying and hiding things. She wasn't at all uncomfortable with it. She was ashamed to admit that she even took a certain pleasure in it. She drew new strength from this situation. Up to this point, she had lived so much for others . . . For her son, for her husband. Now she felt alive. Yes, alive. Finally! Her existence had become richer and more intense. Her happiness had become greater.

Including her conjugal happiness.

She felt better in her head, in her skin, in her body. She sang at home. Which greatly pleased Stéphane. He seemed to have fallen in love with her again, and was proud to find a radiant wife waiting for him at home every evening.

The poor guy, if only he knew . . .

Her concern increased a notch and even turned into fear. A sound in the stairway. Like hurried footsteps.

She tried to rid herself of these gloomy thoughts. What was done was done, it would be pointless to give in to remorse. It would change nothing, it would only spoil her pleasure. What he didn't see wouldn't hurt him. So long as Stéphane knew nothing, she wasn't hurting anyone.

But she knew her husband. He was jealous and capable of brutality. What would happen if someday he discovered the truth?

The answer came in a crash at the door. Suddenly thrown open, it slammed against the wall. That was stupid, she thought, it'll leave a mark on the pale-blue wall.

The man who burst into the room looked determined. He saw her, he saw the bed, and his face twisted with hate. He asked no questions, and simply slowly lifted his rifle.

Christine didn't see the gun, she didn't hear the shot. Her lips were about to say "my love," but the words never came out of her mouth. She was already dead.

Chapter 3

Lit by the gentle winter light, the Roussillon plain extended its villages, vineyards, and orchards as far as the sea. The austere breath of the *tramontane* wind was rumbling around the Sant Martì chapel, looking for a body it could seize. Gilles was leaning against the ancestral walls, contemplating the landscape below him. He loved this bit of land, this place between France and Spain—neither entirely the one nor entirely the other—truly a world apart. In the seven years that he had lived here as a voluntary immigrant, he had learned to appreciate the soul and the heart of Northern Catalonia, warm and proud, forged by borders and by exile, sculpted by the caresses of the sun and affronts of the wind.

After his discussion with Claire, Sebag had taken refuge on this strange butte, a hundred and twelve meters above the sea and human beings. He had climbed it by following the path that led to the silent hermitage. He didn't have the strength to run, this time. He lacked breath, he no longer knew how to breathe.

His telephone buzzed in a pocket of his backpack. Five rings, a short silence, and a beep. A voice message had just been added to the SMS he'd already received. There was an emergency at the police station. He didn't give a damn.

At that moment the only priority was to get hold of himself. For hours, he'd been waiting there. He was losing his grip by constantly going over the moments that had shaken the foundations of his life.

Going into the bedroom, he'd quietly drawn the curtain. An orange-tinted light from the streetlights flooded the room. The quilt covered Claire's whole body. Only her brown, wavy hair was outside the sheet. He sat down on the edge of the mattress and ran his hand through her mane.

Claire had awakened slowly. She turned her head and her eyes blinked several times before sinking into the immobile and infinitely sad eyes of her husband.

"What's going on?"

"I love you."

She smiled at him tenderly.

"Is that so serious?"

He handed her the mobile. The time he had so long awaited and so much feared had come.

Finally.

Already.

He closed his eyes for few seconds and then reopened them. Claire had read the messages and her smile had frozen. She nodded with resignation.

"You had to find out . . . You suspected, didn't you?"

She sat up in bed, threw away the phone, and took Gilles's hands in hers.

"I love you, too. You're the love of my life. I love only you."

This declaration passed over him without moving him. The words he'd found on the telephone had made him impermeable.

"Don't tell me you didn't love him!"

"It wasn't the same, you can't compare it."

Gilles had the strange impression of having been split into two people. He was both the actor and the spectator of a very bad film. With such banal dialogue. He would have liked to be able to change the channel.

"So why, then?"

He didn't recognize his own voice. It was sad. Cavernous. Alien.

"I don't know," she replied after a long silence. "Really, I don't know . . ."

"That's not much of an answer."

"True. But what can I say that won't hurt you? I felt like it, I needed it. It's a matter of a friendship that went too far."

Did he need to know more, Gilles wondered. The truth would necessarily be painful. But silence was even more painful. Questions surged up in spite of him.

"Who is he?"

"A former colleague. Simon. A professor of history and geography."

"Is it over?"

"Yes. Since the middle of July. He left."

"Did it last a long time?"

"Only four months."

He pursed his lips. They turned white.

"'Four months' and 'only' don't go together."

"Probably not."

Gilles waited for the rest. A basic technique of interrogation. When you're a cop, you're a cop for everything, for everyone, always.

"He was living in Toulouse, but his wife is Basque and wanted to go home to be with her sick parents. She's a nurse and it was easy for her to get transferred. He was supposed to join her, to be transferred, too, but the administration made a stupid mistake. Somebody confused Pyrénées-Atlantiques with Pyrénées-Orientales and he ended up here. Far away from his wife and his children."

"So he has children?"

"Two boys and . . ."

Gilles put his hand over Claire's mouth.

"Not that! I can't . . . Besides, I really don't give a damn."

"You asked me, and I'm answering you. I'll answer all your questions sincerely."

"Tell me the rest, the essential part."

"As you wish . . . Simon got here last fall. He felt lonely here, far away from his family. We very quickly became close. I didn't immediately understand what was happening. At first I thought it was just a simple friendship . . ."

"Usually you talk to me about your friends, both men and women."

"That's true. And I never talked to you about him. Probably because I was also lying to myself. We began by having lunch together regularly, and then we had dinner, and . . ."

She decided to stop.

"Did you love him?" Gilles asked again.

Claire sensed that every word could be a poisoned blade.

"In a way . . . but not like you. Never. I told you that, you're the love of my life. You mustn't have any doubt about that. I have certainly never had any."

"Is everything over since he left?"

"Yes. We haven't seen each other again. But we write to each other now and then. It has become a friendship again."

"A friendship?" Gilles grimaced, jerking his chin toward the telephone.

One word in the SMS had struck him more than all the others.

"For me, it's no longer anything but friendship. So far as he's concerned, I don't know and I don't want to know."

"Did you feel bad when he left?"

"Yes and no. A little sadness, but also relief. I wanted to go back to a simpler life. Our life before."

"Our life before . . ." he repeated.

He withdrew his hands from his wife's. As if it could be that simple! Only now did he understand why he'd had so much trouble getting used to the idea that Claire might cheat on him. Despite his fine ideas, his determination to be tolerant and understanding, down deep he thought of fidelity like virginity. Once you've lost it, it's forever. That earlier life no longer existed.

"You've never cheated on me before him?"

"No, never, Gilles, I swear."

She tried to take his hands in hers again, but he didn't let her.

"If he hadn't left, would it have continued?"

"I don't know, I don't think so . . . Simon was staying only one year, he had to leave, it was always like that. I think that was precisely why . . . why I became infatuated. Because this thing had an end even before it began. It was only a parenthesis, Gilles."

"A parenthesis . . . A loving parenthesis?"

"Yes."

A tear rolled down Claire's cheek.

"Forgive me. If I want to be sincere, I can't say anything different."

She put her hands on her husband's face and pulled it closer to hers.

"I love you, Gilles. I love you, I love you, I love you."

He watched the tears fall on the quilt. A quilt she had bought recently. Black-and-white, with words written in gray over one another: You and Me, Today, Tomorrow, Forever. He pulled away and stood up.

"I love you, I love you, I love you!" she cried. "This thing is over! Over!"

His telephone rang again. He rubbed his eyes and got to his feet. He felt dizzy, and had to lean on a rock.

After the confrontation with Claire, he'd felt a sudden need to get some fresh air, and he'd left the bedroom while his wife was continuing to declare her love for him. He'd left without slamming the door. What good would it do to yell and scream? That could calm his anger, not his sorrow.

He'd gotten into his car and started it up. Claire's words kept echoing in his head: "This thing is over!" How could it be over when for him it had just begun?

Chapter 4

The metal shutters on abandoned stores groaned under the whipping of the wind. In downtown Perpignan, one shop out of four remained stubbornly closed, and for several months the Rue des Augustins had been driving up the statistics: here almost every other shop had gone out of business.

"It's spooky here."

Jacques Molina, a police lieutenant at the Perpignan police headquarters, lit a cigarette and pulled up the collar of his jacket.

"And it's seriously cold."

His colleague, Lieutenant François Ménard, looked up at the blue sky. The dull ochre façade of the Hôtel du Gecko was bathed in cold shade, but the sun kindly lent an illusion of spring to its red tile roof.

"Still no word from Gilles?"

Molina looked at his mobile.

"Still not, no."

"He's pushing it . . ."

Ménard pulled his hands out of his raincoat and rubbed them together.

"Don't tell me that with this weather he's escaping work to run on the trails."

Molina smiled:

"When he has pins and needles in his legs, Gilles is capable of running in a storm. But if he does that when he's on duty, he takes his phone with him so he can be contacted. This time I've sent him a message and two SMSes and I haven't heard a word out of him."

"He must be in an area where there's no signal."

"Tut . . . As long as he's been running in Northern Catalonia, he knows every corner of the department and he wouldn't go into an area without relays on a workday."

"Well, then his battery is probably dead! No, really, he's going too far. Already he doesn't come in the morning and now he doesn't respond to emergencies. He's lucky to be in the boss's good graces."

Molina would have liked to defend his teammate, but he was out of arguments. He limited himself to pulling on his cigarette. Ménard glanced at his watch.

"2:45! It was hardly worth the trouble to hurry if we're just going to stand around here."

"I'll finish my cig and then we'll go."

Half an hour earlier, a telephone call from headquarters had interrupted their lunch. After hearing gunshots, the manager of the Hôtel du Gecko had found a woman dead in one of the establishment's rooms. The two lieutenants had hurriedly left the restaurant without taking time to drink their coffee. Their colleagues from the forensic police were already working on-site, but Molina and Ménard were waiting in the street for the—as yet hypothetical—arrival of a third policeman, Lieutenant Gilles Sebag, who had been unreachable since that morning.

Ménard kept an eye on Molina's cigarette, which was almost entirely smoked.

"Shall we go?"

Molina knew that Sebag attached great importance to the first moments of an investigation. The first observations, the looks, the first interrogations, the hesitations, the emotion, the silences and the fear. "Ineffable truths float in the air for an instant," Gilles often said. "If you don't grasp them then, you never will." Skeptical at first, Jacques had ended up being convinced that Sebag's idea was correct. But he didn't think this was the time to talk to Ménard about it. To remind him of these remarks was also to admit that in his opinion only Gilles was capable of gasping this truth. That would not be likely to improve his mood.

Ménard ran an exasperated hand through his crew cut.

"Shall we go?" he repeated.

Molina exhaled a final puff of smoke. Then he crushed out the butt on the asphalt.

"OK, OK! Let's go."

The two inspectors climbed the three steps that led to the lobby. They were about the same height, but Molina had retained a massive physique from his years as a second-row rugby player. With time, he had gained in fat what he had lost in muscle. They nodded to the policeman in uniform who was blocking access to the stairway.

The Hôtel du Gecko was a reputable but rather run-down establishment. Black-and-white photos of Perpignan in the early twentieth century hung on faded green wallpaper. The frames seemed to have been placed randomly, without any concern for aesthetics. The bald old man leaning on the reception desk fit right into this décor.

"Which room?" Molina asked, without any preliminaries.

"Room 34, on the fourth floor," the old man replied in a toneless voice. "Top of the stairway, on the left."

"There's no elevator?"

The old man sighed with a slight shrug of his hunched shoulders. François Ménard took a little notebook out of his jacket pocket.

"Hello, sir. Your name is . . . ?"

"Jordi Estève, Inspector. I've been the owner of this hotel since 1975."

Molina snorted.

"You could have changed the wallpaper at least once!"

"We do that regularly," the hotel owner replied, offended. "Unfortunately, the building is damp—a construction defect—and the wallpaper doesn't last long. And since lately there haven't been many guests . . ."

"One thing explains the other."

"And vice versa."

Ménard coughed. These digressions annoyed him.

"Are you the one who called the police?"

"Yes, I am."

"Tell us exactly what happened."

Old Jordi rubbed his forehead with his rough palm. The top of his skull was spotted with the same reddish patches as the back of his hand. Molina remembered the summer of '75 when his uncle's peach orchard in Vinça had been infected by black scab. In a few days, the fruit and leaves were studded with similar stigmata. A whole harvest went into the refuse bin, a catastrophe. Jacques was still just a kid and he remembered well that this was the first time he'd seen an adult cry. Impressive. He was still marked by that. A scab on his memory.

"I was in the restroom when I heard the shot," the hotel owner explained. "I came out as fast as I could and was able to see a man rushing down the stairs like a demon. He was holding a long box at his side. I think it was a rifle. He saw me, but he didn't stop. I was really scared."

Ménard was taking all this down in his notebook.

"What did this man look like?"

"Well . . . about fifty. Pretty tall, not fat but a little heavyset. Rather long hair, blond, and still fairly thick."

Ménard stopped writing for a moment.

"What do you mean, 'a little heavyset?'"

"Well . . . he had a small potbelly and broad, even very broad, shoulders, but you could see that he didn't have as much muscle beneath them as your partner there does."

Molina thanked him with a nod of his head.

"But you couldn't really say that he was fat," Jordi added.

"And you'd never seen him before?" Ménard went on.

"Never. At least, I don't think so."

"Could you recognize him?"

"I think . . ."

"When the man came out, what did you do?"

"Well, I went up to the fourth floor, room 34."

"Why that room in particular?"

Molina and the old man glanced at each other.

"Well . . . there weren't many guests at that time of day," the hotel owner said evasively. "Besides, whatever the hour, we don't have a lot of guests."

"And what did you find up there?"

Jordi Estève hesitated. He didn't want to remember.

"Uhh . . . Your colleagues are already there, they can tell you. And then you'll see for yourself if you go up."

François Ménard put down his pencil and glared at the owner of the Gecko.

"Nonetheless, I'd like you to tell me, Monsieur Estève . . ."

The old man took a deep breath.

"The lady was sitting down. There was blood on her blouse. I went up to her but I quickly realized that she was dead. I went back down to the reception desk to call you."

"Was she the only one occupying the room?"

"No, she came with her . . . friend."

Another exchange of glances between the hotel owner and Molina.

"But he was no longer there when the killing took place?"

"No, I'd seen him leave about ten minutes earlier."

Ménard underlined the last words he had just written.

"Who was occupying room 34? Do you have the couple's name?"

"Monsieur and Madame Durand."

"Durand . . . Are you sure?" Ménard said, raising an eyebrow.

"That's what they told me . . . But as you know, we are no longer required to ask our guests to show their identity papers."

"Did they pay the bill?"

"Yes. The gentleman paid on his way out."

"Do you have a credit card receipt?"

"The gentleman always paid cash."

Ménard frowned. He moistened his finger to turn a page in his notebook.

"Had they been there for several days? Were they tourists?"

The old man's dried-out lips stretched out. His smile uncovered a row of well-aligned but rotting teeth.

"The gentleman always paid cash."

"So they were regulars . . ."

Molina put his big hands on the counter and tapped the false marble with his fingers.

"They usually came twice a week," old Jordi explained. "Tuesdays and Thursdays."

Ménard carefully noted down all this information. Molina sighed and decided to speed up the interview.

"They arrived at noon and never spent the night, right?"

"I don't spy on my guests," the old man replied. "They always paid for the night."

"But they had no luggage, never had breakfast, and you never saw them in the morning, right?"

Jordi Estève lowered his eyes as if he felt guilty of something.

"That's right."

"Some tourists have odd habits," Molina laughed.

Ménard stopped writing.

"You don't think . . ."

"No, I don't think, I'm sure! A couple cheating on their spouses, that was obvious from the beginning."

"Sometimes you have to be wary of what seems obvious. Your friend Gilles often says that, doesn't he?"

"That's true. But he's never challenged the universal laws of gravity: two people who rent a room in a shabby hotel between noon and 2 o'clock are not there for tourism, they're there to screw. That's all there is to it. Feel free to go on believing in Santa Claus if you want, but I'd prefer that you do it when you're off duty."

Jordi Estève lifted an outraged finger and his face was getting red. But in an argument, as earlier on the rugby field, it wasn't easy to stop Jacques Molina once he got going.

"Yeah, I know, old pal . . . You don't like me saying that your hotel is shabby. Excuse me, but I'm the kind of guy who calls a spade a spade."

"This used to be a fine hotel!" the owner moaned.

"I'm perfectly willing to believe you, but that was then, as people say. Before the war. But which one?"

Molina grabbed the owner's still-raised finger and put it on the counter.

"At ease, soldier! Anything else you want to tell us, my dear Jordi? I mean anything else useful for our investigation?"

"Off the top of my head, no, not at the moment."

Molina jerked his chin toward the stairway and turned to Ménard.

"Are you going up, dear?"

Without waiting for an answer, Molina started up the stairs.

"Stop, Jacques. What are you doing there?"

Elsa Moulin, the new head of the forensic team, rushed over to Molina to keep him from coming into room 34. She took off her mask and put her plastic-gloved hand on her colleague's broad chest.

"Are you crazy? We haven't finished, you're going to mess up the crime scene!"

"Relax, *nina* . . . I wasn't going to come in like that, I know the ropes. I remind you that I was a policeman long before you got your first period. Give me shoe covers and gloves and everything will be fine. You know that we like to have a glance at crime scenes right away."

Elsa looked behind Jacques and saw François Ménard coming down the fourth-floor hall.

"Isn't Gilles with you?"

"He's disappeared without a trace."

"But he's working today, right?"

"In theory."

She went back into the room and came out with a box containing complete kits. Molina took out a pair of gloves and plastic shoe covers and put them on.

"Put on the cap, too," Elsa insisted.

"Give me a break, I hate those things. A guy looks so stupid in them."

"The television crew isn't here and there's nobody for you to hit on here, so nobody cares if you look stupid."

"Nobody to hit on, nobody to hit on . . . That's easy to say."

He looked at her with a winning smile. She had on the usual outfit worn by the forensic team, a white jumpsuit that covered her from head to toe. He gently put the mask back over her mouth.

"I think a fantasy is being born. I don't know whether it's you or just the outfit . . ."

The young woman put her hands on her hips and looked at him with pity.

"You know, you try this on me every time! Are you getting senile, or what?"

"And what do you say back to me?" Molina asked, undaunted.

"That if it's the outfit that excites you I can arrange something for your next conquest, but if it's me, I'll give you a piece of advice: Forget about it."

"I'm well aware that you prefer Gilles," Jacques said, pretending to be disappointed. "But that passion is hopeless, my love, and you know it well. Gilles is a married man and a faithful husband . . . Two defects I don't have. Or rather . . . one I no longer have and one I never really had!"

"Charming . . . I find that really tempting. Excuse me, I've got work to do!"

She turned back toward the bathroom. Her young assistant was still going through the room. Sighing, Molina put on the cap and turned to Ménard.

"Do you want an outfit, too?"

"No, I prefer to stay here. I'll observe from the door."

"Regulations, regulations . . . We'll never be able to change you! You guys from the north really take things too seriously."

"I'm not from the north!"

"I know, you're from Picardy, capital Amiens! You've told me that often enough. Seen from here, it's the same thing. For us Catalans, once you've passed Salses, you're already in the Great North."

"I'm not the only one who repeats himself! How many times have I heard that one! Coming from a guy like Llach, okay, he's a real, and authentic Catalan; but you don't even speak the language . . ."

Molina growled: "I understand it, and that's enough for me."

Although he was proud of the part of France where he had grown up, Jacques often made fun of the militant supporters of Catalan identity, like their colleague Joan Llach. He had always thought that learning the language of his ancestors was a waste of time and energy: in the age of globalization, English was the only language that mattered. To avoid remaining one of the poorest departments in France,

Pyrénées-Orientales had to open up to the world and not withdraw into an excessively restrictive Catalan identity. It was a question of survival!

He went into the pale-blue room and cautiously bent over the woman's dead body. She had fallen in a sitting position and remained jammed between the wall and the bed. Her head was still resting on the edge of the mattress, and her glasses had slipped down her nose. Her dark, empty eyes now looked nowhere except inside. Her skirt, hiked up by her fall, bared a birthmark in the shape of a heart on her left thigh. A bullet had penetrated her heart; death must have been instantaneous. *A good shot or a lucky one*, Molina said to himself. He got up and inspected the bedsheets. He saw nothing and was not surprised. "Adulterous couple = protected sex." In matters of love, that equation was as unavoidable as "two + one = a shitload of problems."

"It's all here," Elsa shouted to him from the bathroom.

She was holding in her gloved hands a plastic bag containing a used condom carefully knotted at one end.

"He threw it in the wastebasket."

"In the wastebasket? Yuck . . ."

"Well, what do you do? Do you throw it in the toilet?"

"Of course!"

"You realize that it's latex and doesn't break down. It's not good for the environment and can stop up your pipes."

"Tell me about it . . . I promise that when I'm at your place, I'll put them in the wastebasket."

"I didn't know you were so religious . . ."

"Excuse me?"

"Apparently you now believe in miracles!"

Molina smiled. He liked this verbal ping-pong game with his pretty young colleague. But he was aware that he was walking a tightrope, because he had the ability to annoy people. An innate talent that he had taken pleasure in cultivating.

"Otherwise, what can you tell me about this case?"

She gestured toward the lifeless body.

"She was killed instantly. A single bullet was fired, a .22 long rifle, in my opinion. The shooter hardly entered the room and probably opened fire immediately. There were no questions, no dialogue. The guy knew exactly what he was doing . . . And what she had done!"

"The case seems as clear to you as it does to me."

Molina glanced at François Ménard, who was following their exchange from the doorway to the room.

"A tragedy of jealousy . . . Get your hands on the husband and the case will be solved!"

"In her purse on the table there you'll find, among other things, her mobile phone and her pocketbook. Her name was Christine Abad, maiden name Lipart. Her husband's first name is Stéphane. She was forty-seven years old and lived in Pollestres. There is also a photo. It shows three people: her, a guy her age, and a young man in his twenties. They're smiling. A happy family. Up until now."

"Yeah. Sad but commonplace. The husband must have wanted to spare himself the cost of a divorce."

"That's not very clever!"

"I was joking. In any case . . ."

He stopped; he was about to start down a slippery slope. But he went on anyway:

"My own divorce cost me an arm and a leg."

"And you regret not having killed your wife?"

"Maybe . . ."

"However, after what you told me a little while ago, she was the one who would have had reasons to kill you."

"Yeah, sure . . . A few casual fucks . . . Women don't kill for so little!"

Elsa didn't reply and went about her work: putting plastic bags in sterile boxes, putting labels on these boxes, and then putting them in the case. Jacques had an irresistible desire to continue teasing her.

"By the way, do you have a boyfriend?"

"That's none of your business."

"Is he the jealous type?"

Elsa sighed loudly. Jacques persisted:

"I ask because when we sleep together, I'd like to know if I need to keep my gun handy."

"Don't worry, that won't happen."

"Ah, so he's not jealous?"

"It won't happen that we sleep together!"

"You're right: I prefer younger women . . . How old are you, by the way? Over thirty, no?"

"Go fuck yourself!"

"OK, OK. You're a little quick-tempered today, you wouldn't be on the . . ."

"Oh, no, stop! Not that one, please, you're better than that. And no, I'm not on the rag."

Jacques realized that he'd gone too far. But he couldn't help it, he liked to exasperate people. In the rugby scrums, he was better than anyone at teasing the opponents. He'd often taken a few hits for doing that, but he'd given some back, too.

"I was just trying to relax the atmosphere," he said, pointing to the still-warm cadaver.

"And you think you succeeded?"

"Uhh . . . I'm not so sure about that."

He noticed that she kept smiling. Exasperating and funny at the same time, that was him all over. He reached out to take Christine Abad's purse and cautiously opened it. Leaving aside the usual everyday women's items, he removed only the mobile phone and the pocketbook. He trusted Elsa; if there had been anything unusual in this purse, she would have spotted it before he did. He opened the pocketbook and took out the family photo and took it to Ménard.

"Can you show this to Grandpa Jordi so he can confirm that the man he saw is in fact the husband?"

"OK. And what are you going to do with the telephone?"

"Find the husband's number and figure out who the lover is."

"You'll wait until I get back to call them?"

"Don't worry."

While Ménard was walking away down the corridor, Molina examined the telephone. Recent calls, favorite numbers, text messages. He had no difficulty in locating the messages from the lover, even though Christine had taken the precaution of putting them in her contact list under the feminine first name "Pascale." Only one SMS was in fact addressed to him—all the others must have been prudently erased after being sent—but it was explicit: "I can't wait to feel you inside me. See you soon." He ran through the other messages but found nothing interesting, much less spicy. But he noticed a number that recurred often. That of a certain Brigitte. Not another lover but a close friend, probably. Maybe a confidante.

"It's OK, the owner recognized the husband."

Molina looked up. Ménard was already back.

"What about you, what did you find?"

Molina showed him the SMS sent to the lover.

"We'll call the husband first," Ménard suggested.

Molina took out his own mobile. He was surprised to have received an SMS; he hadn't heard his telephone beep. It was a message from Sebag.

"Gilles says he's on his way," he told Ménard. "His message was sent about ten minutes ago."

"He didn't tell you where he was?"

"No."

"So we don't know when he'll be here . . ."

"True."

Molina typed in the husband's number and got an answering machine. He left a message. "Hello, Monsieur Abad. This is Lieutenant Molina of the Perpignan police. I'm calling you about a matter of the greatest importance: something has happened to your wife, something serious. Please contact me as soon as possible at this mobile number. You can also reach me by landline at police headquarters. See you very soon." After ending the call, he said to his colleague:

"This case is so clear that I almost wanted to tell him: please come turn yourself in, and don't forget to bring the weapon used in the crime so the technicians can examine it."

Ménard granted him a smile.

"I think that's what he'll understand in any case. So, should we call the lover now?"

Molina put away his own phone and picked up the victim's.

"This might be fun," he said.

He pressed the icon corresponding to the name "Pascale." As soon as he heard the ring, he turned on the speaker. At the third ring, someone answered. Pascale was in fact a man, with a soft, suave voice.

"Hello? Do you miss me already? Are you at home?"

"Sorry, sir. I am not Christine Abad but Lieutenant Molina of the Perpignan police."

The interlocutor remained silent, but his uneasy breathing could be heard.

"This is in fact the police calling you, sir. It's not a practical joke or a trap. I'm calling you with Christine's mobile because she's had an accident, and we'd like to see you as soon as possible."

"An accident? Is it serious? A car accident?"

"I'm not at liberty to tell you at this time, not on the phone. Can you come to police headquarters?"

"Now?"

"As soon as possible."

"Uhh . . . I don't understand. Why me? I'm only a . . . a friend."

"We know about your relationship with Madame Abad, and we know that you are not merely a friend."

"I don't know what you're talking about."

"Yes, you do, you know very well. Once again, this is neither a joke nor a trap, sir. This is not Stéphane Abad who is calling you, it's really Lieutenant Molina. What is your name, by the way?"

Another silence followed this question. Then the low voice was heard again. It was less suave.

"And how do I know that you are really a . . . police officer?"

Molina was beginning to get impatient, but he had to recognize that in his situation, the lover was very right to be careful.

"I can't in fact prove that to you. So here's what you're going to do: You're going to go immediately to police headquarters in Perpignan, where you will say that you have an appointment with Lieutenants Molina and Ménard. And then you'll see very clearly that this is no joke."

"But that's not possible, not right away! I can't, I'm at work, I can't leave just like that!"

"But that's exactly what you're going to do!"

Molina sensed that he was going to have trouble remaining polite.

"Otherwise, I'll send a patrol car—flashing light, siren, the whole shooting match. That always really impresses people, I assure you. But given your situation, a little discretion might be preferable, no?"

The silence that followed was not as deep as Molina had hoped. His diatribe had fallen flat. He'd forgotten an essential element that his interlocutor quickly pointed out to him:

"And seeing that you don't know my identity, where are you going to send your patrol car?"

This time, Molina exploded. The guy was asking for it and he was going to get it!

"It's true that I don't have your name, Monsieur What's-his-name, Monsieur Thingamabob, Monsieur Asshole. But I have your phone number and in less than fifteen minutes I can have your name, your address, your boss's employer number, the color of your children's eyes, and the size of your wife's waist. I advise you not to force me to make this search, because I'm already in a very bad mood . . ."

He paused before striking the fatal blow: "I am presently in room 34 of the Hôtel du Gecko, and I am always in a very bad mood when I'm investigating a murder!"

After making that blunt declaration, he cut the conversation short and looked up. François Ménard, Elsa Moulin, and her assistant had all interrupted what they were doing to listen to this stormy phone conversation. They were staring at him. Molina smiled at them.

"Now I can assure you that Monsieur Asshole is about to shit his pants. As soon as he's washed them out, he's going to go straight to police headquarters with his tail between his legs and we will soon be able to have a conversation with a nice little lapdog."

He handed the mobile to Elsa Moulin. The head of the forensic team put it in a labeled plastic bag.

"If I understand correctly, you are finally going to get out of my crime scene?" the young woman said. "Great . . ."

"We're off to headquarters, yes," he replied before turning to Ménard. "We also have to put out a notice that we're looking for the husband."

He went out on the landing, took off his shoe covers, his gloves, and his cap, which he threw into the room. Before he left, Elsa stopped him:

"It will take us only a few more minutes, so if you see Gilles, will you send him to me right away?"

Ménard made a face. Molina sniggered:

"If it's about a date for tonight, my dear, I warned you: he won't call you!"

"Molina, do you know what?"

"I have a vague idea."

"Go fuck yourself!"

"That's just what I was thinking. Come on, François, we'll go together. It's so much more fun when two are doing it!"

CHAPTER 5

The perfect crime.

Finally!

His plan had worked.

From his observation post, he had seen everything, better than on TV. The couple's arrival, the man's departure, then the husband going in and coming out, and finally the arrival of the useless emergency vehicles and the police. First the forensic team, then the investigators. He hadn't understood very well why the two lieutenants had lingered so long in the street before deciding to go into the hotel. From where he sat, he couldn't understand everything.

But that didn't matter.

A funeral home's black hearse came up Rue des Augustins. Metal barriers along the narrow street prevented any vehicle from parking in front of the hotel. The hearse found a precarious place only on the little Place des Poilus, just in front of him. Two men in dark suits got out and headed for the hotel.

They were going to take the body away.

Poor Christine . . .

She was not necessarily the most guilty, but fate had decided things that way, she'd married an impulsive man, it was the fault of bad luck. At the same time, if she'd behaved instead of cuckolding her husband for weeks on end, none of this would have happened.

He saw one of the undertakers leave the hotel with a cop in

uniform. The forensic team had probably not yet finished in the "mortuary chamber," he'd have to wait. The guy from the funeral home offered the policeman on guard a cigarette, and lit one for himself. As they smoked, they exchanged a few words, probably commonplaces. They looked bored. You had to admit that there were terrible dead times in their trade.

He smiled at his joke.

At least in his own job it was like a reality show on TV: something was always happening. Usually not very exciting things, but from time to time, a few nuggets of truth.

He'd never loved his job as much as he had these last few weeks.

A fat gypsy woman walked in front of the hotel. Wearing a black skirt and blouse, with a simple cardigan over her large shoulders, she was strolling casually along in slippers, despite the winter weather. She was having an animated conversation on her telephone. He couldn't understand what she was saying, but he could tell that she was speaking Catalan. The gypsies of Perpignan were the last who were still using that language on a daily basis. Once her conversation was over, the Woman in Black put her mobile back in her blouse, between her ample breasts.

He took a deep breath. Life could be beautiful once again.

He'd succeeded, he'd taken his revenge.

A perfect crime, yes.

He experienced this result as a kind of liberation. He no longer felt that immense weight on his shoulders, that bitter knot in his stomach. Finally, he was breathing normally. This evening, he would go home with his mind at ease and his soul serene.

For the first time in such a long time.

He was getting ready to leave his observation post when he saw another policeman arriving, one he knew. *My God, he looks completely shot!* he said to himself with compassion, before smiling at his further joke, which was unintended this time. *Christine must look shot, too . . .*

He saw the policeman glance in his direction, but he wasn't worried. The cop couldn't see him. And he would never trace this back to him.

The Eye had achieved the exploit he had so long waited for, so hoped for, so prepared for.

His mission was not over.

CHAPTER 6

"Ah, so there you are! I was beginning to think you were dead. Actually, now that I see the way you look, I wonder if you're not . . ."

Jacques Molina and François Ménard were getting ready to leave the hotel when they met Gilles Sebag in the lobby.

"I'm feeling a little queasy," Sebag said to excuse himself.

"Hmm . . . And does that keep you from answering the telephone?"

"You won't believe this, but I couldn't find it."

Molina stared at his colleague, wondering whether he wasn't deliberately messing with him.

"In fact, I'd left it in my running bag," Sebag explained. "I'd gone on a long run over by Baixas last evening, and I got back pretty late. I was worn out, and I don't know what I ate afterward, but I had diarrhea part of the night and all morning."

Molina shook his head. Gilles looked sad. Whatever he ate must have reached its expiration date at the time of General de Gaulle, the London period rather than the Colombey period.

"You run at night?" Molina asked, astonished.

"Sometimes. I have a headlamp. But in those cases I avoid trails and stay on the asphalt. But why didn't you try calling me on the landline?"

Molina frowned. Once again, he had the impression that they were making fun of him. Very good at discovering other people's deceptions, Sebag turned out to be a pitiful liar. He had learned to invent countless pretexts to justify being late, or even absent, but he usually reserved them for his direct superior, Superintendent Castello, who consented to believe them.

"That's right, that was stupid, we didn't even think about it," Ménard conceded.

Molina remained pensive.

"So, this case, uhh . . . what's it about?" Sebag asked.

"'A tragedy of jealousy,' tomorrow's papers might call it," Ménard replied. "The husband killed his wife in the hotel room where she had just spent two hours with her lover."

"Ah . . ."

"Yeah, even these days that remains a major classic," Molina added. "So you could have spent the whole day on the toilet . . ."

"And the . . . lover was no longer there?"

"No, he'd already left," Ménard answered. "The owner of the hotel unequivocally identified the husband in a photo. We haven't succeeded in contacting him, but we're going to put out a notice that we're looking for him, and we'll also send a patrol car to his home and his workplace."

"We're also going to interrogate the lover," Molina added. "He's supposed to come to headquarters. Do you want us to wait for you?"

"If you want, sure . . . I don't know. It's your call, in fact. For the moment, I'm going to have a look around up there instead."

"Elsa is waiting for you with . . . impatience. It's on the fourth floor."

Without responding to Molina's mockery, Sebag disappeared into the stairwell.

Elsa Moulin took off her cap, shook out her hair, and kissed Gilles hello.

"Oh là là, you're all pale! Are you ill?"

"A little queasy, yes."

As she approached him, the young woman had noticed an unusual sour odor, an odor of perspiration. She thought for a moment that with this case, Gilles must not have had time to take a shower after he ran. But she rejected that hypothesis. Gilles's tired-looking face spoke for itself: he was in no state to run.

"Gastroenteritis?"

"Don't know."

A little voice piped up in Sebag's shirt pocket: "Papa, you've got a message!"

"Excuse me, it's an SMS."

"Amusing way to announce it."

"My daughter recorded that for me and I don't know how to get rid of it. I look stupid, sometimes."

"I find it charming."

"Yes, but when you're trying to look like a hard guy to break a hoodlum and your telephone suddenly calls you 'papa,' it pretty much ruins everything. You don't scare anybody anymore!"

"I can imagine."

Sebag quickly read the message and put away his phone. He remained pensive for some time.

"Bad news?"

Gilles looked up.

"Excuse me?"

"Bad news?"

"Uhh . . . no, no. My wife who . . . I've got to buy bread on the way home tonight. Nothing out of the ordinary!"

He made a quick tour of the bedroom and bathroom before having a look at the body. Then he looked out the window.

"The street is calm and the buildings look quiet," Elsa said. "No point in expecting much from witnesses there. But in any case you don't really need them."

"Jacques and François gave me a quick rundown. So everything is crystal clear?"

"I think so. No need to canvass the neighbors this time."

"Oof. I think that's one of the things I like least about this job: I feel like the sales rep for a product that no one really cares about. As soon as they have a problem, people come to weep on our shoulders. But when they don't need us, they immediately revert to the ancestral antipathy they have for uniforms. It bugs them to have to help us, and they don't even try to hide it. Ah, well, that's how it is. So, anyway, this investigation isn't very exciting!"

Sebag's disillusioned tone astonished Elsa.

"Whoa, you're really out of sorts today . . ."

"Kind of, yeah."

Gilles avoided looking her in the eye.

"You look really queasy," she said sympathetically. "And just before the holidays. That's bad luck."

Sebag gave her a strangely sweet smile. A sad smile, Elsa thought.

"Well, that way I won't put on too much weight."

"Oh, you don't have any real problems in that regard."

"Because I watch myself! But at my age, one minute of inattention and wham, you get rolls of fat."

"Nonsense! You're just right."

Gilles's smile became happier.

"You're too sweet."

Jordi Estève pulled the chain on the toilet. Damned prostate! It seemed to him that he spent half his days in the bathroom. And the other half buttoning up his pants . . . What a stupid idea to go back to the fashion of button-up pants, when there was no finer invention that the zipper . . . Forty times a day that thought came to him. Damned prostate, indeed.

Back in the lobby, he found a man standing in front of the framed photographs hung on the walls. He was a policeman, Jordi had seen him talking with the other two. He coughed. Not because he wanted to attract the guy's attention but because he really had a frog in his throat, so deep down in fact that he wondered if the confounded thing wasn't croaking in his bronchial tubes instead. Or did he have throat cancer? His granddaughter kept pestering him to go to the hospital and have some tests done. He told her that at his age, you had to die of something or other.

The policeman turned to him.

"Not bad, your photos."

"Thanks. My grandfather was a photographer. Most of the pictures of the city around the turn of the last century are his."

"Congratulations . . ."

The policeman came up to him and held out his hand.

"I haven't introduced myself. Lieutenant Sebag. Yes, nice photos. And also very useful."

"They provide good decoration, I think."

"The arrangement is unusual."

"People often tell me that, but I like it this way."

"Yes, very useful," Sebag repeated. "Especially for hiding the traces of damp-rot from the guests."

Old Jordi couldn't help smiling.

"Are you finally going to tell me what happened to Christine?"

The man, very upset, refused to sit down. François Ménard and Jacques Molina had let him stew in his worries for half an hour in the lobby of police headquarters. Long enough to make the pressure rise considerably, but also for them to drink the coffee they hadn't had time to drink after lunch. When they got back from the Carlit, their favorite greasy spoon, they had Christine Abad's lover brought into one of the rooms reserved for interrogations. Sebag had just joined them and sat down in a corner of the room, telling them to conduct the interrogation as if he weren't there.

"What's all this business about a murder?"

The man's blue eyes jumped with concern and anger from one inspector to the other. Molina consulted Ménard with a look before going ahead.

"Christine Abad has been murdered."

The lover's face fell.

"You're kidding."

"Do I look like it?"

"How . . . how is that possible?"

"Sit down."

"Who killed her? When and how?"

"Sit down," Ménard commanded in turn. "Please."

This time the man obeyed. Mechanically. The two inspectors sat down on the other side of a little square table. Ménard laid his notebook in front of him.

"Let's proceed in an orderly way, if you please."

"What happened exactly?" the lover persisted.

"We will tell you when the time comes, but for now, we are the ones who are going to ask the questions. Last name, first name, age and occupation."

"But . . . is she . . . is she really dead?"

"Yes, sir," Ménard replied, with the sobriety of a policeman used to the incredulity of family and friends when faced with this kind of information. "We would like you to answer our questions: last name, first name, age, and occupation."

The man tried to protest again, but when he saw the determined faces of the policemen he finally bowed his head.

"Balland, Éric, 52, sound engineer. I work at the Archipel Theater."

"Are you married?"

Balland acquiesced silently.

"Do you have children?"

"Yes . . . three."

In Balland's voice Molina had recognized a different southern accent.

"Where are you from?"

"Bordeaux. I spent most of my life there. I have been in Perpignan for only three years."

"Have you known Christine Abad long?"

"More than a year. We did yoga together."

Molina almost snorted, but Ménard didn't give him time.

"How long has she been your mistress?"

Balland wrinkled his forehead, making the two bumps over his arched eyebrows stand out. He stared at the two inspectors one after the other and realized that it was pointless to deny it.

"About two months."

"How did you become lovers?"

Docilely, Balland recounted the main lines of their affair. The first looks, the first smiles, the first words. The Hôtel du Gecko as well, and their biweekly habits.

"What was the exact nature of your relationship? I mean, did you love each other?"

"I don't understand what your question means."

Ménard raised his eyebrows.

"But it's clear enough . . ."

"Then let's say I don't see how that is of interest in the framework of an investigation. It's . . . personal."

Despite the shock and pain, Éric Balland had already gotten a grip on himself and was now thinking before he answered. He probably didn't want to feel himself judged. Since Ménard had fallen silent, Molina took over. In the game they were playing, his role was to refocus the witness. To tenderize the meat, as he liked to put it.

"It's up to us to decide which questions we ask."

"I told you: it's personal!"

"That's not a real answer, is it?"

"I have the right to choose what questions I answer. I have come here of my own free will, I'm not in police custody and, I suppose, I'm not a suspect . . ."

Molina interrupted him: "Does your wife know you're here?"

Balland paled.

"What are you getting at? That's . . . blackmail!"

"Already using big words . . . I just wanted to make you understand one thing: the more you put off answering our questions the longer this discussion will last. And the later you get home, the more difficulty you'll have explaining this delay to your wife. We can also come to your home tomorrow morning to ask you the questions you've refused to answer today."

"That's disgusting!"

Overacting his indifference, Molina shrugged his shoulders.

"No more than deliberately delaying the work of two poor government officials whose only goal is to identify Christine Abad's murderer. And whether you loved her or not, I find that absolutely disgusting."

"You know very well who killed her . . ."

"We'll see about that later," Ménard said evasively.

The tension having risen sufficiently, he took over again to reduce it.

"Let me explain to you, sir, how we proceed in the police. In the course of an interview with a witness, we always ask all kinds of questions. Most of them are pertinent, while others might seem incongruous. Some really are incongruous, but it also sometimes happens that questions that seemed incongruous at the time turn out later to be pertinent."

Ménard picked up the pencil he had laid on the table and with a click made the lead project from it.

"It's only at the end of the interview that we decide what is important for the investigation and what is not, what we will keep or not in the record of the interview. Thus everything that you are going to say to us will not necessarily be recorded."

This beating around the bush annoyed Molina. Were it up to him, he would have taken out his telephone and put in the wife's telephone number. Then he'd have the guy by the balls.

"There is no judgment on my part," Ménard went on. "So I'm going to formulate my question differently: "Did you and Christine plan to leave your spouses and live together?"

Balland's eyes opened wide.

"No! Absolutely not."

He realized that his categorical tone might be surprising.

"There was a great deal of tenderness between us, and a great deal of complicity as well. But . . . to answer your first question, I . . . I did not love her, no, and she didn't love me, either. That is . . . everything obviously depends on what you understand by this term 'love.' We loved the time we spent together, but never, never did we imagine living together. Our affair would probably have lasted a few weeks, or even a few months, and we would both have gone back to our little lives."

"Was this the first time you'd cheated on your wife?"

The question had burst forth from the corner of the room where, up to now, Sebag had kept quiet. Ménard breathed noisily. Gilles's clumsy intervention threatened to antagonize the witness again.

"It was the first time, yes."

Balland lifted his strong-willed chin, his square jaw contracted, and his eyes stared unblinking at the policemen. His attitude contrasted with his hesitant tone. Sebag clucked his tongue loudly.

"Hmph . . ."

Balland stared at Sebag, and then the other two lieutenants, as if to find out whether he should respond to this onomatopoeia. Molina came to his aid:

"Consider our colleague a kind of lie detector. In this case, he means he doesn't believe you at all."

Balland ran a finger over his delicate, small lips. Looking at Ménard alone, he answered:

"It does not concern me whether he believes me or not. That is my answer, my only answer. You can record it."

Ménard made use of this to take over the reins of the conversation.

"That will be recorded, Monsieur Balland. Now I would like to come back to a remark you made a little while ago. You said: 'You know very well who killed her.' What does that sentence mean?"

"It's obvious, isn't it?"

"Maybe, but I'd like to hear you say it."

"The murderer was her husband. In this kind of thing, it's obvious!"

"Christine must have spoken to you about him. Was she afraid of him?"

"In general, we avoided talking about our spouses when we were together . . . But she did tell me several times that he was irascible and might prove violent if he learned of our . . . our affair. But I didn't think it could go that far."

"Do you know if he had a gun at his home?"

"Christine told me that he went to a shooting range. With a rifle, I think."

"What kind of rifle?"

"No idea."

"Was Christine Abad afraid of her husband?"

"No, I don't think you could say that. I think she had never imagined that he might . . . go that far. It's insane!"

"Had he already been violent with her?"

"She never told me anything like that. How was she killed?"

Ménard pursed his lips before deciding to answer.

"A bullet to the heart. Probably a .22 long rifle."

"Then it's him, for God's sake, there's no doubt! Why are you wasting your time with me? Have you arrested him?"

"Not yet, but it won't be long. A search notice has already gone out."

Balland took his head in his hands.

"It's dreadful. How can anybody be that jealous? To kill his own wife, it's crazy, it's crazy! I thought that things like that happened only in films."

"You don't spend enough time in court," Sebag suggested from his corner. "And what about you, have you asked yourself what you would do if your own wife cheated on you?"

Balland stared at him, first with astonishment, and then with a glimmer of defiance. He seemed to have no doubt, not about his own reaction, but about his wife's behavior. Molina also deciphered this look and said to himself that husbands who were too sure of themselves were either lucky or fools.

Considering Sebag's question once again off the subject, Ménard resumed the thread of the interrogation:

"What time did you leave the hotel?"

"Shortly before two o'clock."

"And why did Christine stay longer?"

"First, because she had the time . . . I would have liked to stay, too, but I was expected back at work. And then because she liked to linger a few minutes in the room. I often left her a cigarette that she quietly smoked."

His tone had become graver as his answer developed and the last syllables were lost in his throat. Balland bit his lips and sniffed. Ménard asked a few more unimportant technical questions and the interview came to an end.

The two lieutenants stood up and Balland imitated them. They said goodbye and exchanged a few further remarks without interest, but the lover couldn't make up his mind to leave. Uneasy, he shifted his weight from one foot to the other.

A question was bothering him that he finally managed to express:

"Do you think that all this could remain . . . discreet?"

Understanding, Ménard frowned.

"It's a murder, and the press is certainly going to talk about it," he said, nonetheless.

"But all the details won't necessarily be given? All the names, either?"

Ménard scratched the end of his nose.

"We don't control communication, you know. In general, we don't talk with the press. As for the prosecutor, he's not very talkative either. But the information will be in the local newspapers tomorrow, there may be leaks. The lawyers are not bound by the secrecy of the investigation. And neither are the other witnesses."

Perpignan is a small town," Molina warned in his turn. "Your escapades were undoubtedly not a secret for everybody. Some of your colleagues may have noticed things, and also other people in your yoga class. You probably talked about this relationship with friends, and Christine, too. If you imagine that no one knew about it, I can guarantee you that you are mistaken. Perpignan, as I said, is a small town, a very small town."

"We've been as discreet as possible."

Molina sniggered.

"Yeah, I thought so, too . . . That worked for a while."

"In any case, we're going to arrest the husband," Ménard added. There will be a trial, and you will necessarily be called as a witness. I have no advice to give you, but in your place I'd try to get ahead of the curve and tell my wife everything this evening."

"This evening already?"

"Why wait?"

"Tomorrow is . . . is Christmas Eve."

Molina put his paw on Balland's shoulder. He felt like crying "Merry Christmas" to him, but ended up being more indulgent. He'd experienced this, too. Recalling Sebag's skepticism when Balland claimed that he'd never cheated on his wife before, he reassured the lover:

"Be honest about Christine . . . But you're not obliged to tell her about the others . . ."

Balland bowed his head, muttered a final farewell, and left. Molina turned around and noticed at that moment that Sebag was no longer in the room. Jacques hadn't seen him leave.

"So, are you feeling better?"

Sebag didn't move, despite the question. He was standing at the window, watching the traffic calm down on the Avenue de Grande-Bretagne. Night had fallen some time before, and the office workers had almost all gone home. Molina sat down at his desk. He was eager to leave, but his workday wasn't yet over, and might not be anytime soon.

"OK, apparently you're not feeling any better."

He dialed a number on his telephone. Sebag's mobile immediately rang on his desk. Gilles grabbed it, looked at the screen, and then looked up at his colleague.

"Are you stupid, or what?"

"You don't answer me when I ask questions in person, so I've found it more effective to call you. And you see, it works."

"So what was your question?"

"Forget it, I've already got the answer."

Sebag didn't pursue the issue.

"Your guy didn't say anything else as he left?"

"'Your guy'—it sounds like you don't feel very involved in this case."

"Do you find it exciting?"

"It's been a long time since I found this job exciting."

"Now, that's news!"

"What, that I'm no longer excited by it?"

"No, that you ever were!"

"Very funny . . ."

"Thanks. I think so, too."

Molina noticed that his partner had perked up. He thought this might be the right time to mention something that had surprised him.

"What was it with all those stupid questions you asked Balland during the interview?"

"Don't know. They just popped out."

Molina frowned. Not much of an explanation. After a short pause, Sebag continued:

"The guy was just getting on my nerves. He mourned for about three minutes before he started thinking about himself, about saving his family life, when he was the one who'd put it in danger . . ."

Sebag suddenly fell silent. Then he changed the subject.

"What about the husband, any news?"

Before going up to their office, Jacques had reviewed the situation with Joan Llach, who was also working on this investigation.

"No, still nothing. He's not at home, and not at work, either. Joan sent his car's license plate number to all the teams in the field. If he's still in this area, we'll pick him up soon."

"Did you try geolocating his mobile?"

"Yes, but nothing came up."

"Too bad . . . How about the son? Did someone tell him?"

"Julie took care of that."

"That's good. Julie's tactful . . ."

Molina had no trouble acknowledging that: transferred to their department and promoted a few weeks earlier, Julie had already proven to be an effective and subtle psychologist.

"The boy is in business school in Toulouse," Jacques added. "He was on a ski vacation in Font-Romeu. Now he's on his way back and Julie will talk with him in a little while. It would be good for someone to stay with her . . ."

Molina had put the ball in his partner's court and was waiting for him to respond. After all, it was his turn to work a little bit.

"I can do that," Sebag said with apparent relief. "And when we're finished with the son, we'll try to get hold of the father again."

Jacques got up without giving Sebag time to change his mind or for his stomach problem to kick up again. Suddenly he was impatient.

"Great . . . So I can take off?"

"You can."

That morning, Molina had brought a clean shirt and pants to work with him. He took them off the coatrack and started undressing.

"The gentleman is going out this evening . . ." Gilles observed.

"It's impossible to hide anything from you."

"What's she like?"

Molina smiled at the memory of his latest conquest. He'd met her during a wine tasting at the BBC, a trendy bar.

"Young, redheaded, and English."

"How young?"

"Twenty-two."

"Oh, of course . . . you don't deny yourself anything."

"When women like you, what can you do?"

"And he's modest, too!"

"I admit it."

After taking off his shirt, Molina removed his shoes and then dropped his pants.

"Uhh . . . now . . . if you don't mind . . . I'd like to change my boxer shorts."

Sebag turned and faced the wall, where he had hung a relief

map of the department of Pyrénées-Orientales, a gift from Séverine and Léo on his last birthday.

"I didn't know you were so concerned about your personal hygiene," he said, talking to the wall. "And I thought rugby players weren't so prudish in the locker room."

"We're not in a locker room. And you're not a rugby player!"

"True. Would you also like me to stand guard at the door to be sure nobody comes in unexpectedly?"

"It'll be all right."

Jacques had finished putting on his clean shorts. He put the others in his desk drawer.

"OK, you can turn around now."

Sebag did as he was told and allowed himself a slightly mocking smile.

"Did your British girl give you those?"

"Yes, my dear," Molina replied in English. He felt himself blush. He pulled out the elastic band around his belly. On it was written "Thursday."

"And I have a complete set for every day of the week," he explained.

"Nice gift."

"It is, isn't it? Cindy's working part-time in a clothing store."

"And useful . . . You're finally going to know all the days of the week in English."

"Do you think that's why she gave them to me?"

"What else?" Gilles replied in English.

Molina was all dressed again. An apple-green shirt with cobalt-blue pants. He let out a sigh of relief.

"I've wondered if the goal wasn't to make sure that I changed my boxers every day."

"Oh . . ."

Jacques smiled at the joke he was about to make: "Just

between you and me, I'd have preferred another set of shorts! A series of twelve."

"I sense something's coming."

"Shorts with 'January,' 'February,' etc. written on them . . . They'd be less work on a daily basis and they'd save on laundry detergent!"

Sebag laughed loudly and between two chuckles managed to get out a disgusted "yuck!" Molina put on his jacket and left the office, satisfied that he'd given his partner the first and only laugh he'd had all day.

CHAPTER 7

Finally alone . . . alone, goddammit.

He was done pretending, done talking, smiling, and especially trying to concentrate on an investigation that didn't interest him at all and only kept reminding him of his own worries.

Bad luck, all the same! Having to deal with the murder of an adulterous wife by a jealous husband—the very day that he learned that Claire had cheated on him. It was better to laugh about it than to cry over it . . .

Gilles Sebag couldn't do either one.

He stood in front of the open window in his office. He was smoking. Usually he smoked only four or five cigarettes a day. Sometimes more, sometimes less. Since early evening, he had far exceeded his daily ration. The wind outside was blowing the smoke back into the room. Too bad. By tomorrow, nobody would smell anything. And then Molina wasn't going to complain about that.

Across the street from police headquarters, the Carlit's owner was lowering the shutter of his bar-restaurant, making a metallic clatter that disturbed for a few seconds the calm of the Avenue de Grande-Bretagne. Rafel was lingering on the sidewalk, talking with two regulars. Gilles recognized activists in a left-leaning group that supported Catalan identity. They were lighting a last cigarette and no doubt talking about the independence movement that was growing on the other side of the Pyrenees. A year earlier, an unofficial referendum, contested by the government in Madrid, had ended with a big victory for the advocates of independence, and the upcoming regional elections represented the next stage in the struggle. The northern Catalans were following attentively and eagerly the battle begun by their cousins beyond the Pyrenees.

Sebag closed the window and sat down at his desk. It was quiet in the headquarters building. The room he occupied with Molina was on the third floor, far from the offices of the watch.

A bottle of whiskey was standing next to the telephone, as straight and proud as a soldier on his first July 14. Sebag grabbed it. He had gone to buy it at a little corner grocery store just before it closed. He'd bought the cheapest kind. A bad malt. The awful stuff raked his throat and burned his stomach, but it calmed his mind. The dark thoughts had lost their clarity and ardor, and they were now running through his mind at a slower pace. Even the words he'd read that morning on Claire's mobile were gnawing at him less voraciously.

It had become bearable. He took a gulp from the bottle.

Before going out to buy the whiskey, he'd helped Julie interview Maxime Abad. When he learned what his father was suspected of doing, the boy had been shaken—as anyone would have been—and almost fainted. Julie had just managed to catch him, and then laid him down on the floor. They'd called the emergency medics—nothing serious—and then the boy's maternal uncle. The kid mustn't have to face this tragedy alone. His mother dead and his father the killer: there was no good way to become an orphan, but this was one of the worst. Parents who were both guilty and victims, turn by turn, as if in league to ruin his life.

How could he get over all that?

Time dulls all pains, all pains, Sebag had said, annoyed to be thinking about himself as he said it. For a moment, he had been satisfied with himself: He didn't know how he would recover from Claire's infidelity, but he would never plunge his children into such a melodrama.

But that didn't last long.

Between two sobs of pain, Maxime had confirmed that his father owned a .22 long rifle that he used at the shooting range. Then, before leaving, supported by his uncle, he had called his father without receiving an answer. He'd left messages full of love and dignity on Abad's mobile and on the landline at their home.

After the interview, Sebag had decided not to go home. He hadn't really decided, it just forced itself on him. If Claire had been alone, they could have talked; he wanted to, he needed to. To talk to her, to touch her, to convince himself that she loved him. That they loved each other. To draw strength from that. But Léo and Séverine were at home and he didn't think he was strong enough to pretend in front of them. He was saving himself for the next day.

That damned Christmas Eve!

He also needed to think. Was he going to leave Claire or would he try to resume the normal course of their lives despite this misstep? Deep down, he knew the answer. But he also knew that nonetheless, he mustn't try to evade the question. He had to determine how serious it was and weigh the pros and cons in his soul and in his conscience.

Around 8 P.M., he had sent Claire an SMS to tell her that he wouldn't be coming home that night. She had immediately replied. "I understand. I'd so much like to be able to tell you I'm suffering too but you might find that indecent. I can only remind you again that you are the love of my life and that I don't want to lose you. I hope you'll be home tomorrow night. Don't make any hasty decisions. Give us a chance. Give me, the two of us, and the four of us a chance."

He'd read this SMS at least a dozen times since the beginning of the evening. He read it again. Then he looked up. In the windowpane, he saw his father's face. Yes, that pointed face, that straight nose, those long, black eyebrows, that slightly mocking smile. All that he'd gotten from his father. The older he got, the more he resembled him.

He didn't like that at all.

He immediately stopped smiling, put his elbows on his desk, and joined his hands in front of his mouth, as it to pray.

Shit! That, too, was one of his father's favorite positions. Gilles abruptly stood up and yelled:

"Gérard Sebag, get out of my body!"

He reopened the window to light a cigarette. Rafel and his activist buddies had gone away, and the street was quiet. He took a long puff, and the wind blew it back in his face. He breathed in the air full of tobacco smoke. Double benefit, double use, immediate recycling, a good point for the environment.

The whiskey was making his head spin. Damn, it was good! His body was heavy, his mind light. Finally!

"Papa, you have a message."

He didn't flinch. He knew who it was. He'd received the first SMS early in the afternoon, when he was in the hotel room. Since then she had been sending him one every hour. Always the same: "Don't forget that I love you."

It was true that she loved him. He had no doubt about that. She loved him, he loved her, they loved each other, that was the important thing. He had to repeat it to himself like a mantra, focus on that simple idea and prevent all the rest from burdening his mind. Yes, they loved one another . . .

But then why did all this happen? Why all this shit, why this misstep, and why did he hurt so much, why was it so hard for him to accept it?

So hard to forget . . .

The words he'd intercepted on Claire's phone remained engraved on his memory, letter by letter. They made this escapade painfully concrete. He couldn't forget, that would never be possible. It was pointless even to try. What he had to struggle to do was pardon it, not forget it. Pardon it and live with it. Love again, go on loving despite this feeling of betrayal deep in his heart.

That was possible.

Some people became violent—Abad had killed his wife—while others just separated—like Jacques and his wife, for example. But there were also others who continued, despite everything, to go on living or to survive. Yes, but who? Not a single name occurred to him. Those who manage that feat usually do so with the greatest discretion. As soon as people find out what happened, the decisions are no longer made by feelings, but by pride.

People mustn't find out.

Nobody . . . Ever.

Through the open window he heard voices, then car doors closing, then someone coming up from the parking lot. He leaned out the window and saw a patrol car drive off at high speed. The car passed the lifted barrier, turned left onto the avenue, and headed for the Arago Bridge. A little burst of siren to get across the intersection, and then it disappeared into the night. This sudden departure probably had nothing to do with their case. Franck Sergis, the officer on watch, knew that Sebag was spending the night in his office. If there had been anything new regarding Abad, he would have informed him.

Shivering, Sebag closed the window and collapsed heavily into his chair. He allowed himself another swig of alcohol. The level of the bottle was going down rapidly. He was drunk, he smiled. He loved proverbs and was especially fond of giving them his own twist. He opened his mouth and said out loud: *"Il faut soigner le mâle par le malt."*[1]

[1] "The male has to be cured by malt." A play on *Il faut soigner le mal par le mal* ("Evil has to be cured by evil"). Unless otherwise noted, all explanatory footnotes have been added by the translator.

Shouts dragged him out of his torpor. He felt like his mouth was full of cotton. He was thirsty. For water. He got up as slowly as a boxer who has been knocked out, left his office, turned on the light in the hallway, and staggered to the water fountain, leaning on the wall. He drank a cup of water, then another. The shouts were coming from the ground floor. A loud voice was screaming. The same word. Over and over. Sebag frowned; he wondered: maybe Abad had been arrested after all, without him being informed.

He started to go downstairs but changed his mind. First he had to spruce himself up and regain a reasonable lucidity. In the restroom, he splashed cold water on his face and combed his hair in front of the mirror.

His father's face was watching him.

His conjugal torments were reviving painful memories. He was feeling upheavals deep within him. It went far beyond Claire and that . . . that bastard Simon. But he sure as hell didn't want to go digging around in all that shit. He had to get through this alone, overcome the obstacle without breaking the dam he'd constructed and that since his childhood had been holding back the crap.

He went down the stairs step by step, gripping the railing. No, that couldn't be Abad braying like that. Abad had killed in icy rage. According to Elsa, he hadn't said even a word to his wife before shooting her. That kind of behavior didn't fit with the clamor downstairs.

He stopped at the door to the office of the watch, which handled emergencies at police headquarters. The room was badly ventilated and smelled like sweat and lack of sleep. On the wall, a vivid poster the color of end-of-the-night urine listed the emergency phone numbers: 15, 17, 18, 112, all losing numbers in the nighttime lotto. The clock on the wall read 2:16.

In the middle of the room, a solidly-built man was squirming on a chair. His hands were handcuffed behind his back. A long hank of blond hair fell over his massive shoulders. "Samson . . ." Sebag said to himself. Wearing a tank top that was too small for his powerful chest, the guy was in his forties and looked like he had come straight from the gym.

Except that his tank top was spotted with fresh blood. Delilah's blood . . .

"This guy's a real ox," Sergis, the head of the watch, said. "He hit his wife, and when we got there, he punched one of my guys and the other one had to tase him to calm him down. The effect lasted long enough to get him here, but since then he's recovered . . ."

"We have to cut his hair," Sebag said.

Sergis look at him with curiosity. Sebag had thought out loud. All the alcoholic vapors had not yet dissipated. Fortunately, the irate body-builder distracted Sergis's attention.

"I tell you, she's a slut!"

"That's not the point: You don't hit a woman," the policeman facing him said. "That's a serious crime."

"She's not a woman, she's a slut!"

The man's eyes were bloodshot and a thread of saliva hung from the corner of his mouth.

"Do you know that she's in the hospital?" the policeman went on. "They're doing tests on her. You really went at her: she has at least a broken arm and a couple of broken ribs. Maybe even a fractured skull. You're going to do jail time, pal. Several years, probably."

"That's not fair!"

The colossus suddenly stood up, taking with him the chair to which he was attached. His agitation made the muscles on his chest stick out of his tank top. A cop roughly pushed him down.

"What did his wife do to him?" asked Sebag, immediately regretting the question.

"We don't know exactly," Sergis replied. "But you can guess. He doesn't answer questions, just keeps saying 'slut.'"

"I heard that, yes."

"I think we won't get anything more out of him for the time being. We're going to put him in a holding cell to sober up. It might take a while . . . looks to me like he's really plastered."

Sergis signaled to his men to take the guy away. Three policemen approached him, the first one brandishing his Taser:

"Stay calm, pal, or I'll give you another jolt."

The second policeman put a pair of cuffs on the irascible man's ankles while the third quickly took the other pair of cuffs off his wrists, detached the metal chain from the rung of the chair, and then quickly reattached the cuffs. The man followed the policemen reluctantly, swearing all the way. Franck Sergis ran his hand over his cheeks darkened by a carefully trimmed three-day beard.

"I don't know what's up right now but it just goes on and on. Winter must be getting on husbands' nerves. At noon we had a murder, and tonight beatings and injuries . . . I read in an official report that conjugal conflicts represent one-fourth of all acts of violence."

"Do you think that's really new? Maybe today women file more complaints, that's all."

"Yeah, maybe. In any case, there's a lot of violence out there right now."

Sebag nodded, pensively.

"And apart from that, nothing particular last night?"

"A couple that couldn't quiet down their kid and asked us to help . . . More or less calm, actually."

At night, you saw strange people pass through police headquarters, and sometimes there were bizarre scenes.

"No news about your guy, obviously; otherwise I would have let you know. How about you, did you spend a good night up there?"

"It was OK. I've got a comfortable chair," Sebag replied, evasively.

He said goodbye to his colleague and returned to his office. Seizing the bottle of whiskey, he wondered what could lead a man to strike his wife. He had never for a moment been tempted to raise his hand against Claire. That kind of violence was completely foreign to him. The rage he felt would have been more likely to lead him to bang his own head against the wall.

In a crisis, there were two types of people: those who explode and those who implode. He was undoubtedly one of the latter.

He recalled again the text messages he'd intercepted that morning on Claire's phone. They didn't make him close his fists, they gave him cramps in his groin. The stomach upset he'd given to explain his absence was only half-invented. Every word struck him like a punch in the gut. Although he'd always had trouble learning poems at school or the words to songs, he would always remember these accursed phrases.

The first SMS read:

"At this holiday season, I'm thinking about you, my princess, my Heloise. I remember our mad embraces and our passionate discussions about a film, a book, or an exhibit. I miss them, I miss you."

And the second:

"I'm heading into these holidays with a new serenity. I'm rediscovering the pleasures of family life. I hope that everything is going well for you and yours. I embrace you with tender love."

Goddamn son of a bitch!

That second-to-last word made his guts writhe. Anything but that. Not tenderness . . . Sex, all right, a good lay, wild fucking, but not tenderness! And not that complicity regarding films or books. Who was he, that bastard Simon, to embrace his wife, *his wife*, with tenderness? Who was he to call her "my princess"?

He grabbed the whiskey bottle and allowed himself a long swig.

Not that, not us . . . Good God!

For years he'd thought that they were above all that, inaccessible to jealousy, to weariness, to the annoyances of everyday life together, and especially to that way of sleeping around and deceptions that concerned only other people, that existed only in films and not in their real life, not in *their* life!

Well, it did . . . There, he'd said it, it was done: they were just a couple like others, as commonplace, as weak . . .

One among all, one among many.

Goddamn son of a bitch!

He took another drink of whiskey and banged his head against the wall.

A black hole.

He must have sat back down and drowsed off, because a minute, an hour, or several hours later, a hand shook him vigorously.

"Come on, Gilles, we need you. Are you available?"

CHAPTER 8

Sprawled on his desk, his head in his hands, Sebag straightened up. With difficulty, he lifted two eyelids that weighed tons. His eyes flittered about before being able to focus and see Franck Sergis impatiently standing in the doorway to his office. The head of the watch was wearing his jacket, and seemed ready to leave. The swelling under the leather on his right side left no doubt. He was armed.

"The customs men have asked for our help. They intercepted a Go-Fast on the autoroute, but one of the cars managed to get away from them. It exited at the southern toll plaza and is headed for Perpignan."

Sebag got up, took his jacket from the rack, and slipped it on. His movements were mechanical and awkward.

"Are you sure you're operational?" Sergis asked with concern.

"I'm fine, don't worry."

"You sure?"

"I said so, didn't I?"

Franck considered Sebag's state for a long time before saying:

"OK, then, I'm going to trust you on that. I'll be waiting downstairs."

He added before closing the door behind him: "And don't forget to hide the bottle."

Sebag heard the head of the watch run down the corridor. He opened his desk drawer, took out his gun, loaded it, and then slipped it into a holster that he strapped on under his arm. A ring of iron was pressing on his head. He took hold of the bottle with the intention of washing out his mouth and his neurons, but hesitated: alcohol and a gun didn't go together. Wisely, he put both of them back in his desk drawer.

After running water over his head in the restroom sink, he joined Sergis in the lobby.

"All my guys are already out there. We're going to form a team, if that's OK."

"My pleasure."

Sebag handed him his keys.

"We'll take my car, but you're going to drive."

"That's OK with me."

They raced down the stairs that led to the parking lot. Sergis started the motor and roared off.

"A squad car located the suspect's car on the outskirts of the city, at the roundabout in front of the Méga Castillet cinema complex. It had to let him go on toward the Boulevard Kennedy. It's a BMW 4 Series coupe, it's powerful and the guy is driving too fast. It's dangerous, even at this time of night, to chase him through the city."

Sergis turned on the siren and ran a red light in front of the Arago Bridge. Only then did Sebag realize that it was still dark. He looked at the clock on the dashboard. It read 6:15. He put his hand to his forehead and felt a kind of bump; he remembered the wall. So alcohol wasn't the only reason his head hurt.

"We're going to try to cut him off by taking the boulevards," Sergis explained. "It's likely that the guy will try to go that way and head for Narbonne."

The Go-Fast is a classic technique used by drug dealers to enter France over the Spanish border. In general, three fast vehicles follow one another on the autoroute at intervals of a few minutes. The first car spots the customs agents, the second carries the drugs, and the third follows to protect it from any rivals. That morning the first two cars had been intercepted, but the third managed to leave the autoroute at the southern toll plaza and was now driving at breakneck speed through the streets of Perpignan.

Franck Sergis and Gilles Sebag crossed the Basse River and passed in front of the glass-walled offices of the *Indépendant*, the local newspaper. The head of the watch had reasoned correctly, because at the end of the Mercader Boulevard, they saw the last vehicle they were looking for. Sergis positioned his car across the boulevard, but the BMW, after slamming on its brakes, turned right into the warren of narrow streets around the Palace of the Kings of Majorca. Sergis turned his vehicle around and followed the drug dealer. It had taken a fraction of a second for the policemen to size up their quarry: there was just one man in the car. Apparently, he was very young.

The BMW shot down the narrow streets without paying attention to the one-way signs, and what had to happen did: at the foot of the imposing walls of the palace, the fugitive soon found himself faced by a car coming in the opposite direction. The driver leaped out of his vehicle and started running. He was young, in fact. Not more than thirty.

Sebag unbuckled his seatbelt.

"Are you sure?" Sergis said, worried.

"Did you forget that I run marathons?"

Sebag didn't leave his colleague time to question him further about the state of his health. He was already running after the drug dealer.

His head hurt with every step, but his legs and his breath were OK. That was the crucial thing.

The kid first ran alongside the fortress, then began zigzagging in the narrow streets of the city center. He didn't seem to know Perpignan and chose his itinerary solely in relation to the length of the streets. He wasn't going anywhere, and had only one objective: to lose the cop who was chasing him, and to do that, he first had to get out of his sight.

Sebag was aware of that. He had started out by sprinting to reduce the distance separating him from the fugitive, and now he was keeping back. No need to put the pressure on too soon. Being twenty years younger, the kid would necessarily be able to run faster. On the other hand, unless he was used to running, he was going to fade rapidly. Gilles had to manage his race, find the right rhythm, the one that would erase the night's excesses.

Then everything would be possible.

After the Sainte-Claire convent, which is now occupied by the Centre de Documentation des Français d'Algérie, the young man took the ramp that went down to the museum's parking lot. Then he ran down the pedestrian streets of the Réal quarter. Without trying to, and probably even without knowing it, he was moving east. He was running with his hands alongside his body and did not seem to be armed. Sebag did not regret having left his pistol in its drawer; it would have hindered his running.

The headache was going away and Gilles was beginning to feel strong again. The miracle of regular training . . . Gilles remembered his first marathon, that magical moment at the twenty-fifth kilometer when he had felt as fresh as he was on the starting line. Lacking experience, euphoric and presumptuous, he had then decided to modify his race plan and accelerate. A few minutes later he ran straight into the notorious wall at thirty kilometers.

He'd never made that mistake again.

The drug dealer started down the Rue Llucia; he was entering the North African quarter of Old Perpignan. If he continued to the end of the street, he would arrive at Place Cassanyes, where the daily market would be setting up. There he could slip away among the boxes, stalls, and vans.

But fortunately, he didn't know the city!

Still obsessed with searching for short, narrow streets, he turned left toward the gypsy quarter. A mistake. Here people lived at night and things didn't start up again until late in the morning. The deserted street ran uphill, and the kid slowed down. Sebag was playing for time. It was still too soon to pounce.

When he got to the Place du Puig, the drug dealer changed one of his priorities. Hoping to catch his breath, he chose a route that ran down a gentle slope. Rue Saint-François-de-Paule first, then Rue du Ruisseau and Rue de la Révolution Française. Now they were in the downtown commercial center. The ground becoming flat again, the young man's speed decreased once more.

A little patience . . .

The streets were getting broader, but they remained empty. The boy started zigzagging again, one street to the left, the next to the right. He had only one goal, to lose his pursuer, but he couldn't do it. He was getting scared and began to cast worried looks over his shoulder. Each time he did that he lost about twenty centimeters.

Without accelerating, Gilles lengthened his stride. That was enough to shorten the distance.

The kid was now panicking. Only about ten meters now separated them. While continuing to run, he reached into a pocket of his pants and pulled out a knife. With a click, he flipped open the blade. The threat was clear but he had lost another meter.

Rue de la Fusterie, Rue des Cordonniers, Rue de l'Ange.

At each stride, Sebag ate away at the distance. He could hear the young man's gasping breath; his adversary was in agony. Even if he turned around to fight, he wouldn't be lucid enough.

This time Gilles accelerated.

A last turn. Rue Mailly. Gilles sprinted. He got nearer.

He remembered the advice Molina had given him one day about making the perfect tackle. He had listened only vaguely, but he recalled the main lines. "Grab whatever you can, a shirt, a leg, or a pair of balls, anything, and never let go, never, never, never." As they ran by a bookstore, Gilles decided he was close enough. He pounced. His hands slipped over the fabric of the kid's pants before he was able to grab the cuffs right at the bottom.

He didn't let go.

The young drug dealer slammed heavily onto the street. He hadn't had the benefit of well-informed advice and didn't know how to break his fall. Sebag clearly heard a bone break.

He got up first. Looked for the knife, roughly turned over the kid, who was writhing in pain on the pavement. His nose was spurting blood. Sebag grabbed his right arm, moved up to the hand, and found the knife planted in the boy's thigh.

Not a serious wound.

He got out his handcuffs, attached the kid's hands behind his back, and searched him. He had no other weapon, but he did have a big roll of bills, a mobile phone, and his driver's license. His name was Corentin Jacquet; he was twenty-four and lived in Cugnaux.

"Where is that?"

"In the suburbs of Toulouse," the young man gasped, breathless.

Sebag had already caught his breath. He called Sergis.

"It's OK . . . You can stop everything. I've got our guy. I'm taking him to Place Arago, meet us there. It'll be easier. I'll also call the emergency medics."

"Are you hurt?"

"Thanks for your confidence! No, it's the other guy who broke his nose as he fell. He also cut open his thigh trying to play with a knife. He'll need a little care before they take him away."

Sebag took his prisoner to the Place Arago, which was accessible to vehicles. Sergis arrived within five minutes, followed by the emergency medic's van. The doctor had the drug dealer get into the van, but before following him he pointed to Sebag's forehead.

"Did you hurt yourself when you fell?"

Gilles ran his hand over his bump.

"Huh? No . . . it's nothing."

"I think in fact you don't require hospitalization," the doctor joked. "And your client, shall I examine him with his handcuffs on?"

"Does that bother you?" Sergis asked.

"Not especially, given the nature of his wounds."

"Then it's more prudent to do it that way."

The two policemen had just enough time to smoke a cigarette before the door of the van opened to reveal the doctor.

"The nose is broken, but there is no deviation of the septum. I inserted cotton to stop the bleeding, and I'm leaving him to you. There's nothing more to do, the fracture will repair itself. As for the thigh, I disinfected the wound and bandaged it."

"So we can take him away?" Sergis asked.

"Absolutely, he's all yours."

Sergis put the prisoner in the back of their car and sat down at the wheel. Sebag got in alongside him.

"Not worth the trouble to bother with this one, Franck. You've finished your shift, I'll take care of it."

"Are you sure?"

"No problem."

"Are you up to it?"

Gilles was not unhappy to be dealing with this case rather than handling the consequences of Christine Abad's murder.

"You should take off before I change my mind."

"You're right! I'll owe you one, Gilles. This really works for me. My vacation started fifteen minutes ago and I was counting on taking a little nap to be in shape for Christmas Eve. My parents, my sister, and her children are coming down from Cahors late in the afternoon. What about you? You've got family, too, I suppose?"

"Only my wife and children. Afterward they're going to be with my in-laws."

"Without you?"

"I didn't take vacation time this year."

"You wanted to escape the fatigue duty?"

Sebag replied with a smile. He got along well with his in-laws, but there were always too many people at their home over the holidays. Friends, uncles, distant cousins. He didn't like that. Too much noise, too much small talk. And then every time people asked his opinion on cases that had been in the national press, about which he usually didn't know any more than what he had read in the newspaper. Not to mention that among that multitude, there was always somebody who would suggest or even insist that he denounce this or that abuse of police power. Although he was often the first to criticize, internally, the way the police functioned, on these occasions he felt obliged to defend colleagues he didn't even know and who might not even be defensible.

This year, he regretted missing this rendezvous even less than he had in previous years.

After dropping Sergis off at police headquarters, Sebag took the wheel to deliver his prisoner to the regional customs authority. Captain Marceau, who was responsible for customs investigations in the department of Pyrénées-Orientales, received him in a large room where a dozen agents were bustling about. He turned Corentin Jacquet over to a customs agent, who immediately took him away. In a corner of the room three agents were piling brown bricks on an enormous scale. The cannabis resin had been found in the second vehicle of the Go-Fast, a powerful, luxurious 4x4. When they had finished weighing it, a customs officer announced in a loud voice:

"Seven hundred and fifty-three kilos."

Captain Marceau made an approving face. To minimize the commercial and judicial risks, in recent months drug dealers had considerably reduced the quantities brought in on each trip. Today's take was the largest of the year.

"And we arrested five people," Marceau added. "Almost everybody."

"Almost?"

"We thought there were two people in the BMW that you intercepted. The customs men who spotted the group in Boulou saw a passenger sitting alongside your guy. He must have gotten out somewhere before arriving in Perpignan. He'll be the only one of them to have a good Christmas Eve. There's not much chance of our catching him beforehand."

"Good work all the same," Sebag commented.

"We've had that group in our sights for a long time, and tapped some of their phones. It wasn't very hard, in the end."

"They didn't use prepaid phones for this operation?" Gilles asked in surprise.

"Sure, of course. But one of them used his phone to call his wife to ask how their sick child was doing. Since his landline was tapped, we got the number of his mobile and we were able to geolocate it."

"What a moron!"

"That happens more often than you'd think. Fortunately. But we're not obliged to tell the public about that stroke of luck."

"You're going to talk about it?"

"We'll take some photos that we'll send to the journalists. During the holidays, they don't have much to write about, and I hope that they'll embroider on it as much as possible."

Sebag spent the whole morning with the customs agents.

They lent him a computer and he wrote his arrest report on the spot. The coffee they offered him on several occasions was of more than acceptable quality. Around 10 A.M. he received a message from Claire asking him for news. She also wanted to know whether he was planning to return home that night, or whether she should tell the children something. After weighing his words at length, he replied in two short sentences: "I'll be there. I love you." She immediately answered with a simple "Thanks with all my heart." During the night, messages saying "Never forget that I love you" had been interrupted only between 2 A.M. and 6 A.M.

CHAPTER 9

François Ménard was having lunch with Jacques Molina at the Carlit. Located across the street from police headquarters, the restaurant offered a decent and copious daily lunch special at a reasonable price. And the boss regularly gave policemen a cup of coffee or even a quarter-liter of red wine at no extra charge. In exchange, the policemen waved away with their magic wand the fines that the distracted Rafel was always forgetting to pay before the deadline. Ménard consented to close his eyes to these "habits" that he found inappropriate but which had existed long before he arrived in the department. In private, however, he constantly criticized these "Mediterranean customs."

They were starting in on the *plat du jour*, an eel with aioli, when Sebag made his appearance in the restaurant. Molina spontaneously stood up and applauded. Ménard limited himself to raising his glass of mineral water.

"Bravo! We followed your exploit with a slight delay, but it was grandiose," Jacques said to him.

Seeing Gilles's astonishment, he explained:

"We were at the video-surveillance center this morning, and the guys showed us your chase and your final tackle."

Ménard and Molina had in fact spent the morning examining the municipal police's surveillance tapes. The city of Perpignan had about a hundred video-protection cameras, scattered through the city, which filmed the streets 24/7. The policemen at headquarters often requested these images for use in their investigations.

"There was a camera ideally placed on the Rue Mailly," Molina went on. "Really, what a tackle! I'm not sure I ever made a better one, even in my glory days . . ."

Ménard laughed.

"What glory days would those be?"

Sebag didn't leave Molina time to respond.

"What were you doing at the municipal police's video center?"

"We were looking at images of Abad," Jacques replied. We were able to follow part of his itinerary. He parked in a handicapped space at the end of the Rue Foch and the Rue des Augustins, the only parking space available. He got out of his car with his rifle in its case and then went to the Place des Poilus, where he stayed to observe . . ."

"To observe?" Sebag interrupted. "Well, what was he waiting for?"

Gilles frowned. Ménard had also found the husband's behavior strange, but he had paid it no more attention.

"He must have been waiting for the lover to come out. But what's strange is that after Balland left, he still took the time to smoke a cigarette before deciding to go into the hotel."

Ménard paused to observe Sebag's reaction, but his colleague's face remained blank. He seemed to be elsewhere.

"Afterward, on the other hand, things moved fast. Abad remained in the hotel for less than ten minutes, and then he returned to his car with the rifle back in its case. He took the Quai de Lattre de Tassigny, turned right at the light toward the Place de Catalogne, passed the Arago Bridge, and took the northern expressway. We lost sight of him after that."

"And we have no idea where he went," Molina added. "Conclusion: in the end, we're right where we started."

Rafel put a plate in front of Sebag. Gilles spread his napkin on his lap and picked at the eel with the tip of his fork.

"I hope you aren't planning to conclude your Christmas

Eve with a torrid night," Molina said, amused. "There are things more erotic than aioli to spice up an evening . . ."

Sebag smiled wanly.

"What about you, aren't you afraid of driving away your English girl?"

"All she has to do is chalk it up to discovering the local sexual customs and practices."

Ménard let this facetious parenthesis pass and redirected the conversation toward their investigation:

"And you, Gilles? We haven't yet had time to talk about our interview yesterday with Abad's son. I suppose you asked him if he had any idea where his father might have taken refuge."

"Julie thought of that, yes."

Sebag put down his fork and took out his notebook. His memory, for once, failed him.

"Abad's family is mainly from over by Aspres, and most of his friends are in Perpignan and the surrounding areas. No trace of his car, I suppose?"

"None. We called the gendarmes.[2] Nothing to report. It's as if he'd disappeared into thin air."

"We'll eventually catch him."

"I hope we won't find his body rotting somewhere a couple of weeks from now."

"François, I recognize there your legendary optimism," Jacques remarked before turning to Gilles. "By the way, is it true that you spent all night in the office?"

Sebag evaded the question.

"François is right: we can't reject the hypothesis that Abad committed suicide after killing his wife."

[2] In France, there are two main police forces: the *Police nationale* and the *Gendarmerie nationale*. The former is civilian and is primarily responsible for cities and urban areas. The latter is part of the military and is responsible mainly for small towns and rural areas as well as military installations, airports, etc.

"Oh, great!" Molina chuckled. "Is it the idea of spending the holiday with your family that puts you in such good humor? I barely escaped it, in the end . . ."

"You don't have your children with you?" Ménard asked.

"No, never. That's the prerogative of my dear and loving ex-wife. Same as every year. As a result, I'm on duty for Christmas and for the following weekend."

After the meal and coffee, the three policemen got up to pay the bill at the counter. Next to the till, Rafel had placed a crèche. He did that every year. It was partly a tradition, but mainly a provocation. Among the classic characters of the Nativity, the Catalans always add an unusual character: the *caganer*, a famous man or woman shown defecating. A symbol of luck and fertility, the *caganer* was supposed to remind people that at certain times of day, the human condition remains the same for all, no matter what their rank, title, or fame. Molina bent over the crèche.

"So, what did you put there this year? Ah, yes, of course!"

Ménard bent down in turn, to examine a tiny figure with black hair and a white beard crouched over a magnificent turd.

"Who is it?"

"Rajoy," Rafel replied, shrugging his shoulders.

A determined opponent of an independent Catalonia, the Spanish prime minister had managed to unite all the Catalonian activists against him.

"I should have known."

Whereas Sebag and Molina went back to their office with the intention of having a little nap before dealing with current business and going home, François Ménard plunged into the first reports on the Abad case. He reread attentively the transcript of the interview with Éric Balland, and then the forensic team's report. At the end of the day, he called the gendarmes back and gave them his mobile number so they could inform him first if they had anything new on the husband.

It was not very good form to try to short-circuit one's colleagues, but knowing Molina well, he feared that only Sebag would be informed in the event of a new development over the long Christmas weekend. And that would be unfair! He, Ménard, had been there since the beginning of this case, he was the one who had carried out the interrogation of the lover, and it was also he who had had to perform the boring task of viewing the municipal police's video recordings. It was really time that Superintendent Castello, their superior, notice that there was more than one cop at the Perpignan headquarters who could conduct a criminal investigation all the way to its completion.

And because Sebag loved proverbs, Ménard had one of those ready to use as well, a nice hot one that he'd learned from his maternal grandmother. He recited it out loud in his Picard dialect: *"El vertu, é boin pour chès tchurés vius qu'is n'puettë pus."*[3]

[3] "Virtue is fine for curés and old men who can't do it anymore."

Chapter 10

The man was walking rapidly despite his corpulent physique. No time to exercise, he had to get home. Tonight was Christmas Eve, and the girls would be there as they used to be.

When they were still a real family.

On the Quai Vauban, he had to slow down. The crowd was preventing him from moving forward. Latecomers were thronging around the Christmas market's little lighted stands. People essentially looking for a last-minute gift. Merchants and customers were smiling. Despite the crush, it was a genuinely festive atmosphere.

He wasn't looking where he was going and bumped into a man wearing a red costume. Santa Claus turned around and smiled at him. Unsticking the white beard from his pale cheeks, he used his hands to put it back in place. A father thrust a terrified infant into his arms and he stepped back toward a stand decorated with a snowy nighttime mountain landscape. He whispered a couple of words in the child's ear in the hope of eliciting a smile. A flash lit the scene. Santa Claus kneeled to put the child down, then stood up again with difficulty. He pushed up the sleeve of his coat and looked at his watch. Impatient. Santa Claus was expected for Christmas Eve and had no intention of working overtime.

He finally got to the end of the Quai Vauban and leaned on the railing of the Magenta Bridge, just behind an advertising poster. He looked up and smiled: he knew that the halo of Christmas garlands protected him from indiscreet eyes.

He took a mobile phone out of his backpack and put a battery back in it. He also had a gift to give.

To give himself.

He wrote a text message. Only a few words. Carefully considered. A first contact. Just to worry the receiver.

It was time to get ready to fire the second stage of the rocket. Liftoff in a few days.

Merry Christmas!

Chapter 11

The Sebag family lived in Saint-Estève, a large community northwest of Perpignan. Before opening the door to the house, Gilles took a deep breath.

Claire was bustling about in the kitchen and Séverine was in the living room, wearing headphones as she watched a police series on television. The big room faced south and looked out on the sunlit terrace. The wind was blowing dead leaves from the apricot tree onto the blue tarp that protected the swimming pool from November to April. Claire often left the outside lights on. On evenings when she was in high spirits, she said the view of the garden expanded the living room with the promise of the spring to come.

Gilles came up to his wife. She was wearing a gray-and-yellow sheath dress that sensually emphasized her hips and her firm bust. The dress was a gift he'd given her the preceding Christmas. He found his wife beautiful, marvelously beautiful. But he couldn't help wondering if she had already worn that dress for the other man as well.

Claire looked up at him and he gave her a chaste kiss.

"It smells good," he said.

She pointed to the hot oven.

"A guinea hen with chestnuts, I didn't do anything unusual."

"That's my favorite dish."

"I know."

She took his hand and pressed it between hers.

"Your day wasn't too hard?"

"Apart from lasting thirty-six hours, not too."

"I heard on the radio that there was a murder?"

Sebag thought a moment about what he was going to say.

"A pretty ordinary case . . . A drama of . . . jealousy."

He'd avoided the painful word "adultery," so why wasn't he able to prevent himself from immediately adding:

"It ends that way, sometimes."

Claire's lips tensed and her blue eyes clouded over, becoming a sad green.

"Most of the time things go differently. I know that it's the first cause of divorce, but it nonetheless sometimes happens that love is stronger and triumphs over jealousy and suffering . . ."

Gilles just nodded.

"Is Léo there?"

"In his room, on his computer, as usual."

"Do I have time to take a shower?"

Clair sniffed and smiled.

"You have not only the time, but also the duty!"

Gilles gently freed his hand from hers and fled into the bedroom. On the bed, the quilt cover was still the same one as the day before: *You and Me, Today, Tomorrow, Forever*. The sheet retained the shape of a body where his wife usually slept on it. His pillow lay on top of the quilt and was creased. After a difficult and partly sleepless night, Claire had probably taken a nap in the early afternoon, her nose thrust into the pillowcase still imbued with his smell.

He went into the adjoining bathroom, threw his dirty clothes into the laundry hamper, and stepped into the shower. He began by letting the hot water flow over his tired body. Then he abruptly turned the lever in the other direction. The stream of icy water stunned him. His breathing stopped, he groaned, shivered, then shrieked. His breathing gradually became more regular, the cold became bearable. The body could adapt to anything. The mind ought to be able to do the same.

He was drying himself off when Claire came to press herself against his cool skin. She ran her hand over his face and stopped at the bump on his forehead.

"Did you hit yourself?"

He recalled his dialogue with the emergency medic.

"Yes, I . . . I chased down a little drug dealer this morning, and the heel of his shoe hit me on the forehead when I tackled him."

"You're not hurt any other way?"

"Apparently not."

"I don't like it when your work becomes dangerous. I don't want to lose you . . ."

"I don't either . . . I don't want to lose myself."

He'd tried to make a joke, but realized that his remark was double-edged. Just like his wife's.

Claire stood on tiptoe and opened her mouth. They kissed for a long time. Sebag was sorry he'd eaten the eel with aioli, even though he knew his wife was in no position to complain. When their lips separated, she thanked him for coming home. For her and for the children.

"We're spending Christmas together as a family, and then I'm going to my parents' place. You can think about it. But give us some time. You can decide afterward what you want to do."

As in the kitchen a few minutes earlier, Gilles just nodded. He knew that he was prepared to do anything to try to accept, but he was in no hurry to reassure his wife. A petty punishment, perhaps, but he had a right to inflict it.

"And . . . What about him, does he know that I know?"

Silently, she acquiesced.

"What did you tell him?"

She bit her lip.

"That you had read his messages and that I'd confessed everything to you."

"Does his wife know?"

Claire frowned.

"No. Why would she?"

"He might have told her."

"Why would he do that?"

"So he could stop lying, for example."

"The affair is over, we live four hundred kilometers apart, and we'll never see each other again. She has never suspected anything and probably never will. He won't have to lie to her anymore, why do you think he would hurt her by telling her everything?"

He almost told her that he wouldn't allow their couple to be the only one to suffer, but succeeded in controlling himself. Deep down, he clearly sensed that unhappiness can't be cured by another unhappiness. Seeing his somber face, Claire suddenly got worried.

"You're not going to tell her, are you?"

Gilles looked her straight in the eye. Claire's concern was like a balm.

"Probably not."

"Probably?"

"Does anyone ever know what he might be capable of in a moment of . . ."

He hesitated; he was afraid of being too melodramatic. Then he decided the term was justified:

"Of despair."

Claire dug her white canines deeper into her soft lip.

"Don't ever do that, please."

For a moment he thought his wife's sharp reaction came from the word he'd used. His expression hardened.

"Are you afraid for him?" he said coldly.

She put her hands on his stubbly cheeks.

"No, Gilles, I'm afraid for you. Really. That's not the kind of person you are, I know that afterward you'd feel terrible about it."

"So what kind of person am I? The nice fall guy, the understanding cuckold?"

Gilles hadn't planned to get angry like this. He'd come home full of good intentions but rage had overcome him. A tear slipped from Claire's eye. In that pearl he found the strength not to go any further, and to keep to himself all the smutty questions that were banging around in his head. He took his wife's hands and pulled them away from his cheeks. Then he went on in a tone that was firm but less severe:

"I don't want you to contact him again. Ever. No e-mails, no text messages, nothing at all. I can't erase him from your memory but he has to disappear from your life, from our life. Forever."

"I've already told him not to contact me again."

"Did you tell him that in an SMS?

Claire bowed her head.

"I called him."

She immediately looked up.

"I thought that was better, firmer and more definitive."

"And what did he reply?"

"That it would be difficult but that it was preferable for everyone. Then I erased his number from my contacts."

"And will it be difficult for you, too?"

"No doubt. But this affair is over, it should never have happened. I want to do everything I can to save our marriage, our family, I'm ready to do anything to win you back."

He put his hand on Claire's shoulder. She tilted her head to put her cheek on his hand.

"I want to trust you, Claire. But so far as he's concerned, I'm going to be straight with you: If I learn that he has tried to contact you, even once, I'll tell his wife everything. You tell him that. To warn him, you can contact him again. Just once."

Gilles slowly pulled away and then headed for the bedroom closet, which he opened wide. He drew a long breath. He had to get dressed. If only by changing his clothes he could change his mood.

"What do you want me to wear this evening?"

"I like your navy blue shirt with your white slacks."

"A tie?"

"Why not?"

She came over and chose a tie herself. A yellow one with a diamond pattern in sky-blue and brown.

"It'll go very well with your shirt."

The evening went off without a hitch. Sebag managed to fool everyone and even to smile and joke with Séverine and Léo. After his second drink, he decided it wasn't so hard to pretend, and that it even lent one a certain serenity. He recalled the days back when the kids were little and he sat on the floor with them after he got home from work. It took only a few seconds for all his job worries to fade away.

How he would have liked to go back there, to Séverine with her little curls and smiles, to Léo's pure joy, his eyes full of pride as he looked at his father. And the total confidence that he then had in his wife.

The guinea hen with chestnuts turned out to be excellent, as it did every year. During the whole evening, Claire was never far away, and took his hand or touched him every time she could. Maintaining contact to keep him with them in the joy of the instant, to prevent him from escaping to the dark regions of the recent past or to sad nostalgia for older times. After dessert—a chocolate parfait—they gave themselves over to the pleasure of the traditional gift-opening ceremony. The only flaw in the scene was that Claire had really bought him too many gifts this year.

Far too many.

Shortly after midnight, they were alone again in their bedroom. They undressed in silence and slipped between the sheets. Claire's body touched his. Her belly against his side. She laid her hand on her husband's chest and caressed it gently. He turned over on his side, and held her to him. His hand rested on her soft shoulder.

"I love you, Claire, I love you so much . . ."

He caressed her shoulder, then her neck. Then his hand went up to her cheek. Claire pressed her lips to his mouth and they embraced with as much passion as despair, combining saliva and tears in a single kiss. The salty taste turned both of them on.

They made love furiously.

As if it were the first time.

Or the last.

Chapter 12

The light they'd forgotten to turn off on the terrace haloed their room with calming shadows. Claire was drowsing, half-asleep, lost between the soothing of her senses and a dull uneasiness that tormented her body. The intensity of the sex had troubled her. Too many emotions were mixed up in it. Passion, fears, hope, anger, and also a bit of madness; a desire for possession in Gilles, a sense of guilt in her.

The body lying at her side turned toward her. The breathing was short, as if held back, the muscles tense. The wind was moving tentacular shadows on the walls. The moment of escape was over, unhappiness was returning. Fear was boring into the pit of her stomach. She remained stretched out on her back, refusing to turn over toward her husband. Above all, she didn't want to encourage him, she was too afraid of what was going to come. Terrible questions, necessarily terrible ones.

She heard the mouth next to her open and stop breathing. The silence thickened around them. Nothing came out of those lips. Claire regained hope.

Not for long.

"And . . . he . . . was he a . . . a good lay?"

Claire closed her eyes. Her teeth bit into her lip without her knowing it. She had to pay the price. It was probably better this way. Her answer slipped out like a murmur:

"I don't know what a good lay is."

A ridiculous evasion. Gilles wouldn't give up.

"Did he give you pleasure?"

A sigh, a moan, a plaint.

"Yes."

"Every time?"

A gasp, a sob, a strangled scream.

"Yes."

"Did he fuck better than I do?"

Her body stiffened further in response to the bruising words. She concentrated on her breathing to blunt the shock. She counted to ten before reopening her eyes. She turned toward Gilles, looking for help in his eyes. There she found neither tenderness nor love—pain masked everything—and felt lost.

How could she keep her promise to be sincere, to tell him everything, to confess everything, when the truth would add pain to his sorrow?

Simon was no more skilled than Gilles, but he had explored her mature woman's body and revealed new paths to her. Paths toward pleasure that probably hadn't existed before, and that Gilles had given up searching for. An absurd comparison occurred to her. The first summer following their arrival in the department of Pyrénées-Orientales, they had played tourist and visited many, many villages, sites, chapels, and chateaus. Then as the months went by, they started filtering their destinations, giving priority to places they knew they liked and thus closing themselves off from any new adventures. Sex with Gilles had resembled that: assured pleasure, safety, trust, and sweet tranquility. But Claire's intimate landscapes had changed with age, they had grown richer. Sex with Simon had followed new paths, it had had the perfume of uncertainty, of turmoil and adventure. Pleasure had experienced caprices, failures, and beautiful discoveries. Afterward, Claire had been able to gradually guide her husband toward these new sensations and their conjugal relations had been embellished by them.

How could she tell him that without dealing the man she loved another painful blow?

Gilles was still waiting. Claire noticed that she had once again ceased to breathe. She caught her breath, she had found an answer. Neither more false nor more true than a diplomatic formula.

"Not better. Differently."

She felt tears welling up in her eyes and a cowardly relief invaded her. She suspected Gilles of needing her tears. They calmed him, reassured him more than her words of love. She seized his chin and forced him to look her in the eyes.

"You don't understand that that's not the issue. I was not looking for better or worse, I needed something different. That's all. I love you, Gilles. I've never loved anyone but you!"

"That's not what you told me the other morning."

Claire bit her tongue, hoping to make the tears flow that were stagnating in her eyes.

"Please don't play the one who doesn't want to understand. I remember very well what I said."

Claire was bluffing. Like a nightmare, the memory of her confessions had faded as the hours passed.

"I . . . had feelings for Simon, it's true. But . . . they were never in any way comparable to what I feel for you . . ."

She remained evasive. She'd never succeeded in putting into words what she'd felt with Simon. By being too precise now, she was in danger of lying. To Gilles and to herself.

"In his message, he calls you 'my princess.'"

Claire ignored his interruption.

"No doubt there are degrees in love, everything depends on what you mean by that word. But I told you and I'll tell you again as often as you want: you're the love of my life, I want to live with you and grow old with you."

"Then why?"

"You already asked me that question."

"And I'll probably ask you again."

Claire thought for a few moments before answering:

"Maybe for that reason . . . Because I thought that we would always be together and sometimes that idea scared me."

The music of a song by Renaud came back to her. Not one of the best written but one of the most moving, perhaps precisely because of its awkwardness and its sincerity. She began to hum the melody, and then the words as her memories returned.

After all, you don't care
You knew that life's disgusting
That love lasts forever
And that sometimes scares us

It was by taking a breath and feeling salty words on her lips that she realized that she was finally weeping.

You told me what you didn't like
Was lying
That it eats you away
And that you are dying
But it's the truth, I find it sad to cry
And I cry

Gilles came closer and drank her tears as much as her words. Between two sobs, she exhaled the refrain:

Don't throw me away
Don't live without me
Don't throw me away
Or throw yourself with me

When she awoke, she was alone under the quilt. She

remembered that she had heard Gilles get up long before dawn. He'd been restlessly moving around in the bed for a long time before that. He could sleep no longer and he was probably struggling with his demons.

She was afraid.

She loved him. She really loved him. Madly.

And yet she'd cheated on him, she'd betrayed him. And she'd been happier than she'd ever been during that period. She hadn't yet understood what had happened in her. And up to that point she hadn't tried to find out.

The answer she'd given Gilles in the song rang true but it was probably incomplete.

With Simon, she'd felt herself slowly growing younger. She had rediscovered the carelessness of her youth, a little madness in a life that was too well-behaved. She'd given in. With delight.

Then she had managed things.

At the beginning of her adventure, she'd had to consult the websites of women's magazines. She'd informed herself regarding the basic techniques of lying well, the pretexts that had to be invented for secret rendezvous and the art of afterward erasing every trace of a clandestine affair, on the body, on clothing, and in telephones. Her husband was a particularly perceptive cop, and she had been forced to redouble her attention.

Then, after several months had passed, she'd looked into crisis management: What should you do, what should you say, if your spouse discovers the cruel truth? Online, there was a plethora of articles on this subject, to the point that you'd think infidelity had become people's favorite leisure activity. From her reading and rereading of advice columns, she had learned two things. First, that after the "revelation," sincerity was required, the main objective being to restore trust. Then, you had to keep scabrous and unpleasant details from being divulged. Because although we are all aware that we may be seriously betrayed by our spouses—and are thus more or less prepared for that—few of us have anticipated the countless daily hypocrisies that accompany adultery, the micro-betrayals that will strike later on, sometimes from behind, through a word, a sentence, or a memory. It was a constant battle against dark ideas and gloomy questions.

Claire knew that. She'd had ceaselessly to juggle this necessary sincerity and this impossible transparency. Gilles, without doing it on purpose, was not making her task any easier: he couldn't tolerate zones of shadow. He was a man of questions, of questions and answers, they were his job, they were his talent, his virtue and his vice . . .

Claire pushed back the quilt and stretched. She looked at the alarm clock: 9:15, time to get up. She grabbed Gilles's pillow and inhaled its odor. She would have liked to remove the pillowcase and put it in her pocket like a child's blankie.

Yes, she loved Gilles and couldn't imagine a life without him.

She finally got up, put on a dressing gown, and went to the garage, which Gilles had divided into two parts, a workshop on one side and a small exercise area on the other. In the latter she saw his jogging clothes hanging on a rack. He hadn't gone running. He was probably walking the deserted streets of Saint-Estève. She imagined his quick and furious pace slackening—she hoped—as he went. He would soon come back with warm bread and croissants.

When in fact he put those presents on the living room table, she'd already prepared everything. Four bowls of different colors surrounded a slab of butter and two jars of jam, raspberry and apricot, produced from their own garden. A lovely fragrance of strong black coffee floated in the room.

Claire examined her husband's face.

"Did you wake up early?"

"Yes."

"Is it cold outside?"

"Pretty warm. The wind died down during the night."

In the Catalan country the *tramontane* wind out of the north determines how cold it feels as much as the temperatures do.

Gilles took off his jacket and sat down opposite her.

"Would you like some coffee?"

"Please."

Claire got up, went around the bar that separated the kitchen area from the dining room, and came back with the coffeepot. She poured the hot black liquid into a blue bowl. Then she sat down again. She pushed the bowls aside so she could reach across the table and lay her hand on her husband's.

"Do you think we're going to get through this?"

"I hope so. We're going to do everything we can, right?"

"Anything you want."

Séverine came into the living room, putting an end to their conversation. Her eyes were still sleepy and she sat down on her father's lap. She buried her face in his neck. Gilles ran his hand through her brown locks and closed his eyes. Claire felt her heart breaking when she saw her husband letting go like that. He was savoring every last second of cuddling with his daughter; it was a long time since he'd been able to cuddle with his son.

Gilles had always been close to his children. After Séverine was born, he'd even gone on a part-time work schedule so that he could spend more time with them. This had not been well received in the macho world of the police, and it had affected the development of his career. He'd felt blacklisted by both his colleagues and his superiors. They were living in Chartres at that time. Fortunately, after his transfer to Perpignan he'd recovered everyone's confidence, but something in him was broken: he no longer felt any real passion for his work.

They ate breakfast while absentmindedly watching a news

channel. But could it really be called news? Nothing but stories on insignificant subjects such as past Christmas Eve celebrations and the feasts to come on Christmas Day. This year, Christmas fell on December 25. What a scoop!

"Foie gras with apples, is that still what we're having?" Gilles asked.

"Precisely. With a little salmon as a starter and a *bûche de Noël*[4] for dessert."

"The whole shebang, in other words! Great."

He got up and put his bowl in the dishwasher.

"I'll peel the apples. In the meantime, if you don't mind, I'm going to get a little exercise."

"Will you also get the wine, please?"

"Of course. A little Château Mossé 2008 Coume d'Abeille, that will be perfect with the meal. The wine shop is closed and I think it's the last bottle I have. We have to savor it!"

She watched him leave. Exercise would be an excellent outlet.

Léo got up shortly before noon, just in time for the aperitif. Claire had an amber Rivesaltes, Léo and Séverine Cokes, and Gilles a whiskey. Claire frowned when she saw the amount her husband poured for himself. Then she said to herself that for the time being, that was a lesser evil.

She pleased everyone with her sautéed foie gras. She congratulated Gilles on his choice of wine and forced herself to drink more of it than usual. If she didn't, he would.

Her eyes never left her husband. Whether it was the alcohol or dark ideas—maybe both—he seemed to be slowly slipping into a kind of lethargy. He was there without being there. When Séverine expressed her surprise, he said he was tired and needed more sleep. And that was only half a lie.

"Had I known, I'd have taken vacation time after all."

[4] A cake in the form of a yule log, traditional at Christmastime.

"Oh, yes, it would have been great if you could have come with us to Grandpa and Grandma's!"

"Too bad! Maybe next year . . ."

Claire's eyes met his. Next year . . . How sweet those words were and how sincere he looked when he said them! If only the year could go by in a flash and they could already all be together a year later . . . Their suffering over, their insouciance restored. And maybe also their trust.

Gilles's telephone rang just as the coffee was being served. Léo and Séverine had gone back to their rooms and Gilles and Claire were alone again, silent and pensive. Gilles didn't answer the phone; he got up only after hearing the beep signaling a voice message. He listened to it. Twice. Then he put the phone down. He seemed to be hesitating.

"Was it work?" Claire asked.

"Jacques, yes. He's holding down the fort today."

"Something urgent?"

Gilles pulled a face.

"I'm off duty."

Claire understood that the notion of urgency could be relative. Ordinarily, it would take a particularly tragic event to make Gilles leave his family on Christmas Day. But during this troubled time, it might be urgent to forget his personal difficulties by throwing himself into his work.

"Is it important?" she asked again.

"They've arrested the murderer. You know, the husband . . ."

She indicated her assent by batting her eyelids.

"Is Jacques going to question him?"

"Of course."

"Alone?"

"I don't know."

"Do you want to go?"

Surprised at first, Gilles was clearly relieved by this suggestion.

"That might be better."

"Maybe . . ."

"I mean, for the investigation," he smiled.

"I did, too."

Gilles stood up and kissed her on the forehead. Then he put on his jacket. Claire watched him get in the car, start it up, and then drive away. Higelin's[5] hoarse, low voice resounded in her head:

Leave, and above all don't look back
Leave, do what you have to without me
Whatever happens, I'll always be with you
Oh leave, and especially come back to me!

[5]Jacques Higelin, a French composer and singer born in 1940.

CHAPTER 13

As he drove, Gilles used his speakerphone to call Molina. "Congratulations on Abad, Jacques! How did you arrest him?"

"Uhh . . . He turned himself in. He showed up at headquarters less than an hour ago, holding his rifle by the barrel. He put it down on the floor and let the man on the front desk cuff him. He's now in our office. I was about to begin questioning him."

"Can you wait for me? I'm coming . . ."

"What?"

"I'm already on the way. I'll be there in five minutes."

"Are you sure that . . ."

Sebag hung up, not giving his partner time to finish his sentence.

Early on the afternoon of Christmas Day, traffic was at its lowest point, and it took him less than ten minutes to make the trip from his home. He left his car in the empty parking lot at police headquarters. The building was four stories high and fifty meters long, and its walls were the dirty concrete color of a low-cost housing development. Sebag climbed a few steps and entered the lobby. Agent Ripoll was manning the front desk on this holiday.

"Hello, Lieutenant!"

The old cop's loud, hoarse voice was further amplified by a contained pride. Sebag responded with exaggerated deference.

"Hello, Monsieur Ripoll! You are the hero of the day, it seems. My congratulations on having arrested such a dangerous criminal all by yourself!"

Ripoll ran his big, hairy hand over his thinning hair. The uncertain look in his eye betrayed his perplexity. He didn't know whether the inspector was sincere or if, once again, he was making fun of him. Sebag did nothing to help him in this dilemma. He held his personal card in front of the electronic reader and went into the secure part of police headquarters. As he entered the room that he shared with Molina, he ignored his colleague's astonished look and concentrated his attention on Stéphane Abad. First he noticed the man's bare neck and his light-colored hair. Abad was sitting on a chair next to two desks. His head was bowed and he had not looked up when another police officer came in. Sebag walked around him and sat down in his desk chair.

Abad slowly raised his head. He looked exhausted. He must not have slept much for a couple of days . . . His dark, tired eyes looked from under two long, thick eyebrows that nearly met over his nose. His delicately drawn mouth and his rounded cheeks gave the rest of his face a babylike look, despite a nascent beard. Sebag discerned in his features a mixture of gentleness and violence.

Molina began the interview with the traditional questions about identity. Stéphane Abad answered in a weary and monotone voice: he was born on May 28, 1962, in Perpignan, the son of Jean Abad and Pauline Coll; he had married Christine Lipart on June 3, 1994, in Boulou; and for twenty-five years he had been working as a quality-control manager at the Cantalou-Cémoi chocolate company. These details having been duly recorded, Jacques paused. He glanced at Sebag and divined that his colleague was advising him not to ask the crucial question right away. So first he questioned the suspect about what he had been doing since the day of the murder.

Stéphane Abad explained that he had spent these two days—"Two days, really?"—crying in his car, hidden away in the hills above the village of Opoul, an area where few people went. He hadn't received any of the messages that had been left for him because he'd thrown his mobile phone into the Têt River.

"You didn't want to be found?" Molina asked.

"I don't know, I just did it, I wanted people to leave me alone. That's all! I didn't want to talk to anybody."

"Not even your son?"

Abad looked up at Molina. Gilles sensed that he'd only now remembered that he had a son.

"Have you seen Maxime? How is he?"

"He's fine, as you're well aware," Molina replied curtly. "Why did you run away? Did you hope to escape us?"

"I don't know, I don't believe so, I wasn't thinking. I was . . . wasted, I think. I had alcohol with me, and I drank a great deal. I don't remember much."

"Why did you turn yourself in today? Did you run out of stuff to drink?"

"I'd finished it all off, yes," Abad answered without noticing the lieutenant's irony. "But that's not why I came . . . I thought there was no other solution. It seemed to me inevitable. I don't know, that's normal, isn't it?"

"You don't know much, in fact! I hope you'll be more precise on other points."

"Have you eaten?" Sebag broke in. "Are you thirsty? Do you want some water?"

"Yes, I'd like a glass of water."

"Something else? A soda, a chocolate bar, a few madeleines? We have vending machines on the ground floor."

Abad was astonished by his concern. Molina warned him: "The interview might be very long."

"A glass of water would be fine. As for the rest, no, thanks, I'm not hungry."

Sebag stood up and filled a cup at the water fountain in the hallway. He got another for himself. As he came back into the office, he signaled to Molina that he could now ask the fateful question, the one that had been looming from the outset but whose answer had to be clear and sharp, and then written down in black and white in the record of the interview. Jacques shifted to his most solemn tone.

"Monsieur Abad, do you admit having killed your wife Christine on Tuesday, December 23, shortly after 2 P.M.?"

Abad hesitated. He took the time to take a sip of water before answering.

"I'm not certain about the time."

Molina drummed his fingers on his desk.

"We don't give a damn about the time! Do you admit having killed your wife?"

Abad's cheeks flushed.

"Yes."

"Tell us what happened."

Abad took another drink of water before starting to tell his story. In the late morning of that Tuesday, he'd gone to the Hôtel du Gecko. He'd waited for the lover to come out, then went up to room 34. He'd opened the door, seen Christine, and fired.

"How did your wife react when she saw you?"

"I'm not sure, everything happened very fast, I don't think she had time to react . . . Oh, yes, she opened her mouth!"

"And?"

"And nothing. She fell next to the bed."

"She was already dead?"

"I believe so, yes."

"You didn't check?"

"No."

"What did you feel?"

"I don't know."

"Pleasure?"

Abad jumped, as if he'd been bitten. Or slapped. Molina continued: "Relief, then? Or sadness?"

"Yes, perhaps a little . . . Especially a great emptiness."

Molina wrote down these answers and then, after a short silence, resumed his most solemn tone.

"When you fired, it was in fact with the intention of killing her?"

Abad sat up slowly and, for the first time, spread out his body. He was bigger than his slumped position had suggested up to that point. Sebag estimated that he was at least six feet tall.

"Yes," he replied without batting an eyelid.

"Why?"

The question surprised Abad.

"Well, because she was cheating on me!"

"Is that a sufficient reason?"

Abad stared at Molina as if he came from another planet. He jutted out his round chin.

"Obviously, since I did it."

Molina sighed and pulled his chair closer.

"Monsieur Abad, tens of thousands of people are cheated on every year by their spouses—both men and women, I believe equality is complete in that domain these days—but that does not result in tens of thousands of deaths. Fortunately for us—we'd be overworked—and also fortunately for the country, because if everybody acted as you did, adultery would become a plague worse than cancer, car accidents, and cardiovascular disease combined . . ."

He paused, turned to Gilles to be sure that he had appreciated this bit of humor, and then went on: "It looks like you thought it was natural to kill your wife. Why?"

Abad wrinkled his forehead and his bushy eyebrows joined over his nose. He spoke in a voice that betrayed his exasperation:

"I don't know what other men in my situation do or don't do, and I don't give a damn! I didn't put up with her so that she could make a monkey out of me again."

"Again?"

"Yes, she had already cheated on me. At least once! Right after Maxime was born. At the time she admitted it, and I agreed to forgive her and to continue to live with her. But despite all that she did it again."

"So for you that was reason enough to kill her?"

Molina's tone had become less severe.

"She humiliated me. When you're a married woman, a mother, you don't do that. If you don't respect your husband, you can at least show concern for your son!"

"Do you regret what you did?"

Abad took time to weigh his words. Then he looked Molina in the eye: "No. I regret that she did it. She's the one who is responsible for what happened. Not me."

"Why did you wait for the lover to leave the hotel? Weren't you mad at him, too?"

Abad seemed surprised. Apparently, he had never asked himself that question; his jealousy was all in his gut, not in his head.

"I don't understand, he didn't know me," Abad replied after thinking for a moment. "She's the one who cheated on me, not him. I don't give a shit about him!"

Jacques carefully noted down his remarks: He had heard enough on that subject. It would be up to the examining magistrate to investigate further, if he wanted to, regarding the murderer's motivations and psychology.

"At what point did you decide to kill your wife?"

"As soon as I discovered that she was cheating on me."

"When and how did you find out?"

Abad pursed his lips and blushed.

"That same morning. I sneaked a look at her mobile phone and found an SMS that left no doubt."

Sebag felt an icy wave cause his stomach to contract, and his mind disconnected. Don't think anymore, definitely don't think. Molina, who had not divined anything, picked up the file folder next to his keyboard and flipped through it. He quickly found what he was looking for. As usual, Ménard had done a good job. He was a first-class pain in the ass, but his files were always irreproachable. Molina reread the transcript of the SMS Christine had sent to her lover on the morning of the day of the murder. The only one they'd found on the mobile phone.

"What did that SMS that you found say?" he asked Abad.

"Uhh . . . I don't quite recall. Something like: 'I love you, I'm waiting for you.'"

Molina reread what he had before his eyes: "I can't wait to feel you inside me. See you soon." That was close enough.

"Anything else?"

"No, I don't think so."

"When exactly did you discover this message?"

"Around 8:30, before leaving for work."

Molina consulted the timeline Ménard had drawn up. Christine had sent her SMS to Balland at 7:46.

"And you left as if nothing was wrong?"

"Yes. Well, almost. Except that I took my rifle with me."

"You already intended to kill her?"

Again, Abad blushed.

"Uhh . . . I don't know."

Sebag suddenly reconnected with the conversation. As if he had heard a mute signal of alarm.

"And why didn't you kill your wife as soon as you discovered the SMS?" Molina asked.

Abad's eyes flicked away toward the window. He was contemplating the roofs of the buildings across the way, the blue sky, or the past. Sebag held out his hand over the desks. Molina passed him the page that mentioned the SMS.

"I . . . I don't know. I . . . I wanted to be sure," Abad tried to answer. "I think I needed to see them together."

Molina held his nose with his thumb and forefinger.

"But you didn't see them together."

"I was there when they got there, and they came together!"

The surveillance cameras had filmed the lovers' arrival at the Hôtel du Gecko. Molina remembered: they were in fact together. Everything was crystal clear.

Sebag laid down the sheet of paper he'd just read and re-read. Then he asked his first question since the beginning of the interrogation.

"I'm not sure I've understood: Could you tell me again what was in the text message that you intercepted?"

Abad's eyebrows frowned. Astonishment would have made them rise.

"Well, I told you, it was simple: 'I love you, I'm waiting for you.'"

Gilles felt the icy wave pass through his stomach again. He closed his eyes. Had he found such precise, terrible words in the message on Claire's mobile, he would never have been able to forget them: "I can't wait to feel you inside me." He opened his eyes again.

"Are you sure?"

"It may not be word for word, but that was the gist of it. In any case, it left me no doubt."

Abad's tone had hardened and he was breathing faster. Uneasiness or irritation, maybe a little of both. Sebag went over in his memory what had been said during this interview. What he had heard and what he had grasped despite himself during the brief instant when his mind had "absented itself." A few points were worth clarifying.

"How did you know where Christine and her lover were to meet?"

Abad stopped breathing for a moment. Then he decided to be annoyed:

"What's with all these pointless questions? It was mentioned in the goddamn text message, that's all."

"What did it say?"

"Something like 'I'll be waiting for you at 12:30 at the Hôtel du Gecko.'"

"Why didn't you tell us that earlier?"

"Because it didn't seem important to me."

Sebag and Molina exchanged a glance. Jacques looked surprised.

"I don't know any more, I'm tired," Abad explained. "I haven't slept or eaten for two days. It doesn't really matter, does it?"

"The problem is that it doesn't correspond at all to the SMS that we found."

Sebag handed him the transcript that was in the file.

"Then it was in another message," Abad replied after having skimmed the text. One she erased afterward, of course. You can trust that tramp to be careful."

"You know that we can recover everything that was erased from your wife's phone?"

For just a moment—a second, no longer—a glint of arrogance shone in Abad's pupils.

"Then why haven't you already done it?"

"Because it's still complicated and hasn't seemed necessary up to this point."

Abad snorted.

"Then do it. Why would I care? I killed my wife, I confessed, what more do you want?"

"The truth, Monsieur Abad."

"I've already told you the truth: I killed my wife, I waited for her lover to leave and then I went into that fucking hotel. I opened the door to the room, I saw her, and I didn't give her time to say a word, I aimed straight at her heart. I didn't hesitate for a second, I wanted to kill her and I did it. You have all the proof you need against me and you have my confession. Charge me, put me in jail, and let's get this over with!"

Sebag waited patiently until Abad's anger abated, and then turned to his partner.

"If you have other questions . . ."

This sudden passing of the baton disconcerted Molina.

"Uhh . . . Yes, I had at least one. I remember that one thing surprised Ménard and me when we were viewing the surveillance tapes . . ."

He turned to Abad:

"When Éric Balland—your wife's lover—left the hotel, you kept waiting. At least ten minutes, if I remember correctly. Why?"

Abad's face relaxed.

"I wanted to give Christine a chance . . ."

"What do you mean?"

"When we were younger and more . . . in love, she liked to smoke a cigarette alone after sex. It was the sign that she was happy."

Sebag looked at Abad. Something indefinable had changed in his attitude. Here he was telling the truth again, that was certain.

Molina clarified:

"If I understand correctly, you wanted to know if your wife was happy with her lover?"

"Yes."

"And it's because she was happy that you killed her?"

"Yes."

A leaden silence fell over the room, disturbed only by the sound of Molina's fingers tapping on his computer's keyboard.

Gilles rose and went out to drink another glass of water. He felt disconcerted. Physically ill at ease and intellectually perplexed. Something wasn't working. Stéphane Abad had lied to them. About a detail, yes, but he'd lied.

Why?

He drank another cup of water. This murder might turn out to be more interesting than anticipated, or was it just that he, Gilles Sebag, a perceptive cop but a cuckolded husband, was dreaming of an exciting investigation that would distract him from his own troubles? He crushed the paper cup, threw it in the trash, and returned to the office. Jacques had wound up this first interrogation and was putting handcuffs on the presumed murderer.

"You're going to spend the night in custody," he explained. "We'll want to talk to you again tomorrow. And we will give you a chance to confront the witnesses. Then you'll go before the examining magistrate, who will indict you for premeditated murder, that is, murder in the first degree. Between you and me, a murderer who expresses no regrets is likely to get fifteen to twenty years."

Abad's mouth twisted in amazement.

"But she cheated on me!"

"There's no doubt about that."

"I'm . . . I'm the victim!"

"On that point, I advise you to change your story. It no longer works like that these days."

"You're just trying to scare me . . . They'll have to grant that there were extenuating circumstances!"

Molina's face clearly showed his skepticism.

"Society is changing, Monsieur Abad. There was a time, for example, when alcoholism was, for any crime whatever, an extenuating circumstance. Today that is not only no longer the case, but it has become an aggravating circumstance. And you see, I increasingly have the impression that the same shift is happening with regard to jealousy. Everything will probably depend on the makeup of the jury. For your sake, I hope there will be a lot of faithful spouses on the jury. But to judge by the surveys that have appeared in women's magazines, adultery has long since become common in France."

He put his big paw on Abad's shoulder and pushed him toward the door. While Jacques was taking the husband to a cell, Gilles remained alone in the room. He opened his desk drawer and took out the whiskey bottle. One swig, just one. This interrogation had worn him out.

"Case closed," Jacques concluded as he came back into the room. He collapsed in his chair and put his feet on the desk.

"Hmm," Sebag grumbled. "Just how long have you been reading women's magazines?"

"Never have. It was just a way of speaking, something that fit well in the sentence! But as for the survey, it's true, I heard about it on the radio the other morning: more than one man out of two admits having been unfaithful, and almost one woman out of three. In the makeup of a jury, that could turn out to be important."

"True."

"And by the way, what was that 'hmm' supposed to mean?"

"What 'hmm?'"

"When I came back and said 'case closed' you answered, 'hmm.'"

"Right. Hmm."

"Is it this business about the SMS that's bothering you?"

"Among other things . . . Abad isn't believable, regarding either the form or the content. According to the owner of the Gecko, the two lovers regularly went to his hotel. Their text messages no longer needed to say where they were going to meet. Especially since in that kind of correspondence, people always get straight to the point."

"Don't tell me you have doubts about Abad's guilt? The owner of the hotel identified him in the photos, the surveillance cameras filmed him going into and coming out of the hotel, he confessed, and we have the murder weapon . . ."

Sebag stopped him with a gesture.

"No, I have no doubts, of course."

"Then we're not going to worry about details."

"I like details. It's odd, after all, that a murderer who confesses everything and declares loud and strong that he regrets nothing hides things from us, even if they're only details. You saw how he reacted when I pestered him about that SMS: He got mad and launched into a long diatribe proclaiming his guilt."

"Do you really think he's not telling the truth?"

"Hard to say. I'm not sure myself."

"Then we'll have to make the victim's mobile give up everything that's in it."

"That's still a complicated procedure, and I'm not sure that the prosecutor will authorize us to carry it out."

Molina clapped his hands.

"You know what?"

"No, tell me."

"We're really stupid sometimes!"

"I'm willing to believe that, but why?"

"We can just call the lover. A message always exists in two places: the telephone that sends it and the one that receives it!"

Sebag bit his lip.

"You're right, we're really stupid!"

Molina picked up his desk phone and dialed Éric Balland's number. The first exchanges were tense; the lover wasn't exactly pleased to be disturbed at home on Christmas Day for this kind of question. But with a few quick, well-chosen words Jacques made him more cooperative. After asking the policemen to wait a few seconds, long enough to move out of his family's earshot, Balland finally answered:

"I've erased everything, as you might imagine. I always did that as I went along."

After confirming that he and Christine had long since stopped mentioning the place of their usual rendezvous, he added:

"As I told you yesterday, it was never a question of love between Christine and me. We never said 'I love you,' and still less wrote it. If in my position I can be permitted a comment, Abad is putting you on!"

A glass in his hand, Sebag was still going through the Abad file. Jacques had left some time before, and he was going to have to do the same. It was Christmas, after all. And then Claire and the children were to leave the next morning to spend the rest of the holiday with his in-laws.

As he reread the last pages he was surprised by certain details. Something was wrong with the timing. He made comparisons. There was no doubt. There was a contradiction between Abad's statements during his interrogation and the timelines drawn up during the investigation. The presumed murderer was lying about a second point.

It was beginning to be too much.

Chapter 14

The sun was coming up and revealing a blue sky blown clear of clouds by the cold, dry breath of the *tramontane*. He crossed the deserted intersection. Across from him the Ferris wheel put up for the holidays was silently challenging the red bricks of the Castillet, its lighted cabins being slightly higher than the immobile, crenellated towers of the ancient fortified gate. All around the idle merry-go-round, a white-flocked décor imitated the snow that seldom ventured down from the summits to the plain.

He was walking at a pace eased by a long exercise session. On the Quai Vauban, the Christmas market's wooden stands had not yet opened their shutters. The owner of a bar was already setting out tables and chairs on the street and, respectful of his uniform, he greeted him with a nod of the head.

He swaggered. He was proud.

Proud as he had no longer been for months. For years, maybe. Since the shock. It had been such a long time.

Now everything was going well.

Stéphane Abad had turned himself in, he'd passed the night in police custody. Today, or tomorrow at the latest, he would be indicted for murder and then locked up. According to his information, the police hadn't asked many questions about it.

The perfect crime. Really.

For the past two days he'd felt better. His fears were becoming less intense. Even those that he felt on leaving for work in the morning and on returning home in the evening. He was regaining his appetite, his taste for life. Last night he'd slept at least six hours.

After the Quai Vauban, he took the Quai Nobel. Down below, on the left, the Basse flowed clear and quiet in its concrete channel. He paused. Leaning on the brick guardrail, he looked down on the river that ran between two strips of grass that were improbably green for the Mediterranean area. He closed his eyes, breathed, listened. The calm city allowed the river's murmur to bloom

He took another deep breath, raised his head, reopened his eyes.

Across from him, on the other side of the Basse, the consular palace flaunted its pretentious architecture over five stories and a surface of more than four thousand square meters. The seat of the chamber of commerce, the building had been for sale for months without finding a buyer. One couldn't imagine a better symbol of a local economy in complete collapse.

He started walking again, lengthening his stride. He didn't want to be late. And especially not to make himself noticed. Neither by his colleagues nor by his superiors. Anonymous among the anonymous, that was his motto.

More than ever, he had to remain vigilant. He mustn't make any mistakes. The Eye's first exploit had been successful. The work continued.

There was a price to be paid for this tragedy that had struck him. Yes, this tragedy had a price.

He alone knew who was going to pay the bill

And it would be a big one.

His vengeance was just beginning.

Chapter 15

"Good-bye, kids! Have a good time at Grandpa and Grandma's!"

Gilles was trying to be upbeat but Claire wasn't fooled. The day before he'd come home from work with his shoulders proudly thrown back and his mind healthily preoccupied by his current investigation.

But that hadn't lasted.

During the meal, she'd seen his posture change. His back had perceptibly sagged under the weight of dark thoughts. His demons had taken control of him again, and he had turned inward on himself, participating only mechanically in the family conversation.

As they got into bed, she'd feared that further questions would come up. But Gilles had resisted the temptation. He'd lain down next to her in the bed, and to her great astonishment, she had very soon heard his breathing slow.

In the middle of the night a sound had awakened her, a sound she couldn't at first identify. She reached out, but she was alone in the bed. Gilles had gotten up. She looked at the clock.

2:23 A.M.

She heard the sound again. Clear and crystalline. A bottle set on the glass coffee table in the living room.

Gradually she fell back asleep. She'd awakened again later in the night. She hadn't dared move or look at the clock. Gilles was getting into the bed. She felt the cold outside slip under the quilt. This time, she was the one who cuddled up to him. Her husband's heavy, hoarse snoring rocked her back to sleep.

Gilles hugged Séverine and kissed her tenderly. Then he held out the flat of his hand to his son. Léo slapped it and then they did a fist bump. For more than a year, that had been the only physical contact between them. Léo had put an end to cuddles and even to kisses, so Gilles had come up with this young male ritual that his son was comfortable with.

Claire was well aware that her affair with Simon had come at the worst possible time. The children were growing up and Gilles was suffering as he saw them pulling away. Emancipating themselves. To get through it, he'd started dreaming about going with Claire on the trips that the four of them had never been able to take. But now his wife seemed to be escaping him as well.

Obviously, that was not what Claire was feeling. More than anything in the world, she wanted to stay with him, to experience with him this second life without the children, and to grow old with him. He was the love of her life, she didn't want another, she hadn't lied.

Not about that.

She also knew that what she was putting her husband through reawakened other, deeply buried pains. Pains connected with his childhood. With his father, from whom he'd been estranged for a long time. And with his mother, too, of course.

Gérard Sebag had been a philanderer. His wife had put up with it for years before finally deciding to throw him out. But Claire sensed that there was something else, too. A kind of secret that Gilles had never told anyone. Not even her.

The children put their bags in the trunk of the car and got in. Séverine sat in the back, Léo in the front. Claire stood at a distance. Gilles went to kiss her good-bye.

"Have a good trip," he said. "And be careful. You didn't sleep well, I think."

She caressed his cheek with her hand. She liked to feel his whiskers scratch her palm.

"I'm leaving so that we can get back together again."

"I hope we will."

"I want us to."

"I do too. Really."

They kissed again.

"Are you going to be all right alone for a few days?"

Gilles ran his hand through Claire's hair.

"I'll be fine. Provided there's enough work at headquarters."

"This is the first time I've heard you want more work."

"I hope it's the last . . ."

She didn't know what to reply to what was probably more clumsiness than aggressiveness. She preferred to change the subject. But was she really changing the subject?

"Don't do anything silly and above all don't drink too much. Please . . ."

"Don't worry about it, it'll be all right."

"We'll call every night?"

He nodded.

"And we'll send as many text messages as we want, day and night," she went on. "The way kids do when they're in love."

She saw Gilles's face darken. Now she'd committed a blunder, too. She guessed his thoughts; he was thinking about all the text messages she had exchanged with Simon. She would have liked to cry, "Never when we were together, Gilles, never behind your back!" But she couldn't. If some day he asked her, she would tell him, she would even go so far as to swear it. But she would be lying. Some weekends far away from Simon had been very long, and she had not always resisted the desire for some tender words, written or read. Yes, she'd sent her lover messages—sometimes just smiley faces—behind the backs of her husband and her children, and she was ashamed of it. But if Gilles asked her about it, she would deny it. Without hesitation. She would do it for him, for them. And a little for herself as well.

"Forgive me, Gilles. I really want us to write to each other. As often as we feel like it."

She took a step away, caught his eyes, and her lips spoke a mute "I love you."

Sebag stood on the curb until the car had disappeared around the corner. Then he went back in the house. He was in his shirtsleeves, and he was cold. The wind off the sea was blowing big, black clouds through the sky. The air was humid. In the house, he went directly to the liquor cabinet and drank a slug of Scotch right from the bottle. Pure malt, pure defiance. Against whom? His wife, Gérard, life, fate. Against himself.

He was angry at his brain, too. That organ was becoming autonomous. It was unbearable. It was his brain that had awakened him in the middle of the night and manipulated his dark ideas.

What if Claire was still lying . . . Had she really cut off all contact with her lover?

He'd gotten up, dug around in his wife's purse, and found her telephone. Goddamned phone! He hadn't found anything, no message from Simon, no trace in the history.

But that hadn't reassured him. A jealous man is relieved only when he finds a reason for his jealousy.

He had to get out of this dangerous downward spiral. He no longer wanted to be that man. He had to stop. Stop spying on Claire's phone, stop asking her questions. Turn the page.

He was afraid it would be a long time before he could do that.

He took another swig before he put away the bottle. Let's

be reasonable. Not get to work drunk. Calm down, just calm down.

Silence prevailed in the large house. This silence was going to keep him company until his little family returned. Next Wednesday, for New Year's Eve. It would be long and difficult, but maybe it was better this way. He needed to take stock of his situation, to feel what it was like without her, and to face up to solitude.

Fuck, it would be hard!

He got the bottle out again. Just one drop, just a drop. Then he took a shower and went to police headquarters.

CHAPTER 16

François Ménard had arrived early at headquarters and taken things in hand. He was satisfied, he'd done good work: the lineup was ready.

Stéphane Abad was standing with his back against the wall along with four other men of similar stature and hair color. Two of them were police officers at headquarters, while the two others were teammates on the Le Soler soccer team Ménard played with every Saturday.

Abad's face looked tired, but he was clean-shaven. Ménard, who was the same height, had lent him a jacket and had taken care to have Abad's laces put back in his shoes. Perfect! A memory from the beginning of his career led him to be a perfectionist when it came to organizing a lineup. While he was working at the Montreuil police headquarters, an inspector had negligently shown witnesses a suspect without laces in his shoes and wearing clothes wrinkled by a night spent in police custody. The suspect's lawyer had found it easy to get the procedure invalidated.

Everything was set up, and Ménard was now waiting for his colleagues. He at least was being a good colleague.

Sebag and Molina, on the other hand, had deliberately not informed him of Abad's arrest. It was only by calling headquarters late in the day that he had learned about it from that old fool Ripoll. He had immediately come to headquarters, gone to see the alleged murderer in his cell, and prepared for the lineup by calling colleagues and soccer teammates with vaguely similar physiques. That morning, he had brought in Jordi Estève, the Gecko's owner.

His colleagues, always zealous, didn't arrive until after 10 A.M. Molina, in his perennial mocking tone, congratulated him on his efficiency. Sebag said nothing: his mind seemed to be elsewhere, and his face looked almost as weary as Abad's.

The policemen had old Jordi come into the adjoining room fitted with a one-way mirror. The hotel owner didn't hesitate a second: he identified the man holding the number 3, namely Stéphane Abad himself. "And voilà, the job is done!" Ménard crowed. A lot of work for a confrontation lasting three seconds. The investigator's work had its boring and slow moments, but rigor in executing it was one of its nobilities.

Some people tended to forget that.

After thanking his soccer teammates, Ménard brought in a table and four chairs and had Abad sit down. There was no question of allowing this second interview to take place on "hostile terrain," in this case Sebag and Molina's office. His colleagues understood the message. Jacques came up to Sebag and whispered in his ear: "Do you want to conduct the interview?"

"No, you began, I'll let you continue. If I have questions, I'll speak up."

Ménard sat down. He would have questions, that much was certain. He'd read the record of the interrogation and had noted areas that remained obscure. Sebag began by asking Stéphane Abad for a detailed account of his actions on the morning of the murder. In a drawling voice, Abad repeated that he had left for work as if nothing was wrong, but with his rifle in the trunk of his car. However, he hadn't stayed on the job for long. Too upset. On the pretext of a family problem, he'd left again an hour after he got there. He'd driven to the beach at Torreilles.

"We like that place, we often go there in the summer."

He'd taken a walk on the beach, then returned to Perpignan.

"I'm not sure what time it was. In any case, soon enough to be in front of the hotel when they arrived."

"And so you saw them together?"

Abad bowed his head and replied in a low, barely audible voice.

"Yes."

"And afterward?"

"Afterward?"

"Yes, afterward, once your wife and her lover had gone into the hotel, what did you do?"

Ménard took out his notebook and his pen. He had in fact noticed something strange at this point in the presumed murderer's timeline. Before answering, Abad ran his hand through his hair.

"Well . . . I waited."

"You waited . . . for an hour and a half . . . for Éric Balland to come out?"

Abad raised his eyes toward Sebag but did not answer.

"Balland is the lover's name," Gilles explained.

"I know, you told me that yesterday," Abad hissed.

"So answer my question."

"I told you yesterday and I'm going to repeat it: Yes, I waited for that asshole to come out."

"Hmm, hmm."

Abad ran his hand through his hair again. His cheeks got a little pink. Ménard knew Sebag well, he'd learned a great deal from his way of conducting interrogations. He also knew the file well and he divined the tactics. After worrying the murderer over a minor discrepancy, Gilles was going to let him relax for a moment before playing his trump cards. But he felt slightly disappointed: he wasn't the only one who had noticed these discrepancies.

"And once Éric Balland had come out, you still waited, is that right?"

"I was waiting to see if Christine would take the time to smoke a cigarette, as I told you yesterday."

"If she had come out sooner, you wouldn't have killed her?"

"I don't know . . . Maybe I would have anyway . . . But not in the street, in any case."

"Hmm, hmm."

"You don't seem to believe me, but I'm telling you the truth. Christine used to have the habit of smoking after sex. And she stopped smoking about ten years ago. I wanted to see if she had started again . . . with him. That's all. Why don't you want to believe me?"

"Oh, I believe you all right, Monsieur Abad."

Sebag smiled.

"On this point, I believe you. On the other hand, I'm puzzled on other points."

"You're not going to ask me again about the confused wording of that SMS!"

Ménard perked up his ears. That point had escaped him. The record of the interrogation mentioned only Abad's statements concerning the SMS that had informed him of his wife's infidelity, not the policemen's questions on this subject.

"Let's leave the SMS aside for a moment," Sebag agreed. "If we need to, we'll carry out the necessary investigations later on. We have other problems with your timetable: you say that you were in front of the Hôtel du Gecko when your wife and her lover went in, is that right?"

"Uhh . . . yes. Exactly."

"Then can you explain why the surveillance camera next to the hotel recorded your arrival only at 1:33 P.M.?"

Abad's eyes opened wide, then his mouth.

"Goddammit!"

Ménard had always been surprised to see that video-surveillance cameras, though they had initially been controversial in Perpignan as elsewhere, had been quickly been accepted and even forgotten by the residents. Few people were even capable to saying where any of the cameras were, even on streets they traveled every day.

"I probably stayed for a long time in a blind spot."

Ménard jumped in:

"I viewed the images myself, Monsieur Abad. They very clearly show you walking down the Rue des Augustins at 1:33 with your rifle in its case, and taking a position about twenty meters from the hotel. Before that, you weren't there."

"Yes, I was," Abad said stubbornly. "Five minutes before, no, but a quarter of an hour before, yes. And probably in a blind spot."

He took a deep breath and explained:

"To avoid attracting attention, I didn't take my rifle with me at first, I went back to get it. I couldn't say exactly when, but I'm willing to believe you that it must have been at 1:33."

A glimmer of pride or even arrogance flickered in Abad's eyes. One didn't have to be Gilles Sebag to see that he was making it up. But Ménard had no way to refute him; he had viewed the images starting from the hotel owner's call to the arrival of the presumed murderer. It was impossible to contradict Abad right now, first he would have to watch the rest of the video recordings.

Abad took advantage of the silence that had followed his story:

"Is that all you've got? Do you always pester criminals so much with your pointless questions? What is this, anyway, a torture session, an initial punishment? Either you believe what I'm telling you and indict me for murder, or you don't believe me and you let me go. But for God's sake, let's get this over with!"

Sebag calmly laid a sheet of blank paper on the table. On it, he drew two parallel lines representing the Rue des Augustins and a square to represent the site of the Gecko. Then he pushed the sheet and the pencil toward Abad.

"Can you put an X on the place where you waited before going to get your rifle?"

Abad rubbed his head and this time, instead of blushing, he paled.

"I'm tired, and I don't feel well. I want to see a doctor."

He looked at each of the three lieutenants before adding: "I also want a lawyer."

A slate under his arm, Rafel, the owner of the Carlit, came to stand in front of the table at which Molina, Sebag, and Ménard had taken seats.

"Bon dia, tothom."[6]

He showed them the slate on which he had written the three *plats du jour*. Molina suddenly felt happier.

"*Caral! Galtes,*[7] and cooked with Banyuls[8] to boot! I love that! You going to have the same, guys?"

Sebag and Ménard agreed.

"Shall I bring you a little Terrasous to drink with that?" Rafel suggested. Ménard quibbled:

"Another local wine, fourteen percent at least . . . I'll have only a glass. The day is far from over."

"Give us a liter all the same," Molina insisted. "Precisely because the day is far from over!"

The policemen were obliged to grant Stéphane Abad's request. It was the law. They had easily found a court-appointed lawyer who would come in right after lunch to talk with his new client. Finding a physician had been another question. They'd had to make call after call to dig up that rare

[6] "Good day, everyone."
[7] Pork cheeks.
[8] A sweet wine from Banyuls, in Pyrénées-Orientales.

pearl, a doctor who would agree to visit a murderer in a dark cell at police headquarters on the Saturday after Christmas—for the standard fee, which would not include travel costs and would not be paid for months, and then only after he had filled out fifteen forms and made countless phone calls to an administration whose dilatory laziness had now been erected into "good management" because it was one of the best ways of saving the government money. The rare pearl was a pal of Molina's, and after he'd examined Abad and authorized them to continue holding him in police custody, he'd taken his friend aside to whisper this imperious entreaty in his ear: "If you're really a pal, next time please forget me!"

Jacques took a sip of his wine. Then he put his elbows on the table and addressed his colleagues: "What's wrong, guys? Why are you bugging Abad?"

Sebag glanced at Ménard before answering.

"For the most part, he's telling the truth . . ."

"That's right," Ménard agreed. "But it's the first time in my career that I've found myself in such a situation: a basically crystal-clear case with a suspect to whom everything points, a murderer who admits everything and yet who is lying to us on certain points. The least you can say is that it's puzzling."

"He didn't tell us everything about the SMS and his timetable, OK, but apart from that?"

Rafel put three steaming plates on the table. Three impatient forks began digging into slices of brown meat. The *galtes* proved to be as tender as one could wish.

What he says rings false, too," Sebag went on. "Not all the time, but from time to time. Take for example when he told us that he waited for an hour and a half in front of the hotel—that's simply implausible!"

"He said he'd left for a moment to get his rifle . . ."

"And even if that's true, Jacques, can you imagine a guy like him, impulsive and violent, standing around for more than an hour in front of the hotel until his wife had finished getting off before killing her?"

"Hard to imagine, in fact." Jacques had been amused by Gilles's way of putting it, which was uncharacteristically coarse. "And so what conclusion do you draw from that?"

"None, and that's just what annoys me!"

"Yeah. Well . . . All that's just pubic hair in a hippie's mane, trifles, details . . ."

"And the devil is in the details."

Molina frowned.

"Is that a proverb?"

"Yes."

"And you didn't twist it?"

"Uhh . . . No."

"So it's more serious that I thought!"

The interview with the lawyer, a puny little four-eyes, simply supported Stéphane Abad's refusal to answer the policemen's questions. So the latter decided there was no reason to continue the interrogation. Accompanied by Ménard, who had insisted on coming along, Sebag handed the presumed murderer over to the court.

Gilles told the prosecutor, Kazatzky, about their interrogations. The skeptical and haughty look in the magistrate's eyes made Gilles wonder how substantial his suspicions really were. Ménard didn't help him; he remained silent, refusing to step up to the plate. Comfortably settled in a large chair, Hector Kazatsky was looking the two lieutenants up and down, despite his short stature.

"What exactly are you asking for?"

Sebag mentioned the examination of the victim's mobile phone, which he still wanted done, the interrogation of Abad's co-workers at Cantalou, in order to clarify the timetable, and another review of the city's surveillance tapes.

"And then, we could also search his house," he added.

"What precisely would you be looking for?"

"When you do a search, you never know exactly what you're looking for, but sometimes . . . you find it!"

Sebag was well aware that his argument was not pertinent. He'd drunk too much wine at lunch and was having a hard time resisting a terrible desire to yawn. Hector Kazatzky took off his glasses and scratched the sides of his nose with the bows. He thought a long time before putting his glasses down on the black desk blotter.

"I'll authorize another review of the videotapes and the examination of the victim's mobile. But regarding the rest, you and I have other things to do, don't we?"

He abruptly stood up to conclude the interview.

"We have the murderer, the weapon, the mobile, the confessions, and all the proof. That's enough for me. You've done a good job on this case; the file is perfect."

They handed their prisoner over to the two policemen assigned to take him away to the detention center, and then returned to police headquarters, where Molina had decided to celebrate, twenty-four hours early, his departure on vacation. A few colleagues were already drinking with him in their office. When Sebag and Ménard arrived, Jacques opened another bottle of Cava, a sparkling wine made on the other side of the Pyrenees. The cork popped. A vice cop pretended to jump and pulled out his gun as if to return fire. The gag was an old one, but a few people nonetheless laughed.

Molina did not ask them a single question about their interview with the magistrate. He, too, considered the Abad case closed. Like the magistrates. Ménard had promised to review the videotapes on Monday, while Sebag would take the victim's mobile to the head of the forensic team as soon as she returned from vacation. And then . . . *Insh'Allah*. He'd done his job, and in his own view he was morally covered.

The police and the judicial system had defects, routines, and weaknesses that resulted from their lack of time and resources, and also sometimes from their lack of desire or competence. Sebag knew that he wasn't up to doing battle. To avoid getting lost in this job, you had to recognize your limits, and he had long since identified his. He defined himself as a "conscientious loafer": too conscientious to be satisfied with his laziness, but too lazy to move mountains all by himself. Come what might. He'd tried to be a perfectionist, and no one had listened to him. Now he could just wash his hands of this case.

Chapter 17

Sprawled on the living room couch, Gilles was drinking from the whiskey bottle. Before coming home, he'd stopped at shop near police headquarters and was advised to try a strong single malt. Ardbeg-something-or-other, he couldn't pronounce the name. A Scotch from the windy islands, peaty, spicy, and woody. The stuff's alcohol content was supposed to exceed fifty-four percent, enough to warm hearts and minds even in the depths of winter.

The blues CD he'd put in the stereo had long since stopped, and a profound silence reigned in the room, disturbed from time to time by the hum of the refrigerator and, outside, the wail of the wind. Gilles had turned off all the lamps in the house. Only the spotlights on the terrace were still on. The shadows of the palm trees shaken by the wind were dancing like merry phantoms on the living room walls.

Damn, this Scotch was really good!

Gilles was making his way through a thick mist arising from the malty sea spray of the Highlands. Nothing was important anymore, he could accept it all: this job he was tired of, his children who were going away, Claire's betrayal, the love that was withering.

A noise yanked him out of his limbo, a loud and repeated rustling. He slowly turned his head toward the sliding glass door and saw a tiny, furry silhouette scratching the window. The animal stopped when it saw that it had been spotted. It sat down, patiently, on its haunches. Two green eyes were fixed on

Sebag. Slowly, he struggled to get up from the couch and ended up on the floor. He got on his knees. He felt as weak and wretched as someone half-paralyzed after thirty-six hours of Telethon. He put one hand on the couch and the other on the coffee table and managed to get to his feet.

He slid the glass door open and let the animal in. It was a tomcat that belonged to their neighbor, a crazy old woman. The preceding summer the cat had already kept him company when Claire, Léo, and Séverine had each gone on vacation alone. Had abandoned him. The cat rubbed against the bottom of his pants leg and started purring.

"So you're back, pal. You at least haven't forgotten me."

Gilles opened the fridge and took a piece of leftover guinea fowl out of a plastic container. He put it on a plate that he set on the coffee table.

"Merry Christmas."

The cat looked at him for a moment—Gilles imagined that he was surprised—before leaping on the meat. He held it with his paw as he tore at it. Sebag sat down on the couch again and picked up the bottle.

"Here's to ya, cat."

He took a long drink and then had another look at the level of the liquid still in the bottle. It had gone down by a good third. He was drinking too much, that was for sure. He smiled as he remembered the bill. He'd paid a small fortune for this Ardbeg. There was no danger that he'd end up with cirrhosis: this Scotch was so expensive he'd have to empty his bank account and sell his house long before he became an alcoholic.

"Merry Christmas, cat."

He lost himself in the contemplation of the feline devouring its banquet. He could no longer connect one sentence with the next. And it was just as well. He must have dozed off for a while. A moment or an hour. He no longer had any notion of time.

It was late. Or else early. He didn't give a shit.

He reopened his eyes when a hairy mass came to lie down at his side, imitating the rumbling of a fuel-oil furnace. With his hand on the warm, vibrating fur, he sank into a deeper sleep.

He woke up shivering. Claire, his father, in the same room, the same bed, united in a single movement. Fucking nightmare! And so obvious . . . You didn't have to be a shrink to interpret its meaning. So Gérard Sebag would always come back to haunt him. Ten years at least since he'd seen him. Maybe he was dead? No, surely not. Gilles was an only son, a notary would have come to find him. In addition to bad memories, old Gérard certainly also had debts to bequeath to him.

He felt cold.

He crept over to the sliding glass door, which he'd forgotten to close. The cat had taken the opportunity to clear off. He'd paid for his feast with a quick caress, quid pro quo, that was life.

There was no free lunch.

Sebag turned off the lights on the terrace. The night invaded the room. He turned the lights back on. For the first time in ages, he was afraid of the dark.

The dark, silence, solitude, and death.

Carefully, he made his way over to the stereo and put the blues CD back in. No need to change it, he'd hardly heard it.

Lightnin' Hopkins's guitar spread through the living room. A little life, a little soul. He stretched out on the couch and took a few more swigs. He had to do something for this headache.

He was alone. Alone to cope with life.

For years he'd followed his children's growing up with a combination of pride and pain. He'd identified that danger, feared it, and had been preparing himself for it. The other one had stabbed him in the back. Naturally, he'd thought about it often enough but had never really believed it was possible.

"Not that, not us," he'd often said to himself.

"Not that, not us," he'd been repeating to himself, incredulous, for four days.

"Not that, not us," the litany rang in his mind today like a death knell.

Sebag accepted the obvious. Whatever you say, whatever you do, whatever you experience, you remain alone.

Hopelessly alone.

Definitively alone.

Fragile, cowardly hearts, people surrounded themselves with families, thinking they were building a continent. All they created was an illusion. We remain icebergs clinging to each other, shivering, and at the slightest storm, the slightest temptation, we resume our perpetual drift across a frosty ocean.

He took another swig of whiskey and expressed his desperation in a solemn burp.

CHAPTER 18

Lieutenant Julie Sadet was walking at a brisk pace to warm herself up. She'd raised the collar of her overcoat and pulled her hat down over her ears, but the wind was still slapping her nose, eyes, and lips. The weather had grown cooler over the last weekend, and winter, real winter, had arrived. Thanks to the wind, blue skies still prevailed over the plain, but the peaks of the Pyrenees were disappearing behind a mantle of dark clouds. It was finally snowing in the high country, and the ski resorts, which hadn't had enough snow at the beginning of the school vacations, were delighted. Julie was, too. As soon as the students and teachers had gone back to school, she herself would go to hurtle down the snowy slopes.

When she got to police headquarters, she asked the policemen on duty what had happened over the weekend. Apart from Stéphane Abad's arrest, it was pretty quiet, they told her. Five pickpockets, two drunks, a disturbance of the peace, and a brawl in a bar on Saturday night. It was rare, but it did sometimes happen that delinquents also respected the *trêve des confiseurs*.[9]

Then Julie went to look for Sebag in the headquarters cafeteria, a fancy name for three tables and about a dozen stools set up at one end of a hallway across from a vending machine.

[9] Lit., "the confectioners' truce." In France, the period between Christmas and New Year's, when little is done.

Since Molina was on vacation with his sons, Julie was supposed to team up with Gilles all week. A first since her arrival in Perpignan. She hoped to get a lot out of it.

"What can I get for you?" Sebag asked her.

His voice had an unusual cavernous sound; it seemed to come from an endless night. As she climbed onto a high stool, Julie wondered if Gilles hadn't taken advantage of his family's absence and his temporary freedom to engage in all kinds of excesses and follies. But that wasn't his kind of thing.

"Coffee, black without sugar, please."

Gilles put some coins in the machine, which snorted as noisily as a tank running on diesel. He handed her a cup and got himself a coffee. When he perched on a stool beside her, Julie expressed her astonishment.

"You're drinking coffee here? I thought you found it disgusting . . ."

"There are times when you have no choice. The Carlit is closed for the week."

He wet his lips with the black, steaming liquid.

"I repeat: It's disgusting! If I'd known . . . The next time, I'll arrange to take my vacations when Rafel does!"

"You've never considered buying an espresso machine for your office?"

"My children wanted to get me one, but I dissuaded them: I'd drink too much."

Julie scrutinized her colleague. His face was wan, his features tired, and he had big bags under his watery eyes—he must be coming down with something. In his sepulchral voice Gilles told her about the interrogations of Abad, the shadowy areas, the questions, and then the indictment for murder in the first degree. "Curious . . ." was the only commentary she thought it wise to make out loud. It had the advantage of being sober, she thought to herself.

Sober . . . the word made her smile at the obvious fact.

Gilles wasn't coming down with anything, he wasn't sick, he had a raging hangover. That's all. Molina had probably taken his partner, a temporary bachelor, on one of his infamous bar crawls.

Gazing into his coffee cup, Gilles seemed to be wondering what he was going to do. Finish his coffee or throw it directly into the trash bin.

"Add a little salt," she suggested.

"Do you think it would be better?"

"No. But it's good, they say, for the morning after."

In reply he stuck out his tongue at her.

"Yuck, that's horrible!" she laughed.

Then Gilles and Julie went back to their respective offices. Like all French cops, no matter what they were doing at the moment, they always had masses of paperwork. The morning stretched calmly on, and Julie had time to go home at noon to have a quick lunch tête-à-tête. But the meal was cut short by a call from headquarters. Some guy had fallen from the sixth floor of a building on the Rue Auguste Rodin, in the Saint-Martin neighborhood. According to firemen, he was in bad shape but still breathing.

Not being able to reach Sebag, Julie went to headquarters and found him dozing in his office, next to his mobile phone, which he had turned off. She shook him and told him about the situation. They went to the site together. The site of what? Of an accident, of an attempted murder, or of a suicide? That remained for them to determine.

In the parking lot at the foot of a six-story building, the policemen in uniform were trying to keep at a distance rubberneckers whose curiosity was valiantly resisting the icy gusts of the *tramontane*. Sebag raised his voice—which was even thicker than it had been that morning—and finally got the crowd to move back a few meters to let the firemen and the doctor from the emergency team work. The prestige of the uniform was not all that it used to be! People knew that the cops in uniform were only subordinates and they were now more willing to obey civilians.

Julie went up to the emergency team. The firemen were making a circle around the victim to hide him from the onlookers. Inside the perimeter thus established, one emergency doctor was bent over the body while another held the infusion bottle. Sitting near them a distraught woman wept silently. Julie tried to speak to her but got no response.

"She's in shock," the doctor holding the infusion bottle explained. "We gave her a sedative and we're going to take her to the hospital with us. I think you'll have to wait to question her."

"And him? How is he?"

The doctor who was bent over the victim stood up and spoke in a low voice to keep the woman from hearing him.

"He's in critical condition. He has sustained a severe cranial trauma and his spinal column has been affected. It would probably be better if he didn't make it. If his heart gives out during the transfer, we won't go to great lengths to resuscitate him."

The two lieutenants turned back to the onlookers.

"Did anyone see something?" Julie shouted after noting that Gilles, lost in his thoughts, was not going to take the initiative.

In the crowd, three people timidly raised their hands. A mother carrying a baby in her arms, a retiree, and a kid about twelve with roller skates on. She motioned to them to come forward, entrusted the old man to Gilles, took the woman aside, and asked the teenager to wait.

After recording the identities of their respective witnesses and taking down their statements, the two police officers turned to the kid. His name was Martí.

"So, Martí, what did you see?"

"I saw Monsieur Valls jump, Madame. But first I heard

shouting. I was roller-skating in the parking lot, my grandmother gave me the skates for Christmas. I looked up: the shouts were coming from the Vallses' apartment, and . . . I saw him put his leg over the railing on the balcony. He said something I didn't hear, and then . . ."

The boy swallowed before going on, looking down at his feet:

"And then he jumped. He . . . bounced off the car, there, and landed on the ground."

"What did you do then?"

He pointed to the two other witnesses.

"Nothing. The old gentleman and the lady came up. They spoke to Monsieur Valls and then telephoned. The firemen, I think."

"And Madame Valls, did you see her?"

"She came down very quickly, she sat down next to Monsieur Valls and screamed. Then afterward there were lots of people around them and I didn't see any more."

"Do you know the Vallses?"

"A little. They're nice, especially the lady. I live on the next street, but my grandmother is their neighbor, so I meet them sometimes when I come to see her."

The boy's statements corresponded exactly with what the earlier witnesses had said. Didier Valls, a forty-two-year-old accountant, married, without children, had jumped all alone from his balcony. Thus it was clearly an attempted suicide, unfortunate, to be sure, but commonplace.

"Thanks, Martí. You should go home now, this is not something you should see."

Julie took a card out of her wallet and handed it to the boy.

"Here's my number. If anything else occurs to you, you can call me. Don't hesitate. And even if you don't have anything special to say and you just want to talk about what happened, call me. It's important, you know, to talk."

Julie got up. Her eyes met Gilles's and she saw that he approved.

Didier Valls's heart did not give out on the way to the hospital, but the following night, during the operation that was supposed to reduce the bleeding of a cerebral hemorrhage. His wife learned the news when she awoke the following morning, another terrible shock. The doctors gave her more sedatives to help her cope. In the hospital corridor, which stank of suffering as much as of chlorine, Julie Sadet and Gilles Sebag were sitting in front of the door to room 112, waiting for the medical team to give them the green light to talk with Sandrine Valls.

Julie saw that Gilles was dozing on his chair. He was still not in great shape.

"I'm disappointed," she said softly.

Gilles opened his eyes and rubbed them.

"Pardon me?"

"I said, I'm disappointed. I was counting on taking advantage of this week to ask you to go running one of these evenings."

Gilles sat up on his chair.

"Sorry. I'm a little tired. I'm not sleeping well just now."

"Maybe you're out of the habit of sleeping alone?"

"Probably."

He rubbed a slight protuberance on his forehead. An old bump, apparently.

"In fact . . ." he began but then stopped. "In fact . . . I think I'm afraid of the dark."

A smile flickered on Gilles's lips but was contradicted by a voice that had sunk into an improbably low register. Julie hesitated. Was her colleague, usually so discreet, trying to help her out? The first thing that came into her mind was also the stupidest: "Do you want to talk about it?" The lethal weapon against confidences. She avoided the pitfall. Tried to find another way.

"Maybe you should try a different herbal tea . . ."

Gilles's smile became more frank, but he avoided her eyes.

"So, you run?"

A sudden bifurcation. He'd changed the subject. Probably intentionally. Or else she had been mistaken about his state of mind.

"I haven't had much time since I got to Perpignan, but I'm slowly getting back into it."

"Did you run when you were working in Paris?"

"Almost every day, I worked nights and I needed that to decompress."

"I can imagine . . . Where did you run in Paris?"

Julie felt her lips purse. Some memories were painful, even a year afterward . . .

"In the Buttes-Chaumont park. I loved that part of the capital. And you, where do you run?"

"Everywhere . . . On the beach, on the plain, in the hills. That's the advantage of this department: the sea and the mountains, everything is close by. And on foot!"

Gilles's voice was slowly coming back as he talked about running. It had taken on relief, a semblance of gaiety.

"So when shall we run?" Julie asked.

"Uhh . . . As you said, one of these evenings!"

Gilles had been staring at her for a few seconds. The young woman felt that he was wondering about the nature of her proposal. Why couldn't relations between men and women be simpler, more direct, without the perpetual misunderstanding? She knew that some people at police headquarters were already wondering about her and that one day, everything would necessarily become known. She wasn't afraid of the truth but she knew that many of her colleagues would no longer see her the same way afterward.

"Nothing like a little running to get back on track physically and mentally," Gilles said.

Another helping hand, Julie said to herself. But she didn't have time to wonder how to deal with this one, because a young doctor in a white smock was coming up to them.

"I believe you want to talk to Madame Valls? I'm going to see if that's possible now."The doctor went into room 112 and came out two minutes later. During that time, Gilles had regained his composure: he'd taken out his mobile and was reading his messages.

"She's waiting for you," the doctor finally said. "But take it easy. She's still in shock."

"Don't worry," Julie reassured him. "We have only a few simple questions. It's only a matter of an attempt . . . I mean . . . of a suicide."

Sandrine Valls's face seemed to them paler than the walls of the room, whiter than the sheets on her bed. When she saw them coming in, she sat up in bed. And before they could greet her, she said to them:

"All this is my fault, and my fault alone."

She began to sob. The two officers pulled up two chairs and placed them side by side. Julie decided to lead the conversation. Women speak to women . . .

"Tell us, Sandrine, why you think that it's your fault?"

"I wanted to leave him. I've been wanting to tell him for a long time . . . I just couldn't. He was often depressed. When he was doing badly, I didn't want to add to his suffering, and when he was feeling better, I was afraid of making him fall into depression again. But then yesterday we had it out. He got angry, and so did I, and I said some painful things, much too painful. I had never imagined that he would go that far, I don't know what I would have done had I known, but of course I would have acted differently. I didn't want that, I didn't want him to die, I didn't want to kill him, I didn't want . . ."

Sandrine's forearm was outside the white sheet. Julie put her hand on it and caressed it gently.

"Of course you didn't want that . . ."

"It was because of me that he jumped. I'm the one who killed him."

"No, no, you're not responsible, Sandrine. He and he alone made that choice. You've already said that you couldn't guess that he would do that."

"I should have! Over the past few days I'd noticed that he was particularly down. I was selfish. We've been living together for fifteen years, I should have been able to tell that he could do something foolish, I should have foreseen it. When you've loved someone such a long time, you ought to know him well enough to keep things like this from happening!"

"And you didn't love him anymore? Is that why you wanted to leave him, Sandrine?"

On her right, she saw Sebag move, but didn't understand the message. Was she missing something, or did he just want to refocus the conversation on the course of events the preceding day? She decided it was useful to prolong the phase of lamentations. Maybe it wasn't useful for the investigation, but it was certainly useful for Sandrine. The pain had to be expelled. She'd missed her calling, she said to herself. She should have been a social worker or a psychologist instead of a cop! Her taste for action had led her to decide otherwise.

"There was no longer anything between us," Sandrine answered, sadly shaking her head. "We'd been sleeping in separate rooms for months! But he still loved me. In any case, that's what he often told me, and even more often for the past few days. And it's what he told me again just before he jumped . . ."

"What about you? You didn't love him anymore?"

"It happened gradually, I didn't see it coming. And then one day I understood!"

Gilles cleared his throat:

"One day?"

Sandrine turned her head toward him.

"About two months ago . . ."

"The day when you realized that you loved somebody else?"

Julie was astonished by this direct question. Visibly, Gilles was in a hurry to get down to the facts. Sandrine took a tissue from the rolling table next to her bed. She blew her nose. She ended up replying, but she addressed herself to Julie:

"Didier told me that he knew everything, that he knew that I had a lover. I've known Francis since last September, he's the new head of my department. He immediately liked the way I worked and took me into his confidence. Not only in my work. Didier spent all his time belittling me. One day in early November, I was having lunch with Francis when he told me that he found me attractive. Up to that point I'd thought I had only respect and esteem for him, but then I realized that I was having stronger feelings. And above all, I understood that I no longer loved Didier."

She put the used tissue on the table, next to a plastic pitcher. She poured herself a glass of water and took a swallow of it.

"But nothing ever happened with Francis. We saw each other from time to time outside work, at a restaurant, at the movies, and also at the beach. We kissed, but there was never anything else between us. I didn't want to. First I had to leave Didier."

Her plaintive tone took on a sudden firmness.

"I'm not that kind of woman."

Julie felt that on her left Gilles was fidgeting again. This time he was right; it was time to move the conversation forward.

"And did something change yesterday? Something that triggered what happened?"

"Didier told me he knew everything. But he only thought he knew . . . He was convinced that I'd slept with Francis and he refused to believe me when I told him that nothing had happened—naturally, I didn't mention the kisses . . . I got mad and told him that I was leaving him. Things quickly got out of hand, he'd been drinking, a lot, and I got scared: I thought he was going to hit me."

Then Sandrine told them that she had packed a suitcase with her clothes while Didier gave full vent to his anger. He had started throwing the furniture around, first the television set and then the coffee table and the bookcase. Julie took notes. All that fit with the disorder they'd found in the apartment after the emergency team had taken the Valls couple to the hospital.

"He'd started drinking several days earlier," Sandrine went on. "I realized that only when I saw the bottles all over the living room: they were almost all completely empty, when last month we'd gone to Spain to replenish our stock for the holidays. He screamed, he was really drunk, and he was saying incomprehensible things. He claimed to have known everything for a long time. 'Everything.' How could he know everything since nothing had happened!"

Her pain and her guilty feelings didn't prevent her from being offended by what she considered an injustice. Gilles abruptly stood up, putting his hand in the inside pocket of his jacket.

"Excuse me, an urgent call," he explained before going out of the room.

When the door closed after him, Sandrine Valls continued her story:

"All at once, he stopped being angry and began crying. He told me that he loved me, that he had always loved me, and . . . and he went out on the balcony. He didn't even threaten to jump, he didn't even leave me time to do anything, to say something. He put his leg over the balustrade and disappeared. I heard a metallic sound."

Her voice broke.

"The firemen told me that he fell first on a car parked in front . . . before landing on the parking lot."

Sandrine sobbed. Julie got up to get the packet of tissues and handed it to her. She didn't need to know more but she asked a few more purely formal questions to give Sandrine time to recover a semblance of calm.

She joined Gilles in front of the entrance to the hospital. A group of patients in pajamas were gathered around a large ashtray. They were all smoking. Gilles crushed out his cigarette butt.

"Since when do marathon runners smoke?" Julie joked.

"Only real athletes can know the true pleasure of a cigarette . . . Have you ever smoked after running?"

"No, never."

"You should; it's delicious. Even better than after sex."

"Ah, I wouldn't know about that. I stopped so long ago!"

Julie waited for Sebag to show his astonishment before adding with a laugh: "I mean: it has been a long time since I stopped smoking!"

"You scared me there for a moment . . ."

Gilles hesitated. Julie could see that he was going to ask the indiscreet question that all her colleagues were asking themselves.

"And so . . . you've got a boyfriend?"

She hesitated in turn. This might be the time. She knew that Gilles was capable of being discreet. But in the end she decided not to.

"Almost," she replied, with a smile lurking at the corner of her mouth. Maybe I'll tell you someday."

"You're not obliged to do that, I was just asking. Without any ulterior motive, I assure you."

"I know. Faithful husband?"

"For the past twenty years."

"Do such men still exist?"

"Have to think so."

"And no regrets?"

"Almost none."

He winked at her.

"Maybe someday I'll tell you about that, too . . ."

Sebag was smiling but his eyes were veiled in gray mist. The time for confidences had not yet come. It wouldn't be long.

"Do we have another emergency?"

"No, why?"

"You said you had an urgent call."

"Ah, yes."

Mechanically, he put his hand in the pocket where he kept his mobile.

"Uhh . . . It was my kids."

"Nothing serious?"

"No, no . . . uhh . . . not really."

"Then it wasn't so urgent . . ."

"Is that a reproach, Lieutenant Sadet?"

"You left right in the middle of the drama, that wasn't very comradely . . ."

"You'll see when you have children. Mine are teenagers and they already have little need for their father. So for me, when they call, it's always urgent to be there."

CHAPTER 19

Oh, Gilles, are you ready?"

Claire's voice brought him back to life. It came from afar, that voice. From the adjoining bathroom and from the depths of his nothingness. He slowly came to and realized that the same question had already been asked several times. At least three times.

Claire's face appeared in the half-open door.

"Come on, you're not yet dressed? Hurry up!"

Gilles was standing in front of the armoire in their bedroom, overcome by the range of possibilities. How should he dress for New Year's Eve? He reached out to take a jacket. Pulled back. Too dark. He stroked the fabric of another jacket. Very soft. Pleasant. Too brightly colored.

"The range of possibilities," he repeated half out loud.

"What did you say?"

Claire had disappeared into the bathroom again, where she was finishing getting ready.

"Nothing important. I was talking to myself."

"Ah . . ."

Where did he come up with that expression? The range of possibilities. You'd think it came from math, philosophy, or even science fiction. A little of each of them, maybe.

He grabbed a gray jacket. He liked it for the four yellow buttons that decorated its sleeves at the wrist. Or the elbow. Because this jacket could be worn with the sleeves pushed up, which he particularly liked.

He was about to put it on when he realized that he was still naked as a jaybird. He put the jacket down on the bed and chose some shorts. As for the rest, it was so complicated . . .

"How do you want me to dress?" he shouted over the noise of a running faucet.

Claire came back into the bedroom. She was wearing a black satin dress that left her shoulders uncovered but enveloped her arms in embroidered muslin. She was almost ready. Dressed, made-up. All she needed now was a little touch of red lipstick. She looked at the jacket on the bed and took from the armoire an Imperial yellow shirt and a pair of pleated trousers in the same gray as the jacket.

"Do you want to wear a tie?"

"Why not?"

She put a cobalt blue tie on the jacket.

"Hurry, we're going to be late."

"Late, late . . . You always have to exaggerate. For New Year's Eve you're not late so long as it isn't midnight."

"That's right . . . I'm not sure that Fanny and her roast would agree with you."

"Ah, Fanny's famous roast . . . Anyway, it's always overcooked. This year she'll have an excuse."

A loud voice reached them from the living room.

"I'm leaving, Mom and Dad. Good-bye, see you tomorrow!"

"OK, son, we love you too! Kisses!"

Claire and the kids had come back from his in-laws' that morning. Séverine had made only a short stop at home before leaving again with a girlfriend—her name was Chloé, he seemed to remember—and Léo was going to the home of a certain Gabriel. He was going there on his scooter. Not cool! At least he had promised to sleep there rather than come back in the middle of the night, tired and—who knows?—drunk.

He and Claire were to dine with the Chambruns. Fanny

worked with Claire at the Rivesaltes middle school, and Érick was a schoolteacher in a primary school in Espira-de-l'Agly. That was also where they lived.

Gilles was finally ready: it was time to leave.

In the car, he thought again about that moment of absence in front of the door to his armoire. It was not the first time that had happened to him. It felt strange to have his head filled, not with those eternal dark thoughts that seemed to circle round and round, but filled . . . filled with emptiness. Yes, that was exactly how he felt. Filled with emptiness.

In general, it lasted a few seconds. He suddenly froze, no longer moving, no longer thinking, indifferent to everything. The world could have fallen apart and he wouldn't have flinched.

The first time, he'd attributed this phenomenon to alcohol. A facile excuse but one that had not worked for the second time. He hadn't drunk. Or rather . . . not enough to explain such absences.

"Why are you turning here?"

Gilles, surprised, gave the wheel a yank that caused him to go over the white line.

"Excuse me?"

"Why are you turning?" Claire asked again. "That's not the right direction."

Damn . . . At the roundabout, he'd taken the road toward downtown rather than heading straight north toward Espira.

"Sorry, I was lost in my thoughts. Conditioned reflexes! I was going to headquarters."

"Do you want me to drive?"

"No, don't worry, it's all right."

He was forced to make a long detour before he could get back on the right road. Claire was watching him out of the corner of her eye.

These last few days each evening they had had long conversations on the telephone. They had said over and over that they loved each other, they had talked about everything and nothing, carefully avoiding the touchy subjects. And every evening after the call, Gilles had slept on the couch, a bottle within reach. He'd alternated whiskey, vodka, Cognac, and Armagnac. In drinking, as within a couple, routine had to be avoided at any price.

The routine that was breaking them apart right now was the worst of all. That of insistent questions. A new question had just arisen in his mind which, unfortunately, had recovered its acuity and normal activity. He couldn't help himself, he had to ask it. He had to know before he could get there.

"Did Fanny know about it?"

"About what?"

"What do you think!"

He heard a long sigh on his right.

"Why would she have? Do you think I shouted it from the rooftops?"

"She might have noticed it."

"She never gave me any reason to think that."

The headlights of the cars coming in the opposite direction filled the inside of the car with an almost continuous yellow light. The traffic was heavy, everybody was going to a New Year's Eve party. Most people were probably happy, or managed to seem happy. If only the year that was ending had never existed . . .

"Don't make it worse, please," Claire pleaded. "We were always discreet. There was never anything ambiguous between us at school or elsewhere. Nobody ever suspected anything."

Gilles bit his upper lip. Was Claire that naïve or was she deliberately deluding herself to alleviate her guilty feelings? How could she think that first the complicity, then the strong . . . attraction that had bound her to . . . the other guy had remained secret? It took so little, a slight touch, a smile, a glance more tender and lingering than others. He knew that strange vibrations danced around people who were attracted to each other. Most people didn't perceive these vibrations, but they did not escape everyone. Gilles remembered that at police headquarters in Chartres he had been the first to notice the ties between two colleagues. The man was an inspector for public security, the woman worked on the financial fraud squad. They also thought they had been discreet, speaking to each other very little and never being less than twenty centimeters from one another. And yet he had found it out. Long before anyone else. Because everything had ended up being known. The liaison had gone on and the two lovers had finally made missteps. Some ill-intentioned or jealous person had informed the spouses. The woman had gotten divorced, while the man had had himself transferred and tried to reconstruct his marriage far from Chartres. Gilles had never heard how that turned out; perhaps the guy had succeeded.

Workplaces are microcosms buzzing with rumors. If that was true regarding Claire and . . . Simon, the rumors had started to circulate even before their friendship got out of hand.

"You always left in separate cars?"

"In the evening, yes. But at noon, not always, it's true . . ."

"And Pascale and Véronique, they knew about it, I assume?"

Claire sighed again. Pascale and Véronique were two great friends with whom she played sports, sometimes went out in the evening, going to the movies or the theater when the posters didn't appeal to Gilles.

"Pascale, yes, but not Véronique. At the time, Véro was right in the middle of a divorce, she was in very bad shape, and I didn't want to burden her with that."

Gilles sensed that this was half a lie, and he wasn't taken in. Last summer, Véronique had just broken up with her husband, who was cheating on her. She wasn't in the best position to receive that kind of confidence. Claire had probably wanted to avoid being judged, or even condemned.

"And how did you tell Pascale about it? Did you say that you had done something really stupid or that you were having a marvelous time?"

"You know that the truth is that it was a little of both."

Claire's voice remained calm, but he discerned a mixture of tension and pain. He had to admit that this mixture did him good.

"I no longer remember what I said exactly," Claire went on, "but it necessarily revolved around that."

"Did you tell Pascale right away?"

"Almost."

"Every time I've run into her since, she knew and she didn't say anything to me . . ."

Despite himself, his tone had hardened. His anger was growing, he had to control it. But it was stronger than he was.

"And what did I look like her, and to your other colleagues, for that matter? The resident asshole? The guy you laugh at when his back is turned? I never want to see Pascale again, not ever!"

"You won't see her, but I'll continue to see her. How can you reproach her for not having told you secrets I confided to her?"

"And what did she say when you admitted you were having an affair?"

"I don't remember. Not much. She, too, cheated on her husband a few years ago. Xavier had already done the same earlier. They were able to talk about it. They are still together today. Maybe even happier than before. You know, it may be unfortunate but that's the way it is: today, a majority of people have strayed at one time or another."

"I know, I know the stats."

In the contemporary world, life could now be summed up only in figures. The sales of Kleenex, the frequency of sexual intercourse, the price of natural gas, the number of sexual partners before, after, and during marriage, popularity ratings, the efficiency of the police. Would there someday be a Richter scale to qualify the intensity of distress?

Gilles felt like the last of the Mohicans.

"In fact, I'm the one who's to blame, the black cat: I should have cheated on you!"

Claire turned to him and put her hand on his arm to calm the storm.

"Please stop, Gilles. Listen to your heart, listen to my love, and above all, don't listen to your pride. Otherwise we're done for."

He tried to breathe more normally. She was right, so right: it was easier to get over a sorrow in love than a wound to one's pride.

The party at the Chambruns' turned out to be a crashing bore. When a middle-school teacher meets another middle-school teacher and a primary-school teacher, what do they talk about? Stuff that is mortally tedious! Especially for a cop. The reform of the middle schools and the school calendar, the wretched salaries, the lack of recognition, conflicts with the students, the parents, and often both. Kindly, as she served the cheese course Fanny tried to reorient the conversation toward Gilles.

"And you, what are you working on at the moment? An exciting case? Do you have any juicy information to reveal to us?"

Well, no, he didn't have anything interesting to recount. For an instant he was tempted to tell them in great detail about all the cases he was currently working on, about all these couples whose marriages were turning into tragedies. To provoke in that way a debate on adultery in the world and in France, here and now. A petty revenge taken on Claire and a way of testing Fanny and Érick. He knew he was capable of discerning, in their words, their glances, and their tone, what they really knew.

He decided not to do it: He might end up being the only one to suffer from that pointless discussion.

Fanny offered Gilles a second opportunity:

"What about the Benitez case, anything new?"

"No, it's dead quiet and there's no prospect of new investigations."

"So the case will remain a mystery?"

"Probably."

Ah, the infamous Benitez case . . . [10] A mother and her daughter, a candidate for the title of Miss Roussillon, had mysteriously disappeared two years earlier, a few days before the celebrated beauty pageant. The father and husband, Francisco Benitez, a member of the French Foreign Legion, had waited two weeks before reporting their disappearance to the police. An extremely strange thing to do. He had therefore very quickly become the main suspect. The only one, in fact. And under the pressure of the police and the media, the man had spectacularly committed suicide: after having recorded a video proclaiming his innocence, he had hanged himself from a window at his barracks. Without bringing forth any conclusive proof, the investigation had afterward continued to assemble evidence all of which pointed to Francisco's guilt. Information, some of it sordid, was leaked almost every day to the national and local press. The case had become a veritable TV serial that the French, and first of all the people of Perpignan, followed with fervor. At that time, Gilles was having great success at dinners, including the ones attended solely by Claire's colleagues.

[10] An actual case (2013). Cf. https://fr.wikipedia.org/wiki/Affaire_Benitez.

Since Gilles did not take advantage of this second opportunity, the discussion returned to the next school year, the summer vacation that was almost over, and the Christmas vacation, which was never very restful for either teachers or students. "It's going to be a long time until February!" they all lamented in unison.

Midnight finally arrived. The Chambruns uncorked the champagne. People embraced, they drank, and then it was time to go.

Oof.

When Gilles and Claire got home they found the house empty. Séverine and Léo were sleeping at their friends' houses. If they ever did go to sleep . . . They went to bed in silence and lay there, each on his or her own side.

Since they'd left the Chambruns' house, they hadn't said a word to each other. Claire had wanted to drive, and he hadn't insisted. Two cocktails, wine, and champagne, he'd had his dose.

The silence continued. Gilles moved over to curl up next to his wife. Their bodies fit together perfectly. An accident of nature or the force of habit. They had matured together, perhaps they had shaped themselves with relation to each other.

And what about the other man, how was it with him? Gilles succeeded in setting the question aside.

He put his hand on Claire's hip and whispered in her ear:

"When you're with me, like that, pressed against my body, I can't think of anything but us. But as soon as you go away, even a few centimeters, I can't help it: I think about the two of you."

Chapter 20

François Ménard got to headquarters early. He felt fresh and rested, because he had gone to bed early the night before to recover from the excesses of New Year's Eve. As usual, he greeted with a quick nod the woman cop who was on the front desk the day after the holiday.

"Happy New Year, Lieutenant Ménard!" she cried.

He froze. Behind her desk, Martine had risen, she was expecting something. Ménard hesitated, took a few steps toward her, and held out a limp hand.

"Happy New Year . . . Martine. Thanks. And especially good health, huh?"

The woman cop shook his hand.

"Yes, for sure, especially good health."

She grabbed a Post-it that she'd stuck to the edge of the desk.

"Here, by the way, someone called a few minutes ago. A young man who wanted to speak to two lieutenants, a man and a woman, but he wasn't able to give me their names. They questioned him a few days ago . . ."

"What's his name?"

Martine examined the note.

"Abad. Maxime Abad."

Ménard was suddenly interested.

"Apparently the name means something to you," Martine remarked. "Are you the one who questioned him?"

If Ménard remembered correctly, Gilles and Julie had met the young man the evening of the murder.

"I'm also working on this case, yes. What was the call about?"

"The boy just told me he had important information to give you. He left his telephone number. Do you want it?"

She handed him a Post-it that he immediately put in his pocket.

"Tell me, Lieutenant . . . This young man, is he the son of the woman who was killed by his father? I mean . . . by her husband. I mean *her* husband but *his* father."

"He's the one."

"He's young?"

"About twenty, I think."

"He doesn't have brothers or sisters?"

"No."

"Oh, *pobret.*[11] So he'll be left all alone . . . If that isn't too bad!"

Ménard cut her lamentations short and left to call Maxime, who answered after the first ring.

"Thanks for calling me back so fast, Lieutenant," the young man said politely. "Could you stop by to see me today? I have something to show you."

"What is it?"

"I think you'll be interested. It's photos. But I'd prefer not to say more. I'll be home all day. You can come to Pollestres whenever you want."

Ménard didn't have to think about it long. He didn't have much to do and could thus take advantage of the opportunity. The future belongs to those who get up early, they say. And in the police, fortune sometimes smiles on those who get to headquarters early.

Like most of the communes on the Catalan plain, Pollestres is smothered in a web of residential subdivisions. Ménard

[11] Poor kid.

wandered around for a long time in a pitiless labyrinth of streets, circles, and dead ends before he finally spotted a young man. Maxime was waiting for him on the sidewalk.

"You're not the only one who struggles in this area . . ."

Ménard followed the young man into the house. In the middle of the living room, the television was on, simulating a presence in the empty dwelling.

"Would you like some coffee?" Maxime asked.

"I'd rather have tea, please."

As the young man disappeared into the adjoining kitchen, Ménard took off his jacket and sat down on a comfortable L-shaped couch. The insipid images of an all-news channel were appearing over and over on the television screen. He took the remote and hit the mute button.

A few minutes later Maxime Abad returned to the living room and put two steaming cups on the solid wood coffee table. But he remained standing.

"You aren't the one who questioned me the other evening at the police station . . ."

"No. But I'm the one who's conducting this investigation, in fact. I took part in the initial examination and conducted the interrogation of your father and of . . . of Monsieur Balland."

Ménard's blunder caused Maxime to raise an eyebrow.

"My colleagues who talked with you are not available today."

Maxime seemed to hesitate, but finally took an envelope out of a drawer in the big bookcase that decorated the living room.

"I found this among my father's things."

Ménard looked at the envelope without touching it. On it was written Stéphane Abad's name and the address of his company. It was postmarked December 20. François made a quick calculation: Christmas was a Thursday, so the 20th must have been a Saturday, three days before the tragedy.

"Was the envelope already open?"

"Yes, of course."

"Did you handle it much?"

"Uhh . . . yes. And I even showed its contents to my aunt and uncle. They're the ones who advised me to call you."

"OK."

Ménard picked up the envelope and took out three series of photos that he spread on the table. They had been taken in quick succession. The first series showed Christine Abad and Éric Balland entering the Hôtel du Gecko together. In the lower right corner was a time stamp: 12:33. The other two series showed the lover and then the wife coming out separately, Balland at 1:56 and Christine at 2:07. On the back of one of the photos, a handwritten note read: "Every Thursday and sometimes on Tuesday. You know how to reach me."

Ménard shook his head and examined the photos again. Especially the ones showing Christine. She had a light step and a smile on her face. The photographer was talented: you could even see a spark of happiness in Christine's eyes. She'd just left her lover and she was radiant, blooming. It was enough to make a jealous husband furious and violent.

"Should we not have touched them?"

Lost in his thoughts, Ménard took a few seconds before looking up.

"Pardon?"

"I was saying that perhaps we should not have touched the photos and the envelope. Because of the fingerprints . . ."

Ménard dismissed this regret:

"That doesn't matter. We would have tried to lift prints, but we wouldn't have found any. These days nobody is stupid enough to send anonymous letters with his fingerprints all over them."

"The note was written by hand. That can help you too, can't it?"

The policemen shrugged his skinny shoulders.

"Maybe . . . If we test the handwriting of everybody living in the area!"

"But when you have a suspect, that could help you."

"A suspect . . ."

Ménard sipped his tea. It was good and strong but already a little cold. He drank it up in three swallows before turning back to Maxime.

"These photos suggest that someone knew about the affair your mother was having with Monsieur Balland and that he informed your father. Why? Probably in order to take revenge on one or the other of them."

"Or to take revenge on my father!"

"Perhaps . . ."

This hypothesis seemed to him less plausible but it could not be excluded, in fact. But that was not the most important thing: he was going to have to pour cold water on the young man's hopes.

"I understand your anger at the person who sent these, but what crime can he be accused of committing?"

Maxime stared at him.

"He's the one who started this whole mess, isn't he?"

Ménard spread the photos on the table.

"What do these photos tell us? Basically, just one thing: that somebody harbored enough malice or even hatred to spend his time spying and then taking these compromising photos."

He paused long enough to find the right words. Clear but not too harsh. He decided to use first names rather than say "your mother" and "your father."

"But who deceived Stéphane? Not him. Who shot Christine? Not him, either. And nothing allows us to conclude that this mysterious individual wanted his revelations to lead to this kind of tragedy. For the examining magistrate and for the prosecutor, the case is closed, we have to move on. And I don't think that the existence of these photos is enough to lead us to request further investigation. By the way, you haven't told me exactly where you found them."

"In the cabinet where Papa keeps his rifle."

"Curious . . . Did he usually store papers in that cabinet?"

"Only his shooting equipment."

Maxime was replying distractedly. He had not yet digested Ménard's remarks.

"Do you mean that you aren't going to do anything to arrest this . . . this bastard?"

"Do you have any idea who he is? Suspicions, a lead we could pursue? Do you think you know someone who held a grudge against one of your parents?"

"Me? Of course not! But Papa's co-workers or his friends might know something. Mama's friends, too."

"And Éric Balland's friends and colleagues as well. That would be a lot of work and energy spent for an uncertain result. And even if we identified the person who sent the photos, what then? We could charge him with 'invasion of privacy' or 'assault and involuntary violence,' but nothing more. And if his lawyer were half-competent, he'd get off with a suspended sentence or a simple fine."

"What if that man really acted with the intention that things turn out badly?"

"We'd have to be able to prove it."

"That's crazy!"

Ménard talked about budget reductions, fewer officers, policies based on numbers, police efficiency, etc. Seeing that he was getting nowhere, he collected the photos. Then he stood up.

"I'll keep these, of course. They'll be part of the investigation file. Maybe the judge will ask us to investigate after all. You can also get a lawyer and file a complaint against an unknown person on the basis of these photos. That might help move things forward."

"But you don't think that's very likely?"

If François Ménard had been the young man's father, he would have advised him to drop it and start the mourning process immediately, rather than desperately seeking a scapegoat for his pain. But he was only a policeman.

"I promise you that I'll do all I can."

He saw Maxime's shoulders trembling. He should have put a comforting hand on those shoulders, a father's hand . . . He didn't dare. Physical contact had always been difficult for him. He just held out his card.

"Don't hesitate to call me to let me know if you have something new."

Julie Sadet and Gilles Sebag were in an unmarked car, patrolling the streets of Bas-Vernet, a problem area north of downtown. A dozen burglaries had taken place in this sector since the beginning of the vacation, all of them during the middle of the day, and all in the homes of elderly people.

The radio crackled:

"Calling all cars: a man has blockaded himself at number 35, Rue Viollet-le-Duc, Las Cobas sector. Threatening to set his house on fire. Need an OPJ[12] on-site."

"You didn't have plans for noon today?" Julie asked.

"Other than lunch, no."

Sebag opened the glove compartment and took out a revolving light and placed it on the roof of the car.

"Do you know where you're going?"

After two months in the department, Julie was beginning to know her way around.

"Las Cobas is on the other side of the Têt, near Cabestany, I think. I take the fourth bridge to avoid going through downtown, right?"

[12] *Officier de police judiciaire*, an investigating officer.

"Perfect. Step on it, I'll guide you afterward."

Their service vehicle was not yet equipped with a GPS, so Sebag did a search on his mobile.

"I found Rue Viollet-le-Duc, it's near the Lycée Picasso."

At the bridge over the Têt, Julie took the bus lane, passing cars on the right. The radio crackled again:

"The man is not alone. He's holding a woman hostage. The firefighters are on the scene."

The avenue went around the Saint-Jacques gardens, the last bastion of market gardening still resisting urbanization, and then climbed toward the Las Cobas neighborhood. Julie enjoyed audaciously passing a few cars on curves. Sebag's hands gripped the armrests.

"Turn right after the roundabout, then turn right again on the third street afterward," he panted.

The tires squealed as Julie made the turn. A hundred meters on, she stopped the car in front of the security cordon the municipal police had set up. She leapt from the car and greeted the officers. Farther up the street, the firemen were unrolling a fire hose. A thick, dark cloud was rising into the sky. Julie turned to Sebag but he was already gone.

Ménard was driving to headquarters when he heard the first radio calls. He was reluctant to respond, and was relieved to learn that Gilles and Julie were on their way to the scene. He was not a man of action, knew it, and made no effort to suggest the contrary. Sebag was better in that regard, unless shots had to be fired. Gilles had the reputation of being a terrible shot. But maybe that was only one of Molina's jokes.

As he drove, Ménard was running through all the oddities in the Abad case, which was basically so simple. The presence of a malicious anonymous letter-writer came on top of the mysteries of the SMS and the murderer's lies about the time of his acts. Because Abad had in fact lied. Ménard had viewed the surveillance tapes again and no longer had any doubt about that. He'd found an image of Abad shortly before he showed up in front of the hotel, but only three minutes before, as he parked his car in a handicapped place on the Rue du Pont d'en Vesit. On the other hand, before that point, there had been no trace of the murderer in the city.

Strange, really strange.

No matter how much he mulled them over, he couldn't make these oddities hang together. He caught himself wondering if once he'd been informed of the existence of the photos, Gilles would be able to find a connection among all these things. He had to acknowledge that his colleague sometimes had amazing flashes of insight. François saw himself as a little more . . . how to put it . . . laborious. Yes, that was the right word. Laborious. A good cop, hardworking, rigorous, but . . . laborious.

Sebag approached the house cautiously.

On Rue Viollet-le-Duc, the little houses were built adjoining one another. They were "two-faces," as people say in Northern Catalonia. The façade of no. 35 was no more than ten meters wide. The front door was right in the middle, framed on the left by a small picture window, on the right by a garage door. Above them a balcony occupied two thirds of the length of the façade, leaving room for a small window over the garage, probably for the bathroom. In the yard, a pile of clothing, furniture, and various other things was blazing.

"For it to burn like that, the guy must have poured gasoline on it before lighting it," said a deep voice behind him.

Sebag sniffed. Beneath the acrid, powerful odor of the fire there were in fact syrupy smells. He turned around and recognized Captain Carré, who commanded firefighting operations in Perpignan. He was a tall, slender fellow with a determined face. Sebag had already had occasion to admire his efficiency and simplicity.

"I've had the two adjoining houses evacuated," Carré explained, "but I'm wondering if I shouldn't expand the security perimeter."

Two tiled areas divided the space in front of the house. Only a little hedge and a concrete wall about twenty centimeters high separated the courtyard where the fire was burning from the driveway. A white Seat was parked there.

"Are you afraid the car might catch fire?"

"My men have already sprayed it with water, but I don't care if it burns. It's only in movies that cars explode. No, what worries me is that the neighbors saw the owner unload several jerry cans from his trunk this morning. He must have them inside the house."

"Shit!"

"The prefect's chief of staff is supposed to arrive any time now. She's the one who will make the decision."

"Who's inside?"

"A man and a woman. The people renting the place, apparently. Bastien Gali and Véronique Marti. Those are the names on the mailbox. I don't know anything more about them."

Sebag took off his helmet and used his sleeve to wipe his forehead, which was drenched with sweat. Then he realized that it was astonishingly warm. He raised his face to the blue sky and let his skin be caressed for a moment by a malicious sun. He was sweating under his jacket and felt sorry for the fireman, who had to put up with his dark uniform in fireproof material. He laid a hand on Carré's shoulder and went off to find Julie. She was questioning the neighbors, who were kept about twenty meters from the house.

"Do I know Bastien? Somewhat, for sure!" exclaimed a stout man with a mustache. "We meet from time to time in the nearby bistro. He's unemployed, and that leaves him a little time."

"At the nearby bistro . . ." Julie repeated. "So he drinks, then?"

The neighbor's face darkened.

"A little glass from time to time never hurt anyone . . ."

Sebag considered the pudgy, reddish face of his interlocutor, but abstained from making any comments. He was in no position to tell others what to do. Not right now. Replying to another of Julie's questions, the neighbor gestured vaguely toward the house behind him.

"I live in number 12, the wine-colored one."

Gilles had to fight down a nascent smile. "Tone on tone," he almost said. The man introduced himself. Norbert Camard. Former mason. Fell off scaffolding four years earlier. On disability ever since.

"So that leaves you the time to . . . chitchat with Bastien from time to time," Julie remarked. "What kind of guy is he?"

"With me, he's always been very cordial . . ."

She picked up on this excessively evasive answer: "And with other people?"

Camard smoothed his mustache greedily. He was about to badmouth his pal and that didn't seem to displease him at all.

"I've heard that some parents complained. He coaches boys in a soccer club and apparently he yells at them a little too much. And in a match he doesn't always set a good example with regard to the referees."

"Is he violent?"

"I don't think he has ever struck anyone."

"But he's irascible?"

"Yes, you could say that."

"Do you think he could do something stupid today?"

The neighbor ran his hand over his mustache again.

"If he bought jerry cans, it wasn't for a barbecue."

Sebag didn't much appreciate that little joke.

"Did you see him take them in?"

"No, I didn't."

Camard turned to a blond young woman next to him.

"But you did, Muriel . . . You saw him, right?"

The young woman confirmed what the neighbor had said: Bastien Gali had returned home shortly before noon and unloaded a dozen heavy jerry cans.

"He looked crazy, I've never seen him like that. I think he'd been drinking. He told me that I should keep away, that he was going to set fire to the whole neighborhood and everyone would see that he wasn't the chump people thought he was, and she'd see, too."

"She?" Sebag asked with a grimace.

"He didn't say so, but it's clear he was talking about Véro. She came back around noon, as usual. She works at an insurance agency. She's inside with him."

"You didn't try to keep her from going in?"

"Of course I did! I'd been keeping an eye out for her, and I told her that he was like a crazy man, but she went in anyway."

"Do they have children?" Julie asked.

"No."

"And then what happened?" Gilles went on.

"Then there was a lot of loud shouting."

"Who was shouting?"

"Both of them. I couldn't understand anything they said, they were both screaming at the same time. And afterward, Bastien threw Véronique's clothes off the balcony into the yard, and then he started throwing other stuff. I saw jewels, a dressing table, things of hers. Then he emptied a jerry can on them, still from the balcony. At that point I went home to call the police. And while I was on the phone, I heard a kind of explosion. Through the window I could see the fire in front of their place."

"Does he have weapons in the house?"

"I don't have any idea."

"I don't think he does," Camard broke in. "In any case, he never mentioned them to me."

"How were Bastien and Véronique getting along lately?"

The question Julie had just asked was the right one, but Sebag dreaded it. A man who threatens to burn his house down, screaming that he's going to prove to everyone and especially to his wife that he's not a chump . . . You didn't need much imagination to guess the reasons for that anger. But good God! Why did every couple in the department have to tear each other apart just now? Couldn't they leave him alone?

"They were a pretty close couple," Muriel answered. "But it's true that for the last few weeks, things seemed a little tense between them."

"Were they just tired of each other, or was it . . . something else?" Julie probed. "Was he jealous?"

"Who isn't?" Muriel said evasively.

"Did he have reasons for being jealous?"

"I . . . I don't know."

Sebag took Norbert Camard aside. To let Muriel speak more freely with Julie, and because the big guy with a mustache had a mocking smile on his lips.

"So, in your opinion, she was fooling around and that's the cause of this mess?"

"Might well be . . ."

Sebag waited. Norbert was dying to tell him more.

"However . . . jealousy really isn't their thing. He looked around. There was a lewd sparkle in his eyes. "Their thing is swinging . . ."

" . . ."

"When he's two sheets to the wind, Bastien gets talkative. One day he told me that from time to time they contacted other couples over the Internet and then met for a party at their house or at the other people's house."

Well, well, Sebag said to himself. Maybe this case is going to turn out to be a little more unusual than the others. But Julie immediately came to dash his illusions.

"Véronique had a lover," she whispered discreetly in his

"Is Lieutenant Sebag directing the operations?"

"He's one of the first officers who arrived on the scene and I have complete confidence in him."

"I do too," she replied, not looking at Gilles but keeping her eyes on the thick smoke that was still rising from the house's courtyard.

The fire had now gone out. The firefighters' action had been rapid and energetic: the car on the driveway had not burned. Sebag took his mobile out of his jacket. Sabine Henri stopped him. She addressed the fire chief, who had joined them during the discussion.

"If there were a fire, would there be a major risk that it would spread?"

"If he's poured gasoline on the shared walls, we won't be able to prevent the fire from affecting the adjoining houses. We're ready to act, but with that quantity of inflammable liquid, the fire will burn very fast and give off a large amount of heat. There will be a thick, black cloud of toxic smoke."

Sabine Henri needed only a few seconds to make her decision. She had the security perimeter expanded, to the south as far as the intersection with the Avenue du Général Jean Gilles, to the north as far as the Rue Blondel. She had all the houses within this perimeter evacuated. After transmitting her instructions, she turned to Sebag.

"Go ahead, Lieutenant."

Gilles dialed the number of the house's landline. He thought that for making the first contact, it was less intrusive than calling the mobile directly. The telephone rang a long time before someone picked up. Then there were a few seconds of silence.

"Yes, who is it?"

A deep, thick, aggressive voice. Sebag turned on the speaker.

"Lieutenant Sebag of the Perpignan police. I wanted to be sure that everything is all right, Monsieur Gali."

"Yeah, everything's fine, just peachy."

"And everyone is all right there?"

"If you mean . . . my wife, yes, she's fine. She's fine . . . for the moment. Have you had the neighborhood evacuated?"

"Is that necessary?"

"It might be, yeah!"

"Why?"

"Because I've got what I need to set it on fire, that's why, you boob!"

Sebag remained calm.

"Is that what you want?"

"I have to say that I'd like that a lot, yes."

"Why?"

"Because I feel like it!"

"Is that a good enough reason?"

"For me it is, yeah!"

"What did your neighbors do to you?"

Silence. That lasted ten seconds.

"Nothing. Everything and nothing. They take me for a loser!"

"Do you really think so? I've just been talking with them, especially Norbert and Muriel: they seem to me to have a rather good opinion of you."

"Oh, sure . . . Then they're hypocrites. Like that floozy!"

"Who are you talking about?"

"My wife, you moron! She made a fool of me, she did. She thought she could do anything to me and I'd accept it, but she got that wrong! And that other bastard, too . . . They were all wrong, I'm not a loser. Now they're scared shitless, aren't they? And you're scared too, aren't you, copper?"

Sebag took a deep breath. He had to remain focused.

"You're scared, huh, copper?"

"Yes and no," he finally answered.

"What do you mean, yes and no?"

"The neighborhood has been evacuated. If you set a fire, there will be only property damage. Except for you and Véronique. I'm scared for you, Bastien."

"You're scared for me, copper? You don't even know me! She's the one you're panicking about, not me."

"For both of you, Bastien, for both of you. You don't deserve that, either of you. I'm beginning to get to know you and . . . I believe I understand you."

There were a few seconds of silence. Sebag was afraid he'd annoyed his interlocutor by claiming to know him. That was a mistake. He sensed that Gali had barricaded himself in the house to make everyone, and himself first of all, believe that he was regaining control over a life that had gotten away from him. He had to be allowed to nourish that illusion.

"What do you mean, you understand me?"

Sebag could breathe again. Gali had ignored his tasteless remark and had just taken the cue offered him.

"You know very well what I mean . . ."

"Not really."

Sebag counted to five to give what he was about to say a confidential tone.

"You're not the first person to whom this has happened, and you won't be the last."

"What are you saying, copper?"

Sebag glanced at the supervisor and the chief of staff. He wanted to fool them. So he gave them a look that said "the things we have to do in this line of work!" Then he lowered his voice and almost whispered into the telephone:

"Discovering the terrible secret, the hole in the pit of your stomach, your brain retracting, the world collapsing, and then, suddenly, solitude, the incredible solitude . . . But don't make me say more: I'm surrounded by people."

There was another pause of a few seconds.

"What are you up to, copper, you want to tell me the story of your life? And how would you like to do that? How about coming back tomorrow to have a drink with me at the corner café?"

"I can come see you . . ."

Sebag looked up at the chief of staff and the superintendent before adding:

"Now."

"You want to have a little chat at home, is that it?" "Gali said. "Like in the movies, you'll take off your jacket and walk toward the house with your hands up to show that you're not armed? You want to play Bruce Willis? Do cops get a bonus when they do something heroic?"

"I don't want to do anything heroic. I trust you."

"You trust me? You don't even know me! You want to fool me, that's what you want!"

His voice had risen a notch.

"I want to keep you from doing something stupid, that's all."

"Yeah, sure . . . You want to fool me. Bye-bye, copper!"

Bastien Gali slammed the receiver down.

At headquarters, Ménard was reading the Abad file, over and over. But he was making no progress at all. And it wasn't easy to concentrate with the radio constantly spitting out news about what was happening on Rue Viollet-le-Duc. He angrily turned the thing off and took a bite of his tuna sandwich with tomato and mayonnaise.

He took a break by looking over the week's other cases. He learned about the burglaries at Vernet, and noticed that Sebag had been investigating them since that morning. Then he came across the Valls case. Another case being handled by Gilles. Well . . . for an idler, he was certainly all over the board . . .

Ménard flipped through the file. Yeah . . . Nothing exciting. The suicide of a forty-two-year-old man. A relatively ordinary sentimental tragedy. The husband had just learned that his wife was leaving him for another man.

Really, he said to himself.

He thought about his own wife, Corinne. She had given him three children, she still loved him, he thought, and he loved her too. However, questions had arisen a few times. Who had never had questions? Corinne had also probably wondered . . . Their relationship had gone through a period of tension three years earlier. Maybe she had guessed something . . .

Because he hadn't always been faithful. Oh . . . nothing important, just a misstep, an affair that was over and done.

He'd just told a divorced woman that her son was dead. An argument on the village square had gotten out of hand. A refusal to give somebody a cigarette, voices raised, a few punches thrown, and then a knife taken out of a pocket and planted in a sixteen-year-old heart. The woman—Sylvie, her name was Sylvie—had broken down. He was her only son, she'd raised him alone. François had taken her in his arms to comfort her. The physical contact had been exquisitely pleasurable. He'd felt her firm breasts press against his chest. His heart was beating very fast. In his pants, he'd gotten a hard-on. She'd noticed.

Despite the noise of the evacuation that filled the street, Sebag, Castello, and Henri felt a dense silence seep from the telephone. The superintendent was the first to speak.

"You've handled this well, Gilles. It's to be expected that he would hang up the first time. But you've created a link and aroused his interest. Let him stew a quarter of an hour and then call him back."

"I sensed that he was determined," the chief of staff said with concern. "I'm going to have the GIPN[14] called in. It's

[14] *Groupes d'intervention de la Police Nationale*, elite units of the national police that specialize in cases involving hostage-taking, terrorism, etc. In April 2015, they became local units of RAID (*Recherche assistance, intervention, dissuasion*).

procedure. I want them to be alerted first, and then we'll see. We've got time: they have to get here from Marseille . . ."

"If he really wanted to set the neighborhood on fire, it would already be ablaze," Sebag noted. "His act is a call for help, he doesn't want to go through with it."

"So in your opinion Gali isn't dangerous?" Sabine Henri said with astonishment.

"The problem is that he set a challenge for himself. And if we don't do what we're supposed to, he'll be forced to carry out his threat. It's a question of pride now. Between him and her, between us and him, and especially between him and himself. And on top of that, he's been drinking."

"Ah, men's pride . . . ," the young woman felt obliged to remark philosophically. "How many deaths and massacres in its name! How many acts of madness, too. And you, Lieutenant Sebag, it isn't your pride that makes you want to go into that house?"

"No. I don't like the telephone, that's all!"

Sebag was getting irritated. That was unusual for him, but his nerves were on edge, with all these troubles, all this shit . . . What did she know about life, about psychology and philosophy? So far as he knew, those subjects were not central to the ENA's curriculum.

"Obviously, the telephone is safer," Superintendent Castello broke in. "But in such cases, nothing will ever replace direct contact. I agree with Gilles when he says that this guy has no desire to set a fire. In my opinion, he'll want to do it even less if there's a third person in the house."

"You might be right," Sabine Henri conceded. "But I'm going to reach out to the experts on the task force. They have experience with this kind of situation."

The kind of remark that is always pleasing . . . No, clearly, psychology was not her strong point. Sebag watched the chief of staff move away to make her phone call. When he turned back to the superintendent, he noticed that the latter was looking at him. Sizing him up.

"Are you all right, Gilles? Do you feel up to this?"

Gilles knew that an excessively definitive answer would worry his superior.

"I think so, I hope so. But by the way, aren't you on vacation?"

"Uh . . . Yes, but since I had stayed home, I came when the prefecture contacted me . . ."

"What dedication!"

"Go ahead, make fun of me . . . But you don't look so good, Gilles. Is everything OK?"

"A virus that's hanging on. It's the season."

Then they discussed running. Superintendent Castello had resolved to run a marathon before the end of the year, and he was seeking advice from Gilles. But the return of the chief of staff put an end to their conversation.

"At the GIPN they told me that if we have a competent volunteer we could try it."

"I'm a volunteer," Sebag said.

"And he's competent," the superintendent added.

"So go ahead, call him."

Sebag dialed the landline number again. After it rang a dozen times, Gali picked up.

"That you again, copper?"

"My name is Sebag. Gilles Sebag."

"Whatever you say, copper."

Gali's voice seemed even thicker than before. There lay the real danger: alcohol sweeps away fears and inhibitions.

"You're drinking, are you?"

Gilles was now using the familiar *"tu."* When French men talk about drinking, women, or sports, they say *"tu"* to each other. It's instinctive.

"Vodka. Do you like it?"

"I prefer whiskey."

"I have some of that, too."

"Whoa . . . lucky guy. Outside here we've got nothing but water."

"Tough."

"Yeah."

The conversation was dying. Gilles counted to ten.

"How's Véronique?"

"She's scared."

"That's not surprising."

"Sure . . . especially since she doesn't like her new perfume."

He stopped and waited to be asked for more. Sebag played along.

"What perfume is that?"

"Unleaded 98 from Total."

"You poured it on her."

"Affirmative, old pal! She also doesn't seem to like the wet T-shirt contest."

"I understand why."

"You understand me, you understand her . . . You understand everybody, copper."

"It's one of my defects."

"What about you? Do you understand your wife too?"

Gali had taken the bait, he wanted to share his feelings. Sebag had to set the hook.

"I've been trying to."

"Can you do it?"

To mislead the superintendent and the chief of staff again, Gilles made another gesture that meant: "This guy's beginning to get on my nerves."

"Understand, yes. Accepting is harder."

Castello and Henri held their breath; they were looking at each other in a strange way. He'd been too convincing. But it wasn't in vain.

"Are you thirsty, copper?"

"Pretty thirsty."

"I thought cops didn't drink while they were on duty . . ."

"Precisely. For once I could do it, and I don't want to miss the chance."

Bastien Gali took time to think about it. Or rather he pretended to take it. He wanted to talk, that was obvious.

"OK, Bruce Willis, you can come in. With your jacket off, your hands up, and when you get to the driveway, turn around a couple of times so that I can see that you haven't got a gun. Just like in the movies, I love it . . ."

Sebag glanced at his superiors, who gave him a green light.

"Get a glass out for me, Bastien. I'm coming."

"Just a second, I've changed my mind, pal. What have you got on under your shirt, an undershirt or a T-shirt?"

"Uhh . . . an undershirt."

"A little sensitive to the cold, are you?"

"A little, yeah."

"Then take off your shirt and come in your undershirt . . . Like Bruce in *Die Hard*."

"In the film, he was also barefoot. Can I keep my shoes?"

"You're pretty funny, you know? OK, you can keep your shoes."

And then the desire . . . Violent, fierce, shared. Life's revenge on death. A challenge, a combat, a demand. The young woman had grabbed his cock through the fabric of his pants and pressed it hard. Their lips locked together . . .

Stop! Ménard didn't want to remember any more.

He was embarrassed to have betrayed the mother of his children, the woman with whom he had once decided to make his life. No, he wasn't very proud of himself, and on several occasions he had almost confessed it all to her.

But he'd never said anything. What was the point? So long

as his wife didn't know about it, it didn't hurt her. And so far as he was concerned, this foolish act had had no effect on his love. Sylvie hadn't counted. Why take the risk of breaking up a family because of a moment of folly?

A moment of folly . . . But what a marvelous moment! A smile flickered over his lips every time he thought about it. He'd never seen her again. He hadn't tried. Neither had she.

In the file still lying open on his desk, one word caught his attention: Cantalou-Cémoi. Didier Valls held a position as an accountant for the factory where Stéphane Abad worked in quality control. Initially, it occurred to him that this year the *trêve des confiseurs* had been hard on the chocolate company: an employee had killed his wife, and another had committed suicide . . . They'd have to open up a counseling center for the rest of the staff as soon as the vacation was over!

Then he reflected that the psychologists might do better to look into the conjugal relationships of the company's other employees, because after all, these two tragedies sprang from more or less the same source. Strange coincidence.

Coincidence . . .

Sebag took off his jacket and then his shirt, which he handed to Julie. He didn't have his service weapon; he rarely carried it. He walked toward the little house, went through the gate, and approached the remains of the fire that continued to smolder, still emitting thick, foul-smelling smoke. He put his hands up and turned around the first time. Then he went around the fire. He stepped in the black, dirty water that was slowly running toward the little hedge. At one meter from the door, he stopped again and turned all the way around. He glimpsed the silhouette of someone watching him from behind the curtain on the glass door.

Sebag covered the last meter separating him from the front door and knocked. After obtaining authorization, he opened the door and went in. The door led directly into a small living room.

Bastien Gali was waiting for him, sitting on a couch in mahogany leather. His wife was curled up at the other end of the couch. She gave the policeman a frightened look. Between the man and the woman was a bottle of vodka, two-thirds empty. Gilles spotted no weapon in the area, there was a packet of firecrackers on the coffee table in front of the couch. That must have been what Gali had used to set fire to his wife's things. A first reassuring point.

"Come in and sit down, Gillou," Gali said, pointing to a chair.

Sebag took a few hesitant steps. His wet shoes left dark spots on the ocher-colored tile floor.

"Don't worry about that. The housekeeping these days isn't the best!"

Rainbow puddles stood on the floor of the living room, and an intoxicating smell of gasoline floated in the room. Sebag came forward carefully. On his left, he saw a few strangely colored flames illuminating the hearth of a fireplace. Fortunately, the fireplace was equipped with an insert, and the door seemed to be firmly closed.

"I made a little fire, I didn't want you to be cold."

Sebag sat down on the chair. A bottle of whiskey had been put on a low table in front of it. Tullamore Dew. Not bad . . .

"Serve yourself," Gali suggested, grabbing the bottle of vodka and taking a swig. You'll have to excuse me, I didn't set out a glass for you. I prefer to drink out of the bottle."

"Me too."

Sebag unscrewed the cap of the whiskey bottle. He put the bottle to his lips and took a long drink. He wanted to impress Gali, but what the latter noticed most was the sigh of satisfaction that escaped him despite himself when the liquid spread through his veins.

"So, copper, looks like you were thirsty . . . You wouldn't be on the way to becoming an alcoholic, would you? Go ahead, tell me your problems."

The jerry cans were piled up at the other end of the living room, next to the door that must lead to the kitchen: five standing upright, probably full, and five more lying on their sides, empty. Sebag set the bottle down. Gali had a lighter in his left hand and was caressing the thumbwheel. That was less reassuring.

"After you, Bastien, if you don't mind. In a way, you're the one who began, aren't you?"

From underneath a high forehead two dark eyes were looking at him. Gali had a long, straight face; his hair was going gray at the temples. A little three- or four-day beard surrounded a large mouth with a drooping lower lip.

"You're joking! You lured me with your personal problems, now you've got to cough them up."

Sebag took another swig of the whiskey. In the fireplace, the flames had gone out; the fuel had been just paper. The first words were hard to get out, but the rest came easily. He told the truth, just the truth. He didn't invent anything, he didn't hide anything. The alcohol and the adrenaline gave people a sixth sense. Gali could have spotted the slightest lie and the trust that had been established would have been broken . . .

"What do you think you're going to do?" Bastien asked when Gilles had finished.

"Try to forgive her, try to rebuild. Before that happened, I thought that it would be easy to put up with this sort of thing: we've been living together for twenty years and what Claire might have experienced with this guy has nothing to do with what we've shared over all those years. But that was theory. In practice, things aren't so simple. There's the head, and there's the gut. Our organs don't all agree. Despite everything, I think we can overcome this."

He made sure he had Bastien's eye before he added:

"In any case, I don't think that burning my place down is a solution."

Gali nodded pensively.

"You got children?" he asked.

"A sixteen-year-old son, and a daughter who has just turned fourteen."

"That changes everything, doesn't it?"

"That changes things, absolutely. But not everything."

Gali looked at his lighter and struck a brief light. Even though he was in his undershirt, Sebag felt sweat running down his back.

"We've never been able to have kids. Though we had every possible test. In theory, there's no problem. Doctors are stupid jerks!"

"No doubt."

Gali picked up the vodka bottle and put it to his lips to take another swig. Sebag did the same but only pretended to drink.

"So what about you, what's your story? Your story . . ."

"You already know everything. Unfortunately, it's completely ordinary!"

Véronique, who had raised her head while Sebag was telling them his story, bowed it again. Gasoline was seeping from her clothes, just a T-shirt and panties.

"It's never ordinary when it happens to you . . ." Sebag said. "And whatever people say or think, it's always difficult to take."

"Yeah, but why is it so hard, after all? That's the question I've been asking myself for three months and I haven't found the answer."

Sebag recalled what he'd heard about Bastien and Véronique's sexual habits.

"However, I've been told that you weren't the jealous type . . ."

One of Gali's thick eyebrows shot up.

"You done a bit of swinging, haven't you?"

Bastien's mouth stretched into an ironic smile. His lower lip seemed all the heavier.

"You're a good cop, Gillou. You already know everything, it seems."

"Only a few bits and pieces."

Gali took another drink from the bottle before putting it down alongside him. The level was sinking at an alarming rate.

"I know it might seem strange, but swinging has nothing to do with infidelity. On the contrary . . ."

"How's that?"

"I'm not sure I can explain, but I'm tempted to say that it's the opposite of infidelity. It might seem stupid, I know, but I think that it brings us closer. We talk about it together beforehand, and we talk about it together afterward. Yes, it unites us unto death. We both take pleasure with someone else, but we also take it together through these intermediate persons. Do you see what I mean?"

Sebag nodded. Out of neither politeness nor tactics. He could understand: love without sexual exclusivity was perhaps true love. Yes, he understood. He always understood.

"Swinging brings you closer and infidelity drives you apart, is that it?"

Gali gave him a grateful look:

"Exactly! But this time, she did it behind my back, you see, without me, secretly. She no longer had the intimacy with me but with this other guy. That's . . . that's . . . that's just betrayal, goddammit!"

"Who is this guy?"

"One of her co-workers. He's married too, the bastard. When I found out three months ago, she told me that I was the one she loved, that she'd never considered leaving me, that they'd been discreet and that no one at the place where she works knew about it."

Sebag could hardly resist the desire to take a real drink. Here, too, he not only understood but knew. Why did his professional life and his private life have to telescope to this point?

"At first, I was surprised that I was so jealous. A little like you, I told myself that given the way we live, I didn't have the right. But it was too strong for me, I just couldn't do it."

Gali took a big slug of vodka. A real snootful.

"Listen, I'll tell you how unbearable it is: every time we watch a film together and a woman falls into some guy's arms, she's the one I see with somebody other than me, and fuck, I assure you it's painful. However, that isn't the way it usually works . . . Usually you yourself are the one you imagine in the arms of another chick, generally a really great one. But I can't do it anymore, no way! It's torture and crisis every time. The result is that now I watch only game shows on TV."

"I understand why you're mad. Game shows on TV, they're God-awful!"

Gali laughed jerkily. The way a drunkard does.

"And why are you angry today, Bastien?" Sebag asked. "This business is three months old . . ."

"Yeah. Three months that I've been trying to accept it and can't. And then she started up again."

Véronique sat up and tucked her legs underneath her. The gasoline stuck her black bangs to her shining forehead.

"I didn't start up again," she said softly. "I told you, nothing happened."

She had a singsong voice. He thought he detected a Toulouse accent. Bastien didn't look at his wife; it was to Sebag that he replied:

"It seems they only ate together, but I'd forbidden her that, too. I didn't want them to speak or see each other ever again. Ever. I'd already accepted their running into each other at work every day, but I couldn't do any more . . ."

He turned to her:

"What got into you, you slut?"

His hand was playing with the thumbwheel on the lighter.

"I shouldn't have, I know," Véronique whined. "But it has been so difficult between us for the past three months, I needed to talk to somebody."

"Not to him, goddammit! To anybody but him . . ."

Gali had shouted. His index finger pushed on the lighter's flint and lit another flame. Véronique bowed her head again. Sebag held his breath.

Was it really a coincidence?

Ménard pulled the envelope he'd taken with him out of his jacket pocket. He spread the photos of Christine Abad and her lover on his desk. And if ever . . . "Good God!"

In the Valls file he found the name and address of the widow of the man who committed suicide. He dialed the number of the landline. No answer. Then the number of the mobile. Voice mail. He asked for a rapid callback.

Then he telephoned the Cantalou company. At first he got a not very cooperative personnel director, but by moving from one person to another he finally obtained the information he was looking for. The information that opened the door to all kinds of conjectures.

Sebag had to remind them of his presence. In any way he could.

He tapped his chest but he was in his undershirt, he'd left his pack of cigarettes in his jacket.

"You wouldn't have a cig?"

That was the best he could think of, but maybe it wasn't so bad. Gali mechanically rose. From the drawer of a secretary he took out a pack of cigarillos.

"I haven't got anything else, will that do?"

He handed Sebag the pack of Niñas.

"Perfect. The smoke won't bother you?"

"No, because I smoke them!"

Sebag pretended to dig around in his pants pockets.

"Got a match?"

Gali was about to hand him his lighter when he changed his mind.

"Are you nuts or what? You want to burn everything up?"

Sebag put the pack of cigarillos on the coffee table and looked Bastien straight in the eye:

"No, I just wanted to steal your lighter to keep you from doing something stupid."

Gali stared at him, speechless, then broke into his staccato laugh.

"Fuck, what a moron! And I almost fell for it, too . . ."

He sat down again, relaxed, on his end of the couch. Sebag took advantage of this moment of calm.

"What if we just stopped all this bullshit? We could get out of here and continue the discussion somewhere else."

"In police custody, for example? Now you're the one who's being stupid. You're going to throw me in jail."

"Not necessarily. If no one files a complaint, this can turn out differently for you. The judicial system doesn't pardon violence, but it can understand despair."

Sebag had prepared the way. He mustn't push harder. Not right away.

"And how did you find out that she'd had lunch with him?"

Gali's face hardened. The memory must be painful. Sebag was moving onto dangerous ground.

"I intercepted an SMS. The stupid bitch! She knew I was regularly checking her phone after I found out."

He raised his left buttock and took a mobile phone out of his hip pocket. He put it on the coffee table and then pushed it over to Sebag.

"Alain Guibert, that's his name. Easy to find, he's in her favorites."

Sebag didn't pick up the phone. He didn't want to read the messages, it was more than he could stand.

"We just had lunch together," Véronique repeated. "I swear it."

"I told you not to see him, and you went ahead and did it anyway."

Bastien's tone had softened. There was now more sadness than anger in his voice. Sebag had to take advantage of that.

"She needed help, she was unhappy, she didn't go to the right person . . ."

"That's the least you can say!"

"Is that a reason to blow up everything now? You've been struggling for three months to forgive her, and you want to give up? Your battle's over, is that it? You've lost?"

Gali bowed his head. He suddenly felt tired.

"I can't live with her any longer. I'll never trust her again." He began to sob. His voice trembled. "But I can't live without her."

"And that's why you want to set a fire?"

"I don't know what I want, I can't think anymore! I want all this to stop. One way or another."

Véronique's eyes met Sebag's, and they understood each other without saying a word. It was time. In a smooth movement, she unfolded her legs. Her T-shirt soaked in gasoline stuck to her skin, emphasizing the curve of her full, firm breasts. She put her arm around her husband's shoulders.

"I can't live without you, either. And I don't want to."

She caressed his hair. A tear rolled down her cheek.

"If you think we no longer have a future together, then go ahead, burn everything to the ground. I want to die with you."

She wasn't bluffing, she was sincere. She was ready to go, too. Bastien still had his lighter in his hands and his finger was caressing the thumbwheel. It was double or nothing . . . Sebag braced himself. Say something, he had to say something.

"You could get help, you know. There is such a thing as couples therapy.

Véronique coiled up next to her husband, who didn't budge.

"There's no miracle solution," Sebag went on. "But when you love as much as you two do, you have to try everything."

Véronique put her mouth near her husband's ear and whispered to him:

"I love you, I'll do whatever you want."

At least that's what Sebag thought he heard. He continued:

"Each trial we encounter takes on a particular resonance for all of us," he explained. "Depending on our past, our childhood, our upbringing, our character . . . And everything that we've buried, year after year, deep inside ourselves."

Images flooded into his mind. A face, a figure, a house that wasn't that of his childhood, another woman in familiar arms. He added, in a lower voice:

"Or else personal therapy, why not? We spend our lives chasing phantoms but sometimes we have to confront them straight on."

He smiled inwardly. He no longer recognized himself. And that did him good. And he wasn't ashamed of it. That was not only the effect of the alcohol and the gasoline fumes. It was not only because he was trying to prevent a tragedy.

Then he understood that everyone would walk out of this house alive.

"What are we going to do, Bastien?"

"What do you mean, what are we going to do?"

Sebag pointed to the lighter.

"Are you going to burn us all up or are we going to leave the house upright?"

Gali played with the thumbwheel again. A flame sprang up that he let burn.

"I knew there was a trap. Do you think I won't dare set fire to the place with you inside it?"

"Yes."

"Now we've changed styles: it's no longer Bruce Willis, now it's Mel Gibson, *Lethal Weapon*. You're ready to risk your skin to achieve your goal."

"Not at all. As I told you a while ago, I trust you. You're not a madman but a good guy. And whatever she might have done, your Véronique is a good woman, too. You've still got a ways to go together. As I do with Claire . . ."

Gali pretended to hesitate again and then finally threw the lighter to Sebag.

"Here, Gillou, we're going to smoke that cigarillo outside."

"Love to."

"I'm not sure I can stand up. I think I've drunk too much."

He put his hand on his wife's shoulder.

"You've got to stop drinking," Sebag said. "That's never a solution."

"You're right about that, Gillou. Have you thought about doing it yourself?"

"I pay attention: on days off, for instance, I no longer drink in the morning."

"That's a good start," Gali snorted. "And what's your secret?"

"I set the alarm for noon!"

"*Attention!* They're coming out."

François Ménard had turned the radio back on and was following Sebag's exploits. Listening to the messages and orders, he could guess what was going on in front of no. 35 Rue Viollet-le-Duc. Gilles had left the house with Gali and his wife right behind him. Together, they'd smoked a cigarillo. An ambulance had taken the wife away and then Gilles put the guy in his car. Soon they'd be back at police headquarters.

Gilles Sebag, the hero of the day. Once again.

Ménard shrugged. He had no reason to resent Gilles. He could have, though . . . But he hadn't responded to the radio call. Action wasn't his thing. He wouldn't have had the guts to do what Gilles did.

He collected the notes he'd taken. He'd made progress, he had something. Something even Gilles hadn't seen.

Valls and Abad knew each other well, they even saw each other outside work. Two friends, one a victim and the other a perpetrator of conjugal tragedies that arose from their wives' infidelities. These tragedies occurred at a few days' interval, and at least one of the men had learned everything through an anonymous accusation.

Was that really a coincidence? No, certainly not, that was no longer possible!

Chapter 21

As he drove home, Gilles felt an immense satisfaction. Everyone had congratulated him. His boss, his colleagues, the chief of staff. Molina, who was on vacation, had also called him: he'd made fun of him, which was his very special way of weaving a laurel crown.

Beyond this symphony of praise, he was especially happy to have been useful. His work consisted of punishing crimes; preventing them was rarer but so much more gratifying . . . Today, he had kept a whole neighborhood from burning, saved two lives, and even better, saved a couple. At least he hoped he had . . . Bastien Gali had been put in police custody under medical surveillance in a Perpignan hospital. He was to be examined the next morning by a psychiatrist. He would probably be indicted for making death threats, but with a streamlined procedure. However, Sebag clung to the hope that the case would simply be closed. Especially since Véronique, who had also been hospitalized, did not want to file a complaint. Those two loved each other madly and still had a future as a couple.

He felt strong. Ready to accept everything, to put up with anything. Bastien and Véronique's story might have turned tragic, but in a few weeks or a few months it might have a happy ending. Jealousy didn't necessarily lead to the worst.

When he opened the front door, Claire, Léo, and Séverine gave him a standing ovation. They'd heard about his exploits on the radio and the regional TV news.

"You were even on TV," Léo said, his eyes full of pride. "Just for a second, but we had time to see you as you came out of the house. The undershirt was great. But if you want my advice, you need to stop running and start lifting weights."

Gilles savored this moment. His fifteen minutes of fame shone in his son's eyes. Not every father could boast of having seen such a spark illuminate the usually dull eyes of a pimply, silent adolescent. Although Leo limited himself to a manly slap of the hands with his father, Séverine coiled up against him for a tender caress. For a long time, he ran his hand through the mane of brown hair she'd inherited from her mother.

Then it was Claire's turn. Their bodies melted together and their lips met. Léo and Séverine modestly moved away. They had the charming idea of setting the table while their parents kissed.

"I'm proud to be your wife," Claire told him when she had recovered the use of her tongue.

Dinner was excellent. Filets of sole with rice and mushrooms. Gilles had not had time to eat anything since morning, and he was hungry as a bear. As he ate, he told them about his adventure. He avoided certain details of his conversation with Bastien Gali but could not omit the general theme.

"It's crazy to be that jealous," Séverine commented.

"She did cheat on him, though," Léo replied with the brutal certainty of a sixteen-year-old macho. "That's not cool."

"Yeah, but to want to burn down a whole neighborhood . . . The neighbors weren't to blame!"

"That's true."

The parents exchanged looks as neutral as possible and abstained from any participation in this exchange. After dinner, they cleared the table together. Léo went back to hole up with his computer, while Séverine sat down on the couch.

Claire insisted that the three of them watch a film on TV,

Embrassez qui vous voudrez.[15] A comedy by Michel Blanc, with trenchant dialogue and marvelous acting by a bunch of French movie stars. Gilles sat between his two women. Claire pressed her thigh against his and took his hand.

He didn't much care for the film. All about couples and sentimental mix-ups with the inevitable lies and sexual encounters they entailed. So that was all that was left in the world these days . . . He thought again about what Gali had said to him a few hours earlier, and when he saw women in love he too now saw only Claire, and in the men they were embracing only an unknown silhouette. But the day's satisfaction, and also the alcohol to some extent, made a kind of armor for him. Exhausted by all the excitement, he kept dozing off. He lost the thread of the story. It didn't matter: he'd understood the general meaning.

An obvious point woke him up. He needed sleep. For a long time, he hadn't been sleeping enough, and he was exhausted. Under such conditions it was impossible to struggle against his demons. When he felt strong, as he did tonight, he was able to keep them at a distance. He had to recover his energy. Sleep, and then physical activity. He saw no other way of getting out of this.

[15] "Kiss whomever you want," English title *Summer Things* (2002).

Chapter 22

On Monday, everyone was back at Perpignan police headquarters. Around the coffee machine, the policemen wished each other a happy new year. Most of them were talking about holidays, gifts, feasts, and drinking bouts. However, some preferred to talk about the USAP's next match.[16] Only Agent Ripoll and Lieutenant Llach were talking about police matters, but solely regarding their labor union.

"I could lose a hundred euros a month off my pension if they do away with the 'one-fifth' bonus," André Ripoll moaned.

Joan Llach, the local union representative, tried to reassure him.

"But we're not going to let that happen, trust me. We're going to fight. That is a concession we won in 1957, just think of that—1957! The government can't just take that away from us . . ." The reform of their particular retirement plan was arousing discontent among the police. It was in fact proposed to simply eliminate a bonus based on the number of years in service. The subject didn't much interest Sebag. He had just had his coffee at the Carlit, which had fortunately reopened, and he was finishing his first cigarette of the day. Smoking was prohibited in the cafeteria but the policemen had granted themselves a little dispensation: through the open window,

[16] USAP (*Union sportive arlequins perpignanais*) is a rugby team in Perpignan.

they smoked outside, and when the *tramontane* wasn't blowing too hard, it was bearable for everyone.

Sebag put out his cigarette butt in the ashtray attached to the outside wall under the window, then went back to his office. He was tired. The day before, he'd gone to run on the heights above Saint-Estève. Getting back into running had proven difficult.

Molina had not yet arrived, and Gilles was tempted to allow himself a swallow of whiskey. He always had a bottle within easy reach. That was stupid and dangerous, and probably cowardly to boot, but he couldn't seem to regain control over it. Despite Claire's love and affection. Mornings were especially difficult. He woke early, always with dark thoughts and new questions. They matured during the night and wrenched him out of his sleep. Each morning, he had to reinvent his life. A few stretches, a good liter of black coffee, kisses for his kids, and a kiss for his wife. And a good slug of whiskey when he got to work! Too often, that drink was not the last. The slope was slippery, he knew. There was no lack of examples of that in his line of work. He'd seen too many cops, even good cops, go off the rails this way.

He was aware that this was an unhealthy game. A kind of Russian roulette. But he found alcohol less dangerous than drugs. He reached for the handle of his desk drawer.

"Happy New Year, hero!"

Behind his back, the door flew open and Molina, smiling, came and stood in front of him. As he did once a year, he gave him a big kiss.

"And health above all!"

Gilles felt it necessary to ask for news.

"So, did it go well with your sons?"

Jacques's elder son had turned eighteen a few weeks earlier, and the younger was the same age as Léo.

"Mm . . . yes. What a gift to celebrate Christmas Eve on

New Year's Eve! We were at my parents' house and we'd hardly finished off the *bûche de Noël* before the boys left to party at their friends' house. I ended up sitting there like a dope, tête-à-tête with my folks. Great! At midnight we kissed and I went to bed."

"You went to bed at midnight on New Year's Eve? What about your English girl?"

"She went home for a few days. Didn't I tell you that?"

"Maybe I missed that . . ."

"By the way, you don't look any better than when I left. You didn't like the gasoline fumes?"

"I loved them. I sniff my car's gas tank every morning now."

"Otherwise, what's new here, apart from the drama on Rue Viollet-le-Duc?"

"Well, as people say, nothing but old news, nothing to report. Except for this business in Clos Banet, a pair of burglaries in Vernet, and a conjugal argument over by Saint-Martin that ended with a suicide."

"Marvelous. Happy New Year, good health, right? Was it the guy who offed himself?"

"Yes."

"How?"

"As you said: he offed himself. Jumped off a sixth-story balcony."

"Was he badly hurt?"

Sebag told Molina about the fall onto the car, which absorbed part of the impact, and Valls's death the following night, despite the efforts made to save him.

"What was the argument about? His wife wanted to run off with somebody else, is that it?"

"You're a soothsayer . . ."

"Go ahead, make fun of me. OK, so in short it wasn't a big deal. I hope the crooks are going to wake up a little."

He jerked his head toward the floor above.

"Otherwise, the Old Man is going to want to put us on cases involving marijuana and cigarette smuggling again."

Tobacco was sold at half the price in Spain, and trafficking in cigarettes had greatly increased in recent years. In this department where the unemployment rate was among the highest in the country, a lot of people were engaging in that sort of thing. A few months earlier, the police and customs agents had broken up a Mafia-style smuggling network, but trafficking continued in a more ad hoc way: a few cartons bought by individuals in Perthus and La Jonquera were sold illicitly on the streets of Perpignan or in bars whose customers were not very scrupulous. So far as marijuana was concerned, it was the local cultivation of the plant that took off. Seeds could easily be bought on the other side of the Pyrenees, and private plots were becoming more numerous. These neo-farmers often began with two or three pots on a balcony, for their own use, and then expanded their production and started selling it, thus giving themselves a valuable complement to their wages or compensation. Some of them, it seems, even increased their production during the holidays to help pay for their children's Christmas gifts.

"I admit that I'd prefer a little holdup," Molina added. "Something that wasn't too awful, but that would get us out a bit."

"And preferably between 10 A.M. and 5 P.M. . . ."

"Obviously!"

The small conference room on the third floor was almost full for the traditional Monday morning meeting. The first meeting of the new year. When Gilles and Jacques came into the room, Julie Sadet, François Ménard, Joan Llach, and Thierry Lambert were already there. Lambert, the youngest lieutenant, was tanned from having spent two weeks on vacation in the Antilles. He was sitting at the end of the table, each of his colleagues having taken care to keep their distance. The young cop had developed a phobia that had become a genuine vicious cycle: fearing that he had BO, he was constantly spraying himself with a cheap toilet water that his co-workers found unbearable. Thus it was his perfume rather than his odor that they were trying to avoid. Not knowing the real reason for this ostracism, Lambert doused himself even more often with perfume.

After opening a window, Molina sat down next to Sebag and murmured to him: "When Thierry's around, I think about the locker rooms of my youth. Ah . . . the intoxicating aroma of camphor, the acrid fragrance of manly sweat, the bitter effluvia of dirty underpants and damp socks . . . What a delight!"

The superintendent's face wore the somber expression it had on bad days. His right hand rested on a stack of files. He opened one of them and spread out the sheets of paper in front of him. Then he scratched his nose but didn't chew on his lips. "A category 3 storm on a scale of 5," Sebag thought.

"I've received new instructions from the Ministry of the Interior," Castello began, looking at each of the policemen in turn. "Our stats are not good, we're being strongly urged to improve our performance."

The lieutenants immediately translated the message. For the time being, they were going to have to give up substantive work and long-term investigations in order to make their stats look better. A few quick, easy arrests would do the trick, even if they were hasty and made mainly for the media.

"The local police situation has been pretty calm over the holidays—except for Gilles, perhaps. It's high time to get busy."

"Aha! So things were pretty cool!" Lambert exclaimed in a low voice. "Damn, if I'd known that I wouldn't have left over the holidays."

Unfortunately for him, the superintendent had sharp ears. He gave Lambert a lethal look.

"I would ask you to spare me that kind of reflection. I don't need another Molina around this table."

"Even when I keep quiet, I still get it in the neck!" Molina grumbled.

Castello preferred to ignore this remark and return to the essentials.

"We're going to start by reviewing the ongoing cases with the people who were working last week. Gilles, Julie, who wants to begin?"

Sebag left the floor to his colleague, who talked about the series of burglaries. The perpetrators had stolen nothing but cash, jewels (including fakes), and video equipment.

"We think they're young people, maybe even boys."

"How many have we got?"

"Five burglaries last week and five more the week before."

"So if you find the perps, we'll already have ten cases resolved. Perfect."

Superintendent Castello was the first to be annoyed by this obsession with statistics in the police over the past decade. A fixation that was becoming ridiculous because police work remained one of the kinds of work most difficult to quantify. For example, to produce good figures, it was preferable to arrest somebody who had written twenty bad checks rather than a rapist. As for certain domains, such as drug trafficking, all one had to do to make it seem that the situation was improving was to stop arresting people. Castello pointed to Julie:

"Mademoiselle Sadet, you're going to continue to investigate these burglaries; Molina will help you. You will start from the beginning: canvass the neighborhood, collect testimony. I want a serious lead by this evening."

Julie nodded, Jacques grimaced.

"I also have an urgent request from the city regarding

merchants. It's been a hard year for them, between a couple of spectacular burglaries and a lot of shoplifting. We have to reassure them. Llach and Lambert, today you'll go around to all the retailers downtown. Remind them that over the past months we've made arrangements that allow us to respond quickly to the slightest theft. Just imagine that we caught a little gang responsible for several dozen larcenies . . . Bingo for the stats!"

"Walking the beat is a job for subordinates," Llach objected. "Not for lieutenants."

"When we want to be seen by the public at large, yes. But when it's a matter of reassuring a particular category of the population, officers are better. To show that we are taking these things seriously, I want you out there in civilian clothes. And don't hesitate to imitate Belmondo:[17] leather jacket, sunglasses, weapon prominently displayed, et cetera. That will reassure people!"

Thierry Lambert turned to Molina.

"Damn, I'm going to have to buy some sunglasses. I left mine on the plane."

"You've got ski goggles!"

"Are you kidding?"

"No, they'd be great! You could also put on your boots, your down jacket, and especially your mittens. A revolver with mittens, that will really reassure our shopkeepers!"

Castello scratched his nose and pursed his lips. "Category 4," Gilles said to himself, scowling at his partner to encourage him to let up.

"Fine, Molina, I'll change the teams. You'll be more reassuring than Lambert. You're going to be the one out making the tour of the merchants with Joan. I want both of you on the street in ten minutes. Get going!"

[17] Jean-Paul Belmondo, a well-known French actor who often played a tough cop.

The inspectors rose in a great clamor of chairs and recriminations. Only Ménard remained seated. Although his name had not been mentioned, Sebag was starting to follow the others when the superintendent stopped him.

"Stay here, Gilles, I'd like to talk about a case with you."

Sebag sat down again. The three men formed an equilateral triangle around the table. Castello took a file out of his pile. "Abad-Valls case" was written on it in red felt pen. Gilles recognized Ménard's writing.

"This morning François drew my attention to an investigation that you conducted together. You'd already brought certain oddities to light. He found some more. Go ahead, François."

After clearing his throat, Ménard began his account. Sebag listened to his colleague attentively, not taking his eyes off him. The little bastard had acted on his own, and that wasn't right: if he'd acted like a good comrade, he would have spoken to him about his discoveries before going to the boss. However, Sebag tried not to let his eyes show anger or disappointment, only indifference. In his state of mind, that wasn't very hard. Ménard looked only at the superintendent as he talked.

When he had finished, Castello turned to Sebag:

"What do you think?"

"It's disturbing, in fact," Gilles admitted.

"Isn't it . . ."

Castello found it difficult to conceal his pique. His favorite had failed. Part of his annoyance today might have proceeded from this disappointment. *Well done*, Sebag said to himself. He thought his boss counted on him too much.

"It's only a short step to infer that the informant tried to take revenge on the two employees by telling them their wives' dirty little secrets," Castello went on. "I'd like you to follow this lead with François."

Apart from the fact that he had little desire to work with

Ménard after this low blow, Sebag was not very eager to plunge back into these conjugal dramas. He'd had enough of them. He gave, without knowing it, the same arguments that Ménard had used with Maxime Abad the day before, regarding the risks the mysterious informer was taking—or rather was not taking.

"All the same, he caused two tragedies," Castello argued. "And we don't know what his motives are or how many targets he has in mind. Who knows if he has other accusations to make?"

"Hmm . . . yes. I thought that we had enough work and that we needed to improve our stats. Do you really think it's necessary to put two inspectors on this lead—which is interesting, to be sure, but uncertain?"

"That's for me to decide!" the superintendent shot back. "I'm trying, as best I can, to reconcile two irreconcilable things: presenting good figures to my superiors while at the same time maintaining a humane, effective, and vigilant police force. François, have you already thought about the leads to be followed?"

"Sandrine Valls called me this weekend. She wasn't at home, but with her . . . friend. She's expecting us today for a search of the apartment to look for any possible photos. I gave her no details, I remained vague and I didn't mention Abad, thinking that wasn't useful."

Ménard glanced at Sebag out of the corner of his eye, as if he were seeking his approval. Only Castello nodded.

"Then we'll have to go to the Cantalou factory to question the victims' co-workers. The victims, that is, of the *corbeau*,[18] we might say, since Stéphane Abad is not exactly a victim . . ."

"What about him, do you plan to question him again?"

[18] In French, *corbeau* means "raven," but it is also used to refer to a snitch or malicious informer. This figurative meaning later plays a role in the story.

"I don't think that would be very helpful. After having lied, he decided not to answer our questions any longer. I'm afraid he hasn't changed his mind."

Ménard glanced again at Gilles, who remained stolid.

"And finally we still have to examine the telephones. We have Christine Abad's phone in our possession, and soon we'll have Didier Valls's phone as well. Stéphane threw his in the Têt, but I plan to subpoena his phone records. We won't be able to recover the content of the messages, but we can get a list of his calls. On the back of a photo the informer wrote: 'You know how to reach me.' We can thus legitimately suppose that they had already called each other."

"If the guy isn't an idiot, he'll have used a burner phone," Castello objected.

"That's possible. But we can still geolocate his calls."

Castello closed the Abad-Valls file and picked up the other papers.

"Fine, I'll leave it to you. We may be wasting our time on this case, but that's a luxury I still want to allow us from time to time."

In the car, Sebag carefully reread Stéphane Abad's deposition, because he already remembered it only in part. His brain wasn't retaining much right now. After he finished, he called Elsa Moulin. The head of the forensic police had just returned from vacation.

"Do you remember the telephone I gave you ten days ago?"

"Of course."

"It has just become one of your post-vacation priorities. And I'm going to have another one for you."

"Yes, sir, Boss. I'll deliver all their secrets to you by, say . . . end of day tomorrow?"

"Perfect."

A man opened the door of the Vallses' apartment. Although he was fat, he held himself as straightly and proudly as a retired colonel in the gendarmerie. He introduced himself:

"Francis Hubert . . . a friend."

With his mocking eyes and his chubby cheeks that compressed his small mouth, this "friend" looked like a satisfied piglet. Without understanding why, Sebag took an immediate dislike to him. However, Francis, for his part, had been able to be patient and well-behaved with his "mistress," limiting himself for long weeks to the latter's sweet words and tender kisses.

"Come in, inspectors," Sandrine called from behind her friend Francis. "I'm sorry, I didn't find anything. In any case, not yet."

She had been looking for only an hour, she explained. When she got out of the hospital, she had moved in with Francis and had come only twice to this apartment, which, moreover, she planned to sell soon, along with all the furniture of her past. Sebag noticed that she had nonetheless found time to carefully straighten up the living room that her husband had ravaged before jumping to his death. Accompanied by Ménard, Sebag followed her to the office that she and Didier had set up in a room next to their bedroom. They shared the computer.

"We'll have to take that with us," Ménard informed her.

"Go ahead, go ahead, it was mainly Didier who used it. I, you know, computers . . ."

A file cabinet sat next to the desk with its drawers open. Sandrine had taken out the files. She had examined all of them.

"I didn't find any photo or document suggesting that Didier had been informed of my . . . connection with Francis."

Sebag understood that if a woman as orderly as she was had found nothing in this office, that was because there was nothing to find.

"Do you have a recycling bin for paper and cardboard?"

"That's a good idea, I hadn't thought of that."

She led them to the kitchen and opened the cupboard under the sink. Two blue bins stood there side by side. She pointed to the one on the right. It was full. Sebag emptied the contents on the floor and then examined each paper, which he then put in the trash bin. He found nothing but advertising flyers, packaging, and an old issue of *La Semaine du Roussillon*.

Sebag stood up and rejoined Sandrine, who was inspecting with Ménard the last room—a guest room—in the apartment.

"So you confirm that at the time of the argument with your husband, he told you he knew everything?" Gilles asked. "'Everything' was the exact term he used?"

"Yes. He even repeated it several times."

"And he didn't explain what he meant by 'everything?'"

"No, and I didn't ask. I thought he was just saying that to get me to tell him the truth. Especially since nothing had happened with Francis . . ."

This inappropriate, even suspicious insistence annoyed him. Sandrine had loved another man whom she met and kissed as soon as her husband turned his back. Could she say that nothing had happened on the pretext that they hadn't slept together? Was adultery only a matter of sex? He thought again about his own situation and how much the tenderness that emerged from Claire's conversations with her lover had hurt him.

"And you don't know how Didier might have been informed of your . . . friendship?"

Ménard had taken over the questioning.

"No. As I told you, I thought he was bluffing and that he didn't know anything."

"Your husband knew Stéphane Abad, I believe?"

Sandrine's face darkened.

"Yes. They played pool together once or twice a week. I learned what he did, it's awful! My God, poor Christine!"

"Did you know her?"

"Not really. We ran into each other from time to time, but our husbands preferred to meet without us. And then we didn't become close friends, the two of us. All the same . . . Poor Christine."

She ran her hand over her lips. Her chin was trembling. "She probably imagines that she might have met with the same fate," Sebag mused before correcting himself, sarcastically: "Oh, right, *she* didn't do anything!"

"Could you give us your husband's mobile phone?" Ménard asked.

He hadn't asked any other questions about Abad. That was a good thing. Shortly, at the Cantalou factory, it would be time to be more precise. Sandrine handed over the mobile. It was off; the battery was probably dead.

"It's almost new and I was going to give it to my grand-nephew, but perhaps that can wait."

The lieutenants exchanged a glance but said nothing. There was no point in telling her now that the phone would be impounded and that she would probably never get it back.

"You're not saying anything, aren't you convinced by this business?"

His colleague's silence irritated François Ménard. He had the impression that Gilles was mad at him about what he'd done, and that bothered his conscience.

"I'm waiting to find out more. For the moment, we have only hypotheses."

Ménard's hands gripped the wheel tighter. He thought again about the many occasions on which the whole team had been mobilized to follow Gilles's wild imaginings.

"They don't explain Abad's lies," Sebag went on. "And then there's something in your reasoning that bothers me a little . . . I didn't mention it in front of the boss a little while ago so as not to put you in a difficult position, that's not my way . . ."

Ménard had his confirmation: this little jab was significant, Gilles was mad at him.

"I'm listening . . ."

"Accusations of adultery are usually made to hurt the lovers, not the husbands."

Sebag was really taking him for an imbecile . . . He, too, had thought that at first. And then he'd found the response, the argument.

"The first person to suffer from an infidelity is the spouse, isn't it? That is even truer these days, moreover. Since 1975 adultery is no longer a crime. But if there are no longer any guilty parties, there are still victims."

He was proud of his formula, and shot a sideways glance at his colleague, who was sitting in the passenger seat with his eyes fixed on the road in front of him; he made no reply. No doubt his formula was a good one, Ménard thought, it had struck home.

"Today, Valls is dead and Abad is in prison. If the *corbeau* had it in for them, the result may have gone far beyond his hopes."

Since Sebag still said nothing, Ménard asked:

"Don't you agree with me?"

"Yes, yes . . ."

He saw his colleague settle deeper into his seat and frown. He wouldn't have expected him to be such a bad sport. It's true that he wasn't used to being put in his place like that.

Satisfied with himself, Ménard left the north arterial, taking the airport/hospital exit. Founded in Pyrénées-Orientales in the nineteenth century, the Cantalou-Cémoi company now had thirteen factories throughout the world, but its headquarters remained in Perpignan. The firm had recently left its historic but shabby buildings on the road to Thuir and moved into a new, cocoa-colored factory near the airport. A young personnel director received them and escorted them throughout their visit.

After two hours, they had drawn up a complex profile of Stéphane Abad. A very skilled professional, very effective and competent, but demanding in a way that did not make everyone happy. Thanks to the entry badge that each employee held, they had been able to discover that Abad had come to work as usual at 9 A.M. and abruptly left again a few minutes later, explaining that his wife had fainted and that he had to go home immediately.

Didier Valls's personality seemed to have been considerably paler. With the exception of a secretary who gave a favorable description of the accountant, nobody had much to say about him. "Likeable," and "discreet" were the words they most often used.

Ménard thought he perceived hesitations when he asked some of the employees whether anyone in the company might hold a grudge against the two men. Hesitations and fleeting glances in the direction of the personnel director. Each time, François turned to Gilles, who never reacted. Not the slightest click of the tongue.

He finally realized that the most famous lie detector in the department had put himself in sleep mode. Gilles had stopped asking questions and was not even listening to the answers. He seemed to be elsewhere. Obviously, when he wasn't the one who found the lead interesting . . .

Before leaving Ménard decided to make a frontal attack on the personnel director. He didn't usually do that kind of thing, but he had seen that Sebag sometimes got good results with that tactic.

"Why doesn't anyone want to tell me who had recently quarreled with Abad and Valls?"

"I beg your pardon?"

"You know what I mean."

Sebag opened his eyes wide and then stared at Ménard and the personnel director.

"No, I don't have the slightest idea," the latter protested. "Didier Valls committed suicide and Stéphane Abad killed his wife, I don't see why you're trying to stir up trouble here with your completely irrelevant questions."

"They are relevant."

"I really don't see how."

"I am not obliged to tell you, but you are obliged to answer my question. Otherwise I'll come back tomorrow with my colleagues to question your three hundred employees one by one and go through your files. Then we'll be likely to stir up trouble for sure!"

The young personnel director's determination was beginning to weaken. He readjusted his tie.

"Without revealing any secrets," Ménard bluffed, "I can tell you that we fear a third tragedy in your firm. So if you have anything to say to us, say it right now."

Ménard couldn't help glancing with satisfaction at Sebag. Turning back to the personnel director, he added:

"Please tell us, I'm sure it will be very interesting."

Chapter 23

He had to admit that there had been some failures. Everything hadn't gone exactly as it was supposed to. He had sometimes lacked psychology.

It didn't matter much.

The victims were to blame for their misfortune. He couldn't help that. He'd only exposed their weaknesses. Collateral damage, as military men call it.

Nonetheless, he had to redouble his prudence. The main risk, as he knew, was haste. About that he had no doubts. Patience had been the key to his successes up to this point. Patience, along with perseverance, memory, and intuition.

And hate.

His mission had occupied his mind. He was obliged to stay focused, using all the resources of his brain to incorporate the data, to compile them, to eliminate false paths. To compare. And he had to do all that while remaining discreet and invisible.

The Eye had helped him a great deal. Without it, nothing would have been possible.

He swallowed a mouthful of hot coffee. It was his third cup. He needed at least that much to be able to see things clearly. He felt more tired since he'd begun sleeping better. Curious . . . his nerves were probably relaxing . . .

He was methodically carrying out his work, and that way he would not be stopped. The Eye was invisible, and must remain invisible right to the end. What end? He perceived that he'd ear. "Bastien figured it out a couple of weeks ago and ever since things have been pretty bad between them."

"OK," Gilles sighed before turning back to the neighbor to ask him for Bastien's phone numbers.

Camard took his mobile out of his hip pocket, carefully pressed his big index finger on the screen, and gave Gilles the numbers for Bastien's landline and his mobile. Sebag felt a hand on his shoulder.

"We've got a visitor," his colleague told him.

Sebag saw Superintendent Castello crossing the security perimeter accompanied by a young brunette with a severe face. Sabine Henri, the prefect's young chief of staff, shook his hand vigorously.

"Where are we with this?" she asked.

Sebag described the situation in a few sentences.

"So he's potentially dangerous," she summed up.

Her questions rang out, cold and direct. The preceding autumn Sebag had dealt with this young woman who had just graduated from the ENA.[13] He had found her competent and had quickly understood that her distance and austerity were just a pose to establish her authority in a man's world, because she was a woman and only twenty-seven years old.

"A few witnesses heard something like explosions: he may be armed."

"What kind of weapon?"

"No idea. Nobody has seen anything. Just heard . . ."

"Have you established contact with the madman?"

That was the first time that word had been used. It resounded like a verdict. Quick but right.

"I was just going to do that when you got here."

Sabine Henri turned to the superintendent:

[13] *École nationale d'administration*, an elite French graduate school that trains many of France's senior officials.

never asked himself that question. He had a mission to accomplish, a vengeance to take . . . But when would it stop?

When he decided it would, when he felt like it.

Not now. No, not yet.

That was the right answer, the only possible answer.

Taking his revenge had finally calmed him after months of internal tempest. He was not going to stop when things were going so well.

The cops were making progress. They might have found a lead. He himself was surprised that he wasn't scared.

He finished his coffee and threw the paper cup in the trash bin. Another workday was beginning. It might bring him something new, a new hope. In a little while he would pick up his camera and his new mobile phone and set out in search of a new exploit.

That was all he lived for now.

Chapter 24

An area salvaged from former swamps, Salanca is an unusual part of Roussillon. As flat as a tortilla, its orchards, vineyards, and artichoke fields stretch as far as its long beaches of golden sand. Sitting in the passenger seat, Sebag was watching the landscape pass by. Ménard soon left the D83 highway and headed for Saint-Laurent.

They easily found the place they were looking for, a small village house on a one-way lane. On the ground floor was a former shop that had been transformed into a garage. On the faded sign one could still make out the words *Boulangerie Coll.*[19] On the upper floor, the shutters were closed.

Ménard rang the doorbell. Several times. No response.

He dialed the telephone numbers the personnel director had given them. The policemen hadn't called in advance, wanting to have the advantage of surprise. Reaching the mobile's voice mail, Ménard immediately hung up. When he dialed the landline number, they could hear the phone ringing behind the shutters upstairs.

"Nobody. What shall we do?"

"What do you suggest?" Ménard replied evasively.

"We could question the neighbors to find out if our guy left for a long time, but they might snitch on us and warn him."

"We don't have to tell them that we're cops."

[19] Coll Bakery.

Sebag looked at his colleague's long gray raincoat. He himself was wearing a leather jacket and jeans.

"No, we don't . . ."

Ménard had seen where Gilles was looking.

"Well, yeah . . . There's no hurry. We'll come back tomorrow."

Sebag opened the door on the mailbox. There was hardly any mail. Dominique Barrache had not been gone very long.

Not without reluctance and a careful choice of words, the young personnel director had finally put them on the trail of a former guard at the company who had been fired six months earlier for serious misconduct. Stéphane Abad had repeatedly faulted him for his behavior during his nighttime vigils. Barrache spent more time looking at his computer screen than at the surveillance cameras. And he didn't always make his appointed rounds.

"Shall we go back?" Sebag asked hopefully.

"I was thinking that we still have time to go by Pollestres to question Abad's neighbors."

"Go by Pollestres? That's on the other side of Perpignan!"

Sebag looked at his watch. It was almost 5 P.M. The first traffic jams must already be clogging the boulevards and the road along the river. It would take forever to cross the city.

"Whatever you want . . ."

The slowdowns began on the Arago Bridge. It was always difficult to cross the Têt. Sebag had time to enjoy the view of le Canigou.[20] He came this way every morning, but had hardly paid attention to the landscape these last few days. The mountain had put on its white winter mantel and its snowy summits stood out magnificently against the sky reddened by the setting sun. Sebag closed his eyes. It was a beautiful place, this part of France where they had decided to settle seven years earlier.

[20] A peak in the Pyrenees (altitude 9,137 feet) visible from Perpignan.

Obviously, had they remained in Chartres, there would never have been a Simon, but you can‘t rewrite history. And in any case there would have been a Pascal, a Philippe, or a Didier. It wasn’t the opportunity that elicited the desire, but the desire that found the opportunity. The chicken and the egg. An eternal debate.

Abad’s neighbors had not all come home from work. There was no answer at the house on the right, and none at the one on the left, either. However, the old lady who lived just across the street received them on her doorstep.

“It’s a real tragedy, this affair. I’m still all upset about it. Such nice people . . . Who could have imagined this? Christine was adorable, she invited me to tea now and then in the afternoon. I knew him less well, but he was helpful. Several times he came over to make some little repairs for me. The last time must have been about a month ago, he unplugged the kitchen sink. And when I think about little Maxime, what a misfortune! I knew him when he was just a little boy. At the funeral he looked so sad, completely lost. How can anybody recover from something like that? *Pobret!* Now he’s all alone in life.”

She shook her head, putting two white, permanent-waved locks in movement on her wrinkled forehead.

“Maxime came by two or three times for just a moment. I invited him in for tea, but he refused. I hope he’s being well taken care of and that he has friends in Toulouse . . .”

“We hope so, too.”

Ménard had let the old woman express her sadness; now he could move on to serious matters. First he questioned her regarding the personalities and habits of her neighbors, but obtained only the conventional, already known answers. On the other hand, when he mentioned the morning of the tragedy, he got a surprise:

“I didn’t see Christine that day, but I did see Stéphane. Maybe even several times . . .”

Sebag and Ménard frowned at the same time.

"What do you mean, 'maybe even several times?'"

"I saw him—definitely—come home at ten minutes after noon."

The two policemen looked at each other. This contradicted Abad's statements: the murderer had said that between the time he left work and the time he arrived at the hotel he had gone to the Toreilles beach.

"Are you sure about the day and the time?"

The old woman adjusted the pink shawl draped over her shoulders.

"How could I forget a day like that one . . . As for the time, I haven't yet lost my mind, Monsieur. Every morning I go to see my friend Louise, Louise André, who lives two blocks away. We watch a television program together, it's a game show we both like. It's better to watch together than separately, isn't it?"

Ménard nodded approvingly.

"After our game show, Louise watches the regional news. But since I have already seen the news the evening before and they always repeat the same reports, I prefer a different program, so I go home to watch it. And it was as I arrived that I saw Stéphane parking his car in the driveway. Christine's car was no longer there."

"You didn't speak with him?"

"No. Besides, I don't think he saw me, I was still at the end of the street when he got there."

"Did he stay long?"

"I don't know. All I can say is that when my program was over, around a quarter to one, his car was still there."

"Are you sure of that?"

The old lady pursed her lips. She had used a lipstick in a shade similar to that of her shawl.

"Yes, Inspector. I was surprised. Stéphane never came home at noon, he worked a lot and returned only late in the evening.

He didn't take many vacations, either. Poor Christine was often left alone. Especially since Maxime left for Toulouse . . ."

She suddenly interrupted herself.

"What was I saying? Ah, yes! Since Stéphane never came home at noon, I was amazed to see him on that day. And when that evening I learned about the tragedy from my neighbors, I saw the connection."

"What connection?"

"Well, he came to get his rifle, obviously!"

Sebag stared at the old lady. She thought she was Miss Marple! But what she said wasn't necessarily stupid.

"You knew he had a rifle?" Ménard asked.

"Yes, of course. He belonged to a shooting club—it's over by Boulou, I think—and he went there every Saturday morning. Christine was left alone again . . ."

Ménard let her go on about the Abads' life before returning to the strange expression she'd used a few minutes earlier.

"A little while ago you said that you'd seen Stéphane 'maybe even several times.' What did you mean by that?"

"Wouldn't you like some tea? It's cold outside."

François sensed a trap. If they wanted to get short, precise answers, they'd be better off remaining on the doorstep. Sitting in a warm room, they would have a hard time avoiding useless digressions. He declined the offer. And after all, it was a little late to drink tea. Madame Vidal finally answered:

"I had the impression that he'd been sitting there for a long time. And even that he'd been waiting for Christine to leave."

"Why is that?"

"When I went out around 11 A.M. to go to Louise's house, I thought I saw his car parked nearby. That struck me as odd because the car started and backed up while I was approaching it. I couldn't tell whether it was really Stéphane inside it. At the time, I thought I'd made a mistake and paid no more attention, but later on I said to myself that it must have been him."

She stroked her silvery locks with a wrinkled hand.

"But about that—I prefer to tell you, Inspector—I'm not entirely sure."

"But you think it was he and that he was waiting for Christine to leave?"

"Yes. As I told you: so he could pick up his rifle. Are you sure you wouldn't like some tea?"

"We wouldn't want to impose."

"You wouldn't be imposing, you know."

The old lady was already opening her door and standing aside to allow them to enter. Sebag sensed that his colleague was going to give in, out of politeness or Christian charity.

"We would have loved to have some tea with you, but we don't have much time, Madame Vidal. Thank you very much for your valuable information. We'll probably come back to see you regarding other questions."

They hurried back to their vehicle. Before getting in, Ménard put his hand on the roof of the car and asked Sebag:

"Interesting, no?"

"If her testimony is credible . . ."

"She seemed to me in possession of all her faculties."

"You think so? Inviting two cops to drink tea at the cocktail hour, does that strike you as mentally sound?"

He got into the car. Ménard did the same and put the key in the ignition.

"You sound exactly like Jacques Molina. Do you miss him that much?"

Surprised by what seemed to be an attack of jealousy, Gilles did not reply. Ménard started the car.

"I think we've just succeeded in determining an important part of Abad's timeline on the morning of the murder. He did not learn of his wife's cheating by SMS, as he claimed, and he didn't have his rifle when he left work. Instead, he went to Cantalou just as he did every morning. There, he received the *corbeau*'s letter and the photos, and freaked out. He went back to Pollestres and waited until his wife left. Then he took his rifle and went to wait in front of the Gecko. Regarding the exact time of his arrival in front of the hotel and his convoluted explanations of it, I admit that . . . I'm stumped."

"The city's security cameras filmed him at 1:33. We have no reason to think that he showed up earlier. On the back of one of the photos, the *corbeau* wrote: "you know how to reach me." We can suppose that Abad called him, and that was how he learned what time the lovers usually left the hotel. Thus he didn't need to hang around there for hours."

"But why did he lie to us about that?"

Sebag took time to think. He had a vague sense that there was something important there. He didn't answer until they were about to arrive at headquarters.

"Abad did everything he could to conceal the *corbeau*'s existence from us. Showing us that he knew too much about the lovers' schedule would have been too likely to tip us off."

"He didn't hide the photos very cleverly."

"Because he didn't hide them. He was angry, he had them with him when he got his rifle, and he simply forgot about them."

Ménard shook his head.

"Hmm, hmm . . . Those are just suppositions."

"Sorry, I don't have anything else on hand."

"But why did he want to hide the *corbeau*'s existence from us? Especially if his enemy was the guard . . ."

Sebag gave him a sly smile.

"For the moment, the guard's guilt is only a supposition."

CHAPTER 25

Gilles Sebag poured himself a shot of whiskey in a plastic cup. Sitting at his desk, he had momentarily set aside the hypothesis worked out in the car and tried to resolve the problem of probability in order to figure out whether the lead Ménard was following really held water. The terms of the problem were the following: given that the department of Pyrénées-Orientales has—according to a very recent census—452,530 inhabitants, that Cantalou-Cémoi employs three hundred people, and that one third of all women admit having cheated on their husbands, what are the chances that the conjugal problems of two of the Catalan chocolate-maker's employees come to a dramatic end in a period of less than ten days? No matter how much he turned the problem over and over in his head, he could not come to any conclusion. First of all because he'd never been very good at math, and secondly because Sandrine Valls threw the data off by claiming that she had not cheated on her husband!

The only quantitative result he could arrive at was "not much!"

Sebag didn't like chance. Experience had taught him that in police work, aleatory facts could sometimes disrupt the best arguments. But if they were included in one's reflection from the outset, it became impossible to forge serious and credible hypotheses. He had therefore decided that until he had proof to the contrary, chance played no role in the proximity of the two tragedies.

So what did?

A single answer had germinated that was capable of contradicting Ménard's theory: that the tragedy Abad had caused deepened Valls's despair and made it easier for him to act. A slender, uncertain supposition that would suffice for this evening.

He finished his glass and decided it was time to go home.

As it did every evening, his anxiety mounted very fast. He regretted not having drunk a full glass. As he approached his house, the malaise in his gut grew. His pain never disappeared, it just became less acute when his professional concerns took over. Or when he was restoring to sanity a madman holed up in his house. But it remained there despite everything, crouching inside him, like a headache that never goes way.

He recited out loud a line from Baudelaire he'd learned in middle school: *"Sois sage, ô ma Douleur, et tiens-toi plus tranquille."*[21]

He'd always seen his home as a haven of peace in a world gone mad. But the patiently constructed dikes had burst and his little moorage had to struggle against the assault of furious waves . . .

However, he spent a pleasant evening. Claire, Séverine and Léo had gone back to school and had lots of things to talk about. Gilles remained in the background, contemplating his little world.

He'd lived happily with Claire for twenty years. At first it was just the two of them, and then they were four. She had given him magnificent children and he had discovered a passion for his role as a father. He had played it well, he thought. He'd taken a pleasure in it that was as intense as it was unexpected. Léo and Séverine seemed to be flourishing and at ease with themselves. He'd never had major conflicts with them. What more could he ask for?

[21] "Be calm, my Pain, and lie more quietly."

Deep down, he'd always known that there would be a price to pay for this happiness. Life had just presented its bill. He was going to pay it and then happiness would return.

But a typhoon cannot be calmed with simple words and fine resolutions: you can't stop a good shit by reciting Coué's method of autosuggestion while sitting on the toilet. Nature always brings us to heel.

As they were getting undressed for bed, Claire suddenly pressed her warm body against his. Then she pushed him onto the bed and kissed his skin all over before concentrating her attention on one precise part of his anatomy that she caressed, licked, sucked. Overcome by this passionate desire, Gilles experienced a rapid and intense pleasure. He climaxed with happiness.

The moment should have remained fabulous, but this rush of pleasure had devastating secondary effects. Gilles was assailed by brutal, atrocious, rending images. It was still Claire's body, her mouth, her tongue, but it was no longer his body. Direct, raw questions arose in addition to the images. How many times had she done the same thing with him, with the Other, the asshole, the sleazebag?

He abruptly got out of bed.

Claire put on her silk peignoir and joined Gilles in the living room. At first she didn't see his form slumped on the couch. She sat down beside him. It was a bright night, the moon was almost full. Gilles's profile stood out like a silhouette against the picture window. She couldn't see his features, but she could sense that his jaw was tight. She tried to take his hand, but he refused.

"Would you prefer to be alone?"

"I'm not alone."

He raised his arm on the other side and indicated a whiskey bottle. He took a swig from it.

Claire bit her lip until it bled. She got up and, dragging her feet, returned to the bedroom alone. In the doorway, she turned around.

"I made a mistake but I'm not responsible for everything."

"I know."

She would have liked to leave the door half-open. As a sign, a proffered hand. You're suffering, you're not sleeping, neither am I, I'm waiting for you. But she didn't want to hear again that night the clink of the bottle on the glass coffee table.

She closed the door, buried herself in the sheets, and let herself be overwhelmed by sorrow.

Chapter 26

When Sebag arrived at the office the next morning, Molina was sitting straight up on his chair, his eyes riveted to his computer screen, his hand clicking the mouse nervously.

"Are you winning?" Gilles asked.

"Almost . . ."

"The operation 'reassured merchants' is making progress, it seems . . ."

"Rapidly!"

Sebag knew from experience that he mustn't disturb Jacques when he was fully engaged in something like Bubble Shooter, Jewels, or Last Chaos. He sat down in his chair and turned on his computer.

His hand caressed the handle of his desk drawer. He'd thought he would be the first to arrive and that he'd be able to get himself going with a quick swallow of whiskey. A little one, just one. He looked at Jacques, so absorbed in his game. That might do it. He bent down, got a paper cup out of the waste-basket, and opened his drawer. Holding his hands under the desk, he poured himself a drop that he quickly tossed down. Damn, it was good. He felt the warmth flowing through his veins.

Molina had a final spasm before being defeated. Then he furiously pushed the mouse away.

"I've learned what Ménard did. Not cool! When you make progress on a case, you talk about it with your colleagues before going to the big boss . . ."

Sebag shrugged.

"We haven't always been straight with him. You didn't call him when Abad turned himself in."

"It was Christmas Day, he wasn't working!"

"Neither was I, but you still let me know."

"OK, agreed! He screws you royally and you ask his forgiveness. Go right ahead." Uh-oh . . . Jacques had to be dealt with carefully. Prudence . . .

"And when I refer to progress, I'm being nice. Do you believe his theory of vengeance? It's a little shaky, isn't it?"

"I've occasionally suggested riskier hypotheses."

"That's true. But it was you! I have confidence in you!"

"Thanks . . . But I wonder if it's confidence, faith, or blindness."

"A little of all that, for sure."

For the first time, Jacques smiled.

"By the way, I thought of something . . ."

"Tell me."

"You know that I'm a very basic guy, and so I started out from the premise that if revenge is involved, it was aimed primarily at the lover . . ."

"If we start from that premise, there is no longer any connection between Abad and Valls."

"That connection is Ménard's idea, not mine, or yours. And I reconsidered the interrogation of Balland. Do you remember that you were skeptical when he said he'd never cheated on his wife before Christine?"

Sebag absolutely did not remember that.

"Yeah, vaguely . . ."

"If this guy had had other mistresses, we can imagine another husband taking revenge on him. A guy who didn't have the balls to punch him in the face and chose a different method."

Sebag thought the idea pertinent. Unfortunately. He would

have greatly preferred to work on a different kind of case . . . . The burglaries in Bas-Vernet, the merchants, tobacco smuggling, drunk driving, speeding. Anything but these endless cases involving adultery . . .

"I called Balland a little while ago. He's waiting for us where he works."

"Now?"

"Whenever we want."

Sebag rubbed his eyes. He would have liked another glass of whiskey. But Jacques was already on his feet and was playing with his keys.

"You driving or am I?"

Gilles gave his partner a severe look. An idea occurred to him. He too could take a little revenge.

"It's nice this morning, let's go on foot."

"On what?"

"On foot, you know, walking."

"That's what I thought you said."

"Feet are those things you put in your shoes every morning, you know. And what are shoes made for? For walking!"

"I thought they were used only to press on the accelerator."

"They can also be useful for giving a kick in the ass to a colleague who's a little too lazy."

"Stop, I'm scared . . . All right, we'll go on foot: I like new experiences."

The Archipelago, where Christine Abad's lover worked as a sound engineer, was a recently constructed theater that people considered prestigious. Or pretentious. Designed by the architect Jean Nouvel, its four different structures rose over the south bank of the Têt. Molina liked the "Garnet," a kind of flying saucer the color of the traditional Catalan gems. This ovoid edifice rested on a pink cube whose façade was engraved with cultural quotations. All that was not bad. But why had the famous architect decided to add two metal hangars alongside it? While it was being built, Jacques had thought that they were construction sheds. Only later did he realize that they were part of the masterpiece.

"Forty-four million euros for this piece of shit," he complained as they entered the building.

"You're a little harsh."

"I'd be less harsh if Perpignan weren't already one of the most indebted cities in France!"

Éric Balland was waiting for the policemen under the great glass roof of the lobby. He had them sit down around a table.

"Was it really necessary to come here? I could have gone to police headquarters. It's right nearby."

He wasn't trying to conceal his irritation.

"It's right nearby for us, too, and we felt like walking," Molina explained. "We also wanted to find out how you're doing."

"Very kind of you! My wife has thrown me out, she never wants to see me again, and doesn't want me to see my children, either. Not even the dog! Now I'm living alone in a residential hotel just next door. There, now you know everything!"

"Am I mistaken or are you angry at us?" Molina retorted.

Balland ran his hands over his face. His irritation subsided.

"Sorry, you're not to blame for this, it's true. I take responsibility for it, it's my fault, I did something foolish."

"Still, what your wife did isn't cool," Molina conceded to calm things down. "She threw you out for . . . a single mistake. That's pretty hard-nosed . . ."

"Yeah."

Balland seemed ill at ease. Molina saw that Gilles had been right the other day. "It might not have been the first time that she learned about something . . ."

The lover gave him a black look. He wasn't yet ready to let the cat out of the bag.

"My wife didn't throw me out until she'd caught me a second time," Jacques admitted. "How about you?"

"You didn't come here just to talk to me about my private life, I suppose?"

"Yes, we did!"

"Are you joking?"

"Do I look like I'm joking?"

Balland didn't have to look at him long to have his answer.

"I have nothing to say to you, it doesn't concern your investigation!"

"There have been developments you don't know about."

"That's a pretty facile argument to worm information out of me."

"So there is information to be wormed out . . ."

"I have nothing to say to you."

"We can go ask your wife."

"At this point, I don't give a damn."

"Really?"

The two men glared at each other. Molina sensed hesitation in Balland. He stood up.

"All right, then, we're leaving. You coming, Gilles?"

Jacques was using the technique usual in difficult interviews: he established at the outset that he was the one running the show, and then let Gilles develop his questions. Balland waved his arm to get Molina to sit down again.

"OK, you win."

Jacques sat down at the table. He waited for Sebag to take over, but nothing happened.

"I'm listening."

Balland let a few seconds go by before finally saying:

"It was the . . . third time that she discovered something."

"Were they all married women?" Molina asked. "By 'married' I mean, of course, 'in a couple?'"

"Most of them, yes."

Molina raised an eyebrow. Balland's answer had been clumsy, even blundering. He had to seize the opportunity.

"Most of the three or most of all of them?"

"Are all these questions really useful?" Balland moaned.

"Yes, I assure you they are. Answer me and I'll tell you what justifies them."

Balland shook his head several times. He was becoming resigned.

"I've cheated on my wife seven times since we were married. Always with women who were 'in a couple,' as you put it. Contrary to what you think, I was very attached to my family life and I didn't want one of my affairs to become too important, or one of these women to ask me for more than I could give her."

"Could you tell us the names of these women?"

"You're jok—"

Balland interrupted himself. Molina still didn't look like he was joking.

"I can't do that. It's impossible."

Sebag coughed. He was waking up.

"We have learned that an anonymous letter-writer had informed Stéphane Abad of his wife's infidelity. Someone photographed you with Christine in front of the Gecko and sent the photos to her husband."

Sebag paused to give Balland time to take that in. In order to put pressure on the lover, on the way to the theater they'd decided to conceal the other hypotheses they were also pursuing.

"We have good reason to think that this someone also acted with the intention of harming you."

"To harm me? But why?"

"After what you've just admitted, don't you have any idea?"

"Jealous husbands?"

"For example."

"That's nonsense!"

Balland's tone lacked conviction. As he was speaking, he must have been reviewing the list of his conquests and their husbands.

"I really don't see it. In any case, I very seldom knew the husbands."

"That's why we'd like to have a list . . ." Molina said, trying again.

"Out of the question! This business has already broken up my marriage, I don't want to break up anybody else's."

"You're forgetting the Abad couple!" Sebag replied curtly.

"That's true . . ."

"We'll be very discreet . . ." Molina promised.

"I won't do it."

"You have no choice."

"One always has a choice."

"We can indict you for obstruction of justice."

Balland shrugged.

"If you think that will make me do what you want . . . I've lost Christine, I've lost my wife, I may be going to lose my children. I don't want to lose respect for myself."

Molina applauded loudly. In the lobby, faces turned toward their table.

"Bravo! What a speech! It's lovely, but it doesn't get us anywhere. We want a list."

"I won't give you one."

Balland was digging in his heels.

"Do you think someone other than a jealous husband might have had it in for you? A co-worker, for example?"

Molina admired Sebag's attempt at an end run.

"No, I don't," Balland answered calmly. "There's a good atmosphere here, people are cool. We have a great job."

"You don't have other . . . other weaknesses in your life? I don't know, gambling, for instance."

"I occasionally play poker with friends but we don't place large bets. And as I said, they're friends!"

"So we come back then to jealous husbands," Molina concluded. The other day you told us that you knew that Stéphane Abad was violent. Do you recall another husband with a fiery, vindictive temperament?"

"No. As I told you. I didn't know much about them."

"In this city there is a man who has it in for you and who seems prepared to do anything to hurt you. Don't you want us to arrest him?"

"Not at that price. And there's nothing he can do to hurt me: I've lost everything, he has already won."

"Maybe he doesn't consider his vengeance complete. He might want to attack your children?"

"You're trying to scare me, and I'm not fooled."

"We prefer to foresee the worst so that it doesn't happen. You'd be the first to reproach us if we didn't."

Sebag tried a new, parallel approach.

"This accusation led to Christine's death. Don't you want us to catch this guy?"

"Nothing indicates that that is what he wanted. Maybe now he regrets it. And then he isn't the one who pulled the trigger!"

"But he is partly responsible, isn't he? And you don't give a damn whether or not he's punished?"

Balland sighed but did not give in.

"No, I do care, and I hope you'll catch him. But I won't help you. Not in the way you're asking me to. Don't persist. You may think that I'm just a skirt-chaser, but I had feelings for each of the women I slept with, and I've maintained contact with some of them. I won't betray them."

Molina slapped his thighs, loudly.

"OK, fine. So here's what we're going to do: we're going to send you an official summons for another interview at police headquarters, and if you still refuse to cooperate, we'll indict you for obstruction of justice. In the meantime, we're going to investigate your private life on our own, and we won't be tactful or subtle about it. You can trust me, I'm an expert in that domain. We're going to question all your colleagues and all your friends, including your yoga partners. I'm warning you: this may cause damage."

He forced himself to remain firm but he felt a certain respect for Balland's obstinacy. For the first time since the beginning of the interview, Balland took his time before answering. But he did not yield.

"If you have time to waste . . ."

Molina stood up.

"We'll leave it there for the moment. But you'll soon be hearing from us."

"I'm sorry."

"You'll be really sorry. Soon. I guarantee you that."

On the way back to headquarters, Sebag and Molina remained silent for a long time. They had obtained nothing from Balland. Even the final bluff hadn't worked. But was it really a bluff?

"You're not going to mess up his life?" Sebag asked with concern.

"I admit that I'm pretty tempted to kick the anthill."

"First we have to be sure about this line of investigation. Let's wait and see if François gets anywhere. This morning he was supposed to try to find the former guard at Cantalou. I haven't yet had any news about that."

"Yeah, you're undoubtedly right. And then I might have another idea . . ."

"Two ideas in one day, wow! Is it your English girl who's stimulating you?"

"Must be!"

Jacques suddenly frowned. Sebag remembered that he had

found him in a bad mood when he got to work. He avoided any mockery in his tone.

"And what is this new idea?"

"I don't know if you deserve to hear it."

"You have the right to maintain the suspense."

"I'm going to work on it this afternoon and I'll tell you tomorrow. Maybe . . ."

"OK."

"What about you, what are you doing this afternoon?"

"Uhh . . . I'll talk to you about it tomorrow. Maybe . . ."

The "madman of the Rue Viollet-le-Duc," as the media had nicknamed him without much originality, remained hospitalized under police surveillance. The psychiatrist who had examined him feared that he might still be a danger to others and especially to himself, and wanted to have him transferred to the psychiatric hospital in Thuir.

"He's a fool, that doctor. I'm not crazy!"

"Of course not, but you need help and support. Now, if you'd prefer to go directly to jail, I can have a word with the judge."

"Uhh . . . I think I'll try the insane asylum, then. But do you really think I'm going to go to jail?"

"We'll do everything we can to avoid that. I promised you."

Gali was sitting on a chair next to the room's window, and Sebag had put one buttock on the bed.

"Do you think that anything is still possible with Véronique? I love her . . . I miss her already."

"You're the only one who can answer that question."

"But what do *you* think?"

"I'm not a shrink . . ."

Sebag contemplated the blue sky through the window. The weather was incredibly warm. On the way to the hospital he had heard on the radio that the temperature in the department had risen above 20° C.[22] For January 6, that was exceptional.

Gali was still waiting for a real answer.

"Every couple has to find its own way," Gilles explained, "its own way of defining the goal and setting the limits. What one must and wants to accept, and what one can't tolerate. I can't answer for the two of you, or for you alone."

"But you can answer for yourself, and it's your opinion I'm asking for."

"I'm not in a good position to do that."

"On the contrary."

Sebag no longer wanted to talk about himself. But he had to provide after-sales service.

"Frankly, I don't know. First of all, there's the past, which you'll have to cope with, that wound that is going to have to heal. Then, and especially, there's the future: restoring trust . . . Since both of you want it, you've got to try. But above all it's a battle against yourself that you'll have to wage . . ."

After having said good-bye to Bastien, Sebag went down a few floors to visit Véronique in another ward. The young woman had recovered; she would be released the following day. Social services had already found her a place in a center for battered women. She confirmed that she would not be filing a complaint. He spoke to her about nothing else. When he bent down to give her a good-bye peck, he could tell that her hair still smelled of gasoline.

Night had fallen and the wind was coming up. Winter was returning full force. As he got out of his car, Gilles pulled up the collar of his jacket. In front of police headquarters he found Elsa Moulin smoking a cigarette. She handed him her pack.

[22] 68° F.

"Smoking is bad for your health," he sighed, taking a cigarette. "We'd be better off quitting."

"Are you afraid of cancer?"

"No, bronchitis! In the winter, it's risky to smoke out of doors."

She offered him a light. He put his hands on hers to protect the lighter's flame.

"By the way, I've got news for you," the head of the forensic police announced. "I was just about to call you."

"Did you speak to Ménard about it?"

"No. Should I have?"

"We're working on one of his ideas . . ."

Elsa looked at him with curiosity.

"I was just thinking that you didn't look so good. Are you sick?"

"Why do you ask me that?"

"Since when is it Ménard who has ideas?"

Chapter 27

Sebag followed Elsa Moulin into the lair of the forensic police. To reach her office they had to pass through the laboratory. On the white tile drain boards, utensils were piled, each of them more mysterious than the next. Gilles considered his colleagues modern sorcerers who were capable of making objects, fluids, marks, and even dust speak, alchemists endowed with powers that were scientific, to be sure, but obscure for common mortals. For a long time, these cops had borne an image of rigorous, tiresome drudges, people who worked in offices and laboratories, dreary and austere. But over the years they had developed their techniques so far that even the most obsolete beat cop now expected them to perform miracles. Molina loved to repeat that on the basis of a single pubic hair found on a crime scene, these magicians could tell you the guy's age, how long it had been since his gun was fired, the bar code of his last condom, his bank balance, his mother's first name, and that of the postman . . .

Elsa leaned against the doorframe of her office and gestured to Sebag to enter. To get past her, he couldn't avoid grazing her white blouse, which absorbed her form without completely concealing it. The cops in the forensic unit had really changed recently! Elsa Moulin had been running the unit for only a short time, and Gilles had never regretted the departure of her grumpy predecessor, Jean Pages. He liked the young woman's smile as well as her relaxed style, her availability, and her competence. Once they were both seated on one side of the desk, Elsa showed him big piles of copies and a few stapled sheets. She put her hand on the first pile.

"Here you've got the history of the calls and text message sent and received by Christine Abad over the two weeks preceding her death. I've left the calls in chronological order for you, and classified the text messages by their interlocutors. I thought it would be clearer that way. Everything that has been erased appears in red. There's not much to conclude from it other than that her husband did in fact lie to you: there is no SMS that corresponds to what he told you."

Her hand moved to the second pile.

"Here, you've got the same thing for Didier Valls's calls and SMSes. I've classified everything in the same way as for Christine."

She picked up the stapled sheets.

"So far as Stéphane Abad's mobile is concerned, because it was thrown in the river I haven't been able to get from his service provider anything more than the record of his calls. I don't have anything on the content of the text messages."

"A brief summary?" Sebag cut her short.

She pushed one of the two piles of paper toward him. The one that corresponded to Valls's telephone records.

"Have a look at this."

As soon as he had examined the first sheets, Sebag spotted a recurring number written in red. The first SMS went back to Christmas Eve. It was simple and concise: "Your wife is cheating on you." He looked up and smiled at Elsa. There it was, they had proof: Ménard was right.

"Valls didn't answer this first SMS," Elsa explained. "He must have thought it was a mistake. The real exchanges began the next day, and they continued until the day before his suicide. Valls erased everything just before the argument, including the records of this number in the call log."

"So Valls was also the victim of the informer."

"Of *an* informer," Elsa corrected. "There are good reasons to think that it is the same person who sent the photos to Abad, but no definite proof."

"Explain."

"I compared the *corbeau*'s number with those found in Abad's call log: it's not there. On the other hand, I did find another number that recurs several times on the days leading up to the murder. Text messages and even three calls were exchanged. Since this number doesn't appear in the phone's contact list, I tried to identify it, but didn't succeed: it's probably a disposable phone."

"Like the telephone used to contact Valls, I suppose?"

"Exactly. I have not been able to identify the owner of that phone, either."

"So it's probably the same individual using two different disposable phones?"

"Or the same phone with a different SIM card."

"OK, we don't have ironclad proof that it's the same person, but you spoke of good reasons to believe that it is."

"I geolocated the two numbers. We have to assume that they are no longer active, but it seems that both were used in the center of Perpignan, essentially in a sector that reaches from, say . . . the Place Arago to the Conference Center."

Sebag nodded pensively. This time it was certain, it couldn't be an accident. He warmly thanked his colleague and went back upstairs to his office, his arms loaded with documents. For a good hour, he delved into Christine Abad's and Didier Valls's private lives.

These days, there is nothing more intrusive or more instructive than reading people's text messages. Written rapidly and summarily, they reveal everyday life in its raw state, both the great and the very small things in life, details that are insignificant but highly symbolic. Written straightforwardly and without artifice, these momentary states of mind tell us more about a person than the most personal of diaries.

Sebag went through dozens of messages that were probably valuable for determining Christine's and Didier's personalities, but had no direct interest for their case.

He found Christine's correspondence with her lover disturbing. Necessarily. This outflowing of sweet and sometimes sexually explicit words, this profusion of desires and wishes laid out before his eyes, awakened his demons. It was impossible not to draw a parallel, not to wonder what phrases Claire might have exchanged with "her" Simon, what greedy hungers she might have expressed, what satisfactions she might have told him about.

On Tuesday, December 23, at 12:10 P.M., Christine Abad send a final message to Éric. She wrote: "I'm leaving my house. I can't wait to feel you inside me." Sebag felt a sudden unease in the pit of his stomach. As when you realize that you've just escaped a tragedy. Fortunately, he hadn't read his wife's text messages earlier. If he'd read them while the affair was going on, he would probably have found messages of the same kind. And, he was convinced, their marriage would never recover from that.

He took the whiskey bottle out of his drawer, and after drinking a first glass, breathed a long sigh. By beginning with Christine's correspondence, he'd already done the hardest part. He could calmly move on to Valls's.

On Christmas Day itself, after twenty-four hours without a reply, the *corbeau* had sent Sandrine's husband another SMS.

"I have all the proof you need, your wife is cheating on you."

"Who are you?"

"A friend who wishes you well . . ."

"But who are you?"

"My identity doesn't matter, only my information does."

"How can I believe you without knowing who you are?"

"This is your business, not mine. Do you want the truth?"

"What are you after, what do you want from me?"

"I want to reveal the truths that are being hidden from us. Are you ready to see them?"

"Do you want money?"

"I'm not asking for anything."

"How much?"

Getting no reply, Valls dialed the number. The call had lasted only twenty-two seconds. Sebag inferred that he must have gotten an answering machine and left a short message. Two days later, the dialogue was resumed. At Valls's initiative.

"What exactly do you know?"

"If you want answers, don't call me anymore."

The *corbeau* made it clear that he alone was setting the rules.

"OK. What do you know?"

"Your wife has a lover. Her boss. First name: Francis. They seem to be very much in love."

"How do you know that?"

"I know it, I see it. You don't need to know any more."

"What is Francis's last name?"

The SMS received no response. Valls sent another the next day. The mysterious informant knew how to turn up the heat. If he was after money, Didier was ready to shell out a small fortune.

"If you want me to believe you, you'll have to tell me more. I'll give you what you want."

This message got a quick response.

"Don't insult me, I don't want your money."

Sebag frowned. Was the man sincere or particularly devious?

"Excuse me. But you've told me too much or not enough."

"Sandrine has been lying to you for a long time. Be patient. You'll soon know everything."

Despite Valls's numerous attempts to recontact the *corbeau*, this was the last SMS. The last trace of the mysterious interlocutor was a call he made on the morning of Valls's suicide. At precisely 9:45. The conversation had lasted thirty-five seconds.

Just one thing aroused Sebag's interest in the rest of Didier Valls's telephone correspondence. Valls seemed to be very close to a certain Nathalie who also worked at Cantalou. They often set lunch dates, and while many of the messages referred to work matters, others concerned their marital problems, tensions and arguments, their worries and even their suspicions.

Despite the large number of text messages and their very personal character, this relationship seemed not to have gone beyond sincere friendship. Some text messages ended with "love and kisses," nothing more.

And no trace of a message mentioning the *corbeau.*

He'd had a piercing headache ever since he'd begun reading the text messages. In his desk drawer, he found a bottle of paracetamol. He took out a tablet and washed it down with a gulp of whiskey.

No one having answered the door, Julie knocked again. A little harder. This time she heard Gilles's voice:

"Come in."

She opened the door and walked into the room. She saw Sebag rapidly close his desk drawer.

"I was wondering if you were still there," she said. "It's late."

"What are you thinking! I often work late . . ."

Seeing his distant expression, she was concerned:

"I hope I didn't disturb you?"

"Are you kidding? I'm contributing to my own legend as a do-nothing."

"I promise to keep your secret then. I won't tell anyone that you worked hard today."

"Whew!"

Julie smiled. She liked Gilles. She had rarely met a cop with such a great sense of humor, so much humility and talent. He asked her how her day had gone and she told him that she had once again walked the streets of Bas-Vernet and collected interesting new information. Some residents had mentioned a six-year-old girl's game.

"I think the burglars took advantage of the trust inspired by her youth. She stands in front of the apartment building's doors and claims that she's going to see her grandmother: people are inclined let her come in. The problem is that she has not yet been identified. How about you, made any progress?"

Gilles didn't have to be asked twice to summarize Elsa's discoveries for her.

"Wow!" she exclaimed. "This case is getting exciting! I'll have to clear up my burglary in a hurry so I can work with you on it."

"I'd like that."

There was an odd aroma floating in the room that occasionally tickled Julie's nostrils. Her eyes fell on the plastic glass next to the telephone on Gilles's desk. The amber liquid it contained wasn't water, and still less coffee. She wanted to be sure, and took another glass from Molina's desk. She wiped the rim and then held it out to Gilles.

"Will you give me a little?"

Sebag blushed slightly. He opened his drawer, took out the bottle, and poured a shot of whiskey into her glass. Julie put it to her lips. She immediately made a face.

"You have better taste in coffee."

Saying this, she remembered the conversation they'd had a few days earlier. They were in the cafeteria at headquarters and Gilles was criticizing the quality of the coffee. She had suggested that he buy an espresso machine, and he had replied that if he could make good coffee for himself in his office he would probably drink too much of it. Didn't the same go for whiskey? She examined his drawn features, his sad face. Her colleague didn't look so good.

"So, when are we going for a run together?"

"Whenever you like . . ."

"Tomorrow after work?"

"If I don't finish too late . . ."

"You, working late two days in a row? Watch out, if you pull that one on me I'm going to conclude that you're avoiding me. Given the time I've been asking and you've been delaying, I'm going to end up thinking you're afraid to run with me."

"Nonsense!"

"Or that you just don't want to . . ."

"You're kidding."

"Drinking or running, you have to choose!" Julie almost told him. She restrained herself but vowed to force her colleague to make a rapid decision.

Chapter 28

"I think it would be crazy for them to get into the Top 14 immediately."

"I agree with you so far as finances are concerned, but not on the athletic level. They have to be careful not to get too established in the D2 league. Just look at Pau: it took them years to get back into the Top 14!"[23]

Molina was distractedly following his pals' conversation. For once, he wasn't interested in talking about the USAP. He put his lips on the straw and sucked noisily, but without success. He'd already finished his mojito. Three drops of rum, a slice of lime, and the rest in mint leaves and shaved ice. What a scam!

He ordered a beer.

For almost two hours, he'd been drinking and eating tapas with two friends who were rugby fans. They'd gathered around a table on the terrace in front of a bar. Despite the wind and the cool night, the sidewalk was swarming with people all along the Avenue du Maréchal Leclerc. After it was refurbished, this avenue had become a real street of thirst, lively late into the night even in winter.

Jacques had had a full day on the job. In that respect, at least, he was satisfied. He'd met with the heads of five private detective agencies in the Perpignan area. They had all said they'd had no contact with Stéphane Abad or Didier Valls, and

[23] The French Rugby championship competition.

he had believed them all. Or almost. Regarding Àvia Maria, he had some doubts. He'd always had doubts about Àvia Maria. The old woman was too wily and they were too close. With her, he was never sure of anything.

He'd have to talk with Gilles. He'd know.

"Anyway . . . let's hope . . ."

For several days, Sebag hadn't been in the best of shape. Headache, pain in the gut, upset stomach . . . He could say all he wanted, he couldn't fool an old monkey like him: storm warnings were up for his marriage. Such a beautiful, desirable woman, such a confident man, twenty years of marriage—a quadratic equation with three terms and an unknown.

But not all that unknown!

During Gilles's absence that afternoon, Jacques had dug through his partner's desk drawer. Too often lately he'd seen his partner dive under his desk for no reason. And he'd found a bottle of whiskey there, three-quarters empty. As he stood up, he'd put his hands on the desktop and unintentionally awakened the computer, which Gilles had forgotten to shut down when he left. A face and a name had appeared on the screen. Those of Simon Bidol, a teacher of history and geography at the Lycée René Cassin in Bayonne. Jacques found the profile Bidol had posted on the social networks and learned that he had lived in Northern Catalonia the past year. A few more clicks revealed the school where he'd taught: the Collège de Rivesaltes, the one where Claire Sebag taught.

No need to have his colleague's gift for drawing conclusions.

The waiter put Jacques's beer on the table. His two pals were still drinking mojitos. And they were still talking about rugby.

"What was really fucked last season was the scrum."

"No shit!"

Gilles was going through a difficult period and he needed a

helping hand. Work—there was nothing like it for taking some distance. But he still had to be able to lose himself in an exciting investigation instead of tagging along behind Ménard on a lead he'd discovered.

A lead or a pseudo-lead?

If he could prove that François was on the wrong track, that would be great. For Gilles and for himself. Because he also needed to think about something else.

He shivered. The parasol heater set up next to their table was burning the top of his head but a cold wind was finding its way under his shirt. After this last beer, it would be time for him to go to bed.

Since the previous evening Jacques had been in a glum, languid mood. His little English girl had dumped him without warning. He hadn't felt any pain, and ultimately it was that that was making him sad. What was the point of these little flings if they didn't leave you even a little sorrow when they were over?

An unknown figure was approaching a nearby table. The man had his back to him, but Molina recognized the tall stature of Éric Balland. He wasn't at all surprised. The Archipelago theater was not far away and Christine's lover had told them that very morning that he'd been living on the same street since his wife threw him out. Balland must have felt Jacques's eyes on his shoulders, because he turned around and saw him. Then he leaned toward his friends—a man and two women—and all four of them very quickly got up and left.

Molina caught himself watching them go with scorn. Normally, he would have rather admired Balland's success with women. He thought about Cindy again. His desire for the young woman had been strong, and he was moved by the memory of their athletic sexual encounters. But what would remain of all that a week, a month, or a year from now?

He thought about his ex-wife. Where was she tonight? After having dined with their sons, she must have sat down alone in front of her TV. Had she found someone since their separation? Up to this point he'd never worried about that, but tonight jealousy was bothering him. What was up with him? Probably getting old, by God, really getting old! Thinking about Sandrine, he felt melancholic. He missed her. His old friend. Fifteen years together, with fights, of course—a few too many—but also habits, comfort, and complicity. How he would have liked to sleep next to her tonight and feel her warmth against his tired body! He would have probably had a little erection, nothing much, the kind of desire that you could arouse or just let it fade away.

He was tired of lovers and dreamed of a companion, a partner, a sister, somebody with whom he could share something other than a good dose of sweat and a few milliliters of sperm. Ah . . . calmly falling asleep next to a woman without having been obliged to make love to her . . . Complete bliss!

At the age of fifty, the wolf was weeping over his chains. Christ, he was getting old. Old and stupid!

Chapter 29

On the road that led to Saint-Laurent-de-la-Salanque, François Ménard was jubilant. The forensic team's analyses had validated his hypothesis. What a triumph! On the strength of these results—and the complaint against an unknown person filed by Abad's son—the prosecutor had just decided to open an official investigation of the *corbeau.* Superintendent Castello had personally congratulated him and given him a blank check. He was the one who was going to head the investigation.

On the passenger seat, Sebag was keeping his mouth closed. Ménard's brilliant colleague was trying to put up a good show, but he was failing. His face was grim and wore a fixed smile. He hadn't said a word since they got in the car.

Ménard found a parking place close to the village house occupied by Dominique Barrache, the guard who had been fired at Cantalou-Cémoi. He'd finally managed to contact him. The suspect had gone home and was waiting for them there.

He rang the doorbell. A round, bearded face appeared in a second-floor window.

"Come up, it's on the second floor."

The two policemen took a steep, narrow stairway and came out in a small room that served as living room, kitchen, and office all at once. In one corner, another staircase led to the upper level; in another, a laptop hummed on a small table. The screensaver was a photo of Le Canigou. The mountain's summit was covered with glazed sugar that stood out against a pink sea of peach trees in bloom.

"Did you take the picture?" Ménard asked.

"Yes."

"Do you take many photos?"

"It's my passion, in fact. My only vice."

Ménard gazed at the man facing him. An odd physique for a guard. Dominique Barrache stood hardly 5'3" tall and his waistline looked more like an inner tube than a chocolate bar. The cop even wondered if carrying a telephoto lens on his camera wouldn't be too strenuous an exercise for him.

"Please, sit down."

The guard pointed to chairs around a table topped with Formica in an imitation wood pattern.

"Would you like some coffee?"

Ménard followed Sebag's glance at the coffeemaker sitting next to a sink overflowing with dirty dishes. It was half-full of cold, weak coffee. Barrache had been gone for several days and the coffee looked like it dated from before his departure.

"You wouldn't have anything else?" Sebag asked.

"Orange juice?"

"Perfect," Ménard answered after glancing at his colleague.

Barrache pulled three glasses from the pile of dirty dishes and summarily washed them before putting them on the table, which was covered with crumbs.

Then he took an open bottle from the refrigerator and filled the glasses.

"Do you live alone?" Ménard asked, even though the answer was obvious.

"Yes," the guard replied, playing with his wedding ring.

"But you're married?"

"My wife left with the children two months ago. We're going to get divorced."

"Sorry to hear that."

"It's all right. Probably better this way."

Barrache said nothing more about it. He took a swallow of orange juice. He was waiting to find out the reason for this visit. On the telephone, Ménard hadn't told him anything.

"Do you know why we're here?"

"I have an inkling."

This enigmatic and promising response made the hair on Ménard's forearms stand on end.

"I suppose it has something to do with my being fired?"

"In a way . . ."

"And in what way does that concern inspectors from the Perpignan police? I made a stupid mistake, OK, but I didn't steal anything."

Ménard took a drink of the orange juice. It was so sour that it must have been open for a week at least. A joke occurred to him. For once! He said:

"Attempt to poison a policeman. That's going to get you ten to fifteen years."

Barrache, without smiling, sipped his orange juice again.

"Still tastes good to me."

"It's just that we're not used to drinking it all by itself," Sebag joked. "The last times, it was with vodka."

This time Barrache was kind enough to give a half-smile. Enough! It was time to get to the heart of the matter.

"You heard what happened to Stéphane Abad?"

"Of course."

"Did his problems give you joy?"

"I wouldn't go that far. Let's just say that I didn't feel a lot of pain for him. On the other hand, it's too bad about his wife. May her soul rest in peace."

"Were you really angry with Abad?"

"Naturally. I've never understood why he wanted to get me in trouble. I never did anything to him. And it wasn't his job to monitor the guards."

"What exactly did you do?"

"You don't know?"

"Yes, we do. But we'd like to hear it from you."

Barrache put his hand on the table and started collecting the scattered crumbs. They weren't bread crumbs, probably cookie crumbs.

"One night when Abad had forgotten something in his office, he returned and I didn't see him coming. He caught me classifying my photos on my laptop. From that time on, he tried several times to trap me. And he finally succeeded. He snitched on me and the management started keeping a close eye on my work. They noticed that I didn't always make the rounds I was supposed to make."

"You didn't contest these accusations?"

The guard shrugged.

"People who think what I did or didn't do is a fault have never spent a whole night looking at surveillance screens on which nothing ever happens. To keep from falling asleep on the job, everyone finds something to do. Some of my colleagues watch porno films or play games online. I work on my photos."

"What about the rounds?"

"There too I must not be the only one who doesn't always follow the schedule. They make us do ridiculous things. Who's going to burgle a chocolate factory at night? There's nothing to steal there!"

"But all the same, you're paid for that."

"Yeah, that's true. But I was guarding that place all the same! In any case, the company is trying to outsource the guard service, and so first they have to fire the old guards. They jumped on the opportunity."

Barrache swallowed a big gulp of orange juice. Ménard didn't touch his glass again, and Sebag's was still full.

"What are you doing now?"

"I have a job for two months working the night shift at a security company. Even though I don't like this job, I don't know anything else."

"You don't have a degree?"

"I left school at fourteen to get certified as a pastry cook, but I failed the exam. Then I enlisted in the army."

Ménard looked again at Barrache's feeble physique and wondered what assignment the French army had been able to give him. Certainly not in the special forces. A cook or warehouseman at most . . .

"But you have a talent for photography?"

"Maybe."

"What do you photograph?"

"The beauty of things: landscapes, animals, flowers."

"People too?"

"Rarely. I don't like people much. That's also why I work nights."

After that skillful digression—in fact it was a way of preparing the way for further questions—Ménard returned to the main subject.

"What about Valls, did you know him, too?"

Barrache's face darkened.

"What are all these questions about?"

"You must have some idea, don't you?"

"I . . . uhh . . . no."

More than uneasiness, it was fear that Ménard saw in the guard's eyes.

"What was your relationship with Valls?"

"Uhh . . . he was the accountant. Except that he signed my paycheck every month, I didn't have much to do with him."

The guard was lying, that was clear. Ménard rubbed his hands.

"You didn't have any reason to be angry with him?"

"Well . . . no!"

Ménard gestured toward the computer sitting on the small table.

"Are all your photos on your laptop?"

"Well . . . yes."

"And you're sure that you never take photos of people?"

"Well . . . no, I mean yes. As I told you . . ."

"You never photograph couples leaving or entering a hotel? Couples having an illicit affair?"

Barrache's eyes and mouth opened wide at the same time. He was doing a good job of pretending to be surprised. Ménard took out the photos he'd gotten at Abad's house, and after clearing the crumbs off part of the tabletop, laid them on it.

"You didn't take these photos, Monsieur Barrache?"

"Uhh . . . no."

"Are you sure?"

"Abs . . .absolutely!"

"Why did your wife leave you?"

Ménard liked to use opposite techniques. By moving unexpectedly from one to the other, he sometimes succeeded in getting the suspect to entrap himself in his own lies. Barrache drank his glass dry.

"Irreconcilable differences."

"What else?"

"We had been together for fifteen years. Well . . . together is a big word. I worked nights, she's a nurse, so she doesn't really have a schedule. We met only occasionally. We both found it hard, but when I was unemployed again we realized that it was also the reason we had remained together so long. Once I was home all the time, we had one argument after another. But the worst thing, I think, was that except for these arguments, we had nothing to say to one another. As I told you, she left two months ago."

Barrache was more inclined to talk about his wife than

about his photos. Ménard pointed to the photos, which were still lying on the table.

"If we examine your computer, we won't find photos like these?"

The guard looked at him for a long time before answering. He had trouble following.

"Well . . . no!"

"You never take 'pictures of people' you said. Even your children?"

"Well . . . yes. But that's not the same thing."

"Have you missed them since they left?"

"Yes and no . . . Since we were never there, Chloé and Alexis grew up mainly with their grandparents, my wife's parents. When I was home, I wanted to have them with me, but I think they were less happy. Their mother went back with them to live with her parents in Millas."

"Monsieur Barrache, we're going to take your computer with us to examine it."

The guard opened his mouth as if to speak but couldn't say anything. He ran his hand through his sparse beard.

"But . . . There are very personal things on it. Letters exchanged with my wife."

"Where were you these last few days? I was unable to contact you."

"I was in the Spanish Garrotxes,[24] taking photos."

"Is there someone who can confirm that?"

"Well . . . no. I was alone. As I told you, I live alone now."

"Too bad for you. So you're going to come with us to police headquarters."

"But why?"

"Because we have good reasons to think that you took pictures of Christine Abad and her lover, and that to avenge

[24] A remote valley in the Pyrenees.

yourself on Abad and on Valls, you sent them anonymous letters revealing their wives' infidelities, and that you were thus indirectly responsible for a murder and a suicide."

The guard's pudgy body slumped. Ménard was unsure. He always was always unsure at times like this.

"For the moment, we'd just like to question you at somewhat greater length. But if you refuse to go with us, you will be placed in police custody immediately."

CHAPTER 30

Rafel set four dishes of tapas on the table in front of Sebag and Molina.

"Pa amb tomaquet, bunyols de baccallà, polpets à la planxa, et pata negra!"[25]

The owner of the Carlit was doing them a favor. When he got to the restaurant, Molina had complained loudly about the daily special, coq au vin with vegetables. He'd ribbed Rafel about his cooking, which, despite all his talk about Catalan identity, was moving farther and farther away from Catalan values. Rafel had succeeded in calming him only by promising him some local tapas.

"I also gave you a little wine from the Terrats wine co-op," Rafel explained as he opened a bottle. "A Terrassous 2011, a blend of carignan, syrah, and grenache noir. You'll like it."

He filled their glasses with a very appetizing blood-red wine. Jacques and Gilles tasted it in silence, found it supple and fruity, and then clicked their tongues in approval. Satisfied, Rafel headed back to the kitchen.

"So, is the guard the right suspect?" Molina asked.

Sebag frowned; he didn't share Ménard's enthusiasm. When asked probing questions, Barrache had seemed surprised—just as much as necessary—and offended—just as much as he should have. He wasn't overacting, he seemed sincere. Or else he was an excellent thespian.

[25] Bread rubbed with oil and tomatoes, salt cod fritters, calamari cooked on a *plancha*, and dark Iberian ham.

"I'm not so sure about that."

"Ha, ha, Ménard wants to play with the big boys and he's going to fall on his face."

Gilles didn't share Jacques's *Schadenfreude* either. In fact, he didn't share anything. He was still in a bad way, he couldn't seem to get a grip on himself. On the way back, he'd received an SMS from Claire with a nice little note. The kind of words that people exchange for years without really thinking about them, such as salutations or even simple punctuations, and that one day suddenly take on all their meaning. At first he had just replied, "See you this evening," but then added a more affectionate "I can't wait!" But as he was putting away his phone he thought again about the other man—he kept returning to him, he couldn't help it. The words that man had exchanged with Claire had never had time to become banal. They had been powerful, weighed, shared.

So who was this guy who had been able to seduce his wife? And what did he have that Gilles didn't?

It took him a few seconds to notice that Molina was looking at him with a spark of curiosity in his eyes, and another spark of impatience. His partner had something to tell him, but he was letting it come. Jacques gulped down a slice of *pain à la tomate*. Then he licked his fingers and began.

"Do you remember the little idea I had after our interview with Balland?"

"I especially remember that you didn't want to tell me more about it. If you've changed your mind, I'm listening."

"It occurred to me that the photos we found at Abad's place looked like they were taken by a professional. But not by a professional photographer . . ."

He paused before going on to explain:

"But rather by a professional detective."

The idea surprised Sebag.

"I see what you mean so far as the nature of the photos is

concerned, but they weren't delivered the way a private agency would. Abad and Valls received anonymous calls and letters. That has nothing in common with a file provided by a detective agency."

"Objection, Your Honor!"

At that moment Rafel arrived with two steaming plates.

"Messieurs, *el gall*!"[26]

"Even presented in Catalan, it's still a French dish," Molina grumbled, digging his fork into the meat. "Damn! French but delicious."

Sebag let him swallow his food before urging him to explain.

"Valls received anonymous calls," Jacques said. "We know that, we have a transcript. But so far as Abad is concerned, we have no proof concerning the calls. On the other hand, we have the photos . . ."

"So you still think we have to separate the two cases? You really don't want Ménard to be right, do you?"

"You're the superhero, not him!"

Sebag almost burst out laughing.

"And so in your opinion the fact that Abad and Valls both received unidentified calls from the same part of downtown Perpignan is a mere coincidence?"

"Why not? I did a little investigating yesterday and it seems to me that the head of one of the agencies didn't tell me the whole truth. Imagine that one of the detectives is using a throwaway phone. The agency is located in more or less the same part of downtown as Abad's mysterious caller . . ."

"Aha . . ."

Molina took another forkful of *coq au vin*. Then he wiped his mouth on his napkin.

"Have I already talked to you about Àvia Maria?"

[26] The cock.

"Who?"

"Àvia Maria . . . in Catalan, *àvia* means 'grandmother.'"

Molina downed a big swallow of red wine.

"Àvia Maria runs the Catalan Detective Agency, the oldest agency in Perpignan, with a dozen investigators. She was born near Barcelona in 1934. She is descended from Spanish Republicans. She came to France during the *Retirada*."

In February 1939, almost half a million people fled the advance of Franco's troops in Spain. Soldiers and also whole families of civilians crossed the mountains on foot to find refuge in France. In Pyrénées-Orientales, they had been parked in hastily constructed camps, notably on the beaches at Argelès and Saint-Cyprien, and then also at Rivesaltes. This period is known to history as the *Retirada*, which means "retreat" in Spanish.

"In the 1950s, Maria married a Catalan from around here, Jaume Borell, who had just opened this agency. Since the death of her husband from leukemia more than twenty years ago, she's been keeping the place going. An iron hand in a velvet glove, as they say."

"You seem to know her well."

"You better believe it . . . I worked for her when I was a kid."

"You don't say . . ."

"The agency needed a smart kid for certain stakeouts and to tail people. Because of my age, I was less likely to be spotted than the adult detectives. That's where I learned the rudiments of the trade."

"And today you continued to inform 'your' Àvia every time she asks you to."

"Every time I can."

"So she owes you one!"

Molina smiled.

"It's clear that you don't know her: Àvia Maria doesn't owe anything to anyone."

Sebag was beginning to feel a strong interest in this charming grandmother.

"And so that's what happened today with the old lady?"

"She didn't seem very sincere to me."

"But you didn't succeed in getting her to spill the beans?"

"No. She knows me too well. In fact . . ."

Molina scratched his head again and lowered his eyes. He looked like a timid child.

"In fact, I need you to play hardball with her."

Sebag didn't hide his astonishment. When they were working together, it was always Molina who played that role. It was second nature . . .

"That would be a first. It might be fun."

"Could you manage it?"

"Thanks for your confidence! Since I've been working with you, I've learned a lot. Shall we go back there now?"

"I thought we could show up unannounced this afternoon."

"Why go unannounced?"

"Because she doesn't like that at all!"

Sebag remained skeptical about Molina's theory, but he was eager to make the acquaintance of this old woman who had so impressed his partner.

The offices of the Catalan Detective Agency occupied the second floor of a dignified building that looked out on the Promenade des Platanes. The two lieutenants passed through a glass door and found themselves in a small lobby equipped with a desk and four chairs lined up along the wall. A young woman stood up behind the table and gave Molina a kiss.

"Twice in two days, the year is starting well! I hope this time it's me you've come to see."

"Julia, this is Gilles, my partner. Gilles, this is Julia, one of Maria's granddaughters. I knew her when she was little and I even dandled her on my knee."

"But ever since I grew up he has stubbornly refused to do it again . . ."

"It's the very first time I've seen him turn down a pretty young woman," Gilles observed.

"I consider her my grand-niece," Jacques explained, pinching Julia's cheek. "A grand-niece who's mischievous and a tease. I'm sure that if I said yes, she'd be the one to refuse."

"Mean."

"No, not mean. Àvia Maria is here, I assume?"

"The day when you don't find her here, you'll have to look for her in the cemetery. But you didn't call in advance?"

Molina spread his arms wide in a gesture of impotence.

"My partner was in too much of a hurry to make her acquaintance."

Julia walked down a long hallway and gently opened a door at the end on the right.

"At this hour she takes her nap," Molina explained. "For more than fifty years she has been coming to the agency at 7 A.M. and takes a little nap in the morning and a longer one in the afternoon."

"Fortunate lady."

Julia rejoined them.

"You can go in now."

They entered a large, dark room cluttered with files. There were files everywhere, on bookcases, on the desk, on a windowsill, even on the floor. In a corner, a large armchair offered comfort from the headrest to the footrest. It was covered in plaid.

Behind her desk, partly hidden by the files, Àvia Maria showed them a pleasant face. Molina planted resounding kisses on her plump cheeks. If it hadn't been for her steely blue eyes, Sebag could have imagined her at a stove surrounded by grandchildren rather than at the head of a private detective agency. He shook her hand.

"Bonjour, Madame Borell."

"Call me Àvia Maria, please."

"All right, Madame Borell."

The old lady noted this refusal without batting an eyelid. She invited them to sit down and then addressed Molina:

"So you've come back with reinforcements."

"In a way."

Àvia Maria turned to Gilles.

"So you're the one who's going to play the bad cop?"

"You could say that."

"That doesn't seem to be in your nature."

"It's true that I usually like to leave that role to Jacques. But I promise to force myself to play my role."

"I'm expecting you to. I don't like to give up my information without a battle. It's a question of principle. At my age, you don't change."

"So you have information that might be of interest to us?"

"If you're here, it's because you think I do. I sensed yesterday that this big lout here hadn't found my answers very convincing. I know him, and he knows me, so . . ."

"You know each other!"

"Precisely."

"But you and I don't know each other."

"Speak for yourself. Jacques has often told me about your exploits. And I know about the most recent ones: arresting a young drug dealer and preventing a madman from burning down a whole neighborhood. All that in less than ten days, I say bravo!"

"You're well-informed."

"I read the newspapers, I listen to the radio. Among other things."

Sebag noticed that Molina, on his left, was squirming on his chair. He shot him a side glance. His partner seemed to be telling him: "Be careful, she's putting you to sleep."

"Madame Borell," Sebag went on, "I have no desire to play cat and mouse with you. So far as I'm concerned, I'm too old for that. Or not old enough!"

The old woman's eyes smiled at what she could have seen as an affront. Everything seemed to be a game for her. Not easy to handle.

"Jacques undoubtedly explained to you that we're working on two cases that are delicate because, although in different ways, they both resulted in deaths. We're now certain that Stéphane Abad and Didier Valls were informed of their wives' infidelities by photos that resemble in every way the kind that agencies like yours provide."

He had decided for the time being not to dissociate the two cases.

"These are serious matters, two homicides. If it was your agency that provided these photos, you're obligated to tell us that."

Àvia Maria looked at him without answering. Her eyes spoke for her. They said: "You don't scare me at all!"

"We're conducting this investigation at the behest of the prosecutor. You have to cooperate."

When the old woman's mouth widened, it made her chubby cheeks even rounder.

"But I am cooperating, since you're here . . ."

"That's not the feeling I have."

"But you haven't yet asked me any questions!"

Molina burst out laughing. Àvia Maria ran a spotted hand over her blue-black, permed hair. This time her pink lips formed a genuine smile. Sebag felt ridiculous. By playing this unhabitual role he was acting against type and wasn't doing it well. Not focused. Not involved. Or maybe too much involved.

Suddenly he felt a desire to give it all up, go home, pull the covers over his head, and sleep.

Finally sleep. For a day, a week, a year. Forget everything.

Obviously, that wasn't possible.

"OK., Madame Borell, I will therefore very officially ask if your agency has had anything to do with Stéphane Abad or Didier Valls?"

"I promise to ask my agents about that. But some of them are still on vacation."

She looked around the room with its piles of file folders.

"I can also look myself, but that might take a while."

"Don't tell me you aren't computerized?"

"Of course we are. But I'm not! I don't know how to use a computer, and for such important matters I'm the only one who can provide you with the information."

The owner of the Catalan Detective Agency might run her operation with a firm hand, but she was acting like a capricious old lady.

"Do your employees use prepaid phones?"

"Sometimes, when the investigation requires it."

Sebag took out his notebook and opened it to the page where he had written down the number Elsa had found on Abad's phone.

"Does this number mean anything to you?"

She didn't even look at it.

"When my agents use that kind of phone, it is to be discreet. In general, they don't give the number to everybody."

A capricious old woman, yes, that was it. That was *all* it was. He had to find something else. Silence fell on the room. Gilles looked out the window at the sparse foliage of the plane trees on the Allées Maillol. He thought. The old woman was having her fun like a girl, he had to surprise her. That was just what she was waiting for.

Get back to fundamentals, that was the key. Observation, psychology, intuition . . . He stopped contemplating the trees. His eyes grew blurry, he was looking inward. An image came back to him. When they had come into this room . . . the armchair with the plaid . . . he studied the room, examined the armchair. He felt something vibrate inside him.

"Your friend is no longer talking," Maria said to Jacques, astonished. "He's lost his tongue."

The old lady had followed Gilles's eyes and then broken the silence. She was confirming his doubts. He sized her up for a few more moments before beginning to speak.

"Do you know Abad and Valls?"

An imperceptible movement of her lips provided an answer.

"No, not both of them. You know only Abad."

A wrinkling of her eyelids assented. Àvia Maria's interest was growing.

"You worked for him."

He asked no further questions. An interrogative tone would have caused the old woman to clam up. Making an assertion seemed to him the best way to get a response.

"You run an agency with an excellent reputation and you're completely familiar with the law. You wouldn't play around this way if you were the source of the photos Abad received."

Àvia Maria didn't turn a hair, but her breathing became quieter, as if she were monitoring it.

"So if you have already worked for him, it was earlier. Much earlier. Long ago."

He paused.

"Go on, I'm finding this fascinating," Maria said.

Molina was bouncing on his chair. He was loving it. Like a kid at the circus.

"Oh, there, Maria, I recognize my Gilles, and when he has that inspired air of Jesus Christ Policeman, he's redoubtable. He's going to make you spill all your secrets!"

Sebag didn't want to let himself be distracted. He recalled a few elements of the Abad couple's marriage. It all fit together.

He waited another moment before continuing. That was it, now he had his idea.

"Christine Abad cheated on her husband the first time after the birth of her son. She confessed everything to him, and that was a mistake, because Stéphane, who had not been jealous before, became jealous. He started spying on her and asked your agency to help him. At least once, maybe more."

Sebag had taken a risk by being too explicit. But the old woman's attention had not flagged. He wasn't mistaken. With a wave of his arm, he indicated the disorder in the room.

"Among all these files, Madame Borell, you therefore have one that bears the name Abad. You knew that you hadn't convinced Jacques yesterday and you suspected that we were going to come back. So you've already looked for this file and found it. You even reread it during your naptime. And you should have put it back with the others before receiving us instead of putting your plaid over it."

Molina stood up. There was bump under the plaid blanket. He lifted the blanket, revealing a blue file folder. With Stéphane Abad's name written on it in bold letters.

"I suppose there is nothing in this file that would help us in our investigation," Sebag concluded. "You've wasted our time."

"I haven't wasted mine. Jacques has praised you to the skies. You're really fascinating!"

"He's not that good every day," Jacques said.

"You're not going to tell me that you did all this just to meet me?"

"I won't tell you that, then . . ."

Àvia Maria automatically adjusted the embroidered woolen jacket that she wore over a thin turtleneck sweater. Jacques opened the bulging file folder.

"Monsieur Abad came to see us on three occasions over the past ten years," the owner of the agency finally explained. "At his request, each time we followed his wife for several days. But we never found anything. Could you please close the file again, Jacques? Your colleague is right: there's nothing in it that concerns your current investigation."

Molina obeyed and put the folder on the desk.

"So apart from those two mistakes Christine was a faithful wife?" he asked.

"The absence of proof of adultery is not a proof of fidelity."

"But Abad was reassured each time?"

It was to Sebag that she replied.

"A jealous husband can be reassured only by proving to him that he was right to be jealous."

Gilles saw the justice of that statement. When he discovered Claire's fling, he'd felt, beyond shock and pain, a strange and ineffable feeling of satisfaction.

"Since you didn't succeed in 'reassuring' Abad, mightn't he have gone to another agency?"

"I don't think so."

"Why?"

"I would have been informed of that, believe me."

That answer was enough for Sebag. He rose.

"It was a pleasure."

"For me, too."

He held out his hand. She shook it at length.

"And I hope that the next time you'll call me Àvia Maria."

"Count on it."

This time, he couldn't escape it.

But how could he hang on? The interview with Àvia Maria had emptied him out. And he'd drunk too much table wine at lunch. And also a little too much whiskey afterward. Two swallows straight out of the bottle. No, three. Whatever!

Too much, that was for sure. The problem with alcohol is that you drink when you're sad, but also when you're feeling good. He'd been happy with his performance at the Catalan Detective Agency and wanted to celebrate it!

Now he was paying the price.

But he also had to draw on his resources to put on a good show a little later. The run with Julie was looking like another test. How long could he keep this up?

Wasn't that in fact what he was seeking? To collapse with exhaustion and no longer have the strength to think.

After his interlude in the domain of private detectives, he'd attended Ménard's interrogation of Dominique Barrache. The guard had refused to be assisted by a lawyer and had clammed up. He seemed to fear the examination of his computer. François had found in that the confirmation of his suspicions and had decided to put Barrache in police custody.

Gilles, for his part, had his doubts.

But he also doubted his doubts.

Miraculously, his intuition had returned to him long enough for a music hall number before an old madwoman. It had left him again afterward, frightened by the storm that was raging in his skull. The past was mixed up with the present, a mass of warm air and a mass of cold air, the devastating hurricane that even whiskey could no longer calm. Alcohol aggravated his fatigue and deprived him of the strength necessary for his struggle.

No, he couldn't manage it. He was going to look ridiculous.

That idea made him smile. Reassured him. Or worried him. He wasn't sure which. If the fear of being ridiculous troubled him, that was because he hadn't yet touched bottom . . .

Chapter 31

Julie and Gilles were jogging together around the lake at Villeneuve-de-la-Raho. It was the first time she'd run there. Two reservoirs separated by a dike formed this artificial lake. They had been made in the 1960s to serve as a drinking-water reservoir. At least that's what Gilles had explained to her before shutting up to catch his breath.

He really wasn't in good shape.

Julie told him about her day—while he was recuperating—and then she asked him about the Barrache case. Ménard had ordered a graphological assessment to compare the guard's handwriting with that on the back of a photograph. He'd asked him to write "you know how to reach me" with his left hand and his right hand. Barrache had struggled to write these few words. Either he was pretending or he was virtually illiterate. Ménard had returned to Barrache's home in Saint-Laurent to look for other written documents.

"What about his computer?"

"Elsa is working on it. She's trying to restore recently deleted files. We should have the results tomorrow."

As they talked, Julie was imperceptibly accelerating. Gilles's sentences began to come haltingly again.

"You know . . . that I am . . . a mara . . . thon runner," he groaned. "I have to do . . . at least one lap . . . to warm up."

"How long is the lap?"

"Seven kilometers."

"Ah, yes . . . I didn't know you were so pretentious."

"A pretension is . . . an ambition that you . . . can't attain. I'll get there on . . . the third . . . lap."

"It'll be dark by then."

The setting sun was already lengthening their shadows and reddening the few clouds floating in the sky.

"When you get there . . . it'll be dark," Gilles boasted.

"And you think that's not pretension?"

"No . . . it's worse . . .it's . . . braggadocio."

When they finished the first lap, the sun had disappeared behind Le Canigou. The little beach along the lake was deserted.

"Do many people come here in the summer?" Julie asked.

"In July and August, lots of Catalans leave the seaside to the tourists and prefer to come here. There are a few open-air cafes and bars and under the pine groves there are concrete barbecues where families come for 'grill parties.' Cooking meat over an open fire is one of the Catalans' favorite leisure activities; it's almost a sport, and even sometimes a cultural expression." Julie grasped her left foot and pulled it up along her thigh to stretch her quadriceps.

"It's too late for a second lap, I think."

"Shoot," Gilles said, with an unfeigned frown of satisfaction.

He bent over forward. His hands slowly descended to his feet. Julie, stretching her other leg, asked the question she'd been holding back for a long time.

"Not in the best of shape, huh?"

"I haven't been sleeping very well . . ." he replied, after slowly straightening his back.

"You're probably not taking the right potions . . ."

Gilles put his right leg in front of him and raised his foot toward his ankle. Stretching his calf.

"What do you mean by that?"

"What do you think?"

Julie stretched her left arm over her head and pushed on her elbow with her right hand. Stretching the triceps. Gilles was still limbering the muscles in his calves. His dark eyes were fixed on the horizon of the lake, which would soon disappear into the night.

"I don't understand . . ."

"Of course you do . . ."

Gilles was no longer trying to fool her, only to put off saying it. He was ready.

"I've got a sharp nose, you know," Julie went on. "You smell of alcohol, you're sweating it out, it's emerging from all your pores. If Jacques were here, he'd say that this evening it was more like we were running in the back room of a bistro than out in the country."

Julie surprised herself. She'd already adopted the technique fashionable at the Perpignan police headquarters, namely, attributing to Molina everything one wanted to say that was too crude or vulgar. Fortunately, his broad shoulders could bear all that!

Sebag still hadn't reacted. As if he hadn't heard anything she'd said. But he was still stretching the same calf.

"I hope you have friends to talk to when you're feeling bad," she said.

She stretched her quadriceps again and put her hand on Sebag's shoulder to keep her balance and to establish a kind of connection between them.

"We don't know each other well, and I understand that you may well not want to tell me what's wrong."

She changed legs and put her other hand on Gilles's shoulder. He trembled.

"But I want to tell you a secret, if that's okay with you."

Sebag remained mute for a few long seconds before finally answering:

"I'll be a silent as the tomb."

"You'd better! Otherwise . . . you'll be one—a tomb, that is! Do you remember our conversation that other day in the hospital parking lot, after our interview with Sandrine Valls?"

"Uhh . . . yes."

Gilles didn't seem sure, so she decided to refresh his memory."

"You asked me if I had a boyfriend, and do you remember what I said?"

Sebag frowned, he was making an effort to remember.

"Oh, yes, you said 'almost.'"

"That's right . . ."

"You don't have to, you know."

Their eyes met, were frightened.

"I know. But I want to."

She took a deep breath and leaned harder on his shoulder.

"I don't have a boyfriend but a girlfriend. Her name is Marina and we've been living together for five years. There, I've said it! You're the only one at headquarters who knows."

Their eyes met again, spoke to each other. In Gilles's eyes, Julie saw first surprise, a surprise elicited not by the content of her admission but by the admission itself. Then she discerned an emptiness, a fear, hesitation. Then their color changed, and a surrender emerged in them, little by little.

Gilles's lips parted and as the darkness deepened, he finally spoke.

Chapter 32

He turned over in bed. A cold wind was blowing through the dark little room. He pulled the covers up over his shoulders.

He was having trouble sleeping. His fears were coming back.

His revenge couldn't stop there. Out of the question. There was still so much to do, so many guilty people who deserved punishment . . . And so many victims who needed him to finally reawaken.

The Christmas holidays had served his ends magnificently. He hadn't foreseen that. It was a great surprise, wonderful news. An unexpected gift. Probably the best Christmas present he'd ever received. He almost burst out laughing but restrained himself.

This wasn't the time.

The police had made some connections and drawn some parallels he hadn't anticipated. However, that Lieutenant Ménard hadn't seemed so swift. His colleague was more alarming, but fortunately this Gilles Sebag wasn't as good as he was supposed to be.

He was going to have to play a closer game than he'd expected. He didn't want to get caught. Not now. It was too early. Much too early. He hadn't finished. The Eye had other ongoing cases that had to be wrapped up.

He stretched out on his back. Put his hands on his protuberant belly. Listened to his breathing.

Despite his workouts—three times a week, on average—he was getting heavier. Inexorably. His wife had already reproached him for that, before. But what could he do? He spent too much time in front of screens.

He put these pointless thoughts out of his mind. He had to remain focused. His mission occupied his mind, and that was as it should be.

Everything was ready for the next step. He wasn't going to stop when things were going so well. For months, he'd been gathering data, keeping an eye out for suspicious behavior and faces, comparing, cross-checking. It was an enormous task to know everything. Everything about everything . . .

All while remaining invisible.

Now that he was reaping the fruit of this labor, he couldn't stop there. And especially not let *himself* be stopped. In any case, the police had nothing on him.

Absolutely nothing.

He felt a kind of shiver. His broadly deployed antennae were picking up vague waves that made him optimistic. The fetid breath of a new drama was floating over Perpignan.

It would happen tomorrow. Tomorrow at the latest.

Chapter 33

Sebag lowered the sun visor. He was driving on the fast road to Canet and the sunlight reflected off the sea was burning his retinas. As he passed by the Europa swimming pool he vowed to finally take up swimming. The outside Olympic pool was one of the few in France that was open year-round, and he had never really taken advantage of that. Claire, on the other hand, went there regularly. One year, in February, she had even sunburned her back.

Claire . . .

He had to not think about her, above all not think about her.

His discussion with Julie the day before had done him good. He'd slept well. For once. And without having drunk any more.

Gilles hadn't seen it coming. When his colleague had begun talking to him about alcohol, he'd suddenly stiffened, closed up like a clam: who did she think she was, this girl, to preach at him like that? And then there had been that warmth on his shoulder, the trust, and that magnificent gift. Julie's secret. Like a hand held out to him from beyond modesty. He'd lost himself for a moment in the sweetness of her bright eyes and had no longer perceived anything but their breathing in unison. His lines of defense collapsed. He'd been keeping too many things bottled up inside himself, and for too long.

At Canet-Plage, the market was in full swing, despite the

early hour. At this time of year, the seaside resort was inhabited mainly by retirees. They went out early to do their shopping and to warm their sagging skins and old bones in the first rays of the sun. Afterward, they walked along the beach promenade, alone or in couples, a loving dog sometimes replacing a deceased spouse.

Sebag parked in an underground parking garage. Made to hold the summer crowds, it was now almost empty, and he found a spot right near the pedestrian exit. He sat down on the Esplanade de la Méditerranée and ordered an espresso. He was early. With his face offered up to the sun's caress, he sipped this first coffee of the day. To the south, the Albères range, the last mountainous rampart before Spain, prevented a foamy tide from spreading over Roussillon. Everywhere else, the sky was a sovereign blue.

Sebag closed his eyes. Take advantage of the present, savor every happy moment, and stop thinking about the past and making plans for the future. Those were the rules he had to follow.

Nathalie Llop soon joined him. She was a small, plump brunette. She sat down at his side rather than across from him: she, too, wanted to enjoy the sun and the panorama. Sebag began by asking her about her relations with Didier Valls, her colleague and confidant.

"We liked each other . . . we were friends. There was never any ambiguity between us. I'd known him for only ten years, but it was as if we'd grown up together. Or been brother and sister."

Nathalie and Didier often lunched together. Their conversations resembled the content of the text messages he'd read: they talked about everything and nothing, a little about their jobs, a lot about their lives and their problems.

"Didier was a chronic depressive, he was anxious. He was very fragile psychologically."

She was surprised and pained to learn of the *corbeau*'s existence.

"I thought we told each other everything! I knew that he had doubts about his wife's love for him, but I didn't know that he'd learned about this relationship with another man."

"A platonic relationship," Sebag added.

She shrugged.

"What difference does that make since she no longer loved him and wanted to leave him?"

"For her, it's important."

"If that's true, then I understand him."

She stopped a moment and then went on before Sebag had asked another question.

"In any case, it was clear that such revelations would make him do something foolish. I think that in a less depressive period, he might have been aggressive toward her. But here he turned his violence against himself."

"Why didn't he tell you about it, do you think?'

"I have no idea. Really, I have no idea."

She took out a Kleenex and sniffled.

"If he'd talked to me about it, I could have prevented him from doing something so stupid."

Sebag mentioned the guard's dismissal. Nathalie remembered having learned about it from labor union handouts. She'd also read the management's reply in an account of a meeting of the employees' delegates.

"Didier hadn't ever talked to you about it?"

"No."

She'd poked her nose toward her coffee cup as she answered. Gilles waited.

"I tried to talk with him about it on several occasions, but he always refused to discuss it."

Sebag didn't conceal his surprise.

"I don't understand. Why did you ask Didier about this?

It was Abad who was at the origin of the dismissal, wasn't it?"

She ran her finger over a carefully plucked eyebrow bisected by a small scar.

"There was always something odd about that business . . ."

Nathalie fell silent again. She stopped massaging her eyebrow. Her hand slipped through her hair and stopped at the barrette that held it back. Sebag calmly urged her to go on.

"What was it?"

"Dominique Barrache knew Stéphane and Didier. They played pool together. And I think they played for money. I believe there had been debt problems among them."

Sebag held his breath. The guard had just moved from being the only suspect to suspect number one. A semantic detail, but a major advance in a police investigation.

His investigation had just taken a giant step forward. François Ménard should have been delighted, but his joy was tempered by pique. Once again it was that damned Gilles who was the source of the most recent advance. A prodigious stroke of luck . . .

They were back in the house in Saint-Laurent-de-la-Salanque. He, Gilles, and Jacques. With Barrache, obviously. They had obtained a search warrant from the prosecutor and carried out a full search. But they found nothing. Not a single handwritten note with writing resembling that of the *corbeau*; no burner phone, no compromising photo in the numerous albums, nothing but pictures of flowers, animals, and landscapes. Not even newspaper clippings that might suggest that the guard had followed closely the misadventures of his former billiard partners.

"You won't find anything here!" Barrache moaned.

He was standing in the main room, his hands cuffed behind his back, and only occasionally raised his head.

"Oh, yeah . . . You already threw everything away?" Molina barked in his face. "You know that that's a kind of confession, don't you?"

Barrache opened his eyes wide with fright. Molina was doing a great job of playing the bulldog's role. Ménard broke in:

"Why didn't you tell us from the outset that you played pool with Valls and Abad?"

"Because I was sure you'd take me away . . ."

"Did you think we'd never find out?"

"I hoped . . . I've just found a job! It's not exactly ideal to be in police custody while you're in the trial period!"

"Bravo, you succeeded!" Molina growled. "You bet that we were dopes and you lost. Now be a good sport and tell us everything. Why were you so angry at these two guys?"

"I . . . wasn't angry with them."

"That's right, go on taking us for fools. Abad and Valls got you fired and you gave them chocolates for Christmas, is that it?"

Molina slowly rolled up his sleeves and gazed down on the suspect from his 6'3" height. Barrache shriveled. His life-buoy waist doubled in volume.

"Yes, of course I was angry with them! What I meant was that I wasn't angry with them to the point of sending them anonymous letters. How would I have known about their women?"

"That's exactly what we'd like you to tell us. Were you out of a job for long?"

"Four months."

"That gave you quite a lot of free time to spy on their women. It's not very hard, after all, to trail two women in a hurry to go get laid by their lovers: when they've got hot pants they're less vigilant, right?"

Barrache looked desperately at his feet. Molina crossed his arms over his chest.

"I asked you a question. It wasn't very hard, was it?"

"I didn't take those photos," Barrache stammered.

"You shouldn't be ashamed of them, they're good photos. Professional work!"

"It wasn't me!"

His tone was becoming plaintive. Molina clipped him under the chin to make him look up.

"Don't tell me you're going to start blubbering now!"

He turned to his colleagues.

"The guard's trade is going to hell. They're hiring even wimps."

Jacques grabbed Barrache's chin and forced him to hold his head up.

"You must have been delighted when you heard that Valls had committed suicide. And what about Abad? I hope that there you felt some remorse, all the same, when you found out that he'd killed his old lady. She hadn't done anything to you, Christine . . ."

Since Barrache still wasn't answering, Molina pinched his cheek hard. The guard tried to resist.

"But . . . you don't have the right to hit me . . ."

"I didn't hit you."

Molina gave him a resounding slap on the left cheek.

"There, now I've hit you. You see, it's not the same thing. Mustn't confuse that," he said, giving him another pinch, "with this."

Molina raised his arm.

"Take it easy," Ménard said.

Molina lowered his arm. He had a carnivorous smile on his lips.

"Where was I? Oh, yes . . . I was saying that you're in deep shit. We have two dead bodies on our hands. And in both cases we've found photos. You're a photographer—a pretty good one—and you had it in for the two guys responsible for these deaths. Moreover, you're a wimp, a coward."

He raised his hand again, ready to strike. Barrache ducked his head.

"You see . . . You're a coward. A real man would have settled his scores directly with Abad and Valls. But a coward prefers to attack their wives and send anonymous letters."

"I didn't do that, I swear it, I didn't do it."

"You're really getting on my nerves, you know that?"

He hit him again. On the right cheek this time. Barrache shot the other policemen looks begging them to intervene. Ménard decided it was time to move to the following stage. Molina had tenderized the meat enough.

"Why don't you go have a smoke, Jacques, just to relax a little."

Molina pretended to think about it and then went down the stairway. Downstairs, he didn't fail to slam the door. Ménard took the cuffs off Barrache and asked him to sit down.

"What exactly happened between you, Abad, and Valls?"

The guard collapsed on his chair and rubbed his wrists.

"Well, as you know, we played pool. Once or twice a week. But . . . in fact we played for money, and I often won. I'm not good at many things, but I'm not too bad at pool. One time when I won a lot of money, Steph accused me of cheating. Nonsense! How can you cheat at pool?"

"You said 'a lot of money.' How much?"

"Thirty-two hundred euros. For me that's a lot—more than two months' salary. That was last summer, and since then, Steph no longer spoke to me, and neither did Didier. Didier always followed . . . At first I didn't understand that Steph was really mad at me, I thought he'd get over it. It was when he started waging war on me at work that I realized."

"And so he ended up getting you fired."

"Yes."

"So you had every reason to be mad at them."

"Yes, that's true. And . . ."

Ménard held his breath. He sensed a confession coming. He watched Sebag, who didn't budge.

"One evening I went to Pollestres. Steph always left his car outside. I punctured two of his tires."

"Are you kidding me?" Ménard said, annoyed.

"Not at all, I swear!"

As he said that, Barrache had glanced behind him in the direction of the stairway.

"If I'd had the idea of spying on their women, maybe I would have done that and I would have snitched on them, I don't know . . . but I didn't have that idea."

"Are you sorry about that?" Sebag asked.

"Yes and no."

Barrache even gave a half-smile.

"It was a pretty good idea, I think, although a little devious all the same. I don't think the guy who did that thought it would go so far. That's what I mean when I say that I'm not sorry. I didn't want Didier to die and still less Madame Abad . . ."

"Did you know her?"

"No, not at all."

"What about Sandrine Valls?"

"I didn't know her, either."

"Do you have any idea who might have done this?"

Ménard shot Sebag a dark look. His colleague was stealing the show, as usual, by pretending to be sympathetic.

"You believe me? You think it was somebody else?"

"I don't believe anything, I'm searching. You are aware that you're our only connection between these two cases?"

The guard tilted his head to one side.

"Then continue to investigate because I don't know who could have done this, but I'm sure of one thing: it wasn't me. I swear it to you."

Sitting in the backseat next to Barrache, Ménard didn't say a word. Sebag didn't dare turn around, he knew he had annoyed him. He was sorry about that. But . . . on reflection, he didn't give a tinker's damn.

His mobile phone rang. Elsa Moulin. She had probably finished examining Barrache's computer and was coming to report. And he was the one she called. It was enough to completely exasperate François. He turned on the speaker. Molina, who was driving, tilted his head to the right to hear better.

"I didn't find anything that might interest you, anything that seems connected in any way with your investigation. Not even among the recently deleted documents."

"Does that mean that there isn't anything or that you didn't necessarily succeed in restoring everything?"

"I found no trace of any particular procedure of erasure. Like everyone else, your suspect puts documents he no longer wants in the trash, and empties it from time to time. And there was no major erasure over the past few days."

Sebag turned to the guard. He did not seem particularly relieved.

"But you have something else to tell me, don't you, Elsa?"

The three seconds of silence that followed concealed a smile.

"It's impossible to hide anything from you."

Barrache's face fell. He was more than embarrassed, he was devastated.

"May I speak freely?" Elsa asked.

"Around me are François, Jacques, and the main person concerned."

"Ah . . . I'm not sure . . ."

Ménard sat straight up on his seat and gripped the back of Gilles's seat.

"Go on, go ahead, we're listening."

"Well, if you insist . . . I found, obviously, all kinds of

photos, hundreds, even thousands of them, maybe, mainly pictures of landscapes, flowers, and animals . . . but not only that."

"Pictures of his children as well?" Ménard suggested.

"Of course, but not only! I understand why Monsieur Barrache really didn't want us to inspect this computer."

"This is getting interesting," Molina remarked with amusement. "Tell us more."

"I prefer to let you guess."

Sebag knew that the question was addressed particularly to him.

"Is that a challenge?"

"Affirmative. If I lose, I'll take you out to lunch."

"How much time do I have?"

"Thirty seconds, is that enough?"

"OK."

Barrache buried his face in his hands, which Ménard had cuffed again. He was trembling. The first idea that came to Sebag's mind was that the guard was a closet pedophile, but he rejected that idea immediately: that was a crime. Elsa wouldn't have made a game out of that.

Sebag thought. Contemplated the guard's sparse head of hair. Remembered the atmosphere of sadness and loneliness that reigned in his home. The children's room: an almost-empty armoire, two beds carefully made, hoping for a miracle, posters of singers on the walls, with their smiles frozen for "poster-ity." Or for "posternity." He closed his eyes. Saw the guard again standing in the main room: his calm air of a docile sheep, his unevenly shaven, vague beard, his belly-buoy and his short, skinny legs.

The difficulties Gilles was going through made him indifferent to certain things, and ultrasensitive to others. He was a sponge, an enormous sponge, absorbing everything around him. And what he grasped of this invisible world passed through his brain even less than before: it was in his flesh that he felt the pain of tragedies.

Not very focused on his investigations, he was missing—and he sensed this—elementary facts. But when he needed his intuition to play a game, it answered the call. In spite of himself.

He was going to find the answer. He perceived a quivering that he knew very well.

Elsa's tone and concern, Barrache's palpable embarrassment . . . There was hardly any doubt. She had found porn photos or even videos on the computer. He mentally reviewed what he knew about the options offered on certain sites, set aside the lesbians (too classical), hesitated an instant regarding big black men with mammoth dicks (too depressing), and ended up making his choice. By crossing what he believed might be Barrache's taste with what was likely to make Elsa smile, he thought he'd found the solution.

He looked at Barrache's resigned silhouette and felt an immense compassion for this loser, an abandoned father and an illiterate guard. Whether or not he was the author of the anonymous letters, he didn't deserve to be humiliated this way.

"Sorry, I've lost."

And he hung up.

CHAPTER 34

Superintendent Castello was examining the arabesques drawn by Dominique Barrache under Ménard's dictation. A "t" without a right angle or verticality, a "z" as rounded as the "s," "o"s that looked less like a soccer ball than a rugby ball, and moreover placed crookedly on the turf before a penalty kick.

"Is he really illiterate?"

Although the superintendent had addressed him, Sebag let François answer.

"He claims that he has lost the habit of holding a pen and now writes only on his computer."

"Mademoiselle Moulin brought me the result of her examination. It's true that in the texts she found, he makes an enormous number of mistakes. Sometimes it's hardly even phonetic. Some sentences have to be read aloud to be understood."

"We can't exclude the hypothesis that he's trying to fool us," Ménard replied. "The *corbeau* necessarily spent a long time preparing his act. Even the texts full of errors in his digital documents might have been written to deceive us."

Castello frowned.

"You mean, including the awkward, touching letters he wrote to his wife and children?"

"I haven't read them, but why not?"

Castello put the sheet of paper back in the file folder lying open in front of him.

"Do we have clear proof against him?"

"No," Ménard acknowledged.

"Concordant evidence?"

"His new employer had him work several nights in a row in the building of the Dames de France, on the Place de Catalogne. That's downtown, not far from the area where the *corbeau* made most of his phone calls."

"Not very far . . ." the superintendent repeated. "That's not much. We may have arrested him too quickly."

"I was hoping to make him crack."

"It's easier to make a suspect confess when you have solid charges to bring against him."

"Abad received photos to inform him of his wife's infidelity, and maybe also phone calls; as for Valls, he received anonymous text messages and maybe photos. That can't be a coincidence, and Barrache is our only point in common between the two men. He has a mobile phone and moreover he's a good photographer."

"And on the psychological level, is he a good suspect?"

Castello had deliberately turned away from Ménard to address this question to Sebag.

"We can't exclude the possibility that he's an excellent actor," Gilles said prudently.

"In short, you don't 'feel' that he's guilty?"

Sebag gave a sideways glance at François before answering.

"I have trouble seeing him in this role, he's more of a good guy. And if he was the *corbeau*, he'd be racked by remorse."

"That could be just a defense mechanism," Ménard suggested. "He refuses to see himself as guilty, and therefore plays the innocent perfectly."

Castello jerked his chin toward Sebag to ask his opinion.

"Everything is possible . . ."

"But we agree that it can't be a coincidence?" Castello insisted. "And that there is only one *corbeau*?"

Sebag silently acquiesced. Ménard seized the opportunity.

"And that *corbeau* is Barrache. He's our only suspect, and so it must be him!"

The superintendent let a few seconds pass before concluding:

"Indicting someone because we don't have another possible perpetrator is one of the primary causes of judicial errors. You still have twenty-four hours to find me something solid against this guard. Afterward we'll be obliged to let him go. I can't imagine transferring him to the prosecutor with so little evidence."

"Bring him to me here right now and I'll make him talk."

Molina was pacing up and down in the office like a caged animal. He had eaten only a sandwich and was starving to death. Impatient to have it out.

"On the condition, of course, that this Barrache has something to confess."

"To question him again, it would be better for you to be calmer," François Ménard advised. "This morning, you were pushing the borderline."

"I played my role."

"Yes, but it was borderline all the same."

The two policemen looked at Sebag. He agreed:

"The second slap was borderline."

"OK, if you're all against me, you can just play the bad cop next time."

He smiled. He had an idea.

"I'm going to develop a new technique for making suspects talk."

He waited for his colleagues to give in to curiosity. Ménard remained impassive, but Sebag played along and asked him to say more.

"The next time, I'm going to eat a plate of aioli before I question someone. Blowing breath loaded with garlic into a suspect's nose is still not considered an act of torture by the

European Court, and yet, in comparison to that, cattle prods and waterboarding are like a spring breeze compared to the *tramontane*."

He roared with laughter and his colleagues were kind enough to echo him. At that moment Elsa Moulin walked into the office.

"I see that you're having lots of fun in here."

She embraced the three men.

"You owe me a meal," she told Sebag.

"Not sure about that . . ."

She wrinkled her forehead.

"I don't understand! You said yourself that you'd lost."

"I didn't want to hurt Barrache by revealing all that right in front of him."

The young woman looked at the file folder she'd given Castello and which now lay on Sebag's desk.

"It's easy, now . . ."

"We haven't opened it yet."

Molina and Ménard confirmed what he'd said.

"OK, the game continues, then."

For the second time in twenty-four hours, Sebag found himself in the position of the divine wizard. He looked straight into Elsa's eyes and reviewed the hypotheses he had rejected the day before. The same tonalities rang in his head. And rang right.

"I think Barrache is a lover of photos of 'mature' women, as they're called."

He looked for a more precise answer on his colleague's face. He found it.

"Older women with big breasts."

Elsa remained speechless. Molina opened the file, took some photos, and swore.

"Ah, damn, the asshole!"

Sebag smiled. If someday he were to leave the police, maybe

he could have a career on the stage. Although . . . There were events in his life that it had taken him a long time to discover.

"Decidedly, you'll always astonish me," Elsa said. "So I'm the one who owes you a meal."

"Sorry."

"I'm not. I'd have had lunch with you anyway. In either case, I won."

This little game with Elsa, this pleasant flirting, flattered Sebag. It restored his confidence in himself. His confidence in life.

"You're too cute."

"Not enough yet, I'm afraid."

Jacques laid the photos on the desk one by one.

"Well, human nature is curious all the same," he said philosophically. "A guy can write sweet words to his wife and then console himself by beating off to photos of sixty-year-old women giving blow jobs."

After a short pause he added, very prosaically:

"I hope, Elsa, that you put gloves on to examine this computer, because between tears, snot, and sperm, Barrache's keyboard must be one helluva nest of germs. Just imagine the orgy of bacteria between the keys. You could pick up the clap just surfing on Google."

Two hours later, Molina was racing down the stairway, crossing the headquarters' lobby, and bursting out the door. He finally found Gilles smoking a cigarette in the parking lot.

"Come on, let's go! There's an emergency."

Molina opened the door of his car and sat down at the wheel. With exasperating slowness, Gilles crushed out his cigarette and got in alongside his partner.

"Hurry up! There's a nut handing out mail in the street and threatening passersby. There's going to be a ruckus!"

"He's handing out mail? Flyers, you mean?"

"I don't know. Ripoll had several phone calls at the switchboard. He told me it was mail."

Sebag opened the glove box and found a pair of handcuffs that he slipped into one of his pockets. He put the revolving light on the roof of the car while Molina turned on the siren and headed into the traffic.

"At last report, he was at the foot of the Castillet."

Less than a minute later, they arrived in front of the ancient city gate. There was a crowd on the square. People were talking and gesturing. Gilles got out of the car. A lady holding a crying baby in her arms spoke to him:

"He went that way, down Boulevard Clémenceau. Look, he gave me this. He's really not OK, he scared the baby!"

Sebag got back in the car and looked at the paper he'd been given. It was a message sent by a certain Marie-Isabelle Casty to a certain Alain Guibert. It read: "I need to feel your hands on my body, I desire you, I love you."

"Ah, OK. So it's about sex again . . ." Molina said.

"We can assume that it's not the Marie-Isabelle in question who's distributing these messages, and if you want my opinion, it's not the Guibert in question, either. There's another character involved here."

"In love, uneven numbers are always a problem. In short, it's another . . . another cuckold who's going through a crisis! Clearly, there's an epidemic. At this rate, we're going to be able establish a specialized brigade."

He'd hesitated to use the word "cuckold," because he feared that that word could hurt Gilles. But since he wasn't supposed to know, he'd decided to act "as if."

On Boulevard Clémenceau, they spotted stunned passersby looking backward with concern. They had only to follow the stream to find a giant in a tank top handing out flyers to anyone who was willing to take them. He was taking them out of a big rigid plastic bag of the kind found in shopping centers.

"I know this guy," Sebag said.

"A pal of yours?"

"Not really. Well . . . I don't think so. I've seen him before, that's all. But I don't remember when or where."

Molina slammed on the brakes as they came up to the man, who stopped and pivoted toward their unmarked car. His blond hair flew around his bull-like shoulders.

"This isn't going to be easy," Jacques predicted, putting on the hand brake. Let me handle it this time, I'm tired of you taking all the credit. I want to be a hero, too."

"Gladly; he's too big for me. But I promise to bring you oranges at the hospital."

"Thanks for your confidence."

Molina got out of the car and put on his "Police" armband. The giant contemptuously sized him up before turning to Sebag, who was approaching.

"I know you," he said. "I never forget a face."

Jacques kept his eyes on the man, but on his right he saw Gilles nod. So they did know each other. Introductions were made, and they could move on to other matters.

The giant handed Gilles a flyer.

"Here, look at this. One message among so many others. This one is for a certain Miquel. Miquel Rossetto. A lawyer by trade."

Sebag grabbed the flyer but paid it no attention. He folded it and put it in the inside pocket of his jacket.

"How come you're still outside?"

"She didn't file a complaint and the judge was nice to me. He charged me with assault but he let me go on condition that I don't try to see her again."

"And on condition that you behave yourself, right?"

The man scratched his chin and chuckled.

"Uhh . . . I don't remember that part."

"You've been drinking again, too."

"I don't remember that, either."

His red eyes full of defiance constituted a sufficient response.

"You're going to have to come with us," Sebag said.

"Why?"

"You're being aggressive and you're scaring people."

"I'm not hurting them . . ."

Molina had observed the exchange without saying anything, and he forced himself to step in. Otherwise Gilles was going to steal the scene again.

"People don't give a shit about your problems with love or sex. They're just quietly walking along, doing their errands, and you're bothering them. Moreover, you're making kids cry. That's called 'disturbing the peace.' If you don't come with us voluntarily, you're going to find yourself behind bars this time."

"I'm going to come, guys, don't get upset."

The man's mouth twisted and his eyes scornfully challenged Molina.

"In just a minute . . . I haven't finished yet, I've still got flyers to distribute."

And he left them standing there while he took off in the direction of the Place de Catalogne.

"He's defying us!" Jacques grumbled. "Hey there, Hulk, we're talking to you . . ."

The man ignored him and continued to walk away.

"Hang on, Gilles, we're going to have some fun!"

He made a megaphone with his hands and shouted:

"Hey, cuckold, you're the one I'm talking to!"

The colossus reacted as if he'd been lashed with a whip. He turned on his heel and walked toward Jacques.

"What'd you say?"

"You heard me. If you didn't want me to call you that, you shouldn't have been handing out flyers all over Perpignan. By the way, is your Marie a good fuck?"

The man put his bag down in a doorway and then stood right in front of Jacques. He flexed his muscles underneath his tank top.

"Goddammit, you're going to pay for all the others. I'm going to rip your guts out." Molina shifted his weight from one foot to the other to be sure he was ready. Without taking his eyes off his adversary, he murmured to Gilles:

"I'm counting on you . . ."

He said a silent prayer. They'd been working together long enough for Gilles to know what to do. The question was whether he was focused enough. He saw the guy's eyes turn slightly away. Gilles had just taken out his handcuffs.

"Here . . . You'd be better off putting them on yourself."

Molina saw the cuffs leave Gilles's hands and fly toward the giant's face. Instinctively, the giant tried to catch them. That was the moment! Molina jumped, grabbed the raised arm—an enormous arm, thick as a tree trunk—pulled it back with all his strength and twisted it. He heard a cry. The pain forced the man to drop a knee to the ground. Sebag picked up the handcuffs that had fallen on the asphalt and attached the man's hands behind his back. It was over.

"I see that you haven't lost your reflexes," Gilles congratulated his partner.

"Rugby is more useful than marathons in this kind of situation."

"That's for sure . . . But don't tell me that you used armlocks in scrums?"

"No. That was prohibited in my time. But we could still call our adversaries cuckolds!"

Sebag didn't reply and Jacques wondered if he hadn't gone too far in acting "as if." He'd never been good with subtleties. He forced the giant to get up and pushed him toward the car while his teammate opened the door. The guy grimaced with pain as he bent down to get in. His shoulder was probably dislocated. As he passed by, Jacques gave him a knock on the head. He didn't flinch. Now he was as docile as a lamb.

Molina leaned on the roof of the car.

"That is the kind of talent that got me into the police," he explained.

"I suspected that it wasn't your scores in general culture . . ."

Gilles might be upset by his personal problems, but he was always quick with repartee.

"You'd better behave yourself if you don't want me to give you the same treatment," Molina shot back.

"I may not be a rugby player, or a wrestler, but you'd find it hard to do the same thing to me."

"You want to bet?"

"First you'd have to catch me. If you're capable of running forty-two kilometers at twelve kilometers an hour . . ."

"OK, you're right, I've lost in advance," Jacques conceded.

He sat down behind the wheel of the car and they took their package back to headquarters. The streets of Perpignan had already recovered their peace and quiet.

Chapter 35

He smoked too much.

That was obvious, but what could be done about it? He also drank too much and thought too much. Far too much. A constant flow of thoughts. His ideas resembled an impetuous mountain torrent that could be diverted, tempered, and deflected by obstacles, but never stopped.

He was who he was, after all! With his defects and his qualities. He had to live with them! On the whole, other people seemed to manage, but for him it was far more difficult.

He would have so much liked to be different . . . Better. More. And especially greater.

`His cigarette was almost finished. He took out another and lit it with the butt of the first one. Going out for a smoke was the only way he'd found to escape the interrogation of Jean-Paul Casty. The wine-soaked brute that he'd once run into in the offices of the night watch, the one who kept screaming that his wife was a "slut."

He tried to stop the flow of his thoughts. To find another subject. For example, this evening's dinner. What should he take? Flowers, a bottle of wine, dessert? No, not dessert . . . Without having made that suggestion in advance, it was impolite. Usually he let Claire handle good manners. But this evening, for the first time in at least twenty years—maybe the first time in his life—he was going out unaccompanied by his wife.

He felt a hand on his shoulder.

"Have you got a fag for me?"

Gilles handed his pack to Molina.

"Everything OK?"

"Hunky-dory. But we're going to take Casty to the emergency room. His shoulder hurts, and he's no softy. I think it's really dislocated."

"We?"

"Don't worry! I asked Lambert to go with me. He's finishing up the statement and then we'll leave."

Gilles gazed at his teammate. Unusual behavior. Why had he asked for Thierry's help when they would usually have handled Casty together? Had Jacques guessed his hesitations?

" Jean-Paul's a nice guy, after all."

"You think?" Gilles said, surprised.

"His wife gave him a hard time . . . I don't think you want to examine all the flyers we've collected, but if you want a summary, I counted almost three hundred e-mails, handwritten letters, and even printed copies of SMSes. She kept everything. And over the past ten years I found about fifteen different correspondents Marie-Isabelle Casty had a romantic or sexual relationship with. There's a broad range of ages, occupations, social circles and nationalities. In the list, I even found a former municipal councilor, a restaurant owner I know, and a guy I went to middle school with. Frédéric Rofé. He dreamed of working in film. He used to bore us half to death talking about it! Now he's working in the Social Security office. Well . . . when I say he's working, you know what I mean!"

Molina took a drag on his cigarette. On the avenue, the streetlights were coming on one after the other.

"Marie's affairs seem to have been romantic as much as they were sexual. She talks about love and tenderness most of the time. That said, I have to admit that sometimes it's pretty raw, all the same! Despite his bull's shoulders and neck, Jean-Paul has a stag's horns on his forehead."

"And she kept it all, that's crazy . . ."

"Broads . . . what do you expect, even when they've got hot pants, they remain romantic."

Sebag thought about Claire. He knew enough to know that she had undoubtedly deleted messages as she went along, in order to avoid taking any risks. But what feelings did she have at the time when she erased her lover's sweet words? Probably sadness and regret.

Molina was still talking and Gilles made an effort to put the fragments back together. Molina wasn't giving him a summary . . . He was explaining that now and then Jean-Paul had discovered some of his wife's cheating, and that each time, after getting furiously angry and slapping her around, he had accepted the situation. Until he got his hands on all the correspondence and learned the extent of his misfortune.

"It doesn't look like it at first, but hey! Basically, he's just a big teddy bear . . . A giant's physique but a soft heart. He wept like a baby as he told me about his wife. If you want my opinion, loving to that point is no longer love."

He threw his cigarette butt on the ground and crushed it out.

"So, that's not all, but there's likely to be a line at the emergency room. I hope Thierry has finished because now we've got to get going."

Sebag went to a nearby wineseller. He'd made up his mind. Giving a bottle of local wine to people who had recently settled in Northern Catalonia wasn't such a bad idea. On the advice of a professional, he chose a Tautavel from the Domaine Fontanel, a well-known wine at an affordable price.

Back at headquarters, he made a tour of the people held in police custody. Dominique Barrache occupied the third cell. Curled up under a moth-eaten blanket, he was sleeping like a log on the metal cot attached to the wall. Every time he took a breath, his lips opened to let a bubble of air pass. For a long time, Sebag watched him through the cell's glass wall. One conclusion was forced upon him: they had to find another suspect as soon as possible.

When he returned to the lobby, Officer Ripoll approached him.

"Ah . . . Lieutenant. A lady wants to speak to you."

Sebag looked at his watch.

"Is it urgent?"

"Yes, please," a voice behind him said.

He turned around. A woman was coming toward him. Tall, blonde, plump, with brilliant blue eyes that elegantly illuminated her square, almost too masculine face.

"You are?"

"Marie-Isabelle Casty."

Sebag couldn't help but look her over. Under her brightly colored overcoat, she was wearing a low-necked blue dress over tanned skin, despite the season. One sleeve of her coat was empty; Marie-Isabelle's arm was in a sling across her breast.

"I'm sorry, Madame, you've been misinformed. It's my colleague, Lieutenant Molina, who's handling your husband's case."

Officer Ripoll's loud voice resounded in the lobby:

"Jacques has gone to the hospital with the individual in question. You're the only one left, Lieutenant Sebag."

Gilles sighed.

"OK. Follow me."

He led her into one of the three offices adjacent to the lobby, offices intended for filing simple complaints and holding impromptu meetings.

The inspector showed her into a small room that smelled like sweat and fear. He pointed to a chair. She sat down, he remained standing.

"I'm listening."

He was receiving her against his will and made no effort to

conceal it. She felt judged and immediately condemned. She had repeated over and over in her head the main lines of what she wanted to say but could no longer find the words to begin. She ran her tongue over the corner of her lip that was still marked by a scar and took a deep breath. It pulled on her broken rib and made her wince.

"How is Jean-Paul?"

"He's in the emergency room. A dislocated shoulder, apparently."

"And . . . psychologically, how is he?"

"It was my colleague who talked with him."

"But I was told that you took part in his arrest?"

"True. But we didn't have time to talk. It was pretty violent."

"I don't doubt it," she smiled, holding her wounded arm. "Jean-Paul is hot-blooded."

The policemen did not reply. He looked at her, his face closed. She mustn't let the silence last. It would be too hard afterward.

"Do you think he'll go to prison?"

"That seems to me inevitable. He should have gone to prison the first time."

"I spoke to the judge to spare him that."

"And is that the point of your visit here this evening as well?"

"Among other things . . ."

"Then you're wasting your time: we can no longer let him go, he's too dangerous."

"I hurt him so much . . ."

The sentence had come out all by itself. Too quickly. It fell flat.

"He hurt you, too . . ."

She almost thanked the policeman for that formulation but she understood that it was more an escape than an expression of empathy.

"What I did is unpardonable, isn't it?"

"I don't know."

"Does that mean yes?"

"That's not for me to say, I'm just a policeman."

"But you're a man, too."

"Inside police headquarters, I'm a cop before anything else."

The inspector didn't want to be maneuvered onto that terrain. She decided to push him.

"And I'm a slut?"

"Please, Madame Casty."

"That's what you think, isn't it?"

"As a cop, I don't think anything on that subject because you are not accused of any offense or crime. What you did does not fall within the jurisdiction of the courts."

"But it does fall within the jurisdiction of morality, is that it? When a man seduces a women, even if he's married, people say he's a Don Juan. These days, when a woman acts in the same way, whether she's married or not, she's a slut."

The inspector crossed his arms to conceal his embarrassment. She had scored a point, she saw that in his eyes, which had grown gentler. But he persisted in his evasion.

"I have not really understood the point of your visit. You came to plead your husband's cause or . . . yours."

He'd said that in a neutral, almost sweet tone, without true malice but with a ruthless pertinence. The words she'd prepared stuck in her throat. Even though she had so many things to say.

She would have liked to explain that she needed these adventures to be happy, that she needed these men to look at her and needed their caresses to feel beautiful. Yes, she had come to plead his case, she hadn't realized that but that was in fact what it was about. She had consulted psychotherapists, she had tried to understand herself. They hadn't judged her, that was normal, it was their profession, their way of earning a living, but they hadn't helped her, either. Hadn't cured her. She would have liked a man to understand her for once, so that she might someday be able to pardon herself. This cop was so frigid in his politeness . . . She would have liked to scream at him that she couldn't do without the first times—the first desire, the first rendezvous, the first kiss, the first orgasm—that she loved men, their warmth, their intimacy, their tenderness, that she liked more than anything those moments after sex when they told her their life stories, their passions, where they finally revealed all their weaknesses as well as their strengths. She would have liked to shout from the rooftops that all that was not a matter of sex, but of thrills, of life and freedom . . .

And where was Jean-Paul in all that? Jean-Paul was her mooring point, her beacon, her rock. Without him, she would drift aimlessly, driven by her wishes, her desires. Without him, she'd be alone. She loved him. Despite herself, despite everything, despite them.

Who could understand her someday? She would never be anything but a slut!

Silence had fallen in the room. This cop wouldn't understand her. Any more than the others. Even her lovers hadn't understood her.

She thrust her hand in her handbag, seized the envelope, and then changed her mind. What good would it do to hand over the photos it contained? In the end it really didn't matter.

A mobile phone beeped. It wasn't hers. The policeman uncrossed his arms.

"I'm sorry, it's late and I still have work to do," he announced. "Thank you for coming to speak with us, Madame Casty. If you need anything else, don't hesitate to contact my colleague, Lieutenant Molina. As I told you, it was mainly he who talked with your husband."

She rose without a word and left police headquarters. It was time for her to go back to the room in the women's shelter where social services had sent her. There she would find other battered women. They were real victims. Not sluts . . .

Gilles emerged exhausted from this interview and he waited until he had left headquarters to read Claire's SMS. She was just asking him to buy bread if he came by the house before going out for the evening. He replied that yes, he needed to take a shower and change his clothes, and that he would buy bread on the way if there was any left. There was nothing exciting in that, much less romantic, but Claire had shared messages like that one with no one else, he was sure of that. Should he be happy about it? He no longer knew. If little everyday habits constituted a couple's DNA, didn't that explain the significance of parallel love affairs?

Chapter 36

"I'm delighted to finally meet you. Julie has told me so much about you."

"Good things, I hope."

"From time to time . . ."

"You're at it already."

Julie took her girlfriend by the neck and reassured Gilles:

"Marina is teasing you, she can't help it. I even wonder if she isn't a little jealous. Sit down, make yourself at home."

Sebag crossed a thick carpet that muffled his steps and sat down on a fuchsia-pink couch with comfortable cushions. On his right, an ethanol fireplace radiated an exquisite warmth into the room. For a few seconds, he indulged in the contemplation of a yellow flame with bluish gleams that was silently dancing in its glass bubble.

"It's fascinating, isn't it?" Marina said. "That was a gift that Julie gave us one Christmas. The only thing we regret about our move to the South is that we use it much less here than we did in Paris. I could spend whole hours in the dark watching this fireplace."

For the moment, it was he, Gilles Sebag, whom the young woman was observing attentively with her dark, shining eyes.

"Have I passed the exam?" he finally asked.

A dimple appeared in Marina's right cheek. For hardly a fraction of a second. Then it disappeared in a smile.

"Excuse me. It's a *déformation professionnelle*."

"What do you do for a living?"

"I'm a physical therapist. And I can't help examining people the first time: I study their bearing, their posture, and I try to discern their imbalances."

"What's your diagnosis?"

"Your weak point is your back, isn't it?"

Sebag nodded.

"Remedy?"

"Massages, loosening up, modification of the running posture, and probably . . ."

"What would you like to drink, Gilles?" Julie suddenly interrupted.

"Do you have whiskey?"

"I think we have some left. You wouldn't prefer some fruit juice? We make excellent cocktails."

"Not really, no."

"I can offer you a blinker: whiskey, grenadine, and grapefruit juice."

Gilles smiled at his young colleague's insistence on selling him her fruit juices.

"The blinker will be fine. I like the name."

Before disappearing into the kitchen, Julie looked sternly at her girlfriend. Which only increased Sebag's curiosity.

"What were you saying before Julie so abruptly cut you off?"

"It wasn't important."

"On the contrary."

"Well, if you insist . . ."

"Can we say '*tu*' to each other?"

"If you insist."

"I insist."

"Regarding saying '*tu*'?"

"And the rest, too."

Marina looked at the flame in the fireplace before making up her mind.

"Before attending a school of physical therapy I got a master's in psychology, and I like to connect the two disciplines. I think that many of our physical problems come from our psychological weaknesses. Sometimes it can be the other way around, but it's rarer. For instance, an anxious person has tense muscles and stiff joints, and he will be subject to cramps and tendinitis. A depressed person holds himself badly, he has low shoulders, a slightly curved back and neck. The posture is often imperceptible to the untrained eye but it is sufficiently marked to produce headaches and lumbago . . ."

Sebag nodded.

"So according to you, I belong to the depressed type, is that it?"

Marina sucked in her lips.

"I spoke too soon. Julie has often told me how . . . how intuitive you are in your work and I was trying to show you that I can be intuitive too. But I spoke before thinking, I'm sorry."

Julie was already coming back with a tray full of colored glasses. She put a blue lagoon in front of Marina, a blinker with orange tones in front of Gilles, and kept for herself a margarita with lime-green reflections.

"Do you serve your aperitifs in accord with the tastes of each person or only to compose a colorful tableau?" Gilles joked.

"Both, Lieutenant."

She leaned over to whisper in his ear:

"I didn't tell Marina anything about what you confided in me. I promise."

He replied with a nod and a movement of his eyelids that meant "not to worry." Julie grabbed a large cushion, put it in front of the coffee table, and abruptly sat down on it. The cushion adapted to her form and turned into a pouffe. Gilles asked Marina questions about her work. After practicing in retirement homes while she was living in the Paris area, the young physical therapist had realized one of her dreams when she arrived in Perpignan: she was now working in a private clinic specializing in sports injuries. She was no longer working with stiff, tired people who were condemned to gradually lose their mobility—from the bed to the armchair, then from the armchair to the bed, as the song said—but with healthy, muscular bodies that she helped get back in shape for future exploits. In particular, the members of the USAP rugby team passed through her expert hands one after the other.

After the aperitif, they sat down at the table before a rabbit in mustard sauce that Julie had accompanied with vegetables: chard, tomatoes, onions, and mushrooms.

Gilles congratulated her. "I didn't know you had this talent."

"I can make only one or two dishes I was taught by my mother. Once I've made them all for my friends, I turn the cooking over to Marina, who is a real cordon bleu chef."

Julie had opened a Côtes du Roussillon Villages, a nice Haute Coutume 2010 by Catalan winemakers. Gilles savored the final spicy, almost vanilla note on his palate. In the concert of forks and knives, the conversation turned toward their current investigations. Julie had made hardly any progress on the burglaries in Bas-Vernet. However, they seemed to have slowed down after the vacation ended. Then Marina brought in a dessert she had prepared. On a dish with a wide rim, a custard licked the edges of an appetizing chocolate fondant. She took three small crystal glasses out of a wooden cabinet and set them down in front of the dishes before filling them with a coppery liquid with glints of emerald green. Banyuls grand cru from the Domain des Templiers, Gilles read on the label. He wasn't crazy about sweet wines, but since he'd been living in Northern Catalonia he'd learned to like them with dessert. He used his spoon to cut off a chunk of the fondant. In the dish, dark cocoa sauce mixed with the yellow of the custard.

"This is delicious," he said appreciatively after a first mouthful.

"I have to admit that I'm not unhappy with myself," Marina said.

Once the dessert was finished, she suggested they return to the living room.

"Coffee, tea, herbal tea?"

"For once, I'm going to avoid coffee," Gilles answered. "I'm having trouble sleeping just now. Maybe it's that . . ."

"Tea, then? Green, red, black, or yellow tea?"

"It's like the cocktails, you serve them according to the colors?"

"I can also classify them by country: tea from Thailand, tea from China, tea from Japan. Or a rooibos from South Africa, a very relaxing drink that aids digestion. Excellent for having beautiful dreams."

"Can it be smoked, too?" Sebag joked.

Marina disappeared again into the kitchen and Julie resumed their shop talk. But was it really shop talk?

"I heard about your action this afternoon. Really, you have no luck . . . It's as if for some reason everything you do revolves around the same themes."

"However, I remind you that I arrested a young drug dealer before Christmas. So far as we know, conjugal problems were not involved in that case."

"But you left the rest of the investigation to the customs agents! Who knows whether an affair isn't behind all that!"

"Stop . . ."

Gilles picked up the bottle of wine and summarily poured the last drop into his own glass.

"And all of them go in the same direction: it's always an unfaithful woman, never the other way around! I'm cursed."

"That's the law of series, as they say. Or else a social phenomenon."

"Meaning?"

"Manners change. Infidelity used to be mainly masculine, probably because men, by their work and their leisure, were more often away from home and also because it was considered less blameworthy. When a man had relations with prostitutes in a whorehouse, people didn't even call it adultery . . ."

Gilles understood that this spiel was in no way spontaneous. Julie was no longer talking shop. Not at all.

"Manners change, yes, but slowly. Women are freer and, despite everything, it's still often the man who's hitting on women, making the first move. In short, women still have as many offers as they used to have, and let themselves be tempted more easily. A pretty woman often has too many options. Claire is a pretty woman. She cheated on you once, but did you ask yourself how many times she rejected the propositions men were making her?"

Sebag had to recognize that he had never asked himself that question.

"And you, Gilles, how often have you turned down propositions made by a woman?"

The image of Elsa Moulin appeared to him. Other pretty faces he'd also met in recent years. But he didn't need to think long before answering:

"Zero. I believe I could have had a few opportunities but I have never had any explicit propositions."

"And if you had, would you have resisted every time?"

"I . . . I don't know."

Julie had led him where she wanted: to reconsider Claire's conduct with more indulgence. Marina came back into the living room with three steaming cups.

"What were you talking about?" the young physical therapist asked.

"About infidelity in general, and about feminine adultery as a social phenomenon," Julie replied.

"Ah, I see . . ."

She handed each of them a cup.

"It's funny that you were talking about that tonight. I have a patient who is a lawyer specializing in divorce cases and she was just telling me that she has been literally swamped for the past few months. A veritable epidemic. She's a jogger who runs races every Sunday and no longer has time to train during the week. The result is that she got injured two weeks ago."

Marina blew on her cup of tea.

"And regarding social phenomena, she told me that right now a majority of couples are separating at the initiative of men. There seems to be a large increase in the number of cuckolds."

Sebag almost choked on his mouthful of herbal tea. It had a bitter taste. Julie tapped him on the back. Her gesture finished with a friendly caress.

"We talked a lot about that while I was massaging her. About the why, the how, and . . ."

Marina suddenly fell silent.

"And?" Julie asked.

"Uhh . . . I don't know if we can talk about that after all . . ."

She was taking sideways glances at Gilles.

"We also talked about women's pleasure, sex, morality, and so on. It's private, in fact. We still don't know each other very well . . ."

"OK, I know what we need then," Julie said, getting up. "Indica or sativa?"

Marina burst into laughter. Julie addressed herself particularly to Gilles: "I recommend indica. That variety of cannabis has powerful destressing properties."

Sebag stared at them one after the other.

"Ah, OK . . . A little while ago when you were talking about herbal teas and teas, I thought I was in a delicatessen. Now I see that it's a *coffee shop*[27] instead. Why not, after all? That will remind me of my youth."

[27] In French, the English expression "coffee shop" is used to refer to a place where cannabis can be bought and/or used.

They had to wait for the joint Julie had rolled to circulate several times before Marina resumed the discussion.

"So then . . . where to begin?"

"At the beginning," Julie suggested.

She turned to Gilles:

"I think this is going to be long . . ."

Marina took a hit and closed her eyes a moment.

"The first observation that can be made is that contrary to what people have believed or wanted to make others believe for centuries, women are made for love. And I'm not talking about romanticism but about physical love, about sex with a big S!"

"Why a big one?" Julie joked. "Size is not as important as all that!"

Marina didn't allow herself to be distracted.

"As I recall, men's pleasure—and my memories are getting older and older—is a little spasm and it's over. Whereas with us, it's a wave, a storm, sometimes a tidal wave. The female orgasm has long frightened both men and women. That's why it has been so repressed."

"Marina is a feminist," Julie thought it useful to point out. "Her grandmother was even one of the founders of the MLF."[28]

"We don't experience just one pleasure, or even two, as is too often thought, but dozens of kinds of pleasures. Some people compare a woman's body to an Advent calendar with a multitude of windows that just have to be opened . . ."

"Hmm . . . I love the chocolates. Merry Christmas!"

"These windows open up one after the other as time goes by, and as a woman matures, gains confidence, and finds skillful lovers—male or female, of course."

"For her master's in psychology, she chose the sexology

[28] Mouvement de la libération des femmes, a French feminist organization.

option," Julie broke in again, speaking to Gilles. "That was the area in which she got the best grade. On the oral, naturally."

Her blue eyes were reddening. Probably fatigue. After taking a long puff, she passed the joint to Gilles. Marina paused; she seemed to have lost the thread of her lecture. Gilles took hit after hit, hoping to hide behind a halo of smoke. He didn't dare say anything. When women talk about female sexual pleasure among themselves, a wise man keeps quiet. Because he knows that if he speaks, he will at best be taken as pretentious and at worst for an imbecile. The two were not incompatible.

Marina took another sip of herbal tea. Her eyes were red, too. Probably the chamomile. Or the valerian. Who knew . . .

"So," she concluded, "—and this is where the Athenians fizzled out—the longer that goes on the harder it will be for women to remain faithful! And since men, who remain incurable machos, are less inclined to put up with cheating than women are, the number of divorces is going to continue to increase. QED!"

She laughed at her formulation, a thick, breathy laugh. Julie sent a second joint around and then got up to open a window. Sebag sank further into the cushions. As she sat back down on her pouffe, Julie said with alarm:

"Really . . .You seem to have a lot of time to chat, you and your lawyer, during massages . . ."

"In two weeks, she has already had four sessions."

"Is she married?"

"Divorced."

"And . . . uhh . . .does she still like men?"

"Ha, ha, ha! For the time being, yes! She left her husband when she found out that he'd cheated on her. Which just goes to show that that happens in that direction too, sometimes. And after going through a difficult period, she's now in full bloom. She's having a blast!"

She stopped long enough to giggle again.

"Finally, she realized that her guy wasn't such a good lay!"

Gilles felt himself disappearing into the voluptuous couch. Soon he would go down body and soul. Despite the . . . fatigue and the chamomile. Or the linden. Marina went on and on. Her voice seemed to come from farther and farther away.

"The other question that comes up is: can you experience a fully-developed sexuality with one and the same guide all your life?"

The question should have struck Gilles. It barely grazed him.

"All women have several partners during their lives," Julie objected.

"Lucky again! But in general, they have several experiences before they meet their 'sister soul' and after that, hang on!"

"Uhh . . . You wouldn't be sending me a subliminal message there, would you?"

Marina caressed her partner's cheek.

"We never promised eternal fidelity, my love. And even if I don't necessarily plan to cheat on you someday, I don't consider ideal the prospect of never knowing anyone else intimately before I die."

Julie took her girlfriend's hand and continued the caress, but she remained pensive and did not reply.

"That's precisely the big problem these days," Marina went on. "How can sexual fulfillment be reconciled with life in a couple, with a family life? The old morality is no longer of much help to us. Each person has to find her own path."

"It's very comfortable here at your place . . ."

Gilles had said that without thinking. Had he really said it? He doubted it for a few seconds, long enough for Marina's and Julie's responses to reach him:

"You can stay and sleep here," Marina suggested.

"You're joking," Julie corrected her. "He *has* to stay here. I strictly forbid him to leave in that state. And if he resists, I'll handcuff him."

They all broke out in loud, staccato laughter. With each burst Sebag sank further. His heavy body melted into the fabric of the couch while his mind, light, light, light, flew away like Professor Tournesol[29] in an old advert from his childhood. He fled toward the past, or into the imaginary. How could he know? He saw his mother. Smiling in his father's arms. He saw the face of a woman who was laughing behind them. Then another. Then two more . . . Then still others . . .

He opened his eyes. The orange light from the streetlamps lit the living room. He was lying on the sofa bed in his undershorts and a T-shirt. He pulled the blanket up to his chin. Shivered.

He thought about Claire. Looked for his phone. Found it. He had to tell her that he wouldn't be coming home. He opened his text messages. Found one sent to his wife a few minutes earlier. He didn't remember sending it. He put down his phone. Hugged the pillow.

A hoarse sound escaped his throat. He was snoring. While remaining awake. Strange sensation.

The dreams that invaded him again were no longer entirely dreams. Too real, too present. A man was leaning over him and laughing. Gérard. The vile Gérard. And yet, no, it wasn't his father but a man with salt-and-pepper hair despite being barely forty. A face that he had looked for on the Internet and whose frozen image now haunted him.

Simon, Gérard, the same thing, the same laugh. Two first names that were banging against the walls of his fractured skull.

It was time to have done with it.

He threw back the blanket. Got up. His head was spinning, his stomach revolted. Goddamn hangover.

He also had to have done with this stupid stuff—alcohol and the rest.

[29] A character in Hergé's *Tintin* books.

Sebag had the curious sensation of being simultaneously exhausted and full of energy. Full of confidence as well. He had made a resolution. He would go straight ahead. Certain meetings were inevitable. To do what? To do *it*, precisely. He'd see what came of it. Maybe nothing or not much? Too bad! It was time that fear and uneasiness shift sides.

CHAPTER 37

The sun had not yet come up when he arrived at police headquarters. He absentmindedly greeted the young woman cop who was on the front desk and strode quickly to the cafeteria, where he got a large cup of coffee. At home, he followed his wife's advice and did without sugar, but at headquarters, what she didn't know wouldn't hurt her. Just too bad about the little nascent potbelly that had caused him to change the waist size of his pants several times over the past few years!

After ordering a second cup of coffee, he headed for the cells where people in police custody were held. He shook the hand of the officer assigned to guard them.

"Are there many?" he asked.

"Only three, it's pretty calm. Even if the big muscleman Lieutenant Molina arrested yesterday made noise all night. He was either snoring like a chainsaw or blubbering. But his neighbors didn't complain."

"Have you given them their breakfast?"

"I was about to do that."

"I'll take Barrache's."

"No problem."

The officer took a package of cookies and a carton of orange juice out of a cupboard.

"Would you have a tray?"

"Ah, no . . . This isn't the Ritz, here."

"How about a plate?"

"I have one of those. But it's a paper plate."

"That'll do."

Ménard managed to fit the cookies, the orange juice, and the coffee on the middle of the plate.

"Will you open the door for me?"

The officer walked in front of him and unlocked the three padlocks on the door. Then he stepped aside. The tiny room smelled of sweat and cold urine. In a corner, partly hidden by a metal screen, a dark hole was exhaling the early morning perfumes of badly maintained pipes. Alongside it a faucet was dripping into a sink stained by calcium deposits and dirt. Ménard gently kicked the mattress on which Barrache was sleeping. The night watchman opened one eye, then both.

"Sit up," François said.

The guard obeyed without resisting. He put the old blanket over his narrow shoulders. Ménard sat down alongside him and put the plate on his knees. Barrache began by drinking the coffee.

"The food here is getting better; I didn't get any yesterday."

"That's a little gift from me."

With his nose in the coffee cup, Barrache thanked him:

"That's nice but it isn't enough to make me confess to something I didn't do."

Ménard observed the prisoner. Pressing his knees together to keep the tray from falling, he tore off the plastic surrounding the cookies. Three butter cookies frosted with chocolate. Barrache wolfed them down in a few hungry bites. Crumbs stuck to his beard and there was dark chocolate on his upper lip. François thought again of what Gilles had said in the boss's office: "He's kind of a good guy," he'd said, "but we can't exclude the possibility that he's a marvelous actor."

Barrache put the plate down next to him and pulled off the straw attached to the back of the carton of fruit juice. He pierced the little hole with the pointed end of the straw and drank. All at once. Then noisily sucked up the last drops that might still be in the corners.

"A marvelous actor . . ."

Ménard scratched his head. He had nothing against Barrache. In the guard's personal files taken from his house, as in his bank statements, he'd found no trace of another rented space. A bill for a garage, a barn, or a simple storage unit in which the suspect might have kept photos, documents, another computer . . . That had been his last hope.

Or rather his next-to-last hope.

This morning, he had decided to come surprise Barrache when he woke up. He'd hoped to discern in a still half-asleep look, in gestures over which the guard was not yet in full control, some sign of duplicity. But no! Even as he emerged from sleep, Barrache had been the same. A "nice guy," a real one, who probably had a tendency to masochism as well as to fatalism. The ideal profile of victims of judicial error . . .

"Now you know that I'm not the informer you're looking for?"

As he ate, Barrache had constantly looked in his direction with the damp eyes of a sad cocker spaniel. François had to accept it: the guard wasn't an actor, either a good one or a bad one. He seemed simply incapable of the slightest deception. Sincere out of an inability to lie. Ménard didn't answer Barrache's question.

"Did you tell your wife you'd been arrested?"

"Why would I do that?"

"You never know. It might make her want to come back."

Barrache shrugged. The cookie crumb caught in his beard quivered in its hairy nest.

"I can call her, if you want," François suggested.

Ménard understood that he was on the wrong path. He was going to have to admit it to his superior, his colleagues, and Sebag. He wouldn't do it in front of Barrache! People were always responsible for what happened to them. If this guy had been able to defend himself and if he had asked for the help of a lawyer instead of wallowing in the pleasure of being a victim, he wouldn't have spent forty-eight hours in police custody. And he wouldn't have caused him to lose this time that was so precious.

However, Ménard couldn't exonerate himself of all responsibility with regard to this poor dope. Now he was going to try to reestablish a connection between him and his wife. That would work or it wouldn't. They could do whatever they wanted, what they could. But he would have given them a chance.

And afterward?

Afterward, he would let Barrache go and set out in search of another suspect.

Fortunately, he already had a little idea. Cantalou was in fact not the only connection between Abad and Valls. The investigations of the guard had led them to discover another one.

CHAPTER 38

He took a deep breath.

As he went out, he'd noticed that the temperature had fallen overnight. Winter, which had been hesitating up to this point, had finally found its starting point. In the distance, Le Canigou, pale in the mist, was displaying its creamy white flanks.

He took another breath.

He loved the fresh air. He liked the winter when he finally dared to.

He lengthened his stride to loosen up his legs after a night, one more night, during which he had slept fitfully.

On the Place de Catalogne, in front of the former Dames de France building, he jumped when he saw Mylène pass by quite near him. Sometimes he reacted that way. He knew so many people in Perpignan. He was always surprised to run into them here and there in real life. Fortunately, no one knew him. They didn't know who he was, or what he did. He wasn't anything for them. A nobody, anonymous, a shadow that passes by and is forgotten.

But he didn't forget anything.

Mylène, who knew nothing about his life, no longer had any secrets for him. He had given her that name, but obviously he knew her real family name. He knew where she lived, where she worked, whom she frequented, who her husband was. He hadn't yet found a hold on her, but someday he would.

He just had to be patient. She was so beautiful, she loved life so much.

He was smiling when he got to work. No doubt for the first time in months. He opened his locker and put on his uniform.

"You look happy now! Are you coming with us to Aimé-Giral on Sunday? The USAP is playing Carcassonne."

He looked at his colleague for a long time. Why was this fool who no longer spoke to him except to give him orders suddenly talking to him? Because his wife had left him and because he needed new friends? He knew all about him, too.

He saw his own face in the mirror that he'd hung inside his locker: he was smiling again. He smiled too much. That was suspicious. How could you turn down an offer with such a smile of satisfaction? Don't make waves, especially not waves, not now.

"Why not? Can I tell you tomorrow?"

"Sure. I'm going with Max and René. You're welcome to come along."

Tomorrow, he'd find an excuse. Out of the question to waste two hours watching thirty overweight men on steroids fighting like kids over a ball that bounced in unpredictable ways. He had other things to do. He hadn't finished. The mission continued. In it, he had found the best of antidepressants, the most powerful of anxiolytics, and he intended to go on shooting up with them as long as possible. The machine was under way. It was not going to stop. The Eye would wreak still more havoc.

He couldn't repress a spasm of laughter.

CHAPTER 39

Sebag was waiting in his car, which was double-parked in front of the Lycée René Cassin. It was almost noon and groups of students were already coming out through the open gates. Some of the young people were standing around in front of the school, waiting for friends, puffing arrogantly on cigarettes. He was surprised to see so many of them smoking. What about Léo, was he smoking too? Some time ago, he'd stopped complaining when his father smoked at home. That was probably a sign. And cannabis? In France, one young person out of two had already tried smoking joints before the age of eighteen. So why wouldn't Léo do the same? And if he had, how could his father reproach him? Gilles's head still ached from the previous night's excesses.

They had tried to transmit to their children the principles of a healthy life, of decency and sincerity. The result was that Claire had lived in mendacity and dissimulation, while he chain-smoked and got high on marijuana with his colleagues in the evening. Not to mention his alcohol problem: secretly swigging down whiskey at the slightest annoyance, that was not exactly setting a good example!

Do what I say, not what I do.

And now he was about to break away from his personal principles as well as his professional ethics. Damn! Sometimes it was hard to follow the rules one set for oneself. But did that mean he should stop trying? No. Tomorrow he would resume his normal way of life.

Tomorrow . . .

Fatigue closed his eyes for a moment. He had risen silently at 5:30 in the morning. Marina and Julie were still sleeping. He had gulped down a quick breakfast in a nearby bar before getting on the road. He'd arrived "on-site" around 11 A.M., a good hour in advance, which he'd used to make a brief reconnaissance.

A buzzer sounded in the lycée's courtyard and immediately triggered a rush. A turbulent, noisy river flowed out into the street. Among the open, pimply, smiling faces, serious, impassive faces were carefully making their way. Gilles got out of the car and leaned on it. He examined the crowd. Using his status as a cop, he had gotten the information he needed. The man he was waiting for would come out at noon by the main door.

He had no difficulty spotting him. Tall, athletic, with an ease and suppleness in his figure that drew the eye. Gilles managed to put himself in the man's path. He too must have at some point done an Internet search to see what Gilles looked like. He felt stronger for that; jealousy also existed on the other side.

"Could you spare me a few minutes?"

He pointed in the direction of his car:

"We can talk better inside."

Simon Bidol said nothing. His eyes jumped from the car to Sebag.

"We could chat in a bar but I wouldn't want to embarrass you before your students and your colleagues. And your daughter. She goes to this lycée as well, doesn't she?"

Simon Bidol just nodded.

"Are you scared?"

Bidol made up his mind, a little out of curiosity, a lot out of pride. He walked to the car, opened the passenger-side door, and got in. Gilles sat down behind the wheel. He started the car and headed out into the traffic going toward the city center.

"Have you settled into your new life?"

"More or less."

A muffled voice. Restrained.

"You don't miss Perpignan too much?"

Silence again. Gilles watched him out of the corner of his eye. Bidol had a delicate, sweet face that a three-day beard did little to harden. Except for the wrinkles on his broad forehead, he didn't look like he was fifty-one.

"You must be comfortable here. You've got a nice house, a beautiful wife, beautiful kids. What are their names again? Oh, yes. Robin, Victor, and Agathe . . . Agathe is the one who's in lycée, right?"

The history-geography teacher put his hands on his knees. He gripped them. His veins swelled. He had nice hands. Gilles imagined them slipping over Claire's skin. Watch it . . . He mustn't let his anger rise.

"Your wife doesn't know, of course?" Sebag asked.

"No."

Bidol cleared his throat. His answer had been barely audible.

"What would happen if she found out?"

"Are you planning to tell her?"

"You didn't answer my question."

Bidol sighed and looked at the street in front of them.

"You can never tell, but that affair has been over for a long time, so I believe that Michèle would try to understand and forgive. Like you. But she would certainly be hurt."

He paused before adding:

"Like you."

Bidol knew things he shouldn't have known. Anger was growing.

"I asked her to avoid any contact with you!"

"She did that, I promise you."

His delivery was rapid; he was worried.

"I'm the one who contacted her after the holidays. I wanted

to know how it was going. Claire would be extremely unhappy if you left her. I don't want her to be unhappy."

"I forbid you to write to her!"

"I am no longer writing to her. Claire also forbade me to write to her. She answered my message but she made it very clear that it was the last time. There has been nothing else since then."

Sebag felt a mad desire to know the content of that exchange, but he couldn't stoop so low as to ask. And that was all the better! It could only have hurt him.

After driving around downtown Bayonne and crossing the Nive River, he took the bridge over the Adour. By means of a slight movement of his shoulder and arm, he moved the jacket away from his right side, revealing the butt of his weapon. He heard Bidol gulp. Claire's former lover felt an urgent need to speak.

"I'm sincerely sorry about what happened, but what's done is done: we can't turn back the clock. You have to think about the future. Claire loves you, she has never loved anyone but you, and your children also love you. You have to think about them, too . . ."

Gilles took deep pleasure in this moment. He wasn't especially proud of himself, but he wasn't ashamed, either. There was nothing wrong with doing yourself good! Bidol was afraid. Not too much. He was doing a good job of keeping himself under control.

At a roundabout, Sebag turned to his right to take a secondary road that ran along the Adour. Houses became rarer. A dense silence filled the inside of the car. Bidol's right hand had left his knee and rested on the door handle. Gilles drove a few more kilometers before leaving the riverbank and starting down a dirt road that led off among fields and forest.

"Where are we going?" Bidol finally asked.

"You'll see."

The teacher put his left hand in the inside pocket of his overcoat and rummaged around.

"It would be smarter to give me your mobile phone," Sebag advised him. "You're not going to worry your wife or disturb my colleagues in Bayonne for nothing?"

"For nothing?"

"Or for so little . . ."

Bidol reluctantly obeyed, putting his phone in the compartment between the two seats. Sebag slowed down and used a path that crossed the road to make a U-turn. Once the car was headed in the right direction, he stopped. Then he switched off the ignition and pulled out his gun. He flipped off the safety and then put it on the dashboard, the butt pointing toward Bidol.

"What would you do in my place?"

Bidol didn't lower his eyes.

"I'm not in your place."

His voice trembled a bit. That was all.

"And I don't have a gun at my disposal to have fun scaring people."

"Do you think I'm having fun?"

Bidol reflected. Gilles suspected that Bidol knew a lot about his character. He knew very well that Claire and her lover hadn't always been thinking about him, and that they must not have spent much of their precious time talking about him, but he couldn't have always been absent from their discussions.

"I wouldn't like to be in your place."

Bidol let go of the door handle to turn more toward Gilles.

"I know you're suffering and that you didn't come here to have fun. But I also know that you won't hurt me. You want to scare me, and I assure you that you've succeeded."

Bidol glanced at the pistol before looking at Sebag again.

"Because I'm well aware that one clumsy word on my part could change everything in spite of all that."

Two mountain-bike riders emerged from a trail and headed in their direction. Bidol started to reach for the door handle but then changed his mind. They waited in silence until the two bikes had passed the car.

"Whatever you may think at this moment, Claire deserves your love," Bidol continued. "And she has never loved anyone but you. I wanted to leave my wife. But Claire never considered for a second living with me."

One question occurred to Gilles. One of the rare questions that he had been able to avoid asking his wife.

"Why did you have an argument one night at the Deux Margot Cafe?"

"Did she tell you about that?"

"No."

"You were spying on us?"

"No, not that either. I learned about it by chance. Pure chance."

One day last summer, during an investigation into the disappearance of some young Dutch girls, he had laid several photos on the bar at the Deux Margot, a Perpignan bistro run by two former prostitutes from Paris. And without having thought about it in advance, he had slipped a photo of Claire among the pictures of the young women. It was the only photo the owners of the bar recognized. They had talked about the presence of a man with her and about an argument.

"We argued precisely because I had just told her that I wanted to leave Michèle. But for her, our affair was a friendship that had gone too far, and that was all. She got angry and so did I."

Bidol looked at the distant, undulating silhouette of the cyclists. They were coming to the intersection with the road.

"You're jealous of me and I understand that," Claire's lover went on. "But you should know that I was jealous of you, too. And I still am: I would have so much liked her to love me as much as she loves you."

Sebag nodded. In the end, he admired this lycée teacher's guts. He was afraid but he hadn't let himself be thrown off balance. Gilles also admired his words: they were intended to be flattering, of course, but they seemed sincere. Strangely, even though he didn't like manly confrontations on athletic fields, in staff rooms, or in the parking lot at headquarters, he understood what two competitors might feel after a fight. Beyond rivalries and even hatreds, there could be respect. Bidol had won a first round by sleeping with Claire. Sebag had won the second round by keeping his wife. The third, decisive round was going to his advantage.

"You still haven't answered my question: what would you do in my place?"

"I did answer: I'm not in your place."

"In my place . . ." Gilles insisted, "you would tell the whole truth to . . . Michèle?"

"I would be tempted, obviously."

He reflected for a few moments before adding:

"The decision is yours, but I don't think that one injury can be cured by another."

More words that hit home . . . That was the same conclusion that Gilles had come to after thinking about it all the way to Bayonne. But he took care not to reassure Bidol:

"Well, you see, you ended up answering!"

He jerked his chin toward the dirt road in front of them.

"You can leave now."

Simon Bidol looked at Sebag, then glanced at the pistol still lying on the dashboard. He must have thought, for a fraction of a sentence, of all the gangster films he'd seen in which the torturer frees his prisoner so that he can shoot him in the back. Nonetheless, he decided to open the car door. But before he got out he pointed to his mobile phone in the compartment.

"Can I take it back?"

"That would be a little too easy, don't you think? It's only two kilometers to Bayonne, twelve at most to your house. You can walk . . . And then I suppose that my wife's number is registered in it but not necessarily in your memory. So you won't be tempted again."

Bidol accepted the deal.

"As you wish. We aren't going to shake hands, I suppose?"

"You have courage and a sense of humor . . . Don't push it too far, all the same."

"You went to great lengths to scare me. You succeeded."

Bidol carefully got out of the car. Sebag had deliberately stopped next to a muddy shoulder. The history-geography teacher went around the front of the car and came back to Sebag.

"Are you going to tell my wife everything?"

Gilles took out a cigarette and lit it.

"I haven't decided yet. And then . . . you need to be scared a little while longer."

"If you decide that she has to know the whole truth, please let me tell her myself . . . It would be better for her. And maybe for you, too."

"I'll think about it."

Driving back on the autoroute, Sebag drank one can of energy drink after another. His eyes were closing all by themselves, he had to keep awake. After he passed Toulouse, he pulled into a rest stop. First he filled the tank and then parked in an out-of-the-way area. He sat down at a picnic table covered with crumbs and eggshells. He smoked another cigarette.

With Bidol, he'd been trying to keep from being overwhelmed by anger, and now he was waiting for it, hoping for it, wanting it . . .

He still had a score to settle.

He closed his eyes.

He was six years old. So that he didn't have to go to the children's activity center, Gérard took care of him on Wednesdays.

A sales rep dealing in vacuum cleaners, sewing machines, and other household appliances, he took Gilles along with him when he went door-to-door. Some of his customers seemed easier to convince than others. An hour, sometimes two. He was set in front of the television in a living room and waited very patiently. In general, the wait was rewarded. Gérard came out with a smile, and happy to have made a sale, he hurried to find a store where he could buy his son candy. Caramel bars, licorice, chewing gum in a tube or a roll . . . Everything he was usually denied was put within the reach of his desires.

On the condition that nothing was said to Mama. It was their secret, just the two of them.

One day, when he was waiting in a pretty blonde's living room, the television had gone on the blink. Black screen. Gilles was worried, but he waited. A long time. Then he got up and went to look for his father in the long hallways of the apartment. Sounds had guided him. Alarming little cries, groans. Not at all like the soft humming of a vacuum cleaner or a sewing machine. He'd opened the door and seen them. His father, the woman on top of him, both of them naked and sweating. Fear had frozen him on the spot.

He could no longer recall the following minutes. But he remembered very well that that afternoon there was no visit to a store. Gérard had taken him to a toy shop and Gilles had come out with the cowboy outfit he'd long dreamed of having. With the same promise as ever, but expressed with more intensity than usual. Above all, say nothing to Mama.

However, for a six-year-old child some secrets are too hard to keep. Especially when Mama was astonished, worried, and began to ask questions. Harassed, Gilles had ended up confessing. He'd talked about that Wednesday and all the others.

The following Wednesday, he was sent back to the children's activity center. No more television but games instead, no more pretty women but activity leaders who were generally rather kind. In that respect, he wasn't any worse off.

But at home nothing was ever the same again. Gérard was there less and less, and Mama seemed to have lost her cheerfulness. In the evening, she sang only sad songs that she wasn't always able to finish. It had taken Gilles years to put a name to this malady that had struck his mother. Depression. She never really recovered from it.

Gilles crushed out his cigarette between two eggshells on the picnic table. He took out his mobile and keyed in a number. The children had told him that it was still good. Léo and Séverine saw their grandfather once or twice a year and called him from time to time.

One ring, two . . . On the fifth ring, someone picked up.

"Hello?"

"Hello, Gérard?"

"Yes. Who is it?"

An old, slightly trembly voice.

"Gilles."

A long silence.

"Hello, son."

A voice that was on the defensive, surprised, a voice that didn't want to yield to hope.

"How are you, lad?"

"Not so good."

"I'm not so good, either, you know."

Gérard had misunderstood the meaning of his call. Gilles closed his eyes, drew strength from his anger. He had to strike.

"I needed to talk to you."

The breathing on the other end of the line grew tense. Gérard didn't dare believe it.

"You're a real bastard, Papa."

The slap. A long silence. No more breathing.

"I have known for a long time what you think of me."

"I never told you."

"You made me feel it countless times when we were still seeing each other."

"But I needed you to hear it directly."

"You've done that. I hope you'll feel better now."

"I hope so, too."

"Thanks, son."

Gilles was caught up short.

"Thanks for having called me 'Papa.' It's been such a long time . . ."

In the late afternoon he finally got to the Salses hill. From this slight elevation, the whole grandeur of the Catalan panorama was revealed. Framed by the chain of summits dominated by the white mass of Le Canigou, the green plain of Roussillon extended as far as the Mediterranean. Having lived for years with the mists and overcast skies of Chartres and La Beauce, Sebag never ceased to marvel at Northern Catalonia's luminosity, even in winter.

A sudden gust of wind blew his car a little sideways. He gripped the wheel more tightly. The wind socks alongside the autoroute were all horizontal. The *tramontane* was clearing the sky of clouds and, by cleansing the air of impurities, bringing out the clear lines of the horizon. It was the price they paid for the Catalan climate, and it never failed to present the bill.

Gilles was soon home, if not happy—not yet—at least relieved. This escapade had done him good. It would help him to turn over a new leaf, he was sure of that.

Soon.

The next step had to be solving this informer case. They had been treading water for too long. By SMS, Jacques Molina had let him know that Ménard had decided to let Dominique Barrache go. Oddly, it was his wife who had come to get him at headquarters. The mystery of the world and feelings:

through their mistake, the policemen seemed to have given new life to a moribund couple.

In the end, the worst was never certain in this vale of tears. It might turn out that reality was stranger than fiction.

Oh, well, that was over. Let's not get distracted! Sebag said to himself. Let's get back to our main subject, or rather to our *corbeau*!

This investigation had gone on far too long. He gave himself twenty-four hours to take a significant step forward. If he failed, he would personally propose to Castello—after talking with Ménard—giving up the investigation. The *corbeau*'s actions had led to two tragedies, but he was not directly responsible for them. There were other priorities.

As he neared Perpignan on the autoroute, he mentally reviewed the situation. In particular, he recalled in detail their conversations with Barrache. Ménard had been right to let him go. A false lead had just been set aside.

So! Now everything had to be done over from the beginning.

On the one hand, they had in Stéphane Abad a murderer who had been sent photos showing his wife's infidelity. On the other hand, they had Didier Valls, who had committed suicide after receiving an anonymous letter informing him of his misfortune. The examination of the mobile phones by geolocating the calls made—but only by that means—made it possible to assume that the informer who called Valls might also be the unidentified caller who had contacted Abad several days before the day of the murder. Well-founded assumptions, but no conclusive proof.

Thus there were two solutions: either they considered these assumptions insufficient and immediately halted a pointless investigation, or they deemed them sufficiently solid and continued to think about them . . .

So let's continue to think about them . . .

That led to Cantalou, the common point of contact among Abad, Balls, and Barrache, their former suspect. Cantalou was the first common point, but not the only one. There was also the billiard hall . . .

How had he not managed to see that earlier? Abad and Valls played for money. They lost to Barrache, but maybe they often won playing against other adversaries.

Sebag lit a cigarette. He had hardly any reason to be happy about having taken so long to arrive at the conclusion that had been staring them in the face for several days, but all the same, he was happy and thought he really deserved this reward.

He smoked with his mind empty and missed the North Perpignan exit. He drove an extra dozen kilometers and left the autoroute on the south side of Perpignan.

Something was wrong in him.

He pulled into a rest stop after the exit, got out of the car, and walked up and down smoking another cigarette.

His mind remained uneasy. The new lead that he'd found didn't bring him any peace. It was as if he'd taken cough syrup to cure a headache.

What if the truth lay elsewhere?

He stubbed out the cigarette he'd just lit. It was unsettling him more than it was helping him. He sat down in a place hidden by cars, with his legs crossed and his buttocks on the edge of the sidewalk.

He closed his eyes and breathed calmly. A word kept running through his head.

Epidemic . . .

"An epidemic of divorces," those were the words of the specialized lawyer Marina had quoted the preceding night.

The last time he'd heard the term "epidemic" discussed very seriously had been on a television program: specialists were talking about a veritable epidemic of cancers in the world.

Could infidelity be the tumor afflicting couples these days? The parallel seemed to him pertinent. Cancer was spreading over the planet along with the Western way of life: a change in habits and traditions, stress, sedentariness and urban life, the environment, and the increasing longevity of people and couples.

Yes, the comparison was tempting, but so far as his case was concerned, it led nowhere.

Epidemic . . .

He took out his mobile, connected to the Internet, and quickly found the definition he was looking for.

"Epidemic: rapid increase in the incidence of a disease in a given place at a given time." The lawyer, one of Marina's patients, thus found herself overwhelmed by a "rapid increase" in the number of divorces. Could it be imagined that such an epidemic had been raging in Perpignan for several weeks, or even several months?

He realized that this idea might seem ridiculous and yet he kept turning it over and over, and clung to it: there must be an angle from which it would become pertinent.

Epidemic . . .

The definition said that an epidemic was caused by an exogenous factor, a virus or a bacterium involuntarily introduced by a third party. Involuntarily?

Not always . . .

So far as Abad and Valls were concerned, there was in fact a third party and he had acted voluntarily.

Two new images telescoped in his feverish mind. The sponge was giving up its juice. He wasn't controlling anything. His brain had its own life, it captured images, sounds, and sensations that it carefully preserved in order to reproduce them later. Haphazardly, most of the time, but sometimes with a frightening relevance.

He closed his eyes.

Molina's cheerful smile disturbed his reflection. If his partner saw him, he would get down on his knees and pray to Saint Rita for him out loud.

Sebag breathed more calmly. He mustn't let himself lose his concentration. He went back to the images that had invaded him. First of all, Gali's living room. The smell of gasoline floating in the air. No, that wasn't what was important. He shivered. Because the wind was blowing around him that evening, or because he'd been wearing a tank top on that day in the living room? It wasn't clear . . . It wasn't a shiver from the cold, but from fear. Bastien Gali's house was only waiting for a spark to explode and a flame was dancing in the fireplace. A strange, colorful flame.

Of course, of course . . .

He reopened his eyes, took a long breath, and then closed them again.

This time he was in a small room off the lobby at police headquarters. His telephone was beeping, he felt relief, he was finally going to be able to put an end to the exhausting interview with Marie-Isabelle Casty. He held out his hand to her, she took hers out of her handbag. She had just stuck her hand into the bag. Why? Had the young woman come solely to plead her cause or did she have something to show him? She might have. But he hadn't been receptive, and she'd changed her mind.

He felt dizzy. He was out of his mind. No, it wasn't possible. It wasn't his intuition but his imagination that was playing tricks on him . . .

Chapter 40

Sebag stopped his car in front of the red and white barrier that blocked the entrance to the hospital complex. He pressed the button on a voice terminal and gave his name. The barrier immediately went up. He was expected. A young woman assigned to handle the hospital's communications met him and led him across the campus to the reception building. She had him go into a small room. He sat down and waited.

The idea that had come to him as he exited the autoroute had matured in his head all evening and part of the night. However, unlike his somber ideas, it had left room for the rest. While thinking about the case, he had been able to take part in the family conversation. In the late evening he had made love to Claire. The vigor he'd put into the act greatly resembled a bestial and elemental marking of territory but the two of them seemed to have found satisfaction in it. Shortly afterward, they fell asleep in each other's arms.

"I didn't expect to see you again so soon!" Bastien Gali said as Sebag entered the room. "It's a nice surprise."

He bent over to whisper in his ear: "It's unbelievably boring here!"

The nurse who had accompanied Gali left them alone. Sebag went directly to the heart of the matter:

"How did you find out that Véronique had had lunch again with her former lover?"

"Aren't we going to say '*tu*' to each other anymore?"

"That will depend on your sincerity. I don't like people to take me for a fool."

"I don't understand."

Gali opened his eyes wide; he wanted to seem surprised. But his crossed arms and his body that had sat up straight in the chair were playing a different tune.

"Of course you understand me," Sebag went on. "But I'm willing to repeat my question: how did you learn that your wife had seen her colleague again in private?"

"I snooped on her phone, obviously. I told you that the other day, didn't I? I even gave you her mobile so that you could look at it, but you didn't do that. It ought to be possible to find it again if you don't believe me."

"That's not the problem, I don't contest the existence of that message. But I think you discovered it only after you'd been informed about that lunch."

"After I'd been informed? What do you . . . what do you mean by that?"

Gali's eyes widened in exactly the same way as before. His repertory for simulating astonishment was not very diverse.

"Let's cut the crap! Before you let me into your house, you burned something in the fireplace."

"They were old papers . . . love letters that she'd sent me."

"The flames were colored. They weren't papers but photos."

"Oh, right, that's true . . . I also burned our wedding pictures. I was angry."

Gali wasn't allowing himself to get flustered, but he wasn't convincing. Sebag put his cards on the table.

"I think they were photos of Véronique with her colleague. In the restaurant together or kissing, I don't know, but they were photos that had been sent to you. And the person who made them had also contacted you by telephone. I've come to get your mobile."

On this last point, Sebag was bluffing: the hospital administration was holding Gali's telephone, like those of all its patients, and without the owner's agreement it could hand the phone over to him only when he had obtained the necessary authorization from the judge.

Gali said nothing more but his eyes spoke for him. They revealed a mixture of discomfort and respect.

"I'm going to be very clear," Sebag went on. "Either you collaborate completely, or I'm going to change the indulgent report I wrote on what happened at your house. And then you won't avoid prison!"

Bastien bowed his head. If his skull had been transparent, his neurons could have been seen vibrating in all directions. He was ready. Sebag drove the point home.

"You don't owe this guy anything, Bastien. By informing you, he was only trying to make you and Véronique unhappy. Especially since he misled you, because your wife didn't sleep with her lover again. She told you that, she swore it to you, you believed her, and so did I, and we still do, don't we? I don't know what this guy's motives are, but you're not the first person he spoke to. His revelations have already caused two deaths. And at your place, we barely avoided carnage . . ."

He moved his chair closer to Bastien's and put his hand on his shoulder.

"Come on, tell me the truth. It'll do you good."

Gali looked up at him. He was still delaying, but Gilles knew he had won. Finally Gali talked.

A week before—in fact, the very day of his fit of rage—he'd found an envelope in his mailbox. It bore no stamp; it had been put in the box directly. This envelope contained three photos of Véronique sitting with her former lover at a table in a restaurant. In one of these pictures, the man had put his hand on her cheek and she was smiling back at him. On the back of the photo there was a handwritten message: "You will soon know how to reach me."

Within the following hour, Gali had received an initial SMS whose words remained forever etched on his mind:

"Your wife is making a fool of you. She's cheating on you again. Please get rid of the photos and any trace of this call."

Bastien had immediately called, but he'd gotten an anonymous answering machine. Five minutes later, he received a second SMS as a kind of answer:

"Is that really what matters? However, her lover's name is Alain Guibert, and he works with her. But you already knew that. Are you going to continue to let her deceive you this way?"

Gali had flown into a bitter rage: that was when he had decided to go buy cans of gasoline. On the way back, he had received a last SMS:

"Don't forget to erase any trace of my contact with you. Thanks."

"I erased the text messages as soon as I got home. I kept the photos a little longer. I showed them to Véronique and I didn't get rid of them until just before I let you come into the house."

"Do you remember the telephone number?"

"No. But it began with 07, and I think the next number was 15. After that, I don't know."

Sebag consulted his notes. Those figures corresponded to the first ones of Abad's *corbeau*'s number. It was a little early to celebrate, but he felt that he was on the right track.

"You really have no idea who this man is?"

"No, none. I didn't try to find out more. He seemed to be very concerned that he remain anonymous."

Sebag reflected a moment before going on:

"You haven't ever worked for Cantalou?"

"What kind of question is that? No, never."

"Do you play pool?"

"Poker, sometimes, but never pool."

"Where do you play?"

"At home or at my buddies' places."

"Do you go to the Balto?"

"What's that?"

"A downtown bar. Rue du Maréchal Foch."

"No. I don't think I've ever set foot in it."

"OK."

Sebag thanked Bastien Gali, who agreed to let him take his mobile. He stopped off at headquarters to pick up Casty's mobile in the cabinet where people held in police custody deposited their personal belongings, and he gave both the phones to his colleagues on the forensic team. Then he headed for Saint-Cyprien.

There was still one point that had been neglected.

Above the Mediterranean, enormous white clouds looked like a snowy mountain range on the horizon. Sebag easily found a parking place opposite the Saint-Cyprien casino. Marie-Isabelle had just left the women's shelter to take refuge with a friend of her mother's who lived in an apartment across from the marina.

"Jacqueline rents it out during the summer and lends it to her children during school vacations. It's free until February. It's very helpful to me just now . . ."

"Your husband has been locked up, you can go home if you want."

"My home is our home. Without Jean-Paul, I prefer to stay here."

She took him through the small apartment and led him directly to the balcony. She didn't offer him something to drink, or a seat. She leaned against the railing and lit a cigarette. He took one out in turn.

"Please excuse my behavior the day before yesterday."

Behind the curls of smoke, Marie-Isabelle was looking at him without showing any reaction. Her face was closed. The young woman seemed in fact not to have liked the way she had been treated. He decided he had to make a gesture.

"You appealed to the man rather than to the cop the day before yesterday. And the man, you see, also had his personal problems: he couldn't be receptive."

Sebag didn't like misunderstandings and he knew that there had been one, an enormous one, between them. During their preceding conversation, she had used the term "slut." He didn't see her that way, not at all, that term reeked too much of machismo to be part of his vocabulary. If he had something to reproach her for, it wasn't her looseness or libertine inclinations, but rather her individualism. In life, you couldn't have everything, you had to make choices. In his view, Marie-Isabelle was above all an egoist, and of the worst kind: it was all about her, all about sex, and too bad about the collateral damage. She had chosen to pursue her comfort and pleasure at the risk of causing pain to those whom she claimed to love.

But he hadn't come here to reopen that debate.

"Let me say no more about it," he added. "It's the cop who's getting back to you today. I believe you did not come solely to plead your cause the other day, but also had something you wanted to tell us."

Marie-Isabelle Casty didn't flinch. He was going to have to shake her up.

"I'm very eager to see the photos that are in the envelope you wanted to give me."

The young woman's eyebrows shot up, betraying her surprise. She put out her cigarette in an ashtray already full of butts and disappeared into the apartment. Shortly afterward, she returned with a white envelope in her hands. Sebag took several photos out of it. Made using a telephoto lens, they showed the young woman with a fairly bald man of around fifty. He was wearing a leather jacket that barely concealed the beginnings of a potbelly and he was leaning on a yellow motorcycle. In one of the pictures, Marie-Isabelle was languidly kissing him. Sebag recognized the place: it was in Canet, close to the Place de la Méditerranée.

"We had lunch on the terrace. That bastard must have been spying on us for a long time, because that's the only intimate gesture we made that day. I was always very careful."

"Who is the man in the photo?"

"Do you think that really matters?"

"Your informer has already had several victims. We're looking for a connection. It might be women, it might be men . . . At this stage of the investigation, we really don't know."

Marie-Isabelle took a photo and turned it over. As in Abad's case, there was a handwritten message, promising an imminent phone call. And there was a number.

"He left his telephone number, you won't have any difficulty."

"If it were that simple, we'd already have arrested him. Who is the man with you in the photo?"

In the port below them, the wind was clacking the sailboats' lines against their masts. For some people, this metallic sound was like a call to the open sea, to adventure, or to luxury, but for Gilles it was just noise, simple noise. And he wondered if the view of the sea from this apartment would make it worth putting up with all the inconveniences of such a location during the high tourist season, when in addition to the noise of boats in the port there was that of cars in the street, voices on the terraces of cafes, and the music coming from your neighbor's balcony.

"Roger Reddah," Marie-Isabelle sighed. "A childhood friend whom I recently ran into by chance."

Then Gilles asked her the same questions he asked Gali regarding Cantalou, pool in general, and the Balto in particular. In each case she answered in the negative.

"You really have no lead at all for this son of a bitch?"

"None."

"Not the faintest idea?"

"He's a bitter or puritanical man, or else a cuckold who's taking revenge. Probably a little of all three. That still includes lots of people in this area."

CHAPTER 41

Chairs scraped on the worn tile floor of the third-floor conference room at police headquarters. The inspectors were taking their places around the table, one by one: François Ménard, Thierry Lambert, Joan Llach, Julie Sadet, and Jacques Molina. Sebag sat at the right of Superintendent Castello. He noticed Jacques's smile of satisfaction as well as François's vexed grimace.

On leaving the apartment in Saint-Cyprien, Gilles had driven along the marina. It was Saturday, the weather was warm. Couples and families were walking along the quays to admire the yachts and dream rather than make plans. After reflecting for a while to clarify his thoughts, he'd telephoned his boss to tell him about his discoveries.

"We're going to go all out on this case," Castello had concluded. "We can't allow some wing nut to mess with every household in the department."

Sebag and the superintendent had agreed to call a meeting of the team on Sunday.

"Take a day off," Castello told him. "And be ready to launch into a week that's going to be a tough one. I don't have to tell you that a good marathon runner has to know how to build up his strength before the race."

It was silent in the conference room. The lieutenants waited patiently while the superintendent read through his notes one last time. They had all received an e-mail setting forth the main lines of the case; they were on the lookout, attracted by the scent of the prey.

Castello cleared his throat.

"On Saturday, Gilles delivered Gali's and Casty's telephones to the forensic team. Elsa Moulin spent her Sunday making a quick first examination. The same telephone was used to contact two people: Stéphane Abad and Bastien Gali. On the other hand, in the cases of Didier Valls and Jean-Paul Casty, two different telephones were used. But in every case, the calls were made from the same part of downtown Perpignan. Although we might have still had some doubts, now that's settled: there was in fact a single informer and that man is already indirectly responsible for a murder, a suicide, a hostage-taking, and assault and battery. So we have to catch him before he adds another tragedy to his record."

The hunt was being organized, but Sebag knew that it wouldn't be very exciting. It wasn't a bloodhound they needed but rather the exhausting labor of thousands of industrious ants.

"The problem is that for the moment we don't have any idea who the informant is. We've got a huge amount of work to do."

Castello turned to Sebag to ask him to take over. Gilles opened his notebook. He'd done good work that Sunday.

"I see at least three ways to make our way back to this guy. First: we find a connection among the victims. The *corbeau* certainly did not choose his targets at random. So first we have to inventory them."

Sebag looked at his colleagues. Llach, Ménard, and Julie were taking notes. Molina was clipping his fingernails and Thierry Lambert was watching a fly cruising around the room. A fly in the middle of the winter . . . the enigma intrigued him.

"At this point, we know four of his targets, but we can assume that there have been others. Many, many others."

The faces all looked up at him. He'd caught their attention. But first he wanted to review the chronology of the facts as he had reconstituted them, which differed from the order in which the police had discovered them.

"Stéphane Abad killed his wife on December 23, and it was on the same day that Jean-Paul Casty beat his wife. Thus they are the first proven targets. Then we have Didier Valls on December 29 and Bastien Gali on January 2 . . . Each time, the first contact between the informer and his targets goes back to only a few days before the events."

"But according to you, there are other cases?" Joan Llach asked impatiently.

Gilles nodded.

"We came across these four cases by chance, and it is absolutely improbable that chance gave us an exhaustive list of the *corbeau*'s crimes. And moreover . . ."

Sebag joined his hands in front of his mouth.

"And moreover, that would presuppose that our individual was successful every time."

"Successful?" Julie exclaimed. "What do you mean by that?"

Sebag pointed his joined index fingers toward his colleagues.

"Watch out, here we're leaving the facts for simple suppositions. But I think that in fact our *corbeau* is not acting simply for the pleasure of settling scores with unfaithful women; he's hoping that his revelations will lead to tragedies."

Ménard frowned.

"Are you sure of what you're saying?"

"Absolutely not! As I said, this is only a supposition."

Sebag sensed an opportunity to tackle his colleague. Usually he was a better sport. Usually, yes . . .

"When we suspected the guard at Cantalou, we didn't hesitate to attribute to him the intention to deliberately provoke tragedies, so why should we change our approach? If our *corbeau* simply wanted to divulge adulteries, he would have stopped with the first tragedy. But the chronology shows us that he continued."

"What is the likelihood that revealing an infidelity would

lead to a tragedy like the ones we've seen?" Julie said with concern. "Do you realize the implications of what you're suggesting?"

"Yes. I thought about it all day yesterday. In many cases, a couple can overcome such revelations all by itself . . ."

He avoided meeting Julie's eyes, in an attempt to maintain a neutral tone.

"In many other cases, the couple separates. Fortunately, tragedies are rare."

"Have you considered how many facts this man might have known? And how many the accusations he might have made?"

"Regarding the number of facts, I agree with you, it's enormous. But regarding the revelations, I think they were much less numerous. He must have chosen his targets carefully. Otherwise we'd have had more leaks."

He added, in a graver tone than he intended:

"Adultery is one thing and the way in which one . . . in which one learns of it is another. I think this individual very skillfully made his interlocutors' anger mount."

Gilles let his colleagues digest what he'd said. Then he moved on to the second part of his presentation.

"And that shows us the second way of identifying our *corbeau.* Who can have access to so much personal information about people?"

Gilles had already drawn up a list, but he wanted his colleagues to draw up another one spontaneously. A list that might be different.

"It must be his occupation that gives him this information," Llach suggested. "A doctor, lawyer, psychologist, cop . . ."

"A private detective," Molina added.

"A physical therapist," Julie whispered, looking at Gilles.

"A hairdresser or a beautician," Thierry Lambert proposed. "I have a friend who's a beautician in a village and I can tell you that she knows all the gossip in the place."

"That's a lot," Molina observed critically. "We might as well be looking for a needle in a haystack."

Castello raised his arm to stop an exchange that threatened to become discouraging.

"Obviously, we're not going to start monitoring all those occupations. Our first task will be to draw up a list of the *corbeau*'s victims. Gilles will inventory recent crimes that might have resulted from a domestic quarrel. François, Joan, and Jacques will make a list of divorces in the department over the past few months and look into the reasons for these separations. Keeping in mind, to be sure, that the *corbeau*'s victims were not necessarily all officially married."

The three inspectors he'd mentioned fidgeted on their seats. The assignment seemed to them to involve an enormous amount of work for an uncertain result.

"We don't have to draw up an exhaustive list," Castello assured them. "We're after big fish. We're casting a wide net and seeing what we catch. You get all the divorce judgments for the past few months—let's say the last three—initially setting aside the ones involving mutual consent. If you have privileged relations with lawyers specializing in such cases, don't hesitate to make use of them: their information might be extremely valuable in making a first selection. We can't interview all the divorced people in the department—we don't have either the time or the means to do that—so don't hesitate to follow your intuition. And any victim you find must be questioned at length. What we need is to find a connection among them all, that's the best way to find the informer."

Castello glanced at Gilles. They had discussed the investigation together before the meeting.

"Between Valls and Abad, we have two possible connections, their work and their leisure activity: pool. The first connection doesn't work for the other two victims, and the second doesn't really work, either. Except if we consider that the

Balto, the bar where they played, is downtown, not far from the area where the *corbeau* made most of his calls. Might be a good idea to keep that in mind . . . Anything else, Gilles?"

Sebag nodded. He'd said there were three ways of identifying the informer and he had thus far only presented two.

"There's another factor we should never lose sight of during our investigations: the list of unhappy couples we're going to draw up might include our perpetrator."

Astonished, his colleagues stared at him. Julie was the first to understand.

"Is that what you were referring to a little while ago when you said that the *corbeau* was settling his accounts with adulterous women? You think that's his motive, that he himself was deceived by his own wife?"

"You won't have failed to notice that in the four cases we've discovered, the *corbeau* revealed only infidelities committed by women. For the time being, that's only a simple, maybe even a simplistic, hypothesis, but we mustn't neglect it. And here we come back to the different occupations mentioned earlier. If among recently divorced people you find lawyers, psychologists, cops, private detectives, physiotherapists, et cetera, give them priority."

"You will transmit everything to Gilles as you discover it," Castello said. "He's going to coordinate this investigation. As for you, Julie, I would like you to spend the day at the city's video-surveillance center: somewhere in Perpignan there's a man who spends his time following people and taking pictures of them with a telephoto lens. It must be rare for that kind of equipment to be used inside the city. At one time or another, he must have been filmed, and he will probably be filmed again. View their archives, starting with the places where the photos we have in our possession were taken, and first of all the Hôtel du Gecko. You will work with Thierry Lambert."

Castello paused before asking:

"Anything you want to add, say, or object to, ladies and gentlemen?"

Sebag looked at his colleagues. He was well aware that his reasoning had a flaw. And a major one! He was waiting to see if anyone would mention it. He saw Ménard wiggling on his chair. The objection would come from him. François ran his palm over his crew cut, and then waved his hand over his head.

"Yes, I have a question to ask."

Castello gave him the floor. Ménard addressed Gilles directly.

"From the outset, you have been speaking of 'the man' or 'the individual.' What if it were a woman? After all, this way of taking revenge—anonymous letters, murder by proxy—could be that of a woman, couldn't it?"

All the faces turned to Gilles. Ménard's remark contradicted what they had just considered as established.

"The term '*corbeau*' was popularized by Henri-Georges Clouzot's film, which came out under the German occupation,"[30] Sebag explained. "Because in that film, the author of the anonymous letters signed his messages with a drawing of a raven. The film was inspired by a case that occurred in Tulle[31] between 1917 and 1922. It took the police five years to identify and arrest the perpetrator—who was a woman, Angèle Laval, a secretary at the prefecture. One of her victims had ended up committing suicide."

Gilles was aware that his long-winded explanation reeked of Wikipedia. So what? It showed that he had done his homework and that Ménard's criticism had not caught him unprepared.

"Yesterday, after thinking about this case for hours, I considered the possibility that our *corbeau* might be a woman. But

[30] *Le Corbeau* ("The Raven"), 1943.

[31] A town in central France, about three hundred miles south of Paris.

this morning I used only the term 'individual,' which does not in any sense imply that the reference is solely to a man. I could have said 'person' rather than 'individual.'[32] But I didn't want to influence you. I wanted to see if the objection would arise by itself. A priori, most of you think in fact that the *corbeau* is a man. However, nothing in the file allows us to assert that."

Sebag looked at his colleagues, one after the other. Then he stopped at Ménard. From the beginning of this case, François had been nitpicking. Gilles had already discreetly tackled him a little earlier. He couldn't resist the desire to do it again.

"The real question now is: are we following this male lead because it is . . . how to put it . . . intuitively obvious, or because for too long we have wrongly suspected a man—the guard at Cantalou—and are incapable of starting our reasoning over from zero?"

On his left, Gilles noticed Molina's smile. He saw his teammate glance at Ménard and he could almost hear him thinking: "Gotcha! Take that!"

"So we come back to the question: could the *corbeau* be a woman? What do you think, François?"

"Uhh . . . I think we can't exclude that hypothesis."

To make it clear that he considered that answer inadequate, Gilles turned to his other colleagues.

"What else?"

The lieutenants looked at one another. Joan Llach was the first to offer a reasoned argument.

"When a crime is involved, we're usually dealing with men. And the more serious the crime, the greater the chance that it was committed by a man. But above all, it's a question of probability. We shouldn't eliminate anything."

[32] *J'aurais pu dire "la personne" plutôt que "l'individu."* Sebag is saying that the use of the feminine noun *la personne* might have suggested that he was referring to a woman—though *la personne* can also refer to a male person.

"Making use of anonymous letters has something devious about it that might be more feminine," Julie prudently suggested.

"I was waiting for you to say that," Molina commented. "I wouldn't have allowed myself . . ."

"I suspected that," Julie smiled. "I know how tactful you are."

Sebag waited for the chuckling to die down before continuing.

"I've looked into that question as well, and it's true that *corbeaux* are more often women. But most of the time, the letters contain insults and slanders. Our case is different: our *corbeau* reveals precise, proven facts, facts that he himself has brought to light through what was probably long and meticulous work."

The superintendent let a few seconds go by and, since no one else seemed to have anything to say, he concluded:

"So we won't set aside any lead, but to move faster, we'll give priority, at least initially, to leads involving males. Dismissed! We're going all out on this case, but we can't do it for long. Do a good job, I'm counting on you."

The policemen immediately stood up and left in single file. Castello put his hand on Sebag's arm.

"I'm glad to see that you're feeling better and that you're recovering your effectiveness."

Gilles thanked him soberly. He didn't want to get drawn into a personal discussion. Castello was still holding his arm.

"Do you remember that I mentioned a promotion to you?"

Sebag couldn't help sighing. His boss had been talking to him about this promotion at least once a month for the past year. And each time, he'd turned it down. He had made his choice when Séverine was born. To spend more time with his children, he'd chosen a flextime work schedule. Since then, he had gone back to full-time, and had been transferred to Perpignan, but basically nothing had changed for him. His family and his leisure activities had priority over his work. Even if his children were growing up and moving away, even if his wife had cheated on him . . . A new rank and a salary increase meant little to him, he wanted to be able to go home every night as early as possible and go out and run the trails from time to time without feeling guilty about it. His colleagues put up with his escapades and even helped him hide them. It would be different if he were promoted.

"I promise you to think about it again, boss."

"That's right . . . Take me for an idiot!"

After drinking a quick coffee at the Carlit, Gilles began by plunging into the TAJ.[33] Created very recently, the TAJ combined the old police files with the gendarmerie's files. It constituted a major advance for the work of all investigators. Unfortunately, it was still inadequate: ongoing cases seldom appeared in it, and even for those that had already been sent to court, key procedural elements were missing. In the TAJ, you found who did what and when, but as for the how and the why, you still had to call the people in charge of the file or travel to consult their archives. That wasn't too difficult for a case dealt with at police headquarters. On the other hand, it became longer and more complex when it involved an investigation carried out by the gendarmerie.

His work seemed to him even harder than he had thought. The example of Valls's suicide showed that the *corbeau*'s revelations had not always led to the punishment of an adulterous woman. It could easily be imagined that sometimes the cuckold's rancor had been directed against the lover rather than against the wife. Therefore he had to broaden his research.

For hours he consulted, compiled, sorted, classified, resorted, unclassified, ordered cases that ranged from murders—the

[33] *Traitement d'antécédents judiciaires*, a database created in 2011.

former were, fortunately, very rare in the department—to simple nighttime disturbances of the peace. Thus he also made a large number of telephone calls to ask for details or to request that he be faxed the basics of a proceeding.

Late in the afternoon what had to happen happened: a pitiless headache combined with total discouragement. Gilles opened his drawer to take a paracetamol tablet. Next to the box of medicine, the whiskey bottle taunted him. He'd bought it three or four days earlier and a little less than a third of it remained. For a moment, he was tempted to take the pill with a slug of alcohol, but he decided that the time of provocations and childish acts was over. He grabbed the bottle and headed for the door. He opened it partway and looked out. There was no one in the hallway. He stole down the corridor to the restroom and poured the remainder of the whiskey down the sink. With a glass of water in his hand, he went back to his office and swallowed the pill.

Around 6 P.M., Julie reported in. She seemed as exhausted as she was depressed. He offered her a paracetamol tablet, which she accepted.

"Do you know how many surveillance cameras there are in this town?" she asked.

"At least a hundred, I think."

"A hundred and eighty-three, to be exact. And if we tried to review all that in one week, at the rate of five eight-hour days, there would have to be . . . guess how many of us?"

"Stop . . . otherwise I'm going to have to take another pill."

"If I'm not mistaken, it would take fifteen hundred and thirty-seven cops working on it. Do you think that if I ask Castello for help with this, I'll have any chance of getting it?"

"Try calling the minister directly, instead . . . . But weren't you supposed to make a selective investigation focused on the places where the recent photos were taken?"

"That's what I did, and I didn't find anything. And for good reason! All the photos were taken more than two weeks before. And as I told you, in Perpignan the images are kept for only two weeks."

"I thought the law authorized keeping them for a month . . ."

"The law, yes, but not necessarily the storage capacity."

She looked again at the sheet of paper on which she'd made her calculations:

"Do you want me to convert the sixty-one thousand, four hundred and eighty-two hours of recordings into teraoctets for you?"

"Have pity on me . . ."

"It's a question of money. Storing images is expensive. The city of Perpignan has split the difference: only fourteen days of storage."

"Bad luck for us. And otherwise . . . has Thierry been of help to you, at least?"

The youngest guy on their team was also the one about whom his colleagues had the most reservations. His reflections alternated between the most dismaying naïveté and the crudest imbecility. The recurrent joke at headquarters consisted of proposing all kinds of hypotheses to explain how he had managed to get such a job at such a young age. Suggestions ranged from the classic diploma found in a laundry detergent package or in a bad German chocolate egg to an administrative error resulting from his very common last name. The jokes always ended by ardent laments for that other Thierry Lambert who had never gotten the diploma he deserved and was probably vegetating somewhere in an obscure department in northern France.

"He remained focused for a good two hours, I have to admit," Julie replied. "Then afterward he spotted two or three buddies in the images and started following them from one camera to the next. Then he started calling them to ask what they were doing on such and such a day at that hour and in that place!"

"Didn't you refocus him?"

"Since I'm the most recent arrival on the team, that seemed difficult to me. I told him he could do whatever he wanted so long as he kept an eye out for the photographer. In any case, we'll never be able to review more than a tiny part of everything that was recorded so that whether we're doing it chronologically, at random, or while following buddies, it comes after all to the same thing!"

"You're not wrong about that . . ."

"If you want my opinion, this shows the limits of these video-surveillance systems. The number of cameras in a city can always be increased, but enough agents can never be put in front of the screens. And if we had enough agents, it would be better to put them directly on the streets, wouldn't it? In Perpignan, on any given day there are only five municipal policemen monitoring the screens. Five for a hundred and eighty-three cameras—you'd have to be really lucky to follow a crime live."

"Sounds like you'd have to really like channel surfing to do that job . . ."

"For sure . . . if you don't, you get bored."

"The film must not be very exciting: lots of characters but no plot. Perpignan will never win an Oscar with that. At most, a special prize for experimental cinema at Cannes . . ."

Julie's laugh was drowned out by the noise of the door flying open. Molina burst into the room.

"What a fricking crappy day! If I'd wanted to be a scribbler I'd have worked for Social Security, for Christ's sake! The last time I spent a whole day with my ass glued to a seat, I think I was in middle school. I have lines of writing dancing before my eyes and sores on my butt."

"Are you sure it's not your hemorrhoids?" Gilles said.

Jacques glanced at Julie. He didn't like some of his health problems to be mentioned in front of young women.

"Shut your trap, you jerk!"

"Otherwise, what did you get out of this day?"

"Great fatigue."

"And lots of annoyance! I understood that. But what else?"

"Not much, exactly. I found two names of guys who had gotten divorced for serious offenses. You'll be able to compare them with the perpetrators of the crimes that you must have inventoried, but I'd be surprised if you found anything conclusive."

"Why?"

"Just because divorce proceedings for serious offenses always take a lot of time and so these two divorces were begun months ago, long before our *corbeau* went into action."

"Damn, I hadn't thought of that. But do you have other names to give me, too?"

"Yes, of course, I've got a list as long as your arm."

From the inside pocket of his jacket he took out some wrinkled papers. He unfolded them and held them out to his colleague. The first one was covered with grease spots.

"I classified everything in order: contested divorces first, obviously, and then divorces by mutual consent. But Joan will have more precise information to give you. He has a cousin and a nephew who work in lawyers' offices. He'll have stuff about ongoing proceedings. Of course, we can never say where we got our information!"

"And where is Joan now?"

"In Le Soler. He coaches a group of young rugby players every Monday. He told me he'd come by afterward."

"That's nice of him, but I don't want to hang around here until he's finished making his kids sweat! I've put in a hard day's work, too, I've had enough."

"Call him."

Sebag punched in Llach's number but got his answering machine. He left a message. When he was alone again in his office, he compared his research with Molina's. One name jumped out at him. A certain Sylvain Crochet. On the one hand, it was a divorce for "definitive severing of marital ties" decreed on December 12 of the last year, and on the other hand, a complaint for assault and battery was filed only two days later. Except that it was Crochet, the husband, who had filed the complaint.

The case had been handled by one of his colleagues, Estève Cardona, with whom Sebag had recently had problems. He called him and was lucky enough to catch him even though the hour was late.

"I need information about one of your cases."

Cardona remained silent for a long time before answering in an aggressive tone:

"Are you going to find fault with me again? Do you think my work is as bad as all that?"

"Not at all, Estève, I promise. It's just that this case may have a connection with the one I'm working on just now."

A heavy silence. The kind that precedes a storm. He had to quickly defuse the situation.

"I don't know anything about your case, and I urgently need your help for my investigation."

Still no response. OK. After the caress, turn up the heat.

"This morning Castello made the case I'm dealing with his top priority. I can have him make my request if you prefer it that way."

The sigh he heard in his receiver tickled his eardrum

"Beneath your nice-guy airs you're a real son of a bitch, Sebag."

Cardona put him on hold and two minutes later gave him the information he was asking for. Sylvain Crochet had in fact filed a complaint for assault and battery against his wife's lover. The fight had taken place in a shopping mall.

"The complaint was ultimately rejected," Cardona explained.

"It was Crochet who attacked the other guy. But since he's knee-high to a grasshopper and skinny as a rail, he got the worst of it."

Sebag hung up, satisfied. A cuckolded husband who had been humiliated by his ex-wife's lover after their divorce. That was enough to make somebody mad at the whole world. However, there was one problem: the husband in question was a mechanic, a trade that didn't really give him access to the kind of information the informer had acquired.

Nonetheless, Gilles felt he'd just found a fresh lead. At this stage of the investigation, he mustn't be too particular. Joan Llach called him back a few minutes later. Shouts and the dull thuds of a rugby ball could be heard in the background.

"It's not easy to talk with you at the moment, so I'll make it short. In a little while I'll give you a list of names and you can look it over tomorrow morning early, if you want. What I can tell you right now is that I've identified a potential suspect. He's a guy who is in the middle of a divorce for cause because he accused his wife of having cheated on him several times. According to what I was told by my cousin, who's defending him, dialogue with his wife appears to no longer be possible, they're completely at war with one another. And guess where the guy works?"

Sebag was tired, and not in the mood to play games.

"No idea."

"He's a technician with Orange[34] and I don't need to draw you a picture: considering the job he has, he must have access to a large amount of confidential information on customers."

Sebag took in this information with a mixture of interest and reservations. In the list of relevant occupations they'd summarily drawn up at that morning's meeting, no one had thought of a position as a technician with a telecommunications

[34] A global telecommunications company that is now a subsidiary of France Telecom and the main telephone and Internet provider in France.

company. However, there was a catch: this implied that all the victims were customers of the same company, and, as he recalled, that was not the case. He nonetheless wrote down the name that Joan gave him. Thus he had a second lead. The day hadn't been so fruitless after all.

It was time for him to go home. His stomach tensed. For him, this was the most difficult time of the day. He opened his drawer. Oh, yes . . . he'd thrown the whiskey out. He clicked his thirsty tongue. Too bad! Or rather all the better.

He put his hands on his desk, leaned back against his chair, and took deep breaths. About twenty of them, very slowly. Alcoholic crutches were a thing of the past. He'd put the hardest part behind him. They were going to make it. A few more breaths and he was convinced of it. The challenge was to stay that way as long as possible.

At least long enough to have a quiet evening with his family, that would be good.

Sebag already had his hand on the doorknob when he heard two timid knocks. He opened the door immediately and to his great surprise saw Thierry Lambert.

"Ah . . . Evening, Gilles. Are you leaving?"

Sebag had his jacket on and he had already turned up the collar against the *tramontane* that he had heard coming up during the afternoon.

"No, I was going to take a leak!"

Lambert slipped into the room.

"No problem, I can wait."

Gilles sighed and took off his jacket and hung it on the back of his chair. Lambert stood in front of Jacques's desk and started to arrange the objects on it. A pen to the right of the blotter, a paper cup in front of the computer, the mouse properly lined up.

"Are you OK, Thierry?"

"Yes, how about you?"

"Is something wrong?"

"No, no."

"But there is! Something's bothering you, I can see that . . . Sit down and tell me about it."

Lambert sat on a corner of Molina's desk.

"Nobody can hide anything from you, Gilles, you're really very good."

"You think?"

"Well, yeah, after all."

Lambert moved the mouse a millimeter. His furrowed brow showed his concern. Sebag looked at his watch. It was late, he was going to have to hurry Thierry along.

"Did your day at the video-surveillance center go well?"

Lambert's lips sketched an embarrassed smile.

"Yeah, it was fun! At least . . . at first."

Sebag sighed noisily and looked at his watch again. Lambert, lost in his thoughts, noticed nothing.

"And later . . . it was less fun?"

"Perpignan is a very small town, you know, and when you look at the images for a while you always end up spotting somebody you know. Do you know who Denis Barge is?"

"No."

"He's a pal of mine who works at the BAC.[35] We sometimes go out together. Sometimes just the two of us, or with another pal, sometimes with his wife. She's good-looking, his wife. Aurélie—that's her name—is a pretty blonde."

Sebag felt a shiver run down his spine.

"I'm really very concerned," Lambert added, looking down at his feet. "I saw her on the images, Aurélie, she was kissing some guy. And the guy wasn't Denis."

Sebag held his breath.

[35] *Brigade anti-criminality*, a special unit of the *Police national.*

"Such a numbskull, dammit, such a numbskull!" he exclaimed.

It was so obvious that he should have seen it from the outset but he hadn't seen anything.

"Yeah, I know," Lambert went on. "It wasn't very smart to follow her like that from one camera to the next, but I couldn't foresee . . . Now I don't know what to do, I don't know whether I should tell Denis about it. You're right, I'm really a dope!"

Gilles approached Lambert, scaring him.

"No, no, Thierry, I'm the one who's a dope. You . . ."

He put both hands on Thierry's cheeks and kissed him on the forehead.

"You're a genius!"

Chapter 42

With his elbows resting on the desk in front of the keyboard and his head leaning forward, he put his fingers on his closed eyelids and then ran them very slowly over his temples. He repeated this massage several times.

His day at work had exhausted him.

He felt a hand on his shoulder. He opened his eyes, sat up. A colleague was waiting to take over from him.

He leaned on the arms of his chair and got up. The chair's headrest could be adjusted for height and angle, it had lumbar support, the seat was also adjustable, everything had been designed for maximum comfort. Nonetheless! After a whole day without moving, the body stiffened up.

He went to the locker room, opened his locker, and took out his sports bag. A little exercise would do him good. The walk to the gym, an hour of exercise, a good shower, and he'd be a new man.

He strode quickly down the quays along the Basse. The wind was blowing, it was cold. He passed by people without seeing them. He was really very tired. After the guard had been released, he'd decided to slow down. The cops were coming closer. Too dangerous. With his mission suspended for the moment, his mind became freer.

Freer to think, freer to remember, freer to suffer.

He placed his badge in front of the electronic reader and opened the door to the gym. He greeted a few faces he recognized before putting on his gym clothes. A quarter of an hour on the stationary bicycle, three exercises for his pecs, four squat repetitions, and a minimal session for his abs.

Even the boiling hot shower didn't relax him.

When he left the gym, he walked to the bus stop on the Boulevard Wilson. He took a number 9 bus and twenty minutes later he got off not far from his house. He ate alone in the dining room, watching the evening TV news, did the dishes as he listened to *Scènes de ménages*,[36] and then returned to his lair. He booted up his computer, looked over his files—his "current cases"—and changed a few priorities he'd established earlier.

Around 10 P.M. he went to bed with a book, Claire Favan's *Le Tueur intime*.[37] He had time to read only a few pages. When he heard the front door open, he quickly turned out the light.

In the dark, he listened to the sounds of his past life. Keys laid on the table in the foyer, the microwave's buzzer, the tinkling of a plate in the sink, and then the creak of a step on the stairway, the seventh step at the turning. The rest took place too far away, he could now only imagine it. A faucet turned on, the clatter of a glass and a jar of makeup remover on the tiles around the washbasin in the bathroom, the water of the shower running over a warm body, then the door of the bedroom slamming. Finally, the sheets of a bed being folded back and a mattress groaning.

It took him a long time to fall asleep.

[36] A French television series. The title means "domestic rows."
[37] "The Intimate Killer," a French crime novel (2011).

CHAPTER 43

"I see that you've changed the teams. It's kind of a boring task, isn't it?"

The municipal policeman who had opened the door showed them a friendly face.

"It's not always fun for us, either, you know. Enlist, they say: in the police you'll always see action!"

Seeing his superior at the other end of the room, he added in a low voice:

"I'm joking, of course: I love this job!"

He extended a firm hand to Gilles:

"Special Agent Laurent Martinez."

Then he extended a softer hand to Julie.

"We've already met."

"Special agent?" she said with astonishment. "You didn't tell me that yesterday."

"I try to vary my jokes from day to day . . ."

The Perpignan municipal police video-surveillance room had four walls covered with screens. Each wall displayed sixteen different images transmitted live by the city's cameras. At their posts in front of a wall, the operators had two computers, a keyboard, and a joystick to aim as they wished the camera they had decided to follow.

"Look, Johnny is opening his little shop early this morning," a blond operator remarked, turning to her colleague, a chubby redhead.

Gilles and Julie could not resist leaning over to look at the computer screen. In a street in the old part of town, a man in his sixties dressed in a cheap tracksuit had leaned his bike against a wall and was waiting in front of a barred window. He took two blue bills out of his pocket. Forty euros. A hand appeared between the bars and whisked away the bills. A few seconds later it held out in return a small package covered with aluminum foil. The old man unfolded the package to examine its contents. The operator zoomed in and a stick of hash became clearly visible.

"The old guy has been cheated again," the blonde commented. "There's not forty euros' worth there."

"Johnny's experienced: he knows who he can rip off," the redhead replied before focusing her attention again on her own computers.

Sebag couldn't conceal his surprise. The old man had opened his package right across from a camera attached to a building less than five meters away.

"It looks like he doesn't realize."

"Special Agent" Laurent Martinez shrugged.

"Most people forget that the cameras are there, including certain criminals. The rest don't give a flying fuck. We've mentioned this drug dealing to your colleagues and they've asked us to keep an eye on it while they try to determine the source of supply. As for the users, they're in no danger. We know this old guy. He goes to smoke his joint every afternoon on a bench on the Place de Belgique."

A woman came up to them. Svelte, she managed to look elegant in the municipal police force's uniform, navy blue slacks fitted at the waist and ankles and a sweatshirt of the same color with lighter blue stripes across the chest. The stripes undulated gracefully over her breasts. Chief Brigadier Josiane Masson greeted them with authority. The intent look she gave Julie did not escape Gilles. Clearly, his colleague was well-considered here. Josiane Masson took a paper bag off the redhead's desk and handed it to the police officers.

"Chocolate cream puffs. They'll blow you away. Take all you want, Pauline has already eaten enough of them!"

Then she led them to the back of the big room where a desk was reserved for them. It also had two computers, a keyboard, and a joystick.

"I won't explain how to use this," she told Sebag. "Julie has already mastered it."

The radio crackled in the room.

"Checking out a group of young people riding scooters without helmets on the Place de la Liberté. Please secure the area."

The head of the center left them the package of chocolate cream puffs and headed for the walls of screens. Julie explained to Gilles that every time the police went into action, an operator kept a close eye on the zone and the surrounding area to prevent any disturbance or outside interference. It was routine.

"So what about us? What are we going to do now?" Julie asked. "We didn't come back to look at all the recordings . . ."

"No, but we can't move in directly, either. This morning Castello met with the adjunct assigned to the city's security forces. He's going to send us a complete list of the police officers who work here: their personnel files, vital statistics, possible past problems, etc. We decided to bypass the head of the center to avoid the risk of a leak."

Julie pointed to the computers.

"So while we wait we just look at images as if nothing were up?"

"Precisely. We pretend to be working, we're friendly with the staff, and we chat. I think if you handle it well, you could probably worm a little information out of the special agent. And also the boss!"

Julie elbowed him in the ribs.

"Nothing escapes you, does it? And what are you going to do?"

"I like the redhead. I'll deal with the blonde, too."

"You're pretty greedy."

Sebag made sure that no municipal agent was nearby before taking a sheet of paper out of his hip pocket. He unfolded it. It was a copy of a photo taken by the *corbeau*. The one that showed Christine Abad and Éric Balland going into the Hôtel du Gecko together.

"I have to check a little detail. Can you call up on the screen the images from the camera on the Place des Poilus?"

"A recorded image or the live ones?"

"Live ones are better."

Julie typed on the keyboard and the Rue des Augustins came to life on the screen. Stopped in the middle of the street, an artisan's van was blocking traffic. But that wasn't what interested Sebag.

"Can you aim the camera wherever you want?"

"Of course."

Julie worked the joystick. The image shifted toward the north side of the Place des Poilus. A gray blur covered part of the screen.

"Protection of private life," she explained. All the cameras are set so that you can't see inside the apartments."

"That's normal . . . Pivot left as far as you can. OK, that's good. Now all the way to the right. Perfect. Now move downward. Great . . ."

After glancing over his shoulder, Gilles showed the copy of the photo to his colleague.

"What do you say about this?"

Julie didn't need to examine it very long.

"That it was taken in from a position this camera doesn't cover."

"Are there other cameras in this sector?"

"Definitely. We're right in the middle of the high-priority security zone: there are about fifty just in this part of downtown."

With one click, Julie brought up a map studded with red dots representing all the cameras. Another click and the image of the Place des Poilus appeared from a different angle. Julie zoomed in and pivoted the camera from right to left again, then downward.

"There's a blind spot. The same one. The photographer couldn't be seen while he was taking pictures.

She added in a lower voice:

"And he knew that. Our lead might be the right one. There were other photos, weren't there? Of Christine and her lover each alone?"

"Yes. All from the same angle."

She put her hands on the armrests of her chair and raised herself to look at the video-surveillance room.

"So who here could be a talented photographer? If it's a guy we're looking for, there aren't many candidates."

Except for Agent Martinez, who had taken a seat before a wall of screens, only one other man was working in the room. He was handling radio communications with the patrols.

"You don't put too much stock in the hypothesis that the person we're looking for is a woman?" she asked again.

"No, I don't. All this time we've been operating on the premise that the *corbeau* was a man and it's always hard to start over from zero."

Julie nodded. Gilles went on:

"In spite of everything, I have a hard time thinking it was a woman. So let's stick to Castello's instructions: give first priority to men. Out of a staff of twenty-five, only nine men work here."

"For the moment, there are only two."

"They relay one another 24/7. In my estimation, there are never more than two or three at a time. By the way, are you still not smoking?"

"Why do you ask?"

"Because if you went out for a smoke, I'm sure that the special agent would follow you . . ."

"There's a coffee machine in the corridor, that might work, too."

"It might. Have you got change?"

"Yes. But I think I'm going to have to ask someone to give me some . . ."

Julie walked over to the desk occupied by Laurent Martinez. She whispered a few words in his ear and he rose instantly. The head of the center watched them disappear into the hallway.

Sebag took over the joystick. He'd understood generally how it worked, and he moved from one camera to another, following random people in the street, zooming in on this or that person to examine a body type or clothing. He stopped on a group of young people who were talking around a public bench. If he'd been able to read their lips, he could have known everything they said. The discomfort he'd felt at the beginning had already disappeared. See without being seen. He found that amusing. He felt omnipotent.

"You've already mastered it, that's good."

Josiane Masson had come up to him.

"I'm impressed by the quality of your cameras," Gilles congratulated her.

"It varies a lot depending on the model. The development of video-surveillance in Perpignan has proceeded by stages, and in each new phase, the cameras are more effective. The definition of the images is improving, which is particularly important on rainy days and at night."

"I'd never come here. It's impressive."

At the same time that he was saying this, Sebag realized that if he had been better acquainted with this cavern of Big Brother, he wouldn't have lost twenty-four hours wondering how their *corbeau* could be so well informed. That said, even if the man he was looking for worked here, that didn't answer all his questions.

The head of the center was continuing to talk to him about technology, but he'd lost the thread. She was discussing a new generation of revolutionary cameras.

"I didn't understand very concretely how that works."

He was satisfied with his vague formula, which allowed him to avoid admitting that he hadn't followed anything at all. Josiane Masson smiled indulgently.

"I'll show you."

She sat down in the chair Julie had occupied and took over the system.

"This is a camera that films live."

She manipulated the joystick, making the camera move.

"As you've already been able to see with your colleague, you can do almost anything—pivot, zoom in, et cetera."

She typed on the keyboard, clicked with the mouse. Another image appeared. The Place Arago at night.

"This is an image recorded last night."

A plastic bag was flying through the air and got caught on the extended arm of the statue of the French physicist,[38] who had been born in Northern Catalonia. The few passersby were hurrying along, their heads down and their collars pulled up to protect their necks. The *tramontane* was blowing through the heart of the city. The image moved from one side of the square to the other and enlarged certain details, not always for any good reason. It took Sebag a while to realize that the brigadier's hand was no longer on the joystick.

"The movement of the camera is programmed, and you're no longer controlling it, right?"

The brigadier nodded. She put a finger on the screen.

"If a crime is committed in front of the Palmarium at the moment that the camera is pivoting, we won't see anything in the recording."

[38] François Arago (1786-1853).

"Does that happen?"

"Yes, unfortunately. It even happens frequently."

Sebag made a quick calculation. With five operators on average (not including breaks) in front of the screens and sixteen screens per operator, most of the cameras were thus functioning automatically.

"We will no longer have this problem with the new little marvel we're going to receive soon. And the quality of the images will be spectacular."

Josiane Masson stopped the recorded image.

"You see the car there, the one that's heading for the Castillet?"

Sebag spotted a white Audi. The chief enlarged the image so that they could read the license plate. But the more the plate was enlarged, the blurrier the numbers became.

"On an image filmed live, the camera refocuses automatically but here, that is no longer possible. It's like you on your screen, when you want to see a detail better."

"That must be frustrating, too."

"Fortunately, it's not a hopeless situation. We have "20/15 . . ."

"Excuse me?"

The brigadier smiled:

"One of our agents has particularly sharp eyes. I'm sure he could have deciphered that plate. He'll be here this afternoon, we'll show it to him if you want."

"That would be great."

Josiane Masson got up to give her seat to Julie, who was returning with a coffee cup in her hands. They exchanged a few more words, and then the brigadier let them work.

"So?" Sebag asked as soon as Masson was far enough away.

"Special Agent Martinez is thirty-five, he has two daughters, eleven and eight years old. He's a regular cyclist and the *tramontane* doesn't keep him from riding, on the contrary, he takes advantage of the wind to perfect his position on his bike. It seems that's as good as the champion racers' training in wind tunnels."

"You don't say . . ."

"He began working on the streets, but had to stop because of a heart problem. He got divorced eight months ago . . ."

"Ah, ah."

"Don't get too excited! He made it clear with a wink that it was his cheating that had led his wife to ask for a divorce. 'You understand, a man has needs that women don't have,' the asshole even added. I swear you've got some real specimens among you."

"Among us?"

"Among you men!"

"Ah . . ."

Sebag didn't want to get into that debate, he didn't really feel that it concerned him personally. He turned back to the screens.

"We're going to view a few recordings, anyway. Did you look at the camera on the Quai Vauban yesterday?"

"No, not that one."

"Then let's have a look at the film. All we need is popcorn."

Julie handed him the last cream puffs.

"Here, stuff yourself!"

"Thanks."

They ran through at high speed the fourteen days of recording and followed in particular the dismantling of the Christmas market stands, then the removal of the decorations. Gilles noticed that the strings of Christmas light spotted the image with white haloes that made the night recording partially unusable. From time to time, they slowed down the film to look more carefully at a tourist who was taking photos. It was a false alarm each time. On January 9, they spotted Molina walking along the quay with a pal of his.

"Can you imagine a woman working here who sees her husband buying her Christmas gift in a stand?" Julie said. "Goodbye, surprise . . ."

"And if she didn't find it under the tree because he was buying it for another woman . . . Merry Christmas!"

"You're right. I wouldn't like to work here!"

After the camera on the Quai Vauban, they moved to the one on the Rue de Sully. They lingered in this part of downtown where the *corbeau* had made his calls. They were interrupted by a radio alert.

"A woman has had her purse stolen in front of the cathedral. Description: two young men in jeans, sweatshirts, and caps. Probably minors."

Julie and Gilles got up to help find the thieves. They stood behind the desk that Laurent Martinez was sharing with the attractive redhead.

"Talk about an identikit picture!" the "special agent" laughed. "Two teenagers in caps who are surely going to head for Cassanyes . . ."

The heart of working-class Perpignan was the Place Cassanyes, a junction point between the gypsy quarter and a few "Arab streets." Every morning, there was a colorful market there.

"I think I've got them," the redhead contradicted him. "There, Rue du Figuier."

On her screen, two young men were trotting along, frequently looking up at the sky. Or at the cameras. One of the two seemed to be holding something hidden under his sweatshirt.

"We've got a patrol not far away," cried the man who was handling the radio connection. Keep guiding us."

The two operators moved from one camera to another and followed the pursuit.

"It's like in the movies," Sebag murmured.

"Almost," the brigadier corrected him behind his back. "It's not as easy in reality. It requires a great knowledge of the map of Perpignan and the positions of the cameras. Pauline has been working here for seven years, and Laurent has joined us more recently. But he got to know the area earlier, and that's a terrific advantage. He has a feeling for the street."

A patrol intercepted the two teenagers at the foot of the Rue des Quinze Degrés. The officers lifted up the sweatshirts and found only a little backpack. No purse!

"They played us," Martinez understood immediately. "They decoyed us and we fell for it like greenhorns. I'm going to find those little bastards."

He switched over to the images recorded a few minutes earlier by the cameras in the area. Pauline spoke to Sebag.

"Are you the one who arrested a drug dealer about two weeks ago?"

Sebag said he was.

"We followed you live. I have to say that you really amused us. At first, nobody was betting on you, you didn't look to be in very good shape, and then you were . . . uhh . . . less young. But finally you took over, little by little. I was the first to put my bet on you."

"Thanks."

"I'm the one who should be thanking you. Chantal a little less: she had to pay up."

Three meters farther on, the blond Chantal gave her a forced smile over her computers. "There! I've got them!"

On Martinez's screen, two teenagers, crouching on a pedestrian street, were examining the contents of the stolen purse. They opened the wallet and the card-holder and took out only cash. After removing the SIM card, they also took the mobile phone. Then they threw the purse into a nearby trash bin. Finally, they moved off, their heads still hidden in their hoodies. Martinez managed to follow them as far as the

Place Cassanyes, where they disappeared into the crowd in the market.

"We'll find the purse," Masson said, putting the best face on the situation. "The victim won't have to stop payment on her credit cards. She'll even keep all her telephone contacts on her SIM card."

"It's frustrating all the same," Julie said regretfully.

"That's part of the game. The video-surveillance system sometimes gives us the impression that we're all-powerful, and sometimes it makes us feel completely powerless: we're in front of our screens and we can't do a thing."

"How does one move from the street to this room?" Julie asked.

Josiane took several steps backward to let the operators work. Or so they wouldn't hear. She replied in a low voice:

"A few joined the municipal police solely in order to work here. I don't have to tell you that working on the street is hard. Even unbearable for some people."

"Is that why most of them are women?"

"Absolutely. In general, for men this is a stage, either the beginning or the end of a career. It can even be a way of taking a break."

"Laurent Martinez has heart problems, I think."

"Heart problems . . . What do you mean by that?"

Julie realized that her formulation had been ambiguous.

"A cardiac malformation, he told me."

The head brigadier frowned.

"Everyone has his own reasons that are his own business."

Sebag felt his hair stand on end. Her tone was too vague, there was a movement of her body that was not under her control: Josiane Masson had just evaded the question. Maybe she was astonished that her agent had already told the pretty young lieutenant so many details about his private life.

They left the video-surveillance center shortly before noon and went for a run along the Têt. Sebag's body already felt tired from having remained sitting all morning in front of the computer screens. They trotted along at a good pace for about forty minutes.

"I feel better," Julie said.

"I think I'm on the right track. I'm getting a grip on myself."

"And at home?"

"Let's say that I'm managing to avoid subjects that lead to conflict."

Since his return from Bayonne and the call to his father, questions hadn't miraculously stopped flowing into his brain, but he had been able to keep them to himself. An initial victory. Claire had also gotten back into stride to a certain extent. Not too much, either. Just as much as was necessary.

They took a quick shower at Julie's place, gulped down a sandwich, and returned to headquarters. Using his computer, Gilles printed the first information Castello had received from the adjunct in charge of security. They read the documents at the Carlit over cups of coffee. Among the nine men at the center, two were divorced and three were bachelors. The others were assumed to be happily married.

"Well, well, well . . ."

Julie handed Sebag a sheet of paper.

"Does our 'special agent' have a secret?"

Gilles read the note and learned that Laurent Martinez had been stabbed eighteen months earlier during an incident on the streets. Nothing serious, however. But he had later taken leave because he was depressed. When he went back to work, he'd been assigned to the video-surveillance center.

"Cardiac malformation, my ass," Sebag exclaimed after reading the document.

"Might be a heart problem all the same."

"What do you mean?"

"I remind you that he's divorced."

"Yes, but he was the one who . . ."

Sebag interrupted himself.

"You think that he lied to us about that, too? That he might not have been the one who cheated?"

"Someone who has lied once will lie again."

"That's a real 19th arrondissement proverb!"

"No. I invented it. You twist proverbs, I have the right to invent them. I think this one is very practical, you can use it in all sorts of contexts: someone who has stolen will steal again, who has killed will kill again, who has cheated . . ."

She slapped herself on the cheek.

"I'm sorry, Gilles, I spoke without thinking."

"It's OK . . ."

Fidelity was like virginity. Once the step had been taken, it was more difficult to start over. He had told himself that not so long ago, when he was at the bottom of the pit. Stupidities . . . Words, nothing but words. The lesson must have been learned: Claire wouldn't do it again. Ever. To drive away these thoughts, he called Molina. With Llach and Ménard, they were still pursuing the other leads.

"Did you get anywhere this morning?"

"What do you think? That we've just been lazing around?"

Genuine aggressiveness. Molina had something new.

"So . . . . Sylvain Crochet first," Molina began. "He's the mechanic who divorced his wife for 'definitive severing of marital ties' and who got beaten up by his wife's lover, you remember? Ménard found him: the guy quit his job and went back to where he came from, Berry,[39] I think. So we can cross him off the list."

Sebag had turned on the speaker and Julie was listening in on the conversation.

[39] A region in central France.

"So . . . now Henri Sylvert. He's the guy who works for Orange and who is being divorced for serious offenses. Llach talked to him and, believe it or not, he killed two birds with one stone: he crossed him off the list of suspects and put him on the list of victims."

"He was contacted by the *corbeau*?"

"Precisely! But he received only photos, he never got a phone call."

"No kidding!"

"Apparently the guy has his personal enemies, because I also came across another victim of the *corbeau* this morning, and he too received only photos."

"Interesting . . . That gives us six victims at this point, if I'm counting correctly. Did you find any points in common?"

"Not really. Apart from downtown Perpignan. The female technician at Orange saw her lover at the Paris-Barcelone, a hotel across from the train station. As for the mechanic's wife, we don't know anything."

"I suppose there are cameras around the station. I'll check that this afternoon with Julie. For the moment, although your info doesn't confirm our current hypothesis, it doesn't invalidate it, either. By the way, I've got a little job for you, OK?"

"No problem."

Gilles asked Jacques to find out what he could about Laurent Martinez, and then ended the conversation. With Julie, he returned to the video-surveillance center. The morning team had been joined by the famous 20/15. The one who had been presented to them as a phenomenon opened his mouth only long enough to greet them briefly.

"Beneath his gruff exterior, he's a real sweetheart," the chief told them discreetly. "And he has a deadpan sense of humor. He can go for hours without speaking and then make a joke just when you expect it the least."

Sebag waited until they had taken their seats before consulting his list. In real life, 20/15 was called Olivier Carbonnell. He was fifty-two years old, and had been married to Annie Fabre for twenty-six years. A former press correspondent, he had joined the municipal police after being dismissed as part of a downsizing.

The afternoon passed in a soporific calm. Around 3 P.M. Julie went out again to drink a cup of coffee, and this time it was Josiane Masson who followed her out of the room. When Julie returned, she confirmed what Sebag had sensed that morning:

"She likes women."

Sebag grimaced.

"Shit! It didn't occur to me until just now: she could also have been the victim of an unfaithful woman: do you think we have to add her to the list of suspects?"

"Oh . . ."

They both reflected for a few moments before setting that hypothesis aside. Julie spoke first:

"I don't know what to give as an argument, it's mainly just an impression, but I think that a lesbian who had been cheated on and who wanted to avenge herself as the *corbeau* did would attack all cheaters, not just women."

"I rather agree with you. As a woman herself, she couldn't be angry with women in particular. Yeah, I don't think we need to change our priorities: our *corbeau* is a man, divorced or a bachelor, but a man!"

Sebag overcame his boredom by going out several times to the parking lot to smoke a cigarette. The third time he did so, Pauline the redhead joined him.

"Can I bum one off you? I stopped but I can't resist. I don't know what I miss more, the tobacco or the break."

Gilles handed her a cigarette.

"I'll let you take just one puff, I don't want to be responsible for your relapse."

Pauline accepted the deal with a languid batting of her eyelids. She drew on the cigarette before handing it back to Sebag.

After making a few general remarks about their work, Gilles decided to ask more precise questions.

"While I was viewing your archives this morning, I spotted a colleague. When you see someone you know, isn't it tempting to follow him for a while to see what he's doing?"

"Following little hoodlums we've already spotted is more or less the basis of our work. That's what we do during dull moments. We try to anticipate their offenses."

"I wasn't talking about hoodlums."

"I know . . . ."

She held out her hand. He gave her his cigarette again.

"Of course it's tempting," she admitted. "But it's strictly forbidden. A question of ethics!"

"Do the municipal police respect ethics more than the national police?"

She smiled.

"You've seen the conditions we work under: we're on top of one another. It wouldn't be easy."

He took his cigarette back, took a drag on it, and handed it back to her.

"Not easy but not impossible. Don't tell me you've never done that?"

"OK, yes, but I didn't tell you this."

"Who was it?"

He pointed to the wedding ring on her finger.

"Your husband?"

She had just taken two drags in row but nonetheless hung onto the cigarette.

"My son," she finally confessed. "I saw him one afternoon in the middle of downtown when he was supposed to be at the lycée. I had just discovered a few days earlier that in his room he had the materials for rolling a joint. I said to myself that I could find out who his dealer was and have him arrested. Catching him in the act with my son would have really put the fear of God into him."

She took another puff. Sebag took back his cigarette, which was almost completely smoked.

"And then?"

"Then he met a girlfriend in a public park and they smooched on a bench. I'd never been so ashamed."

"What if it had been your husband?"

He was aware that he had rushed the question. But he had just put out his cigarette in the parking lot and the break was almost over. Pauline's mouth twitched several times before she answered:

"That's exactly what I asked myself and I promised myself that I'd never do it again. If my husband cheats on me someday, I'd prefer not to know about it."

Her face relaxed and a raffish spark shone in her eyes.

"Just as I would hope that *he* wouldn't know anything. If ever . . ."

She didn't finish her sentence and turned her back on him. His eyes followed the delicious shape of her ass. Sebag felt himself blushing involuntarily, and he cast a worried eye on the video camera attached to the wall over the door. His telephone vibrated in his pocket and showed him a face. Molina's name appeared on the screen.

"Can you talk freely, Gilles?"

"Yes, I'm outside."

"I've got something new concerning your Martinez. I've just spoken with his ex-wife. They separated by mutual consent but first he tried a procedure for serious offense: he surprised her with another man!"

"You see? That's the second time we've caught this rascal in a flat-out lie."

"Ah, ah . . . this is getting interesting."

"Hmm . . ."

"What do you mean, 'hmm' . . . ?"

Chapter 44

Seated on the grass, Sebag contemplated the city of Perpignan spread out below him. The bleating of sheep occasionally drowned out the urban rumble. The country in the city. A beautiful utopia.

A military fort built in the nineteenth century on a hill south of Perpignan, the Serrat d'en Vaquer had pretty grounds neglected by the Catalans. From this summit, there was a view of the sea, Le Canigou, and the whole city dominated by the Palace of the Kings of Majorca. But nobody came up this far. It was not the solid ramparts that frightened families, but the shady fauna that peopled the bushes at their feet. For years, this area had been the favorite meeting place for homosexuals looking for partners. When he had parked his car in front of the entrance to the park, Sebag had taken care to lower the sun visor on the back of which the word "POLICE" was written in large blue letters. He wanted to discourage certain ardors.

Chubby clouds were galloping over his head. The air remained basically cool, but the sun's rays were caressing Sebag's back through his jacket. Like a foretaste of spring. However, it was only mid-January and it would still be a while before he would see the sunny flakes of the mimosa and then the almond trees' nuggets of snow.

Patience . . . . Life would soon be reborn.

With Julie, they had decided to wait before questioning Laurent Martinez directly, and since the preceding day they had been having him followed by a team. The special agent had left the video-surveillance center in his car shortly after 6 P.M., taking with him 20/15 and Pauline, the redhead. Sebag smiled. With those nicknames, you might have thought they were working on a vice case. Martinez had dropped off his colleagues on the Place de Catalogne and then returned to a small house in the Haut-Vernet neighborhood. He did not emerge until the next day at 7:30 A.M., to go back to work, stopping again at the Place de Catalogne to pick up Carbonnell and the redhead.

Nothing to report.

That morning, still with Julie, Sebag had met Virginie Coste, Martinez's ex-wife. She had told them about the circumstances under which Laurent had surprised her with her lover. It was a Friday. She had spent the afternoon at her lover's home in Canohès, a village about eight kilometers from Perpignan, and they had prolonged their pleasure by talking in her car. They were no longer able to separate. Laurent had arrived on a motorcycle. He'd come up alongside the car, looked inside, and zoomed off again, making his engine snarl.

That night at the house, the argument had been stormy, and the quarrel definitive. Virginie was in love and it was no longer with her husband!

Laurent had always refused to tell her how he had found out about her infidelity, but he knew that she had been with her lover at Canohès since 1 P.M. that day. Virginie was convinced that he had bugged her telephone. She'd quickly bought another one.

The bleating came closer. Accompanied by two Pyrenean Mountain Dogs, the flock of sheep was now feasting right below him. The old shepherd, leaning on his staff, was smoking the cigarette that he had just rolled. Sebag greeted him.

"Let's get back to our sheep,"[40] he said to himself.

[40] "*Revenons à nos moutons,*" a quotation from a medieval farce that means figuratively: "let's get back to the subject at hand."

Had Laurent Martinez used the city's surveillance cameras to track his wife? It was possible. But these cameras could not have led him to the village of Canohès. The hypothesis of telephonic espionage remained plausible.

Hmm . . .

The "hmm . . ." Sebag had uttered when Molina informed him of Martinez's lie regarding his divorce had continued to resound within him. To reason with him. Everything wasn't so simple. There remained knots to be undone. Either Martinez was hiding his game very well, or he was still not the right customer. Despite his little mendacities, the "special agent" seemed to him rather simple in nature, far removed from the probably twisted personality of the *corbeau.*

A sheep had strayed from the flock and was slowly approaching him without ceasing to graze on the grass. One of the two dogs came over to place itself between them and gave a brief bark, a warning addressed as much to the human as to the animal. The sheep raised its head for a moment. It did not become agitated, but calmly rejoined its flock.

Sebag was beginning to glimpse another path to the solution. Laurent Martinez had things to tell them. Perhaps all it would take was a few barks to make him finally put them on the right track.

Chapter 45

Good evening. What brings you here?"

When he opened the door of the little house and found the two lieutenants on his doorstep, Laurent Martinez initially had a radiant smile. But the closed faces of Julie and Gilles turned this smile into a grimace.

"What's going on?"

"Can we come in?" Gilles asked.

Martinez stepped aside.

"Please do. Excuse the mess, I don't have the children this week, so this really looks like a bachelor's house."

They entered a living room full of cardboard boxes. The television was on, and in front of it a pile of laundry was heaped on an ironing board.

"I was about to start working on it," Martinez joked.

Sebag pushed aside a box to make his way toward the sitting corner.

"And when do you expect to finish moving?"

Agent Martinez replied in a less cheerful tone:

"When I feel up to it . . ."

"How long have you been here?"

"Five months."

"Ah, yes, all the same!" Julie exclaimed.

"The house belongs to one of my uncles. He was going to sell it when I got separated. He's lending it to me. But I have to buy back the furniture. You know how it is, a divorce: you give up half of your property."

He took another pile of laundry off the couch and put it on the floor.

"But I still have this couch."

He was already smiling again.

"Please sit down."

He took a box and put it on another one in front of them.

"It'll take me just a second," he added before disappearing into the kitchen.

Sebag and Julie heard water running and dishes tinkling. Martinez came back with three stemmed glasses and set them on the piled-up boxes.

"You'll have something, won't you? Well . . . I mean a glass of wine, that's all I've got."

"No problem that's fine," the lieutenants said.

In the mess, the special agent dug out a bottle. He opened it and filled the three glasses. The sadness prevailing in the room was in furious contrast with the good humor displayed by the municipal policeman.

"So, to what do I owe this honor?"

"We're here because you lied to us," Sebag began.

Martinez stared at him.

"Excuse me?"

"You lied to us about the reasons for your transfer to the video-surveillance center and the causes of your divorce."

Martinez's eyes moved from Gilles to Julie and then from Julie to Gilles.

"What are you talking about?"

"It was after your fight on the street that you asked to be assigned to the center, and not because of some so-called cardiac malformation. As for your divorce, it was your wife who cheated on you, not the other way around."

Martinez couldn't get over his stupefaction. His mouth was open and he gasped for oxygen to feed a brain that was running wild.

"But . . . I . . . but . . . It's per . . . sonal."

He took his glass of wine and drank it dry. Better than the oxygen, the alcohol put his mind back in place.

"All that is none of your business!"

His stupor gave way to anger. He rose from the box on which he had perched one of his buttocks.

"What's all this police stuff? What are you meddling in? Don't you have anything better to do? Since when do you have to reveal your whole life the minute a policeman asks you a question around a coffee machine? Does respect for private life mean anything to you? Do I ask you questions about your life?"

His diatribe had run out of steam. Sebag felt like he was reading Martinez like a book. As he spoke, the municipal officer had realized that the two cops hadn't come about his tall tales, that they must have good reasons for being there and for asking him these questions. Julie took over and explained their investigation.

Sebag examined the living room. Disorder, dirt, neglect. What would his house look like if Claire had left him for her Simon, and he'd found himself alone? Probably in the same state. With a few dead soldiers under the couch. He took the glass and drank a swallow. A bad wine. A fruit juice past its expiration date. He saw many similarities between Martinez and the former night guard at Cantalou. Two men unlucky in love, two depressives, too exhausted by the ordeal for either of them to be capable of duplicity or especially of Machiavellianism. And Gilles understood the reasons that had led Martinez to disguise reality.

Julie was completing her explanations. She implied that they'd thought for a moment that the *corbeau* might be a police officer at the video-surveillance center but were on the wrong track and had come there to confirm that conclusion. Together, they had decided on this tactic before entering the house. It was based on their first question:

"Why did you lie to us?"

Martinez had poured himself another glass of wine. He drank at least half of it and answered without raising his eyes to Julie's:

"You think it's easy to tell a pretty girl that you've gone off the street because you're too scared and that you're divorced because your wife has made you a cuckold?"

Sebag noticed the wink Julie gave him to make sure that the word hadn't hurt him. A real mother hen. Martinez swallowed the other half of his glass:

"My grandfather always said: it's better to be envied than pitied."

Strangely, it was that formula that touched Gilles. Had he been pitied? Claire and Julie had probably pitied him a little, and he certainly pitied himself. But he'd regained control of himself. Everything would go better now.

"Since you have nothing to reproach yourself for," Julie went on, "you can let us inspect your house?"

"Well, go ahead, then . . ."

Julie got up and disappeared into the house. Martinez's agreement without arguing already made it possible to cross him off the notorious list that no longer had a single name on it.

"Do you have a camera?" Gilles asked.

"Yes, I have one. A gift from my parents. So that I could take pictures of my daughters."

He went to get it from a box and showed it to Sebag. It was a very classical compact model.

"Can I look at it?"

Martinez turned the camera on and handed it to him. Gilles made the images pass by. He found only photos of two adorable, smiling girls.

"They're beautiful," he said, handing the camera back to Martinez. "Can I also ask you to write me a note on a sheet of paper?"

Martinez agreed again. As docile as a sheep. Sebag dictated the famous phrase to him, the same one he'd found at Abad's house on the back of a photo taken by the *corbeau*: "Every Thursday and sometimes on Tuesday. You know how to reach me." Then he put the paper in his pocket. He wasn't an expert in graphology but the writing seemed to him completely different. Julie came back to them.

"Nothing to report . . . I even had a look in the garage."

She sat down again on the couch. The serious stuff could begin now. Sebag cleared his throat.

"How did you learn that your wife had a lover?"

The question disconcerted Martinez.

"But . . . why are you asking that personal question again?"

"Was it by following her with the city's cameras that you found out?"

"Are you still suspecting me of being your *corbeau*?"

"No, you're no longer a suspect. But you might have used the city's surveillance system to spy on your wife."

"You're crazy, that's serious, too, as an accusation! You're trying to get me fired."

He tried to pour himself more wine but Julie stopped him.

"You want me dead, is that it? First the attack, then the divorce, and now dismissal . . . You want me to throw myself out the window?"

"Don't snivel: it's better to be envied than pitied, right?" Sebag snapped. "And besides, this is a one-story house."

Martinez made up his mind to answer. He did it hurriedly:

"I bugged her phone. I found spy software on the Internet, I loaded it on her mobile and that way I could follow her movements. One day, I saw she was spending the afternoon in Canohès, where, so far as I was aware, she didn't know anybody. I went there and I saw them together in her car. There, now you know everything. Personally, I've never used the city's cameras to follow anyone close to me, I swear it to you."

There was one adverb too many in his sentence.

"You were a jealous husband?" Sebag asked.

"Not so much . . ."

"Sooner or later, all men and women have suspicions regarding their spouses, but few of them go so far as to bug their telephones."

"All right, let's say that I was jealous!"

"You undoubtedly had serious reasons for being jealous," Julie suggested.

Martinez's tone softened.

"When a woman comes home late more and more often, when she seems absent even when she's with you, when she pays more attention than usual to how she looks, you begin to wonder. That's legitimate, isn't it?"

Julie glanced again at Sebag, who took a slug of rotgut before continuing.

"And you bought software to bug her phone?"

"I don't know what you would have done in my place, but that's what I did."

"I don't believe you."

"You have to have been in my position to know what you'd be capable of doing in such a situation."

Sebag gritted his teeth. Good God! Was he doing it on purpose, this guy, pushing on the places where it hurt? But he mustn't let himself be distracted, they'd arrived at the crucial point, they had to set the hook.

Gilles supposed that Martinez hadn't learned of his wife's adultery, like all the others, simply by photos. His hypothesis was audacious, and at first Julie had rejected it when he'd talked about it. But he'd been able to convince her. A little by the pertinence of his arguments, and a lot by the urgency to try it out. They hadn't made much progress in their investigation, and Castello was not going to delay blowing the whistle to end the game. They had to go all out.

Sebag took a deep breath. Laurent Martinez's answers and his attitude had strengthened his belief. People don't bug their spouses' telephones on a simple suspicion. It was true that he was especially well placed to know that. The "special agent" hadn't yet told them everything. They had to make him spit it out.

Now!

Chapter 46

The wind had turned. He felt it. It wasn't good.

Not good at all.

Annie had returned early this evening. She was smiling, looked happy. They ate dinner watching the evening news on channel 1.

While they were having dessert, the phone rang. Annie answered it. It was Chloé, one of their daughters. She lived in Toulouse and had a job as a nurse's aide at the Larrey hospital. Since she had learned that she was pregnant, she called her mother every other night on average. Little Ugo was supposed to be born before spring.

Left alone at the table, he reflected. For the past two days, the cops had been spending more time with the municipal police. The policemen hadn't limited themselves to viewing the archives. They were hanging around in the video-surveillance room, talking with someone or other. Something was wrong. Lieutenant Sebag wasn't there for the images. This morning, he had even had the sense that he was being followed. Maybe not him directly, but Martinez. That didn't leave him much time before they found their way back to him.

No, it wasn't good at all. They weren't there only for the images.

Not only.

Olivier cleared the table. Sitting on the couch, Annie continued her conversation with their daughter. Chloé had just finished decorating the baby's room. According to what he'd understood, she'd opted for a frieze with little blue bear cubs. Annie found that pretty.

After putting the dishes and the silverware in the dishwasher, he drew a glass from his box of fruity Catalan wine. He was nervous, he needed to relax. Back in the living room, he went up to the picture window, and slowly pulled back a corner of the curtain.

It was then that he saw the car.

Parked about twenty meters from the house, the white unmarked police car sheltered two figures. He shivered. They were there. Already.

There wasn't a moment to lose. He had to make everything disappear.

Still on the phone, Annie was following with astonished eyes his coming and going in the house. He wrapped his laptop and his camera in plastic bags and then disappeared into the garden. He came back to the living room shortly afterward to get rid of a pile of sheets of paper and photos in the blazing fireplace. His wife's concern kept growing.

"What's going on, Olivier?"

He approached and kissed her on the cheek.

"I love you."

He was waiting to hear the doorbell ring in the little house and he jumped when two knocks came at the door.

Chapter 47

Sebag and Julie had parked their car at the curb and hadn't taken their eyes off the house at no. 12. They couldn't stay very long. In this neighborhood of small homes, everybody knew each other and their vehicle would soon be spotted. Even at this prime-time hour when everybody was glued to their TV screens.

The house they were watching had a single level. A recess in the façade sheltered a table and two chairs in white plastic. On the left, the living room's picture window was transmitting bluish flashes onto the little garden, while on the right, the garage door windows cast a yellowish light on the little car parked in the driveway.

Two lights, two universes, two lives.

They were on the wrong track: the *corbeau* hadn't divorced, and he wasn't separated, either. He lived with his wife, but in two parallel worlds. Regarding the rest Gilles had in principle been right, but it was too early to celebrate. Julie looked at her phone to see what time it was. 8:35 P.M.

"More than twenty-five minutes . . . What the hell are they doing?"

"I'm sure that Castello is doing all he can."

Laurent Martinez hadn't dilly-dallied for long. The tactic perfected by the police officers had proven effective. They'd let the municipal officer make his way to the truth, and once he understood, Martinez had been staggered. Frightened, he had decided to confess everything. He'd coughed up a name, thus confirming Sebag's hypothesis. Namely, that the *corbeau* had discovered his vocation by accident and had not been prudent when he made his first denunciation. As they left Martinez's house, Gilles and Julie had had a brief discussion. They had to act quickly if they wanted to conduct a search before the fateful hour.

"This guy must have spied on dozens of people over the months," Gilles had argued. "If we haven't heard about his dirty work before, that's because he's careful and well-informed, and he hasn't taken any more risks since that first time with Martinez. He saw us at the video-surveillance center and he undoubtedly noticed that we were following his colleague. He may be getting rid of all the evidence against him."

"In that case, it might already too late," Julie replied. "And if we don't find anything at his house, we'll have only Martinez's testimony. That might be enough to get him fired from the municipal police but not to charge him with all the other cases."

Gilles took a coin out of his pants pocket and showed it to his colleague:

"Heads or tails?"

"Is that the way you work?"

"Always. Didn't Jacques tell you? My famous intuition is just a legend."

Gilles tossed the coin. It spun in the air and fell on his open palm. Heads. But Gilles felt no relief.

"Shall we go anyway?"

"Banco."

Gilles had let Julie drive while he called Castello. Confronted with the weakness of the evidence in the case, they'd thought it prudent to go through the superintendent in trying to convince the prosecutor to issue a search warrant. Since then, they'd been waiting in the car in front of Olivier Carbonnell's house.

The telephone finally rang. Castello had won, the prosecutor had given them the green light. They got out of the car, ignored the doorbell button next to the mailbox, and walked up the driveway. Julie knocked on the door. A little brunette with a plump figure opened it. Sebag had informed himself; he knew that Annie Carbonnell was fifty-two years old, but she didn't look it at all. Gilles and Julie showed their badges and were direct:

"We'd like to see your husband and search your house."

The door that led from the entry hall to the garage opened and Olivier Carbonnell, nicknamed 20/15 by his colleagues, appeared in it.

"What's this about?"

"You know very well what it's about," Gilles replied.

Carbonnell said nothing and didn't pretend to be astonished. On the other hand, his wife's surprise seemed complete. She said to her husband:

"What's going on, Olivier?"

"Don't worry, dear, it's a mistake."

The search lasted two hours. It was carried out for the most part in silence. The lieutenants at no point justified what they were doing, and the municipal officer asked no questions, limiting himself to observing them with his dark, sharp eyes as he smoothed with his index finger the delicate black mustache that crowned his upper lip. As for Annie Carbonnell, she huddled in an armchair next to the fireplace to watch the rest of her detective series. Season twelve, episode thirty-six, then episode thirty-seven.

After the parents' bedroom and then that of the girls, which they had vacated, Gilles and Julie searched the garage with particular attention. In this space transformed into an office and a spare bedroom, they found a desktop computer but no printed documents, nothing but blank pages of photographic paper.

"Do you do photography?" Gilles asked.

"I used to when the girls were little."

On a shelf at eye level stood a long series of family photo albums. The years were written on the spines, 1993 for the first one, and the current year on the last. Sebag thought about the photo albums that were lying dormant at his house. Claire had spent a lot of time on them during Léo and Séverine's first years, but little by little she had slacked off; smiling kids with golden curls always inspire parents more than pimply, grumbling adolescents. He never looked at these albums. The passage of time had always given him the blues. He pointed to the photographic paper carefully piled next to a high-performance printer.

"Did you move to digital some time ago?"

"I made the shift very early on. Beginning of the 2000s. It's so much more practical!"

"We didn't find the camera, have you stopped taking pictures?"

"The girls are grown up, I sold my Nikon. I'm waiting until I'm a grandfather to begin again."

Olivier Carbonnell had just uttered two sentences of more than twenty words apiece. Sebag observed him attentively. A suspect was often more talkative when he was lying.

"But you still have the paper . . ."

"You can't sell it. And then, I'm optimistic: I hope to have grandchildren before long. My eldest is already twenty-four, and she has been living with her boyfriend for three years. I suppose they must be thinking seriously about having children."

Sebag remained skeptical: the paper hadn't yellowed, it must not have been sitting there very long. Julie sat down in front of the computer. It was on, all she had to do was wake it up. First she looked at the "images" file; it was strangely empty.

"Did you clean up before we arrived?"

Carbonnell replied from the bed, where he had sat down.

"Not at all, if you seize the computer, your experts will tell you: I haven't erased anything. I don't know what you're looking for, but it's not in there."

Carbonnell's serenity worried Sebag. Carbonnell must know about computers and he seemed sure of his knowledge. Would Elsa Moulin prove more talented? She'd have to be. For the moment, they had no other hope. There was also the graphological examination but even if the experts were certain, that would never be a sufficient proof.

Their gamble was in danger of becoming a flop. Too bad, they had to go all the way.

Sebag contemplated the former garage. It was more than a simple office and spare bedroom. He sensed a life in it. A bit of fabric was sticking out from under the pillow. A T-shirt or pajamas, probably. He left Julie to examine the computer and went out into the little yard behind the house. He lit a cigarette. Surrounded by the grounds of the neighboring houses, the Carbonnells' rectangle of earth seemed neglected. Short bamboo stakes stuck in the ground in an X pattern preserved the memory of a former vegetable garden. Rows of tomatoes must have grown there, but now there were only tall grasses. At the back of the garden, a compost pile was rotting the sides of a little shed. It took Sebag only five steps to cross the yard. He opened the rickety door of the wooden shed and pushed on a switch. No light. He took out his telephone and had a look at the place in the light of the screen. He moved a few tools, a few bags of potting soil, but found nothing that might have been intended for anything but maintaining a vegetable garden. He had to force himself to close the door again. Before returning to the house, he threw his cigarette butt on the compost pile.

"Do you admit to having informed your colleague Laurent Martinez that his wife had a lover?"

"Yes. And that was a serious mistake on my part, I should never have done that."

Sheltered by his thick eyebrows, Olivier Carbonnell's dark eyes remained fixed on Sebag.

"How did you come to have that . . . information?"

"By accident. I was working in front of my screens and I recognized Laurent's wife. I saw her going into a store downtown, a printer's shop. Then I saw the metal shutter go down, and she didn't come out again. It was noon, and I took my break. When I came back an hour later, I put the images from the same camera on my screen. The metal shutter was still down, and it stayed down for a little while longer. Then it was raised and Virginie came out."

His eyelids half closed, sharpening his look even more:

"What would you have done in my place?"

Sebag did not reply. Even though their search had produced little, they took 20/15 with them, put him in police custody, and let him spend a night—a short one—in a jail cell. Early in the morning, they put him in an interrogation room. Behind the one-way mirror, Castello followed this first interview. Investigations would be begun across the board later in the day, but for the moment, they didn't have much evidence against Carbonnell and he knew it.

"All that was in violation of the rules, I admit that, and if I had it to do over again, I wouldn't do it. But since we can't turn back the clock, I take responsibility for what I did."

Clever. 20/15 had decided to make concessions on the main evidence against him, Martinez's testimony.

"That was already almost a year ago, and I haven't done it again in the meantime."

Sebag decided to launch a first attack.

"However, that was also how you learned about your wife's infidelity."

"Excuse me?"

"Your wife is cheating on you, isn't she?"

Carbonnell ran his index finger over one eyebrow and a smile appeared at the corners of his lips.

"You worry me, Lieutenant. Do you have information I don't know about?"

"You sleep separately from your wife, you've given up the house to live in the garage. That's not the sign of a happy couple."

"I've had problems sleeping, and when I do sleep, I snore. We've decided by common consent that it was better this way. We have been together for almost twenty-seven years . . . How long have you been married?"

Sebag did not reply and laid the photos of Christine Abad and Éric Balland on the table in front of Carbonnell.

"Did you take these pictures?"

The municipal police officer contemplated the photos.

"I'm seeing them for the first time."

He looked up at Sebag before adding:

"Who is it?"

Sebag shook his head, the question rang false. Then he laid down the photos of Marie-Isabelle Casty and her motorcyclist lover.

"A pretty woman," Carbonnell remarked. "And very good photography. A real paparazzi photograph."

Carbonnell was displaying too much confidence. Gilles noted that Carbonnell's pride might cause him to make mistakes. He handed him a pen and a blank sheet of paper to have him write the *corbeau*'s sentence. Carbonnell did so with a disconcerting naturalness. Gilles took back the paper and compared it with the original. Not entirely the same, but not entirely different, either. He could already imagine what would happen—an expert opinion, a contradictory expert opinion, et cetera. In any case, the results of the analysis, if they were someday to be useful, would be so only for the court. To indict Carbonnell, they would need more evidence.

When he was placed in custody, the policemen had stated their accusations to the suspect. Sebag repeated them, and Carbonnell rejected them again:

"I have nothing to do with this business and I think that none of my colleagues could be this *corbeau*. It's not only a question of professional ethics . . . It's simply technically impossible: how can you spy on people without your neighbor noticing what you're doing?"

"That is in fact one of the questions we're asking ourselves. It would probably require immense amounts of memorization and precision, and also a great deal of rigor and an incomparable talent as a physiognomist. I'm sure that you will explain all that to us in a little while."

Gilles had the suspect taken back to his cell before taking Julie out to drink a cup of coffee at the Carlit. Molina and Ménard soon joined them, and together they drew up a list of the tasks that had to be done during the day. Sebag and Jacques were to make the rounds of the newsagents, service stations, and supermarkets. What a chore! After a second coffee, they separated: they had to find something concrete before evening, and there was a lot to do.

"So, what have you got?"

Castello was pacing up and down his office, round and round Gilles and Julie. Sebag opened his notebook and then summarized the investigations carried out during the day. A slender harvest. First of all, the examination of the computer had not been conclusive. There wasn't much on the hard disk; only a tenth of its space had been used. And nothing, absolutely nothing, had been recently deleted. When Carbonnell had booted up this computer on the evening the search was made, it was for the first time in two weeks.

"Elsa thinks he must have another one, probably a laptop."

"She thinks?"

"She's convinced of it. Carbonnell has a Facebook account and an e-mail account, but the passwords for them are not in this computer's memory. He has to type them in each time to access the accounts."

"Maybe he doesn't trust his wife."

"Elsa was able to access the Facebook and e-mail accounts. They contain nothing very personal, and in any case nothing that he would have to hide."

"Maybe he's paranoid."

"Maybe . . ."

"But you didn't find the alleged second computer in the house?"

"No."

"Any more than you found the throwaway phones your suspect is supposed to have. On this question too, you've come up empty-handed."

"By definition, throwaway phones . . ."

"Can be thrown away, I understand. Anything else?"

"With Jacques, we visited about fifty sellers of these disposable phones to show them photos of Carbonnell. Two of them thought they'd had him as a customer."

"They think or they're convinced?"

"They think . . . They have dozens of customers every day, they can't be certain about anything."

Julie spoke up:

"Our colleagues on the forensic team compared Carbonnell's photographic paper with the paper used by the *corbeau*. It's the same brand, but they can't certify that it comes from the same batch. I found the place where it was sold: a supermarket at the Porte d'Espagne."

"Several hundred people must have bought photographic paper there in recent weeks, especially over the holidays. It's no more conclusive than the rest."

The superintendent didn't conceal his annoyance. He had

intervened personally with the prosecutor and he wasn't happy about the investigation's lack of progress.

"At his house, Carbonnell has a card that gives him access to an athletic club near the Promenade des Platanes," Sebag went on. "That's exactly the part of downtown where the *corbeau* made his phone calls. After work each day, he had himself dropped off at the Place de Catalogne and walked to his bus stop, which is located near this club. In short, it is proven that he was often in this area."

Castello opened his mouth to make another objection, but Sebag beat him to it:

"As hundreds of other people probably also were, that's true. But if we include all these elements—the photographic paper, the disposable-phone sellers, the athletic club—there aren't that many people left."

The superintendent scratched the tip of his nose.

"You think you can convince the prosecutor with that? Because if you intend to ask him to extend police custody for Carbonnell, you're going to have to take the lead. Don't count on me this time."

Castello sat down behind his desk and put both hands on the blotter. He bit his lip.

"This is becoming a mania to rush things. First Ménard with the guard, now you with this municipal cop. We don't arrest people just like that, for a trifle. I trusted you."

"And you can continue to trust me. He's our man, I sense it."

Sebag knew how to cajole his boss. Castello gave him a restrained but slightly indulgent smile.

"You still have to prove it."

He looked for a paper on his desk, found it, read it.

"I see that police custody began at precisely 11:17 P.M.? So you still have the whole evening to make a significant step forward."

He dismissed them with a martial gesture and the two lieutenants found themselves back in the hallway.

"Shall we go back to Carbonnell's house?" Julie proposed.

Sebag hesitated. He didn't want to offend his colleague.

"Would you mind if I went alone? I think Madame Carbonnell has things to tell us and that it would be easier to speak with her one-on-one. Less official, so to speak."

"As you wish, but keep me informed."

"I promise."

Chapter 48

The dancing light of a computer screen was still illuminating the driveway. Gilles could make out a dark figure curled up in a chair. He knocked. The murmur of the TV set stopped and the door opened.

"How is Olivier?" Annie Carbonnell asked without any other greeting.

"He's fine."

"Why are you holding him? What are you accusing him of?"

When they'd taken Carbonnell away, Gilles and Julie hadn't told his wife anything. Gilles knew that she had contacted a lawyer but their suspect had rejected any representation.

"May I come in?"

She stepped aside and pointed in the direction of the living room. He sat down on a couch.

"Would you like a tisane?"

"Yes, please."

"*Saveur du sud?* A mixture of mint and licorice."

"Perfect."

Gilles would gladly have chosen a different blend, a mixture of barley and malt, but for the past several days he had been trying not to drink too much. Two or three glasses a day, wine or whiskey, depending on the hour and the place. Never between meals. He no longer had a bottle in his desk drawer. When this stage was over, he would limit his consumption of tobacco as well.

Annie Carbonnell set two steaming cups on the coffee table, along with a saucer and a sugar bowl. She sat down on her chair, tucking her legs under her. She wore a shirt that was too long for her. A man's shirt.

"Are you finally going to tell me why you arrested my husband?"

Sebag said he was, and summed up their suspicions in a few sentences.

"But why would he have done that?" she exclaimed when he had finished. "It's madness!"

Sebag looked straight into Annie Carbonnell's hazelnut-colored eyes.

"We think he wanted to take revenge on unfaithful wives."

Annie's eyes clouded. Her face tensed and unattractive wrinkles appeared between her mouth and her nose.

"I don't understand what you mean . . ."

Sebag had no doubt: she was lying. The only question he asked himself was whether she was lying to protect herself or to protect her husband.

"You've never cheated on your husband?"

"No . . . Absolutely not."

"How long have you been sleeping in separate rooms?"

"But that . . . that . . . has nothing to do with it."

This time her astonishment seemed to him sincere. She gave him the same explanations as her husband, insomnia, snoring . . . Sebag was beginning to see the outlines of this couple's strange relations, the weight of what was not said and of silent suffering. He removed the tea bag from his cup and put it on the saucer.

"Didn't your husband ever tell you that he knew?"

Her mouth opened and her chin trembled. Her eyes became vague, she was looking inward. Toward a recent past that she was seeing in another light. Her hesitation lasted about ten seconds.

"I don't know what you're talking about!"

Sebag did not reply. He sipped his tisane and went on.

"We think Olivier anticipated our arrival and that he got rid of compromising objects, such as a laptop computer, for instance, a telephone, and maybe also a camera . . ."

"There again, I don't know what you're talking about."

She had replied too quickly, almost cutting him off.

"How long has this little game been going on between you two? How long have you been cheating on him and how long has he pretended not to know about it?"

"I don't know . . ."

"But I do! You're protecting him, that's normal. You've just realized how much he has suffered because of you."

Sebag bit his lip. He'd just been clumsy. The "because of you" was excessive. It would only imprison the wife in her guilt and thus in her blind support for her husband.

"Where might he have hidden those objects?"

This last question he had asked himself. Annie Carbonnell wouldn't tell him any more. He got up and went to the garage. The bed was unmade and the mark of the dust left by the computer had disappeared. Olivier's sports bag was lying on the floor, open and empty. A perfect homemaker had been there. A short night in the imprisoned husband's bed, a bit of housework, collecting dirty laundry. Gilles picked up the bag and searched it again. He remembered that Julie had done that rapidly without hiding a grimace of disgust at the strong odor that came from the still-damp sports clothes. He plunged his hands in the various pockets and corners of the bag, felt a hard little object under his fingers, and managed to pull out a key. He sat down on the chair in front of the desk to examine his discovery. A key to a padlock, apparently. Like the ones used in locker rooms, whether at work or at a gym. Carbonnell was probably keeping something besides a pair of gym shoes in his locker, but he couldn't have hidden a laptop there just before their visit.

He leaned backward and made the flexible back of the chair creak.

His eyes scanned the shelves. A few books, magazines, comic books, and the long series of family photo albums. He focused on the last ones, 2014, 2015, and suddenly stood up. Hadn't Carbonnell claimed that he no longer took pictures of his daughters since they'd grown up? He grabbed one of the albums. Opened it.

Goddammit!

He took the album under his arm and found Annie in the kitchen. He put the album on the table and let her look through it. As soon as she looked at the first page she went pale. On the second page, she almost fainted.

Annie Carbonnell flipped through the pages without stopping to look at the photos. The black of her hair accentuated the sudden pallor of her face.

She abruptly closed the album.

Without saying a word, she emptied the cups of cold tisane into the sink and put them in the dishwasher. She pulled the string and the label off the bags and then threw them in the big salad bowl that already contained vegetable peelings. She put her hand on the handle of the window that looked out onto the backyard but changed her mind. For a few seconds, she shifted from one foot to the other without knowing what to do with the salad bowl. Finally she set it down on the countertop.

Sebag reopened the album at random. The two pages contained photos of Annie on a beach in the company of a tall man with close-cut hair. She was reading, he was looking at the screen on his telephone. Nothing compromising. He turned the page. On the right-hand page, one saw her from the back, walking hand in hand with the same man, and on the left-hand page they were kissing.

"I'll ask you again the question I asked a little while ago,

Madame Carbonnell," Sebag said softly. "Have you never cheated on your husband?"

She opened her mouth but no sound came out. Gilles pulled up a chair and asked her to sit down. He opened several cupboards before he found the one that contained the liquors. He took out a bottle of plum brandy. It was about 100 proof, it would take something at least that strong. He found two little cut-glass goblets and filled them. Then he set one in front of the spouse still in shock. She seized it and emptied it in one draft. She coughed and then managed to stammer a few words:

"It's . . . not . . . possible."

"Astonishing behavior, isn't it?"

He refilled his own glass. He had to maintain the connection, not let her sink back into silence.

"Didn't he ever show you that he knew everything?"

She shook her head. He turned more pages.

"He was following you, spying on you, photographing you. And he classified the pictures in the family photo albums."

"It's . . . it's crazy."

She put her hand on the glass.

"It was the madness of love. He continued to love you in spite of everything."

"How he must have suffered . . . He must have decided to move into the garage after he discovered everything. And I believed that he really had insomnia!"

"It probably wasn't all feigned. His behavior didn't change, he hadn't become more distant? Wasn't there anything that might have tipped you off?"

She took another swallow of plum brandy. He did the same. Despite its strength, the eau-de-vie emitted delicious aromas. He put the glass down.

"Olivier was already distant," Annie continued before correcting herself. "We were already distant. I . . ."

A tear rolled down her cheek. As transparent and clear as the eau-de-vie.

"I haven't had feelings for him for a long time. Physically, I mean."

"But you still love him?"

"I don't know."

"Why didn't you leave with your lover, then?"

"Marc isn't free, he has a wife, children. And then . . . I'm not sure that we're made to live together. Our tastes are . . . different."

She put her glass to her lips again.

"I didn't want to hurt our daughters, to break up our family life. Olivier didn't ask me to explain myself even when I came home late, he never seemed to suspect anything. I . . ."

She paused.

"Deep down, I think I knew that he knew."

Gilles put his hand on hers.

"You saw him hide the computer yesterday, didn't you? Where is it?"

Annie abruptly retrieved her hand and let her arm hang by her side.

"I've hurt him enough, I'm not going to betray him!"

He nodded.

"So you know. So it's here."

She looked down at her glass.

"I understand you, Annie, I understand. But I'm going to find it. Without you, in spite of you."

He searched the garage again. For a long time. Then the girls' room, then the parents' room. Without the slightest success. He went back to Annie, who was in front of the TV in the living room. She'd taken the bottle of plum brandy with her and its level had gone down significantly. He remembered that he hadn't finished his glass.

He went back into the kitchen, emptied his brandy, and

then poured himself a glass of water from the faucet. The green salad bowl that had held the peelings and the tea bags was drying on the drying rack. Annie had probably washed it after emptying its contents on the compost pile.

He suddenly recalled the woman's hesitation, her embarrassment.

In the cabinet under the sink, he found the garbage can, and examined it. The peelings were there along with the tea bags, on top of a pile of detritus in plastic. Annie hadn't gone out to throw all that away in the garden as she usually did. He opened the kitchen door and walked over to the shed. Without hesitating, he thrust his hands into the compost. He pulled out the heavy plastic bag. He quickly wiped it off.

By the light of the neighbors' window, he could distinguish the rectangular form of a laptop computer.

CHAPTER 49

Gilles Sebag led Olivier Carbonnell into the interrogation room. Leaning over the table, Julie and Molina concealed the evidence. When Gilles gave them the signal, they moved away, and Carbonnell shrank back when he saw his laptop as well as a camera and a telephone. Gilles had discovered the camera by continuing to dig around in the compost; he located the telephone that same day in a locker at the gym. Carbonnell had undoubtedly put it there as a precaution, to frustrate any possible geolocation.

Gilles gently put his hand on the suspect's back and made him sit down.

"I think we have things to say to one another."

Carbonnell's shoulders sagged.

"I spoke with your wife yesterday, Olivier. She has seen the albums, the photos on your laptop, she knows everything. She tried to deny it right to the end. To defend you."

Carbonnell stared at him. His eyes were empty. Was he seeing anything? Gilles didn't try to rush the confessions. They would come when he was ready. Julie, who had gone out, returned to the room with a coffeepot and a sack of pastries. Jacques set glasses on the table and they ate in silence like old friends. Carbonnell chewed slowly. The muscles in his jaws bulged under his greasy skin.

Once they'd eaten enough, Sebag brushed away the feast's crumbs.

"It was no accident that you discovered that Madame Martinez was cheating on her husband, was it?"

He'd decided to leave personal questions aside for the time being. Carbonnell raised an interested eyebrow before assenting with a movement of his square jaw.

"And you'd immediately told your colleague about it without thinking?"

That was the hypothesis that Sebag had formulated to Julie before talking with the special agent. Carbonnell assented again. Thus Sebag had guessed right, but it wasn't his pride that needed to be stroked.

"That was your only mistake."

He put his hand on the laptop.

"I took a quick look at it this morning. I'm impressed by the amount of information you were able to collect without ever being noticed by your colleagues. You must have a fabulous memory."

Carbonnell's lips trembled at the edges.

"I can't complain about it. It was the only positive thing that my teachers said to me during the whole time I was in school."

The first words were out, the rest would be easier. Carbonnell had kept too many things bottled up inside him these last months. And with the evidence against him spread out on the table, he no longer had any reason to keep silent.

"Did the idea come to you after you'd told Martinez about his wife's infidelity?"

20/15 nodded.

"Laurent's wife didn't love him anymore, but she couldn't make up her mind to break up their family. I did him a favor, in fact. When I realized, I was furious and I decided to put things right. To see to it that the unfaithful people were the primary victims."

He'd said "people" rather than "women." There would be time later on to have him dot the "i"s.

"It must have been an enormous task," Gilles limited himself to saying.

"I spent a huge amount of time on it, that's for sure."

This time, the corners of his mouth actually rose.

"I began by discreetly aiming my cameras toward certain hotels. I was looking for hotels of moderate standing, neither too expensive nor too tawdry. I was always willing to volunteer to keep watching the screens over the lunch break. It was rush hour for that kind of . . . leisure activity, and at work I was more at peace. I spied on the public parks and parking lots: when the lovers separated in front of their cars, there were often mad kisses."

His voice had faded toward the end. Carbonnell looked at his empty cup. Sebag took the coffeemaker and filled it, along with the three others.

"I spotted couples and I followed people. Not only with the cameras. Once I'd noticed a few regular rendezvous, I used my days off to complete my work. I stood in front of hotels and then followed the lovers."

On the computer, Sebag had discovered dozens of named files. A hundred and twenty-three of them. They included not only family names, but also addresses, occupations, and the telephone numbers of the wives, the lovers, and the husbands. Carbonnell also wrote down license plate numbers. Thanks to them and his position as a municipal policeman, he must have had access to a certain amount of valuable data.

"Is that how you came across Christine Abad and Éric Balland?"

"Among others . . ."

"How about Sandrine Valls?"

Sebag had asked this question carelessly, though it had been bothering him. By what extraordinary chance had Carbonnell also been led to follow the wife of a colleague of Stéphane Abad's and thus to trigger almost simultaneous tragedies involving these two employees at Cantalou? A coincidence that had long sent their investigation down the wrong path . . .

"I informed myself concerning other husbands and learned that Abad frequented a downtown bar and that he was friends with a certain Didier Valls. I decided to follow this guy . . ."

"Why?"

"Just like that, on a whim . . . I had gradually begun surfing videos and the Net, moving from one individual to another without any motive other than the impulse of the moment. It was as good a move as any, and here's the proof! From Didier Valls I moved to his wife Sandrine, and then I managed to find her lover."

"An incredible stroke of luck all the same," Molina remarked.

Carbonnell turned to him.

"You could say that . . . In that domain, unfortunately, when you seek, you find."

Julie, annoyed, spoke up:

"Sandrine Valls had a friend, not a lover. She'd never cheated on her husband."

Carbonnell raised his right eyebrow and spoke to Gilles:

"Is that what she claimed?"

"Isn't it true?"

20/15 chortled.

"Then you have to explain what they were doing together on certain late afternoons when she followed him to his apartment on the Quai de Hanovre . . ."

So the "virtuous" Sandrine, contrary to her repeated denials, had crossed the Rubicon long before her husband's suicide.

"What a damned liar and diabolical hypocrite!" Sebag fulminated.

"Nonetheless, with Valls you made a blunder," Julie insisted. "You hadn't foreseen that he would jump out the window."

Carbonnell shrugged his hefty shoulders.

"That's true. But that's how it is. It was his choice. I was only the messenger."

After his initial admissions, Olivier Carbonnell was now unveiling his line of defense.

"Do you know the song? 'The first one who tells the truth has to be executed.' When journalists reveal politicians' turpitudes, some people attack them rather than the corrupt officials. They say the journalists were manipulated. Even the judicial system sometimes prosecutes them: they call it 'violating judicial confidentiality.'"

"Cheating on your spouse is no longer a crime!"

Julie wouldn't give up.

"And that's undoubtedly a mistake made by our society. These people have betrayed their spouses, their families, they've lied to them. I've revealed their offense, and it's up to their husbands to judge them."

Gilles noticed that Carbonnell had said "husbands" rather than "spouses," but didn't have time to point that out. Julie was pursuing her attack:

"To judge them and sentence them?"

"Most of them just get divorced."

"But that doesn't satisfy you. You want them to beat their wives, to kill them."

"I'm only the messenger, I don't have blood on my hands, Mademoiselle."

"Call me Lieutenant, please!"

Carbonnell shot her a black look. He didn't like being put in his place by a young woman cop. Sebag decided to shift to the topic of responsibility.

"You chose your interlocutors, didn't you? Stéphane Abad had the ideal profile for you: he went to the shooting gallery, he had a weapon at home. Jean-Paul Casty was a good candidate: a violent man, a brute who beat his wife. And Bastien

Gali? Out of work, depressed, he was going to do something stupid, and you knew it . . ."

Carbonnell nervously massaged the palm of one hand with the other.

"I contacted lots of people, and as I just told you, most of the couples simply separated."

"In the majority of the cases, you limited yourself to sending photos, but with the men I've mentioned—and with a few others, I suppose—you had a special contact: you telephoned them."

"I chose those who seemed to me most likely to keep quiet about me. With the others, I took no risks."

"Those you harassed, you wanted to push them to their limits. Because you'd chosen them especially for their inclination toward violence, isn't that right? Go on, dare to tell me the contrary."

Carbonnell stopped massaging his hand and furiously crossed his fingers. The joints immediately whitened. He bowed his head.

"I was only the messenger."

"The messenger for what, for whom? Up to this point, you've suggested that you attacked 'individuals,' 'unfaithful people.' The way you talk, you'd think they had no gender . . . But it was women you had it in for, wasn't it? That's obvious for everyone, so why not just say it?"

Charbonnell raised his head and opened two frightened eyes. One would have said that he was only now realizing the ferocity of what he'd done.

"I was only the messenger," he repeated again. "I didn't harm anybody."

Behind the one-way mirror, François Ménard and Superintendent Castello were following the interrogation. The lieutenant kept looking at his boss out of the corner of his eye and was enraged to see him exulting. His protégé was triumphing and conducting the interview very effectively. Ménard had to admit that Sebag had once again unraveled the complicated knot of the plot.

And yet it was he, Ménard, who had put him on the trail . . . He who had discovered the existence of the *corbeau.* True, he'd taken the wrong path because of that damned guard, but who wouldn't have fallen into that trap laid by chance? A stroke of bad luck. He had not deserved that, really. He worked diligently, rigorously, and punctually. In this case, he pulled the chestnuts out of the fire and now it was Gilles who was finishing the cooking and would serve them up to the prosecutor on a golden platter . . .

At the beginning of his career, an old inspector had told him that to be a good cop, you had to be lucky. For sure! From that point of view as well, Sebag was one hell of a policeman . . .

"I began last May, when I learned that Martinez's wife was leaving him. Laurent told other people that he was the one who was leaving, but he couldn't lie to me."

After the skirmishing, Sebag had decided to back off and get back to the facts. Carbonnell became talkative.

"When I wasn't sure that I could remember what I saw on my screens, I took notes on my telephone: I made it look like I was writing text messages."

He smiled, as if pleased with himself.

"One day Martinez told me that the girls in the office were talking about me because of that: they thought I had a mistress! I didn't deny it; it suited me."

He complacently smoothed his delicate mustache with his index finger.

"In the evening, when I got home, I closed myself up in the garage and entered everything into the computer. I completed certain files by making use of the Internet. It's amazing how some people lack the most elementary prudence. I created false profiles for myself on Facebook—a man and a woman—and made lots of friends. Even if people pay a little attention to what they publish on their pages, they're less careful in the comments and especially in their 'likes.' It's easy to see special relationships emerging between people."

Sebag wanted to drink a little coffee, but it was already cold. He pushed his cup away. Molina took the opportunity to speak up:

"What astonishes me is that people have so completely forgotten that there are a hundred and eighty surveillance cameras in this town!"

Carbonnell chortled:

"And do you yourself always think about them?"

"Nevertheless . . ."

"Oh yeah? And when you began to understand that a well-informed man was telling husbands about their wives' infidelities, did you immediately think that he must be an operator at the Perpignan video surveillance center? Of course you didn't! And yet you often work with us. Why do you think that after the polemics there have been all over France regarding video surveillance, the government officials who installed it no longer publicize our successes? So people, and especially criminals, will continue to forget about us, that's why!"

He smoothed his mustache again.

"In fact, do you know who is the only citizen in this town who is constantly aware of the presence of these cameras?"

"No," Molina said.

"The mayor of Perpignan! He told us that one day when he was showing the center to a group of journalists. He was joking, but I'm sure it's true: it bothers him that some of his employees can follow everything he does."

Carbonnell took the time to contemplate the three lieutenants and savor their surprise. Sebag closed the parenthesis Jacques had opened:

"All the same, it's unbelievable. I can't get over the fact that you were able to collect so much personal information."

Carbonnell winked at him. He was ready to go on and on.

"I had an advantage. I have a little secret I haven't yet told you about."

Sebag winked back at him.

"What is it?"

"I can read lips."

"Ah, the scoundrel!" the superintendent exclaimed. "I'm not sure that the CNIL[41] foresaw that possibility. An ability like that in a job like this one leads inevitably to a violation of the right to privacy!"

"The journalists are going to have a field day with this one," Ménard replied.

"We don't have to tell them about it."

Castello pinched his nose.

"Although . . . Why hide it from them? After all, it's relevant to the debate about video surveillance . . ."

Behind the one-way mirror, Carbonnell was continuing to explain. He'd learned to read lips long before he started spying on people. He'd acquired the skill little by little. A gift he'd cultivated, even during evenings at home in front of the television. To the point that he could now no longer tolerate the dubbing of foreign films.

The superintendent turned to his lieutenant.

"What about you, François? Do you pay attention to the cameras when you're walking down the street?"

"Absolutely not."

[41] *Commission nationale de l'informatique et des libertés*, a French government agency whose task is to prevent information technology from being used in ways that violate human rights.

Julie had had the good idea of bringing them more coffee. "Old habits die hard," Sebag thought. Why did everyone think it was normal that the only woman in the office play the role of hostess? When the cups had been refilled, Gilles launched into the most personal phase of the interrogation.

"How did you learn that your wife was cheating on you?"

Carbonnell looked down into his coffee cup.

"Through social networks."

He put his hands around the plastic cup. His gaze was lost in the blackness of the coffee.

"What do you mean by that?" Sebag asked.

20/15 slowly raised his head.

"I noticed that one guy was very present on her page. Too present."

He put the cup to his lips, blew on the hot liquid. He was less talkative on this painful subject, but Sebag wasn't worried: the mechanism was running.

"In fact, I think nothing had yet happened between them."

Carbonnell put down his cup without having drunk from it.

"Maybe if I'd shown my jealousy at that point, none of this would have happened."

"But you didn't do anything?"

"No."

He put two sugar cubes in his coffee and stirred it.

"A few weeks later, I bugged her telephone and discovered everything."

His voice rose from his gut; it came out muffled and cavernous.

"And you still didn't do anything . . ." Sebag said.

"That's true."

"Why?"

Carbonnell's mustache sagged.

"I think I was scared . . . Scared that she would leave me . . . That she'd take off with that guy . . ."

"Did you also follow them?"

"Yes."

"And you photographed them as well."

"Yes."

"And you classified the photos in the family albums."

Carbonnell smiled.

"It's crazy, isn't it?"

"A little masochistic, for sure!" Molina remarked.

"Why did you do that?"

"I'm not really sure. Maybe there was some masochism involved . . . I think I would have liked Annie to discover all that someday, even much later on, and understand that I knew, that I'd accepted it, and that I was ready to do anything to save our marriage, our family life . . ."

"And you continued to live together like that, as if nothing were wrong?"

"Yes."

"That must have been terrible."

"You can get used to anything."

"Why didn't you hide those albums before we got there?"

"I didn't think of it, you didn't give me enough time. I hid the computer and the camera, and burned a few compromising papers in the fireplace, but at that moment I wasn't thinking about the albums . . ."

Sebag let a few seconds pass before continuing:

"You said 'you can get used to anything,' but to do that you had to find a distraction. Spying on other unfaithful wives, for instance."

Carbonnell looked up.

"I got caught up in it, that's true. That . . . task completely obsessed me. It prevented me from thinking about Annie. It did me a lot of good, otherwise I'd never have been able to hold on!"

"Some people paid a heavy price."

20/15 fidgeted on his chair and opened his mouth, but Sebag cut him off:

"I know, you were only the messenger, you've already said that, but you're lying. To yourself first of all, perhaps. It's time to face up to the truth, Olivier: your goal was to make these husbands do to their wives what you didn't have the courage to do to your own."

"Is that what you think?"

"It's obvious, isn't it?"

"You're probably right . . . I never asked myself that question. I found an initial relief in the pursuit, and then another in . . . the punishment."

"You could have stopped after the first tragedy . . ."

"I didn't know about it."

"You didn't want to know."

Carbonnell started rubbing his hands again.

"I don't know how to explain it: I didn't want to hurt them, but it did me good that they suffered . . ."

"And that they died?"

Carbonnell pushed his right thumb into his left palm, harder and harder.

"Only one died."

"Her name was Christine."

"I know. Does Annie know?"

"Yes. I told your wife everything."

"What did she say?"

"That she didn't know that you had suffered so much."

"Is that all?"

"Yes."

"She still loves me?"

"I don't know."

"She didn't say that I was a bastard?"

"No."

"Then maybe she still loves me a little. Because I am a bastard . . . not a messenger, a real bastard."

*

Castello watched Molina handcuff the suspect. Olivier Carbonnell was going to be handed over to the court and a prosecutor would indict him before putting him in detention.

"There's still work to do!" the superintendent exclaimed. "Informing all the *corbeau*'s victims will take time, but it has to be done so that they can file complaints."

Molina took the *corbeau* away. Sebag and Julie followed him. Gilles turned out the light before leaving the room. With his face in the dark now, Castello rubbed his hands together.

"At least a hundred criminal acts revealed and resolved at the same time. That's excellent for our statistics. The year is beginning well!"

EPILOGUE

He parked his car in front of the garage door and laid his head on the steering wheel. He felt exhausted. He hadn't slept much the two preceding nights, coming home late and leaving early. However, the end of the investigation had cleared his mind. Like a purge taken at the right time. All these sad stories of adultery settled at one go! He was finally going to be able to turn the page, several pages even, all at once.

Finally.

He was exhausted, yes, but for the first time in a long time, serene. He raised his head.

There were no lights on in the house. Strange. However, he could have sworn that a small light had gone on in the entry hall when he'd shut off the engine. He got out of the car and quietly locked the door behind him. Then he put his hand on the door of the house and pushed. It was open. He went in and perceived a slight noise in the direction of the living room.

The sound grew louder, became noise and then music. A few notes of a piano alone, soon accompanied by a trumpet. The pure voice of Ella Fitzgerald filled the room, soon joined by the hoarse timbre of Louis Armstrong. Gilles recognized "They Can't Take That Away from Me." The first evening they spent together, in a cellar where a jazz group was playing. Twenty years ago already.

Gilles moved forward silently in the large living room. A lamp went on in their bedroom and Claire appeared against the light. He could only see her silhouette but he would have recognized her anywhere. She was so beautiful, she pleased him so much . . . She approached him, swinging her hips. She was wearing a silk negligee so short that it stopped at the lace on her stockings.

She'd pulled out all the stops.

Gilles devoured her with his eyes. He wanted to think of nothing but her. Of no one else, not even the children. Claire must have firmly suggested that they go spend the night at their friends' houses.

She came to press herself against him; her teeth chewed on his lips.

"I'm ready to do anything to win you back," she murmured.

"I love that 'anything.'"

"You haven't seen anything yet."

She took a few steps backward. Gilles could see a bottle of champagne in an ice bucket on the dining room table. Claire filled a single flute. Returning to him, she took a sip from it before kissing him.

"I've never tasted such good champagne," he told her.

Ella and Louis were now singing "Isn't This a Lovely Day." Claire lifted the glass to Gilles's lips. The bubbles tickled his palate, the coolness of the alcohol caressed his throat. Gently, Claire made him turn around until his buttocks were resting on the edge of the table. Then her body molded itself to his. He felt the hard tips of her breasts tracing words on his chest. Claire started undressing him.

The songs that followed would never belong to anyone but them.

When Claire let his shorts fall to the floor, Memphis Slim's nimble fingers were caressing the keyboard. The quickened rhythm was a boogie. "Shake that Thing." The piano was soon followed by the moans of a harmonica: "Speak Now Woman." Gilles deciphered the message. He gripped his wife's buttocks, lifted them, and put them on the edge of a table. Then he got on his knees. Elvis's hot, powerful voice replaced the harmonica and electrified them. "See See Rider." Gilles got up and kissed Claire before penetrating her. The songs followed one another at a furious pace. "That's All I Want" by Sonny Boy Williamson, then "Hold On! I'm Comin,'" by a superb duo, Eric Clapton and B.B. King. Finally "Good Times" by Lightnin' Hopkins, backed by a guitar and an increasingly urgent drum. Urgent. Gilles and Claire didn't hear the end of the last piece, which they greeted with groans rather than applause.

Afterward, they dined by candlelight at the other end of the table. Claire set out canapés, smoked salmon, a jar of taramasalata, and a few sushi rolls. They ate as they devoured each other with their eyes. One bottle of champagne was not enough to slake their thirst. Claire opened another one.

After dessert, they sat down on the couch. They hadn't touched each other during the meal and their bodies were already getting hungry again. They cuddled, caressed one another, and assured themselves of the solidity of this new desire. Then they made love, slowly. Surely. Tenderly.

Standing in front of the picture window, Gilles was drinking a last glass of lukewarm champagne. He'd turned on the lights on the terrace and was contemplating the garden in its wintry nakedness. Shadows populated it, enriched it, sublimated it.

It suddenly became obvious to him: their marriage could emerge from this ordeal greater than ever . . .

He wouldn't go so far as to say that this painful business had been a stroke of luck—no, that he would never say—but he thought that it had allowed them to test the strength of their relationship. Could anyone know how much he loved life before having one day nearly died? Claire had gone to see what else there was, she hadn't left. She remained, perhaps even more in love with him than before. He had confronted the torments of jealousy, the dark side of his soul, and he had returned from the struggle surer of himself. Surer of them. They hadn't chosen each other at random twenty years ago, or for lack of someone better, either.

Love, even after all this time, couldn't be a long, peaceful river. There was still an impetuous torrent with swirling eddies. Gilles didn't envy couples whose life was uneventful, without storms, without temptations. They lived more on comfort than on love.

He heard steps slide behind him. Claire had just gotten out of the shower. She pressed her wet belly against his buttocks and put her arms around his torso. In the garden, the shadows continued to dance.

This garden would have been less beautiful lit by a stronger light. It wasn't the intensity of the sun but the nuances of the shade that made the beauty of a landscape . . .

Acknowledgments

My thanks to my friends in the police forces of Perpignan, Toulouse, and other cities, whose information and advice helped me make this fiction credible. I won't give their names here because I don't want to embarrass them and because I'm not a snitch.

Thanks to my first readers, Hélène, Alain, and Sébastien, for having agreed to correct my prose within the strict deadlines I'd set for them. Here I will limit myself to mentioning their first names so that readers cannot blame them for any errors or incoherencies that may have escaped their scrutiny.

Thanks to my editor, Jimmy Gallier, for the confidence he has had in me since 2009 and the patience he has shown this year.

Finally, my thanks go to Toinon, Fantine, and Margot, who have supported their "papa" tenderly in difficult moments. My children, I love you.

About the Author

Phillippe Georget was born in Épinay-sur-Seine in 1962. *Summertime, All the Cats Are Bored* (Europa, 2013), his debut novel, won the SNCF Crime Fiction Prize and the City of Lens First Crime Novel Prize. His Inspector Sebag series includes *Crimes of Winter* (Europa, 2107), *Summertime, All the Cats Are Bored* (2013), and *Autumn, All the Cats Return* (Europa, 2014). Georget lives in Perpignan.